Defending Our Home
Loyalist Families of Dundas County and the Battle of Crysler's Farm

A War of 1812 Novel

Canadä

www.accesscopyright.ca or call 1-800-893-5777.
Borealis Press gratefully acknowledges the support of the Government of Canada through the Canada Book Fund (CBF).

Library and Archives Canada Cataloguing in Publication

Doering, Ronald L.
Defending our home : loyalist families of Dundas County and the battle of Crysler's farm / Ronald Doering.

Includes bibliographical references.
ISBN 978-0-88887-437-5 (pbk.) – ISBN 978-0-88887-443-6 (bound)

1. Canada--History--War of 1812--Fiction. 2. United Empire loyalists--Fiction. 3. Dundas (Ont. : County)--Fiction. I. Title.

PS8607.O435D43 2012 C813'.6 C2011-907971-2

Cover design: Constance Rose Zonta
Cover Image - Mural by Adam Sherriff-Scott,
courtesy of the St. Lawrence Parks Commission (taken from original painting on display at Upper Canada Village, Morrisburg, Ontario).
Map, page 249: Lossing, Benson J., *Pictorial Field Book of the War of 1812*. New York: Harpers, 1869

Printed and bound in Canada on recycled acid free paper.

Defending Our Home
Loyalist Families of Dundas County and the Battle of Crysler's Farm

A War of 1812 Novel

Ronald L. Doering

BOREALIS BOOK PUBLISHERS

Borealis Press
Ottawa, Canada
2012

This book is dedicated to AKM

"Tread softly stranger, reverently draw near,
the vanguard of a nation slumbers here."

Plaque over the gate of the old Loyalist Cemetery at Williamstown,
Eastern Ontario.

November 10, 1813

Dear Allie,

John says there's going to be a battle tomorrow so I want to leave you this letter. I'm sorry for what I said last week. I love you and if I get through tomorrow, I'm going to try to be a better husband. If something happens to me, I need to know that you will always tell the baby and J.T. that their father loved them very much.

I hate the Yankees for this invasion. I can't bear to think that we could lose our home to them again.

Love,
Thomas

CHAPTER 1
SATURDAY JULY 23, 1813
Dundas County, Upper Canada

"Do you know much about Canadians?" the farmer asked the soldier.

"No, I don't," the soldier replied.

"Know anything about their background or where they came from?" the farmer continued.

"No. Not at all," replied the soldier. "Where do they come from?"

"Well," said the farmer, "they're a mixed bloodline that goes back to seventeenth-century France, but after all this time here they are now a distinct breed, I would say. A good number have come up from Quebec and now quite a few have gone south to the States. One of their real strengths is that they can take the cold weather. They're small and tough and really hard-working. Canadians are high-spirited but also gentle and reliable. And as you can see, they crave affection."

"I can see that," said the soldier as he stroked her black hair. "What's her name?"

"Her name is Bessie," said the farmer, Jacob Doran. "Pretty little thing, isn't she?"

"Yes, she's a beauty all right," replied the soldier in a thick Irish accent. He was Sergeant Marmaduke Kearns, 2nd Battalion of the 89th Regiment of Foot. "I came to the Canadas last year with Colonel Morrison. I miss being around horses. We had a black filly like this back at our farm in County Cork. She's a great little horse. Lovely neck. Honest eyes."

"The rest of the men should be here soon," Jacob said, trying to reassure the soldier. "I don't always get a good turnout. The men have a lot of work to do on their farms this time of year."

"That's all right. I'm in no hurry. It was good to get away from the fort on this grand day. How long you had this girl?" asked the soldier, still stroking her long black mane.

"I bought her just last month from a Canadien who lives just above Montreal. I'm going to give her as a gift to my new step-daughter. I'm getting married in September to the widow Cook. Her youngest daughter is Maria. She'll be twelve tomorrow. She's a beautiful little thing. Takes after her mother, know what I mean?" Jacob said with a smile. "I'm a very lucky man. I got two grown boys from my first marriage. You'll meet them this afternoon. Most of the men from Matilda should be here by two o'clock." He paused and looked down the road. "I don't know how many men will come from Williamsburg. It's a good hike to here."

"No mind. We'll do a few drills with whoever is here at two. I have to be back to the fort by dark. You think Private Smith over there is a little strange now, you should see him when it starts to get dark." The Sergeant pointed to the older soldier, who was pacing back and forth beside the barn, talking to himself and occasionally to an old black sow lying in the sun beside the chicken coop. He was short and mostly bald. His ears stuck out and pointed forward, much like the old sow he was talking to. His rugged face made him look over 60 but he still had the lean, wiry body of a much younger man.

Jacob and the young redcoat were standing in the yard beside Jacob's barn. It was a beautiful summer day. Jacob had a tidy two-storey clapboard house with several outbuildings including a lovely new barn. His property was on the river, near the Rapids du Plat, Lot 3, Concession 1, Matilda Township, Dundas County, just at the border of Williamsburg Township. The old Indian trail around the rapids was still visible in front of the King's Highway.

Sergeant Kearns was still a young man of only 28. He had a swarthy complexion, with black curly hair, big bushy black eyebrows, and a large scar on his left cheek. He was a natural leader who had come up the ranks in just 14 years.

"Some of the men should be arriving soon. I should put this little lady back in the barn. Come and I'll show you my animals." Jacob beckoned to the soldier as he led the Canadian horse to the barn. "Come on, girl. I know you don't want to go in on this nice day but we'll be doing some shooting, and that could make you jumpy."

They entered the barn through the large double doors at the front. Jacob tied Bessie beside another horse in the first stable to the left. Patting the other horse on its back, Jacob explained to the soldier: "This is Buck. He's been with me for twelve years. Great horse. Don't know how we would've managed without him. Big fellow for a Canadian. A full sixteen hands. I've lent him out to others so he's got lots of offspring along the river. That's why I had to get Bessie from away. I expect we'll have a colt for Maria by next summer. What do you think, Buck, are you up to it, old fella?"

Both men smiled. Jacob then showed the soldier his pair of oxen in the next stall on the left and then the two cows in their separate stanchions. The pens on the right were empty. He explained that this was for when the hogs came back in the fall. The large double doors at the back of the barn opened to pasture. Above the stable and pens, on both sides, hay was stacked to the open roof rafters. The fresh hay gave the whole barn a beautiful sweet smell.

The soldier took in a big breath as he stood and gazed out into the back pasture where several sheep were grazing. Just outside the back door, off to the right in the shade, was a fenced area: muddy at one end but perfectly clean at the other. At the clean end was a large white sow nursing several little piglets that were pushing and climbing over each other, causing quite a commotion. The sow was completely undisturbed.

Sensing that the soldier might not understand all the fuss, Jacob explained to him: "This old gal had twelve little ones this time, all lived, but she only has a place setting for ten, so as soon as she lies down you get all this pushing and shoving. Doesn't seem to bother her though. Have to keep them penned to protect them until they're weaned. Otherwise, we let the hogs run wild to feed themselves outside until freeze-up. 'Root, hog, or die,' we say. They're a tough breed. The piglets will be six weeks old by the end of August. If they all live, they're going to take a lot of feed this winter, but I'll get good money for them in the spring. The army pays top dollar . . . But, I keep forgetting, I suppose if the Yankees invade this fall, who knows what will happen. What do ya think? Are they coming?"

The soldier looked at Jacob and shrugged his shoulders. "Colonel Pearson says we have to be ready, even if it isn't likely. I'm told that he has contacts at Ogdensburg who say that it's already too late in the season for an invasion, but you hear a different rumour every day." Pointing to the large scar across the left side of his face which also caused the left eyelid to droop, the soldier continued: "I got this at Fuengirola three years ago. We lost three hundred good men in Spain that day. I'll fight if I have to. I'm a soldier, but war has no glory for me. I hope the Yanks stay at home."

The men walked back through the barn to the yard beside the house. The older soldier was still pacing, but then he stopped and took off his hat and said something to the inside bottom of his hat.

The Sergeant noticed Jacob looking at the soldier talking to his hat. "Don't mind him, Mr. Doran. He's completely insane but he's a pretty good soldier. Steals though. You have to watch him."

"Can you make out what the poor man is saying?" asked Jacob.

"A lot of the time he seems to be talking to his mother. When he's talking into his hat like that he pretends that there is a picture in there of her. But one of the men checked one night when he was asleep and there was no picture in his hat. When he teased Smith about it the next day, he got head-butted so hard that he got his nose broken. Blood everywhere. Nobody teases Private Smith any more, especially about his mother."

"Did he come over with you last summer?" asked Jacob.

"No, that's the thing. He just showed up one morning last fall at Kingston wearing an old uniform. No identification. No first name. If it's his coat, he used to be a sergeant because you can see where the three stripes used to be. Strange duck. Tough as nails. Eats anything. Hasn't had a bath in a year, I would guess. Steals like a gypsy, then denies it. Always polite to officers but it's too thick to be real. I wouldn't believe a single thing that comes out of his mouth. He knows quite a bit of Spanish so he must have served in Spain. Hates Frenchies. We had to explain to him this spring that the Canadiens are not really French—not like Napoleon French. I hope he believes us. Have you ever seen anybody's ears stick out like that?"

Jacob didn't reply. He couldn't be sure Smith couldn't hear him and this was not a man you wanted to be on the wrong side of. Jacob changed the subject and asked: "Would the two of you like to come into the house for a cup of tea while we wait for the men to arrive? They should be here soon."

"No, no thank you, sir. You wouldn't want Smith in your house, believe me. While we're waiting is there anything we can do for you?"

"No, thank you, Sergeant. Let me go into the house for a few minutes. I'll be right back."

With that, Jacob went inside. He was starting to worry about why at least some of the men hadn't arrived by now. So many of them just didn't seem to take their militia duties seriously enough. He didn't want the Irish Sergeant to think that they were just a bunch of unreliable farmers who didn't understand their duty. Duty and responsibility were very important to Jacob. The young men who hadn't fought in the last war didn't take the Yankee threat seriously enough and were too quick to say that if it came to a fight in the Eastern District, the redcoats would easily handle the amateur Yankees. That's what Bourgoyne thought.

Jacob returned to the yard with bread and cheese for the two British soldiers. When Smith stopped pacing to take the food, his head started to jerk occasionally and he had a slight tic in his lower jaw. Then, surprisingly, he made a little bow and spoke in a clear slow voice with what appeared to be a slight Welsh accent: "Thank you, kind sir. You are very gracious . . . may I be so bold as to ask, sir, do you not have any women on this fine estate?"

"No, Private Smith. I'm a widower."

"Don't get me wrong, sir. Not asking for myself. Can't get it up any more anyway, you understand? I was tortured down there by the Froggies. Asking for the Sergeant here. He would be a fine catch for a good colonial girl. I was just talking to my dear mother about it this morning. She agrees." His chin tic returned.

The Sergeant rolled his eyes and shook his head. "That's enough, Private," he said. "Thank you for the food, Mr. Doran."

"It is my honour, Sergeant. We're grateful that you are here to help our men. They need some infantry practice. You know, we're better shooters than marchers. Unless they were at Ogdensburg, the young men have never been in battle."

"Don't worry about any of that. Hopefully, your farmers won't have to be real soldiers." The sergeant took a bite of the cheese. "Good cheese. Make it yourself?"

"Yes," Jacob replied, "we're pretty self-sufficient now."

"Lovely place you have here. You must be proud of your home. Great new barn."

"Yes, we had a bee here the last summer before the war. Built the barn in one day. Rafters are all hemlock. We've come a long way since '84. See that log chicken coop over there? That was our first house. Whole family lived in that one-room log cabin for the first six years. The winter of '87-'88 we nearly starved. Those were tough times."

Just then, a group of men appeared, coming down the King's Highway from the west. These were the men from Matilda Township. It wasn't long before the men from Williamsburg began arriving from the east. Some came on horseback but most walked.

The men greeted each other warmly. They ranged in age from 14 to over 60. Some of the older men wore three-cornered hats and a few had straw hats, but most were bare-headed. They wore homemade farm clothes. None had uniforms. Some of the older men spoke Dutch or German to each other but most of the younger men spoke English. Some of the men lit up their long Dutch pipes while they stood in the yard in front of Jacob's house. Most stood staring at the river as they spoke.

By two o'clock, about 40 men had arrived. Jacob stood up on the steps at the side of his house. As a lieutenant, he was the most senior officer of the Dundas militia present, so he called the men to order. For most of the men, just getting into ranks seemed to be a complicated manoeuvre. Jacob explained to the men that two soldiers from the 89th had come from Prescott to help out with the drills. He introduced Private Smith and Sergeant Kearns. He then turned the men over to Sergeant Kearns, who jumped up on the step beside Jacob.

Sergeant Kearns explained that Captain Merkley, Captain of the Dundas militia, had asked Colonel Pearson for some help in improving some of the skills of the men. He explained that he had brought some extra powder and balls to distribute to them. These were not to be used for hunting but were to be saved in case they were needed, in the event of an American invasion.

The men were divided into four groups. Sergeant Kearns began to show the men some elementary marching drills. He explained the various musket positions while standing at attention. He brought Private Smith forward and used him as a model. Private Smith seemed to enjoy the attention. He did the drills to perfection.

Most of the farmer-soldiers seemed quite bored as they were ordered to repeat certain manoeuvres. Their lack of enthusiasm for the task and their clear lack of competence embarrassed Jacob.

After a couple of hours, Sergeant Kearns stood up on the step again and explained to the militiamen that they could be quite important in the defence of Dundas County if the Yankees decided to invade that fall. The Dundas farmers didn't seem that impressed.

Two of the men in the ranks were the Marselis brothers, Peter and Garrett. They were the younger brothers of Jacob's soon-to-be wife, the widow Catherine Cook. When the men were ordered to stand down to take a break, Jacob came over to speak to Peter and Garrett, who explained that their other brother Thomas hadn't come because he was clearing trees from his land back on the fifth concession. When Jacob pointed out that this was not the first practice drill that Thomas had missed, the two brothers were quick to assure Jacob that Thomas would make the next one.

Sergeant Kearns and Jacob put the men through a couple more drills and dismissed them at four o'clock. Some of the men started to head home while others lingered in Jacob's front yard getting caught up on the news.

Jacob thanked Sergeant Kearns and Private Smith for their help. He apologized that only 40 men had come. He explained again that this was a bad time of year to be away from the work on the farms. He hoped to himself that Sergeant Kearns didn't realize that there were over 200 men in the two flank companies of the Dundas militia, meaning that over 160 of the men had not even bothered to show up. Sergeant Kearns didn't seem concerned about the low turnout and thanked Jacob for his hospitality. When Private Smith made a little speech to say goodbye, strangely, he spoke in a distinctly Cockney accent.

Jacob's two sons, John and David, stayed on to visit with their father. All of the young men admired the new horse, but Garrett was especially excited. After about an hour, with the rest of the militia gone, Jacob asked Garrett to bring Bessie out into the yard, put on a harness, and lead her over the road to the river to cool off and get a drink. Garrett loved horses and was a natural horseman. As Garrett crossed the King's Highway out of easy hearing range,

Peter quietly explained to the others that their mother Oma was talking about selling Garrett's U.E. acreage which he had gotten the year before. She thought they could get 30 dollars for it because she had been told that was about what 100 acres on the back concessions were selling for now. She thought they could use the money to buy him a horse, he loved horses so much. Jacob offered to check with Mrs. Bouck, who might be willing to sell her late husband's horse. It was a good Canadian, a son of Buck.

The men sat on the front steps of Jacob's house looking at the river and watching Garrett and Bessie. Jacob smoked his old Dutch pipe. He had been upset by the low turnout but now he was relaxed. He reflected on how blessed he was to be sitting here on the steps with his two sons and Catherine's two younger brothers. It was a beautiful warm late afternoon. His crops were looking good. And in only 50 days he would be marrying the beautiful widow Cook. Just the thought of Catherine made him blush a little. He had never thought a man his age could be so in love.

"Come on, Father, come and join us. It'll be great." David was talking to his father, who was startled out of his daydreaming.

"What? What did you say, son?" Jacob could see the young men taking off their clothes.

"Garrett is yelling and laughing. Listen. He wants us to join him for a swim. There's no one around. Let's go." By now they were all giggling like little boys, throwing off their clothes onto the ground. John was trying to get his socks off when his brother pushed him. He fell over laughing.

"We're coming," Peter yelled to Garrett. "We're coming. Let me guess; it's not too cold once you get in, right?"

John finally got his socks off. He stood up and boldly threw off his underwear.

"Bare balls, right?" he shouted to his brother.

"Bare balls it is," said his father.

~~~
~~~

Three miles down the river at Lot 21, Concession 1, Williamsburg Township, Dundas County, Thomas Marselis, the older brother of Peter and Garrett, was not clearing his land. This was just an excuse that the brothers had made up to protect Thomas from more criticism that he wasn't doing his share. Most of the other Dundas County farmers had taken part in the drills that had been organized over the summer. Several of them had even seen action at the Battle of Ogdensburg earlier that February. Most had at least served as artificers constructing a bigger fort at Prescott that spring and summer. Thomas never had.

Handsome blond-haired Thomas Marselis wasn't clearing trees from his lot. He was making wine in the little shed behind his cabin on the St. Lawrence River. He was a young man of many enthusiasms but soldiering wasn't one of them. He had been born with an insatiable curiosity.

Last spring he had devised a new technique for collecting maple sap. Last summer, he had devoted many hours to starting apple trees from seeds and to beginning a new orchard on his cleared land. That these trees would not produce fruit for many years did not concern him. He had experimented with four or five different varieties. He planted several seeds that he had been given by John McIntosh, his neighbour on the back concession, as John had been impressed with a tree that he had found a couple of years earlier on his farm which produced a particularly sweet-tasting crisp apple.

This summer, Thomas had taken his old love of beekeeping in a new direction. He had learned the basics of beekeeping from his father as a boy and he had taken over management of the family hives after his father's death. In the four years that Thomas was away, his brother Garrett assumed the role of beekeeper and doubled the number of hives. Garrett's patience and mild manner suited the bees and Garrett's honey had achieved something of a local reputation by the time Thomas had returned. In the previous year Thomas had tried to make wine from the honey but the results were not good. This spring he had met a man from Glengarry who made a beautiful mead and Thomas obtained his recipe and a better sense of what he had done wrong before. He knew now he had to boil his equipment and take greater care to minimize the amount of lees that got into the drink. The Glengarry man's recipe was for a mead he called cyser. It called for the addition of apple juice. Thomas had also purchased from the man a piece of hose that was of much better quality than the one he had used earlier. The new hose would help him do a better job of siphoning.

So, this fine day in July, while many of the other men from Dundas County were doing their duty at militia practice, Thomas was at home with his son JT showing him his new mead-making equipment and explaining what they would be doing later in the fall. JT was now three and a half years old. He loved to be with his father. Thomas explained to his son that later in the fall when the apples ripened, they would have to be picked, crushed, and strained. The honey would have to be collected from Garrett's hives, the wax separated for candle-making, and the pure honey added to the apple juice with yeast to make the mead. JT loved to see his father so happy and enthusiastic.

"Well, partner," said Thomas to his son as he took his hand, "let's go and see how your mother is making out with your poor little sister. There's nothing worse than a summer cold."

As Thomas and his son came around to the front of the cabin, they met Oma coming out the door. Thomas and JT could see immediately that Oma was not happy about something. Before Thomas could even ask what was wrong, Oma stopped, put her hands on her hips, and snorted contemptuously:

"That wife of yours! She won't listen to good sense. I was just trying to help."

"What's wrong now, Mother?" Thomas asked quietly, and held his son's little hand even more tightly. There was no disguising the tension.

"She never listens to me," Oma continued, "and every time I try to be helpful she turns on me. She's an ungrateful child!"

"She's not a child, Mother."

"Go ahead, stick up for her. You always do. You don't see the side of her that I do."

Thomas picked up JT, who was staring at his grandmother. JT had seen Oma like this before. Then he looked away and hugged his father's neck.

"It's all right, son. Everything is going to be all right," Thomas whispered to his son and then looked at his mother, shaking his head. He said nothing more as he walked past his mother towards the cabin door. Oma stomped off towards her house which was next door, just across a small field.

Thomas carried JT into the cabin and found Allie sitting on their bed, nursing baby Aleda. Allie didn't look at her husband but Thomas could see from her eyes that she had been crying.

"I'm sorry, Allie," he said.

"Sorry? What good is that?" she snapped, wiping her eyes. "You have to speak to her. I can't take this any longer. You think I'm happy that the baby has a cold and a fever? You should have heard what she said to me. You'd think I gave Aleda the cold!"

"What can I say?" Thomas pleaded.

"You can say that you will go and speak to her and tell her to stop interfering. I can't take this any longer. She treats me like a child."

"All right. I'll speak to her," he replied.

"No. No you won't." Allie's voice turned more bitter now, more biting. "You won't say anything to her. You're afraid of her like everyone else. I can't take this any longer."

"Let's talk about this later when the children are asleep," Thomas said as he put JT down. JT didn't walk away. He hugged his father's leg while he kept staring at his mother. Thomas put a reassuring hand on his son's head.

"Allie," he said, pulling JT tight to his leg, "JT and I love you very much, don't we, JT?"

"We love you, Mommy," JT said.

Allie turned her head and looked at the two of them standing at the foot of her bed. She looked down and saw the baby now asleep at her breast.

"I'll put the baby to bed now," she said softly, the anger and bitterness now drained away. "You boys get your chores done and I'll cook supper."

~ ~ ~

Late that same afternoon just before supper, in the city of Washington, in the new building that was called the White House, James Madison, President of the United States of America, took pen in hand and wrote, "approved and adopted," on an Executive Order. The fateful decision was made. Abandoning the Lake Erie and Niagara frontiers, the bulk of the American armed forces were to be concentrated at Sackett's Harbour at the eastern end of Lake Ontario, to prepare for what was to be the decisive assault on Montreal. With the defeat of Montreal, both the Canadas would soon follow. Unbeknownst to the Loyalist families settled along the north shore of the St. Lawrence River, they were about to be thrust directly into the path of the largest military invasion ever mounted against Canada.

Chapter 2
August 19, 1813
On the St. Lawrence River

"It doesn't get better than this, Thomas."

Thomas didn't respond to his brother Peter right away. In fact, neither man had said anything for some time. The beauty of the river, the trees, the spectacular red sunset—the summer evening was so beautiful, so tranquil, that both men seemed content to just paddle and enjoy the moment. Occasionally the rhythmic sound of their paddles in the water would be interrupted by a voice from the shore. While they were well out into the river to take full advantage of the current and to track a straight course to the point, voices travelled easily over the water, especially those of the children playing along the river bank, enjoying the last hour of light. Thomas and Peter knew most of the families but they made no effort to call out to anyone along the shore. Trying to yell out greetings as they went along didn't seem right. Breaking the tranquility of this wonderful summer evening was just not something either man wanted to do.

The loons had no such hesitation. But their haunting calls only added to the perfect natural beauty of the place. Occasionally there would be a slight warm breeze from the shore, pungent with the fragrant smell of the large pines that still dominated the land between and behind the settlers' cabins.

"Yes, beautiful," Thomas finally replied, his voice trailing off, his mind in another place. In spite of the pure serenity on the river, or perhaps because of it, Thomas was melancholy, even sad. After he had finished his chores, Thomas had gone into the cabin to say goodnight to Allie and the children. Allie had been cool, unresponsive, distant even. He had thought to ignore her mood. He had seen this so many times before. But he didn't. He should have left it alone. He wished now that he had said nothing. When he reminded her, almost pleading, that he hadn't left her alone all summer, that he would be back tomorrow night, that Garrett would do the morning chores—none of this consoled her. He explained that his father had taken him when he was a boy and he had promised to now take Peter. Peter had been talking about it for weeks. None of this placated her. His reasonable argument delivered in his usual calm way actually seemed to make her angrier. His self-assured tone always did. It seemed to her that he was talking down to her.

Finally, she looked up at him. "Oh yes, it's always me, isn't it?" She said it this time with an edge of bitterness that surprised him. He shook his head. He felt as if he had been hit in the stomach. She saw that her words had inflicted the intended wound. She looked away again and walked over and picked up the baby.

In her hurt, little-girl voice she said to the baby, "If he loved us, he wouldn't leave us, would he?"

By this time Thomas knew there was no point in extending the conversation. He pushed open the door and then turned around. She was still looking away, putting little Aleda back into the crib. Thomas waited for Allie to look at him but she wouldn't.

"I love you both, very much, and you know it," he said firmly as he went through the door. Then he heard her shout at him, "Fine, go off with your Indian friends. Go see your squaw."

Thomas did not go back. He kept walking to the river where he knew Peter would be waiting. He couldn't get Allie's words out of his mind. He was determined, though, to not let her ruin this trip. But the quiet silence of the evening, the paddling that was so natural to him, and the lack of conversation left his mind defenceless against her words. Then, just off the stern of the canoe, a swell erupted with a loud splash, jolting Thomas back to the present.

"*Tabernac*! What was that?" Peter exclaimed.

Thomas was still a little disoriented and mumbled that he didn't know. He hadn't seen anything, had just felt the swell and heard the splash.

"*Tabernac*!" Peter repeated. "That was too big for a fish and we are too far out in the current for it to be a beaver or muskrat. Let's start to head back towards the shore. That's the point over there, isn't it?"

"All right. I'll turn us in. I don't know what that was. We can ask John. He'll have an idea."

Thomas swung the little birch bark canoe towards the southern shore of the river and then through the fast water in the narrows at the eastern end of Croil's Island. Now the paddling was easier. "What does '*tabernac*' mean? Where did you learn that expression?" asked Thomas.

"I guess I got it from the bateaux men, Jean Louis and Luc," Peter answered. "I don't know what it means."

With quickened strokes, combined with the current, the little canoe made the final mile to the point on the northwest corner of Long Sault Island in less than 30 minutes, just as dusk turned to darkness. As they came around the point, turning into the bay, the Marselis brothers had before them a most remarkable sight. There were at least ten large elm bark canoes, each with a pine torch called a fish light at its bow casting a lurid glow upon everything around. The canoes had square ends, were about 20 feet long, and held three or four people in each. Standing in each canoe was a man with a spear held over his head. The spearman would stay very still until, suddenly, he would thrust the spear into the water. In one of the canoes closest to the Marselis brothers, the man at the stern could be seen pulling the spear out of the water with a large fish flapping madly. This fish was over two feet long and the Indian in the stern of the canoe was yelling something to the others as he was clearly struggling to try to get the big fish into the boat.

Closer to the shore, excitement erupted in another canoe as

another sturgeon, coming up to the surface, attracted by the light of the pine torch, was impaled by a thrusting spear.

Young Peter Marselis had never seen such a sight. Lit only by the flickering light of the pine torches, there being no moon yet on this night, other Indians could be seen leaning over the sides of their canoes, rising with spears over their heads, waiting momentarily and then thrusting down, usually crying out at the same time with a blood-curdling whoop.

Peter couldn't contain his excitement.

"*Tabernac*! Look at the size of those fish! Why didn't we bring spears?"

"Keep paddling," replied Thomas. "We have to get closer so I can make out which one is John. He will outfit us . . . *She:Kon*!" Thomas shouted towards the Mohawks. "That's Mohawk for 'hello,'" Thomas explained to his brother.

As they got closer to one of the Indian canoes, someone shouted something and moments later from another canoe Thomas and Peter heard a voice call out to them in Mohawk.

"Over here, Thomas. I'm waving our torch. Paddle over here."

Thomas saw the waving torch. He turned the canoe and in less than a minute pulled up beside John Sunday's canoe. Also in the canoe, at the stern, was another old Indian. Peter reached out to grab the gunwale of the Indian canoe and immediately noticed the large fish that seemed to fill the whole bottom of the canoe. It was still flapping, its tail splashing water into Peter's face.

"It's a good one," John said in Mohawk. "Hold the canoe steady and I'll try to quiet this big fella. He must be fifty pounds."

John took a club that was hanging from a belt around his waist and, with one firm stroke, the big sturgeon went still.

"Here, Thomas," said John, switching now into perfect English, "take our spear and torch. Smoke and I will take our fish to shore and come back out. See what you can get before we come back."

Peter imagined that years later he would be telling the story of this magical summer night. How he and Thomas speared fish until well into the night. How the warm summer night was pitch black except for the pine torches. How there was no wind and how the smell of fish was everywhere. How the Indians would stand so steady and silent until, with a great whoop, they would thrust their spears into the water and then struggle to haul the great fish into their canoes and club them into submission. And how at one certain moment, the school of sturgeon just disappeared.

"Where did they go?" Peter asked his brother.

"Nobody knows. They school into this bay like this three or four nights right around this time every year. It's a mystery. Equally mysterious to me is how John and Smoke seem to know exactly when they're coming. I got the message three days ago to come tonight."

Thomas and Peter followed the rest to the shore where there was already a large bonfire on the edge of the beach. Nearby, on a makeshift table, several of the Indians were already gutting the fish and then throwing them into large wicker baskets. Others began to gather around the fire, enjoying the good time, lighting their pipes.

Peter looked across the fire and saw his brother laughing and talking with John and others. Thomas seemed so happy, so completely relaxed, so evidently comfortable speaking Mohawk with such warmth and enthusiasm. He was very different from the quiet and brooding Dundas County farmer who had set out just hours before. Peter could see why Thomas enjoyed these trips so much. It made him happy to see his brother so happy. To Peter, his brother seemed more relaxed than he had been all summer.

Exhausted from the paddling and the excitement and exertion of the fishing, Peter curled up on the grass just above the beach and fell asleep.

When he awoke it was dawn. He saw that Thomas was already up and sitting on a log beside the fire—or had he been there all night? Thomas was talking quietly with John Sunday and two other Indian men. An older Indian woman came down onto the beach with chunks of fish skewered on long thin rods. She handed each of the men his own rod and then leaned into the fire holding several rods over the red coals. Peter could smell the fish being grilled on the open fire. As he rose to go down to the fire, Thomas saw him and called out:

"Get yourself a cup from the table over there and come down for a cup of tea and some fresh fish."

Peter got the cup and walked down to the fire. One of the Indians shuffled to one side on a log, leaving a place for Peter to sit down. Thomas took the old black metal teapot from the grill on the fire and poured Peter a cup.

"This is Sasenowane and this is Big Jacob, Peter." Then, in Mohawk, Thomas told the men that this was his younger brother Peter. He told them that this was the first time that Peter had ever gone sturgeon fishing. The two young Indian men nodded and smiled at Peter. One of them took out a little leather pouch, removed from it a pinch of tobacco, and offered it to Peter. Peter smiled, waved it away, and awkwardly said "Thank you," turning to Thomas.

"Please tell him that I don't have a pipe but I appreciate the offer. I don't really smoke much."

Thomas explained this and then said to Peter, "John and the others think they know what nearly capsized our canoe last night. Apparently they have been seeing seals all summer. Nobody has been able to spear one yet. They stay out in the deep water and are just too fast."

At first Peter thought they were making fun of him, but no one was laughing.

"Are there really seals all the way up here? Have you ever heard of this, Thomas?"

"I have heard of it," said Thomas, "but never saw one. John says that some elders tell stories of seeing them below the Long

Sault Rapids and some years ago one was caught in a net. That same year they caught a shark just above Akwesasne ice fishing. Can you imagine? This far from salt water?"

John pulled his fish from the fire and gingerly pulled pieces of it from the rod.

"Good stuff," said John in his gentle voice, reaching over to give Peter an opportunity to take a piece. It was hot to the touch but Peter grabbed a piece, flicking it into his empty cup to let it cool for a moment. John took another piece. It didn't seem to burn his fingers.

"Good stuff," he repeated.

The Indian woman came back to the beach, this time with a large frying pan filled with bannock. John explained to Peter that this was his older sister. She nodded and smiled when John said something to her in Mohawk.

"She says you look like your brother," John explained to Peter. "Her English name is Rachel."

The Indian woman stared intently at Peter. She smiled again.

"Peter?" she asked.

"Yes, my name is Peter. *She:kon*," Peter replied nervously.

"*She:kon*," she replied with a smile. "I knew your father—a good man—and wife Elizabeth. Johannes dead now. Elizabeth live?"

"Oh yes," said Peter, "still very much alive." He could not imagine his mother being a friend of this woman but he was excited by the idea.

"I will tell my mother that we met today. I am sure that she will be pleased to know that you are well," Peter said slowly, enunciating every syllable. The Indian woman smiled but said nothing.

"Oma knew Rachel in the Mohawk Valley before the war," explained Thomas. "In the winter of '79 when Father couldn't come home, John and Rachel took food to Oma at our farm at Turloch. Oma was alone there with four children. You've heard this story before, Peter. Rachel was one of the main women who helped."

Peter wondered why his mother had never spoken of Rachel or tried to make any contact. Rachel used a long knife to slice off pieces of bannock. She spoke to each of the men in Mohawk as she handed them a large slice. When she came to Peter, she stuck her knife into one of the larger pieces and extended it to him.

"Good," she said to him, "good Indian bannock. More fish? More tea?"

"No, no thank you. It's delicious. Thank you," Peter stammered his reply.

Rachel smiled at him and returned to the others to join in the conversation, which had become quite animated.

Peter couldn't take his eyes off Rachel. She was probably sixty years old. She was strikingly beautiful. Her thick black hair was pulled back to reveal a broad forehead. But it was her eyes that could not be missed. Deep and black, her eyes gave her face an almost fierce, cold appearance, until she smiled. When she smiled her whole face shone with a warmth and deep intelligence that stirred Peter. When she smiled he thought she was the most beautiful woman he had ever seen.

Peter watched her pour his brother some more tea. When she bent over, she revealed ample brown-skinned breasts, highlighted by a carved wooden cross hanging from a leather band. Her white blouse was embroidered with blue thread.

Peter had seen Indian men from time to time before, usually going by on the river. But this was his first truly close encounter. If Rachel was what all Mohawk women looked like, Peter could now better understand why his brother had once left home to be with one.

Thomas got up from sitting beside the fire to shake John's hand. John took his hand but brought his big left hand around Thomas's shoulder to pull him in for a big hug. He said something and they both laughed, their bodies shaking together. Thomas shook hands with the others and yelled out to Peter that it was time to go. Peter and Thomas loaded up their share of sturgeon in the bottom of their canoe. With "thank yous" and farewells all around, the brothers pushed off from the shore, waving again to the Indians on the beach, both men digging deeply with their paddles into the black water.

It was going to be another hot summer day, but the wind had come up from the west.

"Against the current and against the wind, this is going to be a long hard day's paddle today, Peter," said Thomas. "Are you up to it?"

"I'm good," Peter replied.

"So what did you think?" asked Thomas.

"About what?"

"About night fishing for sturgeon. About John and his family?"

"Great. Thanks again for bringing me. Fine people."

"Our father thought the world of John. They were like brothers when they were together. Father brought me here first the summer before he died. I've often thought that maybe he sensed something. He did get tired from the trip but I thought at the time that it was simply because I was too young to do my half of the paddling. I was only fourteen and skinny for my age."

Thomas was an excellent sternsman. In spite of the wind and the current, he was able to keep the canoe on a straight course, but the work was strenuous. Neither man spoke for some time.

The stretch along the southeast corner of Croil's Island was particularly difficult because the river there was so narrow. Thomas kept them close to the shore to stay out of the current but twice they got out of the canoe and lined their way along the shore. It felt good to stretch their legs. When they got to the western end of Croil's Island, the river was wider and the current less strong but the wind was worse as they became more exposed.

By now they could see Cook's Point in the distance but the wind continued to freshen, bringing whitecaps to the water. Thomas turned them directly into the wind to cut straight through the waves even if that meant staying out farther into the river than the course they had used to come the evening before. The course actually took them away from the shore towards the American side.

By now, both men had to really bear down and paddle faster and deeper. In the circumstances, talking wasn't easy, but Peter couldn't wait any longer.

"Rachel is a beautiful woman. If she helped our family so much, why hasn't Oma ever spoken of her or tried to keep any contact? Why hasn't she come by our home?"

"It's a long story." Thomas tried to put his brother off but he knew his curiosity was natural.

Peter didn't give up so easily. "I'm not going anywhere," he replied.

"I don't know the whole story. I was young. Ask Catherine or Lena," Thomas said. He took another stroke and continued, "I didn't know that she was going to be there this year. This is the first time I've seen her in several years. She lives at Tyendinaga usually." Changing the subject, he continued: "By the way, John thinks that the Yankees are going to attack us this fall. His cousin at Tyendinaga reports that they are building many boats and assembling already a lot of men at Sackett's Harbour. He says that they know that Fort Henry is too hard to take so they will go around it and try to take Montreal before winter."

"Jean Louis said the same thing last week," replied Peter. "But Luc says that he heard the same rumour last fall but nothing happened. Luc helped some officers from the 89th last month at the rapids and he heard them say that Fort Henry was the more likely target."

The two men resumed their silence; the paddling was getting harder. The wind was increasing and dark clouds were gathering in the western sky.

"I think we are going to have to cut in towards shore to get out of this current and maybe get into the lee of the shore. It's not going to be easy cutting across these waves," Thomas said, with a tone to his voice that worried Peter. As they swung to the right, the waves began to hit the port bow of the canoe, splashing up water that flew with the wind into Thomas's face.

"*Tabernac*," shouted Peter, "we got to get closer to shore. My shoulders are killing me."

Thomas did not reply. He was getting wet. He wished now that he had stayed closer to shore after they had gone around the point. He hadn't expected this turn in the weather.

The canoe was beginning to take on a little water from the continuous spray. This, combined with the cargo of sturgeon, meant that the canoe was riding low in the water. Too low in the water, Thomas began to realize.

Both men were now paddling all out. The black storm clouds in the west were growing, and then one of them crossed the sun and cast a vast dark shadow over the river. The water got blacker, angrier.

Thomas had to decide whether to turn into the wind and head directly west up the river to cut cleanly through the waves or to continue towards shore but risk taking on more water. A crack of lightning, with a roaring thunder clap moments afterward, helped him with his decision.

"Paddle, Peter. We've got to get out of this shit and get to the shore before the storm hits."

Thomas was nervous and angry at himself for not being more cautious about the weather. He knew better. It wasn't that many years before that he had got caught like this on Lake Erie—too far from shore in a storm. In that case the storm had come up from the northeast, catching them in canoes that were already overloaded with fur. The rain-soaked hides so weighted the big canoe down that the gunwales were too close to the water when they turned cross-wind for shore. Thomas shuddered and put the tragedy out of his mind.

"Dig in, Peter," he urged, "we're almost to shore."

Both men paddled frantically, ignoring their aching muscles. Another lightning strike. This time behind them. The wind got worse but there was still no rain. Whitecaps rose on their left and more water splashed into the canoe. Both men paddled faster and deeper.

But before they reached the shore, the wind subsided somewhat. The brunt of the storm passed to the south over the American side. Thomas swung the canoe to the west into the little wind that was left. Exhausted, the two men laid their paddles across the gunwales, resting their arms on them, panting and very relieved.

"*Tabernac*!" said Thomas. Both men started to laugh with nervous exhaustion. Thomas bailed out the water that had accumulated in the bottom of the canoe. The men resumed their paddling. The hot sun and warm breeze partly dried their shirts, even if their pants and boots stayed wet. Closer to shore and with the reduced wind, they began to make good time. They were close enough now to see the cabins along the shore. They responded to the occasional wave and shout from settlers along the shore with a single wave from their paddles. The wind died down completely and they were making good progress.

"What were you saying about Rachel?" Peter resumed his questioning.

"I didn't think I said anything. I think I told you to talk to your older sisters."

"Is Rachel married?"

"She's too old for you, Peter."

"I didn't mean that. I meant 'where is her husband'? Does she have any children?"

"She has a son."

"How do you know?"

"I met him that first time when Father brought me down to the Bay to go night fishing with John's family."

"Where is he now?"

"I understand that he lives at Tyendinaga with his wife's family."

"Where is his father?"

"His father is dead."

"Did Rachel ever remarry?"

"Not that I know of. Are you done now?"

"Why doesn't Oma have contact with John and Rachel?"

"I told you I don't know all about that. Ask Catherine, Elizabeth, or Lena."

Peter sensed that he wasn't going to get any more information out of Thomas on this subject. He continued to paddle hard to keep up with his brother. His arms and shoulders ached. But talking took his mind off his aching muscles and there weren't many opportunities like this to talk privately with Thomas. He resumed his interrogation.

"Did Father ever talk to you much about the war?"

"Not much. He never volunteered much. He would answer questions if you asked him."

"Didn't you ever ask him about the war?"

"Not often. I remember, though, that on my fifteenth birthday, the summer before he died, we walked back to the fifth concession to look at some of the land that had not yet been granted from the Crown. You won't remember much about that summer; you were only ten. But that summer Father wasn't feeling well. Funny what we remember. I remember that walk that August 9th so well. It was one of the few times that Father seemed to want to talk about the past. Looking back now, it's clear that he was not well and I think he sensed that he might not have a lot of chances to talk to me alone. He was uncharacteristically forthcoming. He was a pragmatic man of few words so I remember being surprised when he turned to me and said that he loved Oma very much but they were different people. Hardship, he said, had hardened Oma, but it had softened him. The war and the Yankees' treatment of Oma made her stronger but also angry, angry and bitter. She still carried all that anger. For him, losing everything, knowing that his decision to join Sir John had had such fateful consequences for his family, watching his brother die in his arms, living in the refugee camp at Sorel when he thought he was going to die—all this, for him, led to resignation, not anger. Then he said, almost off-handedly—we were walking, he wasn't looking at me—that he knew that Oma thought that other people believed that he was too accepting, that his passive nature was a sign of weakness. 'Acceptance,' Father said, 'is wisdom, not weakness.' Oma never understood that."

Peter didn't know what to say. He wasn't used to Thomas being so open. Thomas, Peter knew, was just as reserved as his father. Thomas, too, wasn't one to talk about his feelings or to offer up philosophical theories. All the more surprising to Peter, then, that Thomas resumed his reflections on his father.

"I don't think Father was weak. I think he knew that we only live once and happiness only comes from accepting our circumstances. Get pleasure from the little things in life and try to accept what life brings. Live and let live. What good does it do to carry around anger, regret, and bitterness? Look what it did—look what it does—to Oma."

"Well," replied Peter, "she sure hates Yankees, if that's what you mean. Don't you?"

"No," Thomas explained, "I don't even dislike Americans. It's America that I don't like: the America that sees itself as superior to all others, that thinks that it has the right to come up here and take us over. But I accept that they won the first war and we lost. We've got to get over that and learn to get along with them. This shouldn't be hard. We have so much in common, but they must come to understand that we don't want to be part of them."

By late afternoon they could see John Crysler's big yellow house. They were almost home. Thomas's thoughts returned to Allie. She couldn't complain that he was late. He was looking forward to seeing little son JT and baby Aleda. He sighed deeply. He turned the canoe towards the shore.

Chapter 3
Sunday September 12, 1813
Williamsburg Township, Dundas County, Upper Canada

It was only mid-morning but already Oma Marselis's summer kitchen was filled with the wonderful smells of berry pies, johnny-cakes, and fresh doughnuts. Oma seemed happier than she had been in a long time. Baking and having everyone home—all the hustle and bustle—reminded her of some of the wonderful holidays she'd had when Johannes was still alive. She thought of how much he would like to be here now. For a few moments she was lost in another time, but then she seemed to deliberately shake herself, stand more upright, and will herself back to the present. She wiped her hands on her apron, shaking away any remaining flour, and turned to face the back of her oldest daughter Catherine, who was just taking another two pies out of the old oven: "Well, Mrs. Cook—the widow Cook—do you think we have enough food?"

Catherine turned and, with a big smile, set the pies down, came over to her mother, and gave her a big warm hug. Still holding her, Catherine whispered in her mother's ear.

"You look so happy today, Mother, just like your old self. It makes me happy to see you, well, looking so happy."

The two women were still holding each other when Allie came flying into the kitchen, slamming the summer door and startling everyone. Allie immediately sensed that she had disturbed some intimate moment. Then again, this was nothing new. She always seemed to be on the outside. She was carrying baby Aleda on her hip.

"There's my beautiful girl," said Oma.

Allie knew that Oma was talking about her baby, not her. Oma had never called her beautiful, ever. But Allie did notice that Oma seemed happier than normal. Letting go of Catherine, Oma put her arms out to take the baby from Allie. Still no greeting to Allie. When Catherine noticed this she finally beckoned to Allie and said:

"Come here, Allie, try one of my doughnuts. Would you like a little honey on it?"

Allie seemed grateful that somebody had noticed her. She took a doughnut from Catherine as Oma was fussing over Aleda. She looked at Catherine, wondering with her eyes what had come over Oma. Catherine smiled knowingly, then announced to the room, "Isn't this nice. Here we are, four Marselis girls. As Dad would have said, it doesn't get better than this."

Oma was in such an uncharacteristically good mood because her oldest daughter, Catherine Elizabeth Cook, age 43, mother of five, was getting remarried to Jacob Doran. Everybody was pleased about the marriage. While Jacob was over 60, balding, and somewhat overweight, he was a good-looking man who was well respected in the community, financially secure with his own frame house and large barns, and everyone knew that he loved Catherine deeply. He had wanted her for years and now couldn't believe his luck that the best-looking widow in Upper Canada had agreed finally to marry him. Oma didn't have to worry about Catherine any more.

The wedding was to be at four o'clock in the little Lutheran church, the second Protestant church to be built in the Canadas. As a favour to his friend Jacob and as a tribute to his old friend John Marselis, Captain Crysler had graciously offered to provide his big new home for the reception after the wedding. Captain Crysler was providing the roasted pork, potatoes, and vegetables. The Marselis women were making the desserts. Jacob was providing the fruit punch and other beverages. It promised to be one of the biggest parties in Williamsburg in some time.

Oma gave Aleda back to her mother, saying nothing to her. Allie looked straight at Oma, who said nothing and went back into the house. Allie took Aleda outside to look for her niece Elizabeth Schwerdfager who was looking after Allie's other child, JT.

Alone in the summer kitchen, Catherine looked around, counting her blessings. She remembered watching her father and husband working together to build this kitchen in the summer of 1800. Catherine was pregnant at the time. She remembered being so happy, never thinking that her husband would die before Maria was born and that her father would die a couple of months later.

Catherine's three oldest children, John, Catherina, and Christina, had all married in the previous two years so now she had only George, 17, and little Maria, 12, still at home with her. Maria already liked Jacob and would learn to love him—just as Catherine would, in time. Jacob had bought Maria a new colt for her "wedding" gift and a beautiful new stove for Catherine.

Catherine was not so sure how George was adjusting. He had always been polite with Jacob but never reciprocated Jacob's efforts at a closer relationship. Jacob had said not to worry, that these things took time and he was a fine young man. But Catherine did worry. George had seemed so restless and moody lately. He had even snapped at her last week saying that she still treated him like a little boy. Maybe she was going to have to try harder at letting go. She worried about him in a way that she never worried about John. John was only five years older but he had always seemed so mature. John was ten when his father died and he seemed to become a little man overnight. He had always been old for his years. Now John and his new bride Catherina would take over her house. They invited George to stay in his old room and live with them but George scoffed and said that he didn't want to live "with the love birds."

With the last two pies in the oven, Catherine started to clean up the kitchen. Oma came back out to the summer kitchen and, without saying a word, joined in with the cleaning up. She didn't seem so happy any more. Catherine looked at her mother but didn't say anything. Oma looked at her daughter and finally said, "What? What are you looking at? Do you have something you want to say? Spit it out."

"What's wrong, Mother? You seemed so happy just a few minutes ago."

"I have one of my headaches. Do you mind?"

"Is that all?" Catherine's eyes met her mother's squarely. Oma said nothing. She took the pot of hot water from the stove and poured it into the sink onto the dirty dishes. She gathered up the remaining dishes and put them in the sink, finally turning her face to her daughter, hands on her hips.

"Did you see the way Allie looked at me?"

"Oh, for God's sakes, Mother, you didn't even say hello to her. You could at least try to be civil to your own daughter-in-law."

"Don't tell me what to do in my own house. You saw how she snapped at Thomas yesterday."

"Not this again."

"Don't 'not this again' me. You know as well as I do that she tricked Thomas into marrying her. She nags poor Thomas all the time. I know he's not happy. Mothers can tell these things. She's manipulative and she knows that I've always seen through her. Always putting on airs. There. Now I've said it. Are you happy now? Do you want to wash or dry?"

"I'll dry, Mother," Catherine sighed as she picked up the tea towel.

The two women, who had been through so much together, stood beside each other doing the dishes without speaking. There was nothing more to say.

The silence was broken when George came through the summer door, greeting his mother and grandmother. He went immediately to the bowl of doughnuts.

"Love your doughnuts, Oma," George said, smiling at his mother.

"Don't eat too many *olykoeks*, young man. These are for your mother's big reception tonight. But here, take a couple more," Oma said as she passed the bowl to George.

George was a tall, handsome boy with thick blond hair and deep blue eyes. He had a pleasant open face like his mother and, until recently, had always seemed to have a happy disposition.

"Where's Uncle Thomas?" he asked.

His mother took a couple more doughnuts out of the bowl and handed them to George.

"Here," she said, "take these to Thomas. He's still out in the barn finishing the morning chores. Help him finish up as he's running a little behind. Then maybe you can go with him to Cook's Tavern. Jacob has paid for two casks of beer so that the men can have a few drinks before the wedding. Thomas has offered to fetch them with his wagon. Be a good boy and go help him."

"I'm not a boy, Mother."

"You'll always be my boy, but all right, be a good man and go help your uncle."

George glared at his mother, shook his head, and without saying a word, wheeled about and went out to the barn. Thomas was coming out of the barn just as George came up to the door.

"Good morning, George," said Thomas with a smile. "Let me guess. Just as I've finished the chores you've come out to help me, right?"

"I just got here. Mother said to come and give you a hand to get the casks of beer from Mr. Cook. Here are some doughnuts she sent. Can I help?"

"Sure. They're not that heavy and I'm going to take the hand wagon. I think that's the easiest way to bring them back here. Grab the wagon over there and let's go. It's a lovely morning for a walk. And maybe you can tell me what's bothering you. Your mother asked me to talk to you. She's worried about you. Is it the marriage? Jacob will take very good care of your mother. He's a good man."

"No. No, it's not that. I'm fine. Never better."

"Whatever you say. I'll push the wagon half-way there and then you can push it the rest of the way."

Thomas and George walked east along the King's Highway which wound along the north shore of the St. Lawrence from Montreal to Kingston. It was a gorgeous sunny day. Like every other traveller on this road, both men found themselves staring at the great river as they walked along.

Every quarter mile or so, they would pass the home of one of the original settlers of Dundas County. These families had acquired their properties by lot and were deposited on them in the summer of 1784 to create a new home out of the ancient forest. Every Loyalist refugee from the United States received a free grant of land from the Crown and every son and daughter of a Loyalist was also entitled to a free lot when they came of age. The lucky ones, like Johannes Marselis, got lots right on the river, on what became the King's Highway. The area along the St. Lawrence River was called "the front." Loyalists who didn't get lots along the front had to settle for lots along the back concessions which were set out parallel to the King's Highway that ran all along the front from Kingston to Montreal.

The original settlers built crude log cabins from the trees they cut to create land to farm. By 1813, most of the families had built small frame houses and the original log buildings were used as barns or outbuildings or, as in the case of the Marselis farm, the original log cabin was upgraded and used by a son until he built his own home on his loyalist grant.

Just a mile and a half east from the Marselis farm, Thomas and George came to the largest house in Dundas County, the big new two-storey yellow frame house of John Crysler. Crysler's farm was at the corner of the Nine Mile Road which ran north to the First Concession Road. A quarter-mile past Crysler's farm, they walked past Charles Jones's farm, then the Bouck place, then John Haines's farm at Davis Point, and then over the Bush Creek Bridge to the Fetterly family farm. When they came to the next farm,

George seemed nervous as Mrs. Casselman looked up from her garden at the edge of the road and waved to the two men. Just after Casselmans', the road swung right to follow the river to Cook's Point. Looking out over the river, Thomas noticed large billows of smoke on the other side.

"Guess some Yankee is burning brush," Thomas said, breaking the silence.

"Yes," replied George slowly. "Actually, Uncle Thomas, there is something on my mind. I wanted to wait and talk to you about it after the wedding but I might not get a better chance than this for a while. You have to promise me you won't say anything to Mother. I don't want to upset her before the wedding."

"I promise. What's the problem?"

"If anybody should understand you should, and I'm hoping you'll talk to Mother. I thought about it a lot. I'm not ready to be another farmer. I want to do what you did and get away from this boring place. My friend Adam Bouck and I are going to Montreal to join the North West Company. He's just waiting to hear back from Mr. Fraser. Adam heard that there was a party heading west at the end of the month. We want to be on our own. See the buffalo."

"You're a little young for heading out west."

"How old were you?"

"All right. Fair point. My circumstances were different, but that's another story. Why don't you put it off till next year? There are millions of buffalo. They will still be there next year. They'll always be there."

"Adam and I have talked about this all summer and our minds are made up. We are going no matter what Mother says."

"What about young Margaret? Everybody thinks you're a perfect match. Everybody thinks you're eventually going to marry and have a family. What will Margaret think? What will your mother say?"

"Margaret is pretty. She'll find another man very quickly. There will be lots of men come calling as soon as I'm gone. As for

Mother, I've tried to explain that I'm not the marrying kind. Margaret was her idea, not mine."

Thomas was about to reply when he looked up and saw George's face. George looked away and gruffly wiped his eyes with the back of his hand.

"What's wrong, George?" asked Thomas. "Tell me what's eating you."

George looked at his Uncle Thomas and then looked out over the river. There was no wind. There was silence except for the occasional whistle of the tree toads that loved this hot late summer weather.

Still looking out over the river, George finally replied in a quiet voice: "I'm in love with Sally Casselman but she doesn't love me. She's only a year older than I am but she treats me like a little boy. She almost laughed at me when I told her I loved her last month. I think she likes James. I can't get her out of my mind. So I spoke to Adam and he's agreed. We're going west, just like you did. We're good in a canoe. We'll see the buffalo and have a great adventure just like you. And Sally can marry James or Simon or whoever. I don't care." George turned now to Thomas. "I knew you'd understand, Thomas. We're planning on leaving at the end of the month. I can't face Mother so I want you to explain all this to her after I leave."

Thomas wasn't sure what to say, but he was saved from replying since they were just rounding the corner to the tavern.

"Damn it, George, all this heavy talk and I forgot to give you this wagon. Did you get into all this to distract me so you wouldn't have to take your turn pushing this thing? That does it, you're pushing it all the way home."

Both men laughed. Thomas put his arm around George.

"Come on, George," said Thomas. "We will talk about your plans tomorrow. Let's get this big wedding behind us. Let me buy you a beer. You're not the first young man to be rejected by a beautiful girl. Maybe you're giving up too quickly. Sometimes they like to play hard to get. In fact, I've got a better idea. If rich old Jacob Doran can buy two barrels of beer for the wedding, I think he should be willing to buy a couple of beers for the two thirsty men who are soon to be his relatives. We'll just get Michael to add it to Jacob's bill. Forget about women for now. I have had my share of problems with them; come to think of it, more than my share. Hell, I've got problems now, but this is no time to get into that. Come on, young nephew; some day you'll laugh about this tragic time."

Thomas ruffled George's blond hair as they stepped into the tavern. Apart from a window on the south side overlooking the river, the tavern was dark and the two men had to wait for a few seconds for their eyes to adjust. The air in the tavern was remarkably cool, yet pungent with the smell of beer and tobacco. Before Thomas and George could really make out who was in the tavern, Michael Cook's distinctive voice bellowed out, "Well look at this. Thomas Marselis and young George Cook. We don't see you two in here very often. Sit right here. Levi, move over and make room for our guests. Don't mind Levi, boys, he's already pretty much gone."

Levi, who had been slouched over the bar, snorted and grudgingly shuffled to the next stool.

The publican continued: "Sit down here, boys. I have the two casks waiting for you but you look like you could use a drink or two on this hot summer day."

He placed mugs of beer before Thomas and George and then poured himself one.

Levi grunted something and tapped his empty mug with his pipe.

"I think you've had enough, old man. Bossy is waiting. It's time to go home and sleep it off."

Levi angrily grunted something again but neither Thomas nor George could make out what he was saying.

Thomas intervened. "George here had an idea, Michael, just

before we came in. George is about to become Jacob Doran's stepson. He thinks that Jacob would insist on buying a beer for all of us to celebrate this great day. What do you think, Levi?"

"Right. Right on," Levi exclaimed, "you heard him. Pour me a beer and pour it to the top. Right to the top."

The beer was poured to the top but it was clear that a lot was going to be wasted. Levi's left hand was shaking holding his pipe and as his right hand came up from his lap to the bar it was shaking uncontrollably. George moved away to avoid the spill that was coming. Old Levi saw George move and a slight smile came to his face.

"No fear, lad," he said clearly. "I'm an ol' drunk with a bad case of the shakes. The drink has been me master since the war. But I can still focus me muddled old mind and milk me bossy with a firm and tender touch. And I can pick up this mug and ne'er lose a single drop."

With that clear declaration, he stood and straightened his back. He firmly placed his old Dutch pipe on the bar. His right hand immediately relaxed and the shaking stopped. He reached forward, firmly grasped the mug, and lifted it up before him, the grip as solid as an oak.

To further emphasize his miraculous achievement, lifting the steady mug a little higher, chin thrust forward, Levi spoke.

"A toast gentlemen. A toast. First, piss on the Yankees. Let 'em come and we'll kick their arses again. Second, we give our thanks to Jacob Doran and his generosity. The old fart doesn't deserve a lady as beautiful as the widow Cook and the least he could do is buy us this drink. Lucky bastard. Third, did I mention the friggin' Yankees? Yes, I guess I did already. All right then. Gentlemen, the King."

With that, Levi slowly and surely brought the mug to his lips, not wasting a drop; all of it reached its intended destination. He gave a little salute, picked up his pipe, his hands now shaking again, and gave another little salute. When he straightened himself up, he was actually surprisingly tall, providing for a moment a hint of the powerful man he must have once been. He limped to the door, head held high, and turned around.

"Please extend my best wishes to the wedding party and to all the beautiful Marselis girls, even to their irritable old mother. She wasn't always so sour and she too was a beauty in her day. Your father was a fine man, young Marselis. And you, young Mr. Cook, you probably don't remember your grandfather. Johannes Marselis was a good man. Yes, a good man. A brave soldier. He was right beside me when I got this at Klock's Field."

With that he tapped his wooden leg with the knuckles of his right hand and went out the door of Cook's Tavern.

Watching all this from the little table at the back of the tavern, beside the window overlooking the river, were two young soldiers. Because of the bright glare from the window, they were almost invisible from the rest of the tavern, which was otherwise empty on this hot September day.

One of the soldiers got up from the table and walked over to the bar. He was a tall young man with a rather swarthy complexion. With his dark hair, fine features, deep brown eyes, and tight-fitting fancy green uniform, his good looks were noticed even by the men at the bar.

"Excuse me, sir," he said in a thick but clear French accent, "excuse me, but would you be kind enough to give us two more of your fine ales?"

As Michael Cook was pouring out the two drinks, the young soldier turned to Thomas and George, offering to shake their hands as he made a slight bow and formally introduced himself.

"Excuse me, gentlemen. Allow me to introduce myself. I am Captain Jacques-Clement Herse, Canadian Voltigeurs."

After shaking hands, he stood erect, and before Thomas and George had an opportunity to say their names, Herse continued: "I beg your pardon for this interruption. My friend and I couldn't help but hear your conversation with the old soldier. We are taking advantage of Mr. Cook's gracious hospitality while we are waiting for Captain Jackson to return. He has gone to get our wagon repaired. In the meantime, gentlemen, would you be kind enough to accept our offer of another of Mr. Cook's fine ales?"

"We accept your kind offer, sir," replied Thomas with uncharacteristic formality. "I am, sir," he continued, "Thomas Marselis and this is my nephew George Cook."

"Excellent," said Herse, "and perhaps you would be kind enough to join my friend and me at our table beside the window."

Thomas and George moved to the table. They were duly introduced to Lieutenant Guillaume-Francois de Lorimier of the Canadian Regiment of Fencible Infantry. De Lorimier was a shorter man of stocky build. He spoke excellent English with only a slight trace of a French accent. De Lorimier was clearly the shyer of the two soldiers. With thick brown hair and otherwise clean-shaven, he had a dark complexion with high cheekbones. He had warm brown eyes with noticeably long eyelashes.

Herse did most of the talking. He explained that he and de Lorimier were stationed at Prescott and had just received a fortnight's leave. Herse was going home to see his family near Montreal and de Lorimier was going to visit his wife who was expecting a baby. The men had hitched a ride with Captain Jackson of the Royal Artillery, who was taking a wagon to Cornwall to get some additional ammunition. Private Samuel Adams of the Dundas militia was helping Jackson. Thomas and George were quick to point out that they knew Private Adams well and that they were both also members of the local Dundas militia. Herse explained that the artillery wagon had broken down and that Captain Jackson and Private Adams had gone back up the road to find Mr. Strader who, Private Adams had said, could fix the wheel.

Herse had just ordered another round of drinks when Captain Henry Jackson, R.A., came into the tavern. Captain Jackson was a big man, splendidly dressed in the blue uniform of the Royal

Artillery. He had large bushy sideburns. Captain Jackson explained to the men that the wheel was not fixed yet and wouldn't be until noon of the next day. Private Adams had taken the opportunity to walk on home to visit his parents for the night. Jackson explained that the soldiers could pay Mr. Cook to sleep on the floor of the tavern or find a comfortable place outside, as it was still quite warm. Thomas, however, insisted that the soldiers come back to the Marselis farm. There was fresh hay in the mow, no better place to sleep. Captain Jackson declined the kind invitation. Thomas insisted and provided the additional inducement of an invitation to the wedding reception. There would be lots of fine food and music. When Captain Jackson saw how excited the two young Canadian officers were to accept Thomas's offer, he agreed, but insisted that they would pay for their lodging. Michael Cook agreed to board the Captain's horse for the night.

The five men had one more for the road. Then another. As they finally stepped outside they were momentarily blinded by the bright sunshine of the glorious afternoon. The two young officers took turns helping George with the wagon carrying the two casks of beer. Thomas and Captain Jackson took up the rear. With the beer and the sun and the pleasant breeze off the river, all of the men were in fine spirits as they finally turned into the lane of the Marselis farm.

Garrett, who had run out to see them, met them at the gate. He must have been watching for them. He was wearing his best clothes and his hair was neatly slicked down.

"You're very late," Garrett said to Thomas with a little smile and a twinkle in his eyes. "Oma angry. Thomas bad boy," he said in a serious low voice.

Thomas reached out and hugged his younger brother and then put his arm around him.

"I know," he replied, "I know. Allie won't be too happy either. Not to worry. Now let me introduce you to our new friends, these handsome gentleman officers."

Thomas did the introductions, maintaining the almost theatrical tone of formality. He wasn't mocking his guests and they knew that. It was just a little game. The soldiers were immediately enchanted by Garrett's puppy-like enthusiasm and natural warmth. George, though, was worried and looked a little pale.

Thomas decided that this was not the best time to introduce the soldiers to the family and anyway he and George did have to get ready for the wedding ceremony, and he realized that they were very late. He instructed Garrett to take the soldiers to the barn and show them where they could wash up. He explained that they could relax in the shade of the barn or go out into the orchard just behind the barn. The apples weren't ready but Garrett would bring them out some cheese and bread. There should be a nice breeze out there. He explained that the wedding was at four o'clock in the little Lutheran church just down the road. They were welcome to come to the service but he suggested that probably wasn't a good idea considering the circumstances. The soldiers understood. Thomas would be back in an hour or so and everyone would walk back together to the reception at the Crysler house. He urged them to make themselves at home. He and George had to hurry and get cleaned up and dressed for the wedding.

Back at the house, Thomas and George did get some angry words and cold looks, but everyone was so busy getting ready to go to the wedding that they got off easier than they had expected. Except for Allie. All she said was, "How could you? Your own sister's wedding. And look at George." With that, Allie picked up the baby and turned away to join the confusion of the others rushing to finish things and start the walk to the church. Allie was right about one thing. George wasn't looking too well. Thomas helped him wash his face and comb his hair. The two stumbled into the church just moments before the service started. As they slid into the last pew at the back, Allie glared at Thomas with undisguised contempt. Oma looked at Thomas and just shook her head, with more of a look of sad resignation than anger. Catherine was so glad that they had made it that she gave the two men a smile and a little wave. George waved back with a sheepish grin.

The bride was beautiful. The groom was so nervous and happy that he wore a permanent awkward smile. He still couldn't believe his good luck that this beautiful and accomplished woman (some said the most beautiful woman in Dundas County) would be marrying this 60-year-old, more than a little overweight farmer with no hair.

The flowers were beautiful. The late afternoon sun came through the little windows on the west side bathing the whole room with a golden warmth. It was a wonderful moment for everyone. An unforgettable moment.

In the years ahead, however, it wouldn't be Catherine's beauty or Jacob's happiness that was most often recounted about that happy day. It wasn't Lena's lovely solo. It was, just as the ceremony had ended, just after Jacob had kissed his bride, the sound that George made vomiting in the back pew that would be told and re-told in the years to come. This was a family story that George would never live down.

~ ~ ~

By the time that Peter and Garrett and the soldiers arrived at the Crysler house, the party had been well under way. The hall of the house was the largest room in the largest house in Dundas County but it was still so full that most of the guests were milling about outside. Through the open door and windows you could see the dancing inside and hear the clapping, along with the fiddles. Children of all ages were running in and out of the house. Before the soldiers could make their way into the house, an elderly woman brought them glasses of mead on a silver tray. Toasts all around to the King.

Peter and Garrett proudly introduced the soldiers as various neighbours came by to greet them. Particularly pleased to see the soldiers was Captain Merkley, the commanding officer of the

Dundas militia. He was a large man in his early sixties. He had fought with Sir John in the first war, and settled in Dundas County in '84, but he still spoke English with a thick German accent. He was very proud when Captain Jackson made a point of telling everyone how lucky they were to have such an experienced officer to lead the militia. Inevitably the discussion came around to recounting the great victory against the Yankees at Ogdensburg the previous winter.

As darkness fell, the elderly lady who was serving the mead lit two torches outside by the rose bushes. The flickering torches and the rising moon over the river gave the warm evening a silvery glow. In spite of the warm temperatures, it was too late in the season for mosquitoes. When the fiddle music stopped for a break, many of the guests came outside to catch the light breeze coming off the river.

In the yard beside the house some of the older children were playing a game with a ball. Among them was the master of the house, young John Pliny Crysler, who paid particular attention to Maria.

De Lorimier was uncomfortable with all the new people and the attention he was getting. The drinking all afternoon had also made him a little melancholy. He was happy to have this diversion but anxious to get home to see his wife.

When Garrett asked Herse and de Lorimier if they wanted to go into Captain Crysler's barn to see his horses, de Lorimier was pleased to use this opportunity to get away from the crowd. Herse declined. He couldn't take his eyes off of the young woman in the blue dress.

The young woman in the blue dress also saw Captain Herse out of the corner of her eye. In fact, she had seen him earlier through the window. All the young women inside were talking about the handsome soldiers outside.

Herse walked towards the Crysler house to get a better view. He could see that the beautiful young woman in the blue dress had her blond hair pulled back in a bun. Even from this distance he thought he could tell that her eyes were blue.

Herse wasn't inexperienced in dealing with young women. At 24, he had enjoyed the company of many young women in Montreal. His parents had even picked one out as an excellent marriage prospect. She was a notary's daughter. His mother had called Florence "a perfect catch," but Herse wasn't thinking of Florence or anyone else. The girl in the blue dress was the most beautiful creature he had ever seen.

Just then he saw her take her friend's arm and the two walked deliberately towards him. He wasn't ready for this. She thrust her hand forward to shake Herse's hand.

"I am Elizabeth Schwerdfager," she said, "and this is Alzina. Are you a friend of Peter Marselis?"

"Yes," Herse stammered, "and I am pleased to meet you. I am Captain Jacques-Clement Herse, Canadian Voltigeurs. Peter and Thomas were kind enough to invite us to this beautiful reception as we are spending the night in Williamsburg. I am on leave on the way to Montreal."

"Thomas is my uncle. I am living with him," said Elizabeth. "I'm helping his wife Allie with their two young children."

"That is very kind of you, Mademoiselle Elizabeth. Are they here this evening? I don't see Thomas."

"No. Allie isn't feeling well. They told me to come to the reception so that she could rest. I think they wanted me out of the house."

Alzina just stood there staring at Herse. Herse was unaware of her presence. He couldn't take his eyes off of Elizabeth. She fascinated him. Montreal girls weren't usually so forward but Herse admired her forthrightness. She was so self-confident. So direct.

Elizabeth continued: "Alzina and I wanted to come over and welcome you to Williamsburg. We hope you will come inside, as the music should be starting up again very soon. Do you dance, Captain Herse?"

"Yes, yes I do," replied Herse. Why did this young woman make him feel so awkward?

"Come along then. Let's go in to the dance," Elizabeth said as she took one arm and Alzina took the other. The two of them marched Captain Herse inside the house.

It was a grand room. The bride and groom were sitting at one side but most of the guests were standing as the fiddle players were starting to tune their instruments. Elizabeth proceeded to introduce Herse to everyone. He couldn't remember any of their names as he was somewhat overwhelmed by Elizabeth's enthusiasm. All of the faces seemed to blur together. The music began. He was dancing with Elizabeth. Then he was dancing with Alzina. Then he was dancing with an older woman who held him so tightly he could hardly breathe. Then he was dancing with Elizabeth again. In the days ahead, Herse tried to remember that evening but the details eluded him. In the evenings and nights ahead, he tried to recall the order of events but all he could remember was Elizabeth. The way she danced so nimbly. Her blue eyes and blond hair. Her full lips. Her slim waist and full breasts.

Chapter 4
September 21, 1813
Williamsburg Township, Dundas County, Upper Canada

Lot 25, Concession 5 was four miles in from the front. There was still no road open to it but there was a good cleared path that roughly followed the old Indian trail north from the St. Lawrence to the Petite Nation River. The northern half of the lot was entirely covered with large white pines, the soil being sandy there, while the southern half was mixed hardwood—mostly maple with some birch and cedar. There was a small, perhaps one-acre, clearing at the northeast corner. In the clearing, sitting on a stump, was Thomas Marselis.

He had awakened before dawn and quietly slid out to leave Allie sleeping with the two children. He always enjoyed the walk back to his lot. He had been granted the hundred acres from the Crown as the son of a Loyalist. He had petitioned for it in 1810 when he returned from out west. Within a couple of summers he had cleared enough to have a small crop and a garden but the deer ate almost everything he planted that was above ground. Only the potatoes and turnips survived.

The situation at the home on the river had become increasingly intolerable. With two small children, there was just not enough room in the log cabin that had been his father's original house, even with the two extra rooms that had been added. Allie was constantly unhappy living so close to Oma, who lived in the new house right next door with Peter and Garrett. Thomas was now determined to clear more land to have a larger field and to acquire enough logs to build his own cabin for Allie and the children. Allie's father had offered to lend him some money to get him started and he had assured Thomas that he could provide most of their furniture and some farm animals and implements and Thomas could use his pair of oxen any time he needed them. But Thomas had declined the offer.

He had been working as time allowed on his own lot, but to get cash he spent most of the spring working for Mr. Baker and then he spent two weeks in July working for John Crysler at a dollar a day to help bring in the hay. His brothers had been very helpful when they could spare the time, as had his brother-in-law Lewis Schwerdfager. He was especially grateful for Lewis's assistance in providing his oldest daughter Elizabeth to help Allie, but that had made the cabin even more crowded.

Last night he had told Allie that there was just too much to do to have even a partial cabin ready for the winter. They would have to put up with the existing arrangements until next summer. Allie knew this but still she went into one of her moods. When she wouldn't stop crying, Thomas had left and slept in the haymow. Garrett heard the commotion and came out of the barn to keep Thomas company. Garrett always became sad and worried when he heard Thomas and Allie fighting. He was always afraid that Thomas would leave again. Thomas tried to reassure his brother that some arguing between husbands and wives was normal. Thomas said that he was mostly to blame, as he should have built his own cabin by now. He admitted that he hadn't stayed as focused as he should have. He couldn't blame Allie for being unhappy in the current circumstances. Garrett said that he didn't remember Oma and Poppy fighting like that. Thomas told his brother not to worry. They had to get to sleep, as tomorrow would be a busy day.

When they awoke in the morning, Garrett offered to do the chores with Peter and after they were done, he and Peter would come up to the lot and help do some more clearing. Thomas hugged his brother and assured him everything would be all right.

On the walk back to his property that morning, Thomas worried about how sensitive Garrett was to family tension. Thomas could put up with Allie's tantrums—what choice did he have?—but he resented how much Allie upset Garrett. Garrett wanted everybody to be happy.

By mid-morning, Thomas had cut four more pines, sawed them into eight-foot lengths, and stacked them beside the pile of sawn cedar boards that Allie's father had given him earlier in the spring.

The weather was still warm and pleasant. As there was no wind, Thomas decided to burn some brush and small logs. A few more pails of ash would bring in some much-needed cash. Before he started the fire, however, he heard someone shout his name. It was Garrett. He was coming down the trail with Peter and young George Cook. The men were carrying their axes and a large crosscut saw.

Peter explained that Oma had suggested that if enough logs could be felled and cleared before freeze-up maybe a bee could be organized so that at least the shell and roof of Thomas's cabin could be erected and he could work on the interior through the winter.

Thomas accepted the offer and the men set about picking out the best trees for logs. This was a good time of year to work in the bush, as it was too late in the season for mosquitoes. The men had made good progress by mid-afternoon. They sat down to eat the lunch that Oma had sent of apples, cheese, and some of her oat cookies.

While they were having their lunch, Peter took the opportunity to make an announcement. Jacob Doran had just learned that Mrs. Bouck was willing to sell her late husband's horse for 40 dollars and Jacob was willing to buy Garrett's lot on the fifth concession as an investment for that amount. Thomas and George thought that was a wonderful idea. George slapped Garrett on the back:

"What do you think? Great idea, eh?"

Garrett didn't respond. He was confused. What did Peter mean? Whose horse? Peter went through the explanation again. When Garrett finally understood, he was so full of joy he had to do a little dance. He twirled around with his arms in the air. Garrett had a wonderful open smile. He grabbed Peter to give him a big hug and soon the two of them were dancing about.

Garrett's joyful enthusiasm was always infectious. His apparent happiness rubbed off on those around him. Watching Peter and Garrett, Thomas grabbed George and they, too, did a little jig, until George tripped on a stump and they both fell to the ground laughing. In later years, Garrett still remembered this happy time: "the time we did the silly dance in the bush before the war."

Garrett's life had not always been so happy. He received and gave love unconditionally but he had sensed from an early age that he was different. He was 12 when his father died. It was Garrett who found his father in the old barn. He wouldn't go into the barn for months after that. He was 17 when his sister Nancy died. He had spent months sitting with her. During that sad time, he gave Nancy a new kitten, a cat that seven years later he still slept with every night. It was the only barn cat Oma allowed in the house. It was now a large black tom, but it was still called "Nancy's kitten." It was just days after Nancy died that Thomas went out west. Garrett never understood Thomas's explanation for why he left. The death of his sister in July of 1806 and the departure of his brother the next month had had a dramatic effect on Garrett. By the late fall he became so ill that he didn't want to get out of his bed in the morning. He ate so little that everyone thought he was dying of some disease. He came down with a chest infection that winter. His mother thought he had contracted consumption. A doctor was brought from Kingston and he gave Oma the devastating news that people like Garrett rarely lived past adolescence and that Garrett was dying. It was a "scientific fact," he said.

But Garrett's inner spirit didn't know about this medical certainty. When spring came, his cough improved. Two calves were born. Sally had another litter of puppies. Garrett got his appetite back. By summer he had made a complete physical recovery. Emotionally, though, he would never fully recover. He lived his life for the moment, resigned to the expectation that tragedy was always just around the corner. He never fully trusted the happiness of life again. He once confessed to his sister Lena that he thought he was dying that bitter winter of 1806; that he had prayed a lot as Reverend Schwerdfager told him to do, but it hadn't saved Nancy and prayer had no effect for him either; that he had done a lot of thinking in his bed, especially at night when he couldn't sleep for the coughing, and he had come to realize that you can't change most things and that, if he got better, he would choose to be happy; that he would try very hard to not let sad thoughts come into his mind; and that, if he got better, he would commit himself to help his family to be happy and to accept that sometimes bad things happened.

There were no bad things happening this beautiful September day in Williamsburg Township, Dundas County. The men finished their break and resumed their tree-cutting. Garrett, however, couldn't get his mind off of the horse.

"When do I get my horse?" he asked Peter.

"I think Jacob is going to try to bring it Sunday when he comes to church."

"Is it a boy horse or a girl?"

"I don't know."

"Does the horse have a name?"

"I'm sure it does. It is fully grown. It's not a colt. But you can give it another name, if you want."

"You can't just change somebody's name. Anyway, the horse would be confused if I used another name. What colour is it?"

"I don't know."

"Does it come with a saddle? I need a saddle."

"I think it does. We'll get you one if it doesn't."

"I'll take good care of it."

"I'm sure you will."

"Did Oma say I could have my own horse?"

"Yes. I think it was mostly her idea."

"Did anybody tell Maria I was getting a horse?"

"I don't know. Maybe."

"Maria and I can go riding together."

"She will like that."

"You and Thomas can borrow my horse. You can ride him any time you want."

"Thanks," said Peter, "that would be nice. I'm not much of a horseman but Thomas is. He would love a horse if he could afford it."

"Thomas and I can share my horse."

"That would be nice. Your horse could help out back here building Thomas's cabin. Maybe we could rig up something so that he could pull a wagon."

"And a sleigh. Pulling a sleigh in winter would be good."

"Yes. That would be nice . . . Now take the other end of this log and we'll roll it over to that pile."

The days were getting shorter and by seven it was getting dark and time for the men to return to the front. Peter had already left an hour earlier to start the chores.

While they were walking back, Thomas thanked George and Garrett again for their help. He was walking beside George and took the opportunity to ask him whether he was still planning on carrying out the idea he had discussed with Adam Bouck.

George replied that he was meeting this Sunday after church to finalize the arrangements.

"You didn't say anything to Mother yet?" asked George, warily.

"No," said Thomas, "I didn't think I was supposed to until you gave me the final word. Anyway, you should speak to her yourself. By the way, have you had any further conversation with Sally?"

George replied that he had not and then, surprisingly, Garrett said: "Are you talking about Sally Casselman?"

Thomas and George had not thought that Garrett, who was walking several feet ahead, had heard or even been paying attention to their conversation. Thomas knew that George's plans and the whole matter of Sally were a big secret. The men kept walking and then George asked tentatively:

"Why do you ask, Garrett? Why do you think we were talking about Sally Casselman?"

"Nothing, really."

"What do you mean 'nothing, really'?"

"She was talking about you yesterday with Elizabeth."

"She was talking about me? She mentioned my name?"

"Yes. She told Elizabeth she thought you were very handsome."

"When? When did she say that?"

"Yesterday. I told you. Yesterday. Hey, look, look over there, look at the big red cardinal."

"Never mind the cardinal. What else did Sally say about me?"

"Nothing else."

"What do you mean? Nothing else?"

"It was just girl talk. Elizabeth said that she liked the soldier—de Lorimier's friend, I forget his name—and that is when Sally said something else about you that I didn't understand."

"What else?"

"I don't know. I just told you. It was just silly girl talk. They don't think that I pay attention to their silly talk. They ignore me unless they want me to do something for them."

Thomas looked at George. George looked very unsettled. Thomas couldn't resist. He put his arm around George and gave him a playful poke on the shoulder:

"Well, young George, maybe Dundas County doesn't seem so boring any more. What do you think, eh?"

By the time that Thomas got back home it was almost dark. Elizabeth met him at the door. She told him that Allie had taken the baby and JT to visit her parents. Her father had picked her up that morning with his horse and carriage and would bring her back tomorrow afternoon. Elizabeth told Thomas that she had left some bread, boiled eggs, and pickles on the table. She was going down the road to the Straders' as they were having a bonfire by the river in front of their house. Adeline and her father were bringing their fiddles and there was going to be a sing-along. She thought Thomas should join them, as he was alone that night. Peter and George, and maybe Garrett, were coming. Elizabeth said that she would be spending the night with her friend Barbara.

Thomas could see that Elizabeth was looking forward to a party and a break from babysitting. She loved parties. He also concluded that he was too old for most of the group so he encouraged her to have a good time but said he was tired after a full day working at his lot. He would go to bed early tonight.

Thomas sat at his table eating his supper, alone except for his old dog Gunner, under his chair. It was unusual for the little three-room cabin to be so quiet. The sun was down now but there was still a lovely red sky over the river. Tomorrow would be another sunny day.

As the room became dark, Thomas realized that he was missing Allie and the children. For all his problems with Allie, he still missed her when she wasn't there. He knew that she had probably gone to her parents' home because of the fight they had had the night before. Was missing someone proof of at least some kind of love?

He stepped outside and sat on the old wood bench, looking across the road to the river. It was a lovely warm evening, still more summer than fall. A bonfire party tonight was a good idea; there wouldn't be many more evenings like this before the cold would begin to come.

He heard some hammering in the new barn and he could see a light in the little window of the front stable. He would have liked to go and see what was being done but he knew that if he went over he risked his mother seeing him. This was not a good evening to be explaining where Allie was. He was in no mood to have another conversation with his mother about his wife. There was nothing more to say. Talking about it didn't make anything better. Talking as a solution to problems was highly overrated, in his opinion.

He and Allie just needed time. She was young and had been spoiled by her parents. They had been through a lot in just three years. Thomas did not accept his mother's theory that Allie had gotten pregnant deliberately as a way to get Thomas to marry her.

Thomas knew that he didn't love Allie the way he had loved Yakonwita. It wasn't the same. But she was a good mother and beautiful. Her parents had been very kind and helpful. He and Allie just needed time. That was it; they just needed time.

He went back into the cabin to get his pipe and some tobacco. When he came back out he saw Peter coming across the field towards him. He was carrying a small jug in one hand and a little three-legged milking stool in the other.

"Good evening, old man. You look a little lonely and glum sitting here by yourself in the dark. You look like you could use a little party."

Peter sat down on the bench beside his brother, removed the cork from the jug, took a big drink, and handed it to Thomas. Thomas smiled, took a drink, then started to cough.

"Whew. That is strong stuff. Is this your new batch?" he said, taking another drink.

"No. This is some of Adam's grog left over from the wedding reception. He gave it to me because he didn't want to carry it home. I hid it in the barn."

"That's Garrett in the barn now?"

"That's Garrett. I just came from there. He insists on building a new stable for his horse. There's no talking him out of it. He can be so stubborn. He says it can't wait until morning. He's using the north end of the sheep pen."

"Oh well. If it makes him happy. He sure is excited about that horse. That was a good idea you and Oma had. You're not as dumb as you look. Give me another drink of that rotgut."

"Here, but that's the last one. We have to save the rest for the party. We should get going."

"No. No. I'm not going anywhere. You go ahead, if you like. It's been a long day."

"I'm not taking no for an answer. Even Oma thinks you should take advantage of Allie's absence and go with me. She thinks you've been working too hard lately. Her poor little boy. She doesn't realize what a lazy old hound dog you really are, and that Garrett and I do all the work around here."

Thomas smiled. He said nothing, just shook his head and then stood up. "All right," he said, "let's go for an hour. A little drink and a smoke never hurt anybody. We won't have many more evenings like this."

As soon as they stepped out on the highway they could see the fire just a mile down the road. Soon they could also smell the wood smoke and hear the fiddles and singing.

The fire was on a small, elevated point beside the river. A couple of dozen people surrounded the fire seated on logs and benches. The Marselis brothers were warmly welcomed when they arrived. On a log, back from the fire, Elizabeth was holding hands with a boy until she saw Thomas come over to sit beside her. Thomas recognized him as one of the young Merkley boys. He shook his hand, asked him his name, and sat down between him and Elizabeth.

"You're getting to be a big fellow. How old are you now?" Thomas asked.

"I'm fifteen, sir, almost sixteen," he stammered.

"When will you be sixteen?"

"Next summer."

"Is your father or mother here tonight?"

"No sir. My father is on artificer duty at the fort this week. My mother is at home with the twins and the babies. She let me come here with my Uncle Alfred to make sure he doesn't get too drunk and to help him home if he does."

"I see," said Thomas. "I thought Elizabeth here was going to be with her friend Barbara. Where is she?"

"She's gone for a walk with her friend. She'll be right back," Elizabeth explained.

"I see," said Thomas, standing up and walking towards the fire. "I'll be right back. Got to get this thing going."

Thomas lit his pipe with a stick from the fire. He could see that Peter was sitting on his little stool sharing his jug with a couple of other young men. Their faces glowed from the fire as they sang and clapped and stomped their feet to the music with great enthusiasm.

Thomas didn't feel like singing so he returned to the log where Elizabeth and the young Merkley boy were sitting. This time he didn't sit between them but instead pushed the boy closer to Elizabeth and sat down beside him, saying nothing but taking a long pull on his pipe.

The three of them sat there without speaking cuddled up on the log, watching the fire and listening to the fiddling and the singing. Elizabeth was unusually quiet. Some people started to dance little jigs. Peter and his friends started to sing louder. The moon began to rise out of the river. Elizabeth whispered something to the Merkley boy. Thomas smoked his pipe and tapped his toe to the music.

It was the Merkley boy who finally spoke: "Elizabeth says that you went out west with the fur trade for several years. I'd like to do that. How old were you? What was it like?"

"I was twenty. It was interesting."

"What was it like?"

"Saw some beautiful country but it was a lot of hard work. Sometimes we paddled twelve to fourteen hours a day. Sometimes it was too hot. Other times it was too cold. Mosquitoes and black flies could eat you alive."

"My father told me that you can speak like the Iroquois. Is that where you learnt to speak Indian?"

"No. I learned a little Cree and Ojibway out west. My father was a fluent Mohawk speaker. He taught me a little when I was young. When I came back to Upper Canada after two years out west I ended up in Grand River country with the Six Nations and I stayed there nearly two years. That's where I learned Mohawk . . . enough about me. What about you? What do you do besides chase girls?"

Thomas gave the boy a friendly poke and pushed him closer to Elizabeth. Elizabeth stood up, arms firmly at her side. First she had an angry look, then she broke out into a big smile.

"Nobody chases me, Uncle Thomas. I do the chasing . . . Now, why don't we stop all this talking and move our log closer to the fire and join in the singing. Shall we?"

Turning to the Merkley boy, Thomas affected a serious voice:

"Here's a little lesson for you: the only way to get along with women as stubborn and as strong as Elizabeth here is just to generally go along with what they want. Just give in. That's been my experience." Turning to Elizabeth, he said, "I believe you are absolutely right, Miss Elizabeth Schwerdfager, so let's move this log and join the party."

A little later Barbara arrived with her very unhappy mother standing behind her, the mother's hand firmly on Barbara's shoulder.

"Barbara and Elizabeth are leaving now," said the mother to Thomas. "We'll bring Elizabeth back tomorrow morning. Are you ready, Elizabeth?" It was clear that this was an order, not a question.

By now the party was winding down anyway. Uncle Alfred was a little unsteady but he could still walk home. Peter's jug was empty so he was ready to go home too.

Walking back along the road under what was now a bright moonlit sky, once they got away from the fire, both men noticed what a beautiful clear night it was. The light from the moon reflected off the river to cast strange shadows on the sides of the trees.

"Well, that was interesting," Thomas said. "Elizabeth is quite the young lady. Louis and Lena have a handful with her."

"As the oldest of seven, she's had to grow up pretty fast. She's strong though, just like her mother. Speaking of which, I did what you told me to do. I asked Lena about John Sunday and his sister Rachel. She told me to talk to you. Why is everybody so . . . so, I don't know, so secretive about her? What don't I know?"

Without any further hesitation, walking along the road in the dark, looking out at the river, Thomas finally told the story as he had heard it from his older sisters Catherine and Lena many years before:

"Apparently, our father had some kind of disagreement with his father in Schenectady. In 1760, when our father was just nineteen, he left for the Schoharie Valley to clear some land that was given to him by his uncle. He had 150 acres near Cobus Kill. The land was beside a Mohawk village. Father was taken in by a Mohawk family the first winter when he became ill. He lived with them for five years but then something happened. I don't know what. By this time his father was dead and he returned to Schenectady. He was in New York City for part of a winter and then he ended up at Stone Arabia on the Mohawk, when he met our mother and married her in '69. He was twenty-eight. She had just turned nineteen. Catherine was born the next year."

"I have heard a lot of this," Peter interrupted his brother, "so what is the big secret?"

"I'm coming to that, Peter. You asked me what I know," said Thomas. "Our father joined Sir John's King's Royal Regiment of New York in August of '77. In the winter of '78, he wasn't able to come back home from Canada. Oma was the wife of a Tory alone with four young children surrounded by many rebel families who treated her badly. You have heard the stories. Father got word back to the Mohawk village and they provided protection and food. That was when Oma learned of a part of our father's life that he had not fully told her. She had known that he had lived with the Mohawks for a while but she didn't realize how long or how close he had become to them."

"John Sunday was part of that village?" asked Peter.

"Yes. They were very close. In fact, John joined the Loyalist forces and fought the rebels alongside our father. John's brother was killed at the Battle of Klock's Field and John was with Father when Uncle Gar was killed the same day. They both lost their brothers on the same day."

"So Father knew Rachel too?"

"Yes. Very well. They were lovers."

"Father and Rachel were lovers? How do you know?"

"He told Mother the winter of '83-'84 when they were in the refugee camp at Sorel. Catherine was just thirteen and remembers what an awful winter that was. Mother was pregnant with Nancy. We had lost everything, all because Father had joined the Loyalist side. Mother's family disowned her. Her own brother fought for the rebels. Imagine it, apparently he was at Klock's Field, he could have been trying to kill his own brother-in-law. Anyway, Father became very ill in the refugee camp. The doctor, Dr. Smith, told him that he was dying. He confessed to Mother about Rachel and—this is the part that only a few of us older children knew—he and Rachel had a son. Father took me to meet him the year before he died. His name is Jeremiah."

"*Tabernac*!" exclaimed Peter. "I've got another older brother and he's an Indian. What else haven't you told me?"

"That's all for now. Anyway, we're home. So that you won't wake everyone, you can sleep with me if you promise not to snore . . . It's been a long day and we have a lot of work to do tomorrow."

The two brothers went into the cabin. Thomas lit the lantern. In the middle of the table was a fresh bowl of Oma's doughnuts.

"Say what you will about our dear old mother, she's a helluva cook and we'll never starve to death as long as she's alive," Thomas said as he took a doughnut and sat down at the table across from his brother, who was already sampling one.

Just four years apart in age, the brothers had grown even closer in the last four years since Thomas had returned home and moved into the cabin next door with Allie.

"Poor Alfred Merkley," Peter said, "he sure is a slave to the alcohol. I guess he can't help it but it's killing him. He's not the man he was just ten years ago."

"It is sad," replied Thomas, "probably why he never married. Or maybe, because he never did. What about you? Twenty-three and still a bachelor."

"I've got my hands full with Mother and Garrett."

"Seeing Alfred like that tonight reminded me of the time—the summer after Father died, I would have been sixteen, you twelve—when Alfred's sister-in-law came up from the States to visit. Do you remember?"

"Yes, I do," Peter replied, "and she brought her two children. The girl was your age and I recall that you two got along very well. She was a pretty thing. I remember the boy, Luke, was about my age. I remember he had a bone-handled knife that he said was made by a coloured man. Funny what we remember. I loved that knife. He was big like all the Merkleys."

"Yes, she was pretty." Thomas was still thinking of the girl. "Wonder what happened to her. Thinner than I like, but beautiful. They returned to Stone Arabia and never came back. Oma's theory was that the mother came up to Canada to see if she could marry her brother-in-law after her husband died but she left at the end of the summer to go back to the States. Oma said she just wanted Alfred's farm."

"It would be interesting to see them again," Peter said. "Luke and I were good friends that summer. Remember all the pickerel we caught? I suppose he's now in the Yankee militia and getting ready to come up here to kill us. Probably coming with all our American cousins. And we will be trying to kill them."

"Strange and sad when you put it that way, Peter. How did it all go so wrong, that it has come to this? What folly. When will we ever learn?"

"Well," replied Peter, "let's keep one thing straight. We're not attacking them. The Yankees are invading us. There is a difference."

"You could kill Luke? You could run him through with a bayonet?" asked Thomas, making a thrusting motion with his arms.

"I guess I would have to if he was attacking me," Peter replied, "or, maybe you're right, maybe I couldn't if I recognized it was Luke. Let's hope it won't come to that. Anyway, let's not talk any more about wars. You're right, it's time to hit the sack."

Chapter 5
Saturday September 25, 1813
Williamsburg Township

Oma woke early. She dressed and made herself a cup of tea. Peter and Garrett still were not awake. Oma had a lot of things she had to do that day, but she decided to treat herself and go outside and sit on the front steps to have her tea and look at the river. It had now been 29 years since she and Johannes first stepped off the boat onto this land to start over. There had been so many changes, but the one constant had been this view of the great river. The big oak was still there too—Johannes had refused to cut it down.

They had pitched their tent on this same spot that June day. She had been 34 years old then, with five children and very pregnant with Nancy. Thinking back on it, she wondered now how she ever coped. The three girls had been 10, 12, and 14. They had been so strong all through the war and at the refugee camp at Sorel. She was so proud of them still. The experience had made them strong, independent women. Catherine had given her six grandchildren. Lewis and Lena had six, and Christy Ann had seven. With Thomas's two little ones and Maria's baby, she had many healthy grandchildren. Counting them she was counting her blessings.

Then she thought of Nancy. Nancy, who was born in a tent that first summer in Upper Canada before Johannes built the first log cabin. Nancy, who bravely endured months of vicious pain until blessed death finally came to free her from it. Oma would never forget finding her dead in her bed early that July morning. If she were alive today she would be 29 years old.

Then she thought of Johannes. It would be 12 years this October 16th since he passed away. She still missed him so much.

She had dreamt about him just the other night; he had been playing with the dog in the summer kitchen. Why would she dream something as strange as that?

She wasn't worried about her Peter. He was a good boy and would get married some day and have a family. But she worried every day about Garrett. She had no doubt that the other children would look after him when she died. That wasn't what she worried about. It was his vulnerability now that worried her. He loved too much; he hurt too easily. Oma knew that one needed resilience above all other things—how else could one cope with the many setbacks and heartaches of life—and she knew that she had taught this to all of her children, but Garrett was different. Since the year Nancy died, Garrett seemed to be generally happy but always fearful, always sensing that the happiness wouldn't last. Not that she herself was an expert at happiness. Oma knew that she was sometimes too quick to anger, too domineering, too judgemental. She knew that with the exception of Catherine, who seemed more like a sister to her than a daughter, she was too controlling of her children. This, however, she told herself, was acceptable because she was just trying to protect them. Even if they didn't always realize it or appreciate it, she was doing it for their benefit. They would all come to understand this in time.

Take the case of Thomas, for example. She had seen through Allie from the beginning. She knew that Allie had used her good looks to seduce Thomas that summer he came home. She told Thomas that Allie wasn't right for him but he wouldn't listen to her. He only married her because, he said, it was the right thing to do. And now look at the situation. Her Yankee parents had always spoilt Allie. She might usually be a good mother—Oma would give her that—but Oma knew she wasn't a good wife for Thomas. Allie didn't understand Thomas the way his mother did. A man needs more than beauty in a wife. Beauty is just skin-deep. Thomas never was a good judge of women. At least Allie wasn't an Indian. That was one good thing about her.

Her tea was done. Her hips were starting to hurt so she stood up. She closed her eyes and felt the sun on her face. She could smell the river. She thought again of Johannes. He loved this time of year—warm and no mosquitoes. She was remembering making love to him years ago one warm September like this, when she heard her name spoken. She opened her eyes, startled, disoriented for a moment. It was Allie standing in front of her.

"Heavens, child. You startled me. Why did you sneak up on me so?" Oma barked at Allie.

"I didn't sneak up on you. I just came around the corner and spoke your name because your eyes were closed. Are you all right?" Allie asked.

"Of course I'm all right. Why wouldn't I be? You shouldn't sneak up and startle people. Now I think I feel one of my headaches coming on. See what you've done?"

"I'm sorry, Oma," Allie replied with a sigh.

"Well, what is it? What do you want?"

"I just came over to see Peter and Garrett. Thomas left earlier this morning to go back to our property to get an early start. He asked me to tell Peter and Garrett to meet him there after they do the chores. Are they not up yet?"

"I'll get them up now," Oma replied as she turned and walked through the door, leaving Allie standing outside alone.

"Thanks," Allie said, shaking her head in frustration. "I'll go back to my cabin now." Walking back to her cabin, Allie knew that Oma was now in the house and couldn't hear her say, "It's been very pleasant visiting with you, Oma. I'm fine, thank you for asking. You big fat-assed Dutch cow."

By mid-morning Oma had got Peter and Garrett up, fed them breakfast, and packed them a lunch. Peter couldn't help Thomas today as he had agreed to work for Mr. Barclay for the day. Garrett would have to go back to the property on his own. Oma saw her sons off, mopped her kitchen floor, made two pies, and put them in the oven. She tidied up the boys' bedroom, did a wash, and hung up the clothes on the line in the back. As it was such a clear warm day, she decided to air out the house by opening all the doors and windows, but then she saw that some wasps were coming into the house so she proceeded to close them all. Just as she was closing the windows in the front, she saw, coming down the road from the west, two horses with riders and a carriage being pulled by a horse. She went outside for a better look.

It was Jacob and little Maria riding the two horses and Catherine riding in the horse and carriage. At first she was annoyed that no one had told her they were coming (she hated surprises) and then she realized how happy she was to see them. This was the first time that she had seen them since their wedding.

This was also the first time that Oma had seen Maria's horse. Maria seemed so proud and grown-up on the horse. Maria was 12 but she was tall for her age and she looked much older. She had a lovely open smile with gleaming white teeth. She was wearing a floppy straw hat tied with a large yellow ribbon. Garrett had given her this hat the previous summer. Jacob dismounted, leading the horse he had been riding towards Oma, and explained that the purpose of their visit was to deliver Garrett's horse, and this stallion was it. Oma stroked the black horse's head and confirmed how thrilled Garrett was going to be. Everyone was looking forward to seeing Garrett's reaction. Catherine tied Buck, who had been pulling the carriage, to the hitching post at the side of the house, and went inside with Oma for a cup of tea. Jacob and Maria crossed the field to show Allie and her children the new horses.

Allie was thrilled to see Jacob, Maria, and the horses, and so were her two children. Allie was also grateful for the attention, and even affection, that she had always received from Maria and Jacob. Maria was a naturally loving little girl who had always admired her Aunt Allie, who was young and so beautiful. Jacob, too, had always gone out of his way to be kind to Allie. Perhaps as another outsider, he knew how hard it was to fit in and be fully accepted by the large close-knit Marselis family. Even though he was 40 years older than she, Allie always felt a special bond with Jacob.

Maria had also wanted to show her horse to her cousin Elizabeth, who she knew was staying with Allie and Thomas. Allie explained, however, that Elizabeth had gone to her parents' home for the weekend. Then she asked Maria if she would like to come into the cabin to help her feed Aleda, who was just waking up from her nap. Jacob agreed to stay outside and play with JT.

Jacob had an easy, natural way with young children. He lifted JT up onto the saddle of Garrett's horse and, hanging onto the three-year-old boy with one hand, he led the horse with the other out the laneway to the King's Highway, where he noticed two horsemen riding towards them from the east.

As the two men on horses came closer, Jacob was pleased to see that it was the two Canadien soldiers, Lieutenant de Lorimier and Captain Herse, approaching the Marselis farm. They both waved to Jacob. Returning to the fort from their fortnight leave, this time on family horses, de Lorimier and Herse were stopping at the Marselis home ostensibly to bring small gifts to say thanks for all the warm hospitality they had been given two weeks earlier. In Herse's case, however, after the initial greetings were extended to Jacob, his principal motivation for the visit soon became quite evident.

"So where is everybody?" Herse inquired of Jacob.

"Peter has a day's work at the Barclays. Garrett and Thomas are working back at Thomas's lot for the day. Oma is in her house with Catherine. Maria is in the cabin helping Allie with Aleda, and JT and I are walking Garrett's new horse," he replied.

"Garrett has a new horse? That's wonderful," said de Lorimier. "When did he get it?"

"He hasn't got it yet. I brought it here this morning so he is going to have quite a surprise when he comes back later this afternoon. Good-looking little horse, don't you think?"

"Fine horse," de Lorimier exclaimed as he rubbed the horse's nose.

Herse couldn't wait any longer. "And where did you say Elizabeth was?" he asked with poorly disguised fake nonchalance.

"Oh yes," replied Jacob with a smile, "I forgot that you had met our Elizabeth. She is with her family for the weekend. Come, tie your horses here and we'll get Allie to get you a drink. Have you eaten?"

De Lorimier insisted that they did not want to intrude. They had stayed at the Cornwall Barracks last night and planned to be back to the fort before dark. A drink of water would be quite sufficient, and he wanted to give a gift to Oma. He also had a small gift for the new bride, so it was fortunate that she was here. De Lorimier tied his horse and proceeded to walk over to Oma's house.

Herse, too, tied his horse but returned to an earlier thought. He casually inquired of Jacob where Elizabeth's family lived. Before Jacob could answer, Allie came out of the cabin carrying Aleda, with Maria at her side. They were pleased to see Herse and asked about de Lorimier. Maria proudly showed Herse her new horse and then led her over towards the house to show de Lorimier. Herse played with JT for a few minutes while Allie got some water. Jacob picked up Aleda to bring her closer to Garrett's horse, letting her touch the horse's nose and ears. When Allie returned with the cup of water, Herse took the opportunity to ask, purely in passing, where the Schwerdfager farm was from here. Allie saw Jacob's smile and said that she thought it was a very long way off. Jacob agreed, saying that he understood it to be at least a two-day ride. Maybe three, said Allie. Perhaps, on second thought, it might even be four days away, mused Jacob, until he couldn't keep it going any longer. When he started to laugh, Allie giggled in a way that she hadn't in a very long time. Jacob affectionately put his big left arm around Allie, their two bodies shaking in unison as he gave Herse a playful poke on the shoulder with his right hand. They finally explained to the forlorn and confused Herse that Elizabeth Schwerdfager's home could be reached by horse in less than half an hour.

"Why do you ask?" said Allie, still giggling, not wanting the fun to end. "Are you blushing, Captain? Jacob, I think the Captain is blushing."

Herse finally got the joke. He returned the playful poke to Jacob, although with somewhat greater force. Jacob feigned serious injury and started laughing again, and that set off another round of giggling by Allie. JT was confused. He had never seen his mother being so silly or laughing so much.

Oma insisted that the young soldiers stay for supper. De Lorimier graciously declined. Herse seemed agitated. Maria urged de Lorimier to stay. Allie offered to make dessert. Catherine argued that the Marselis boys would be disappointed if the soldiers left before they got home. Herse admitted that they could still get to the fort without it being too late if they left right after an early supper. Oma insisted that it was no trouble to just add some more potatoes and vegetables to her fish stew. More discussion ensued. It was obvious that de Lorimier was hopelessly surrounded. A compromise plan was struck. Herse would ride over to the Schwerdfager farm just for a quick visit with Elizabeth and to extend his greetings to her parents. De Lorimier and Maria would ride back to Thomas's lot and deliver Garrett's horse to him and suggest an early return to the front. The Dorans and the soldiers would head west right after an early supper, before it got dark.

Catherine insisted on one variation. She and Jacob would babysit Aleda and JT so that rather than de Lorimier having to lead Garrett's horse north, Allie would ride it back to the lot. She was an accomplished rider. Allie could then walk home with Thomas.

In less than half an hour, de Lorimier, Maria, and Allie rode into the clearing at the south end of Thomas's lot to find that Thomas and Garrett were inside the cabin just finishing the top row of logs. With their hammering, Thomas and Garrett had not heard them approach. There were still no windows cut in the log walls, the only opening being for the door on the west side. De Lorimier motioned to Allie and Maria to dismount and to lead the horses quietly closer to the cabin, keeping to the south side so they couldn't be seen. As they got closer to the south wall they could hear Thomas and Garrett talking inside. Maria was bursting with anticipation and excitement. Allie too had to fight back a giggle. De Lorimier was pleased to see how much they were enjoying the game. Suddenly, de Lorimier's horse shook himself, making a snorting sound. The three froze, then listened carefully to determine whether the brothers had heard. They were relieved to hear the conversation inside continuing, indicating that their secret was still alive. De Lorimier motioned to Allie to slowly lead Garrett's horse to the open door and then hold him there. As Allie led the stallion towards the door, de Lorimier leaned down and whispered something to Maria. When Allie had the horse at the door, Maria called out Garrett's name twice. They heard the conversation and hammering inside stop. Then Maria made a loud naying sound and then, half giggling, she said in a high-pitched voice, "I am Garrett's horse. Where is my master, Garrett Marselis?"

She then made another loud naying sound. The three pranksters could not see Garrett, but they could hear the excitement in his voice as he kept repeating: "Thomas, what is this? What is happening?" And then he shouted, "There is a horse at the door!"

Allie gave the stallion a pat on his rear and the horse went through the door with Allie right behind him laughing. She saw Garrett's face, especially his shining eyes. It was a look of sheer unadorned joy that she would never forget. Thomas, too, saw his brother's face and thought that he'd never seen anything more touching. Then he saw his wife's face; he knew that he had never seen anything more beautiful.

Then Maria ran through the door, entering the roofless shell of the log cabin. She kept jumping up and down giggling. Garrett hugged the horse's neck; then he hugged Allie and Maria. He still wasn't sure what was happening but whatever it was, he was enjoying it. When de Lorimier came through the door, Garrett couldn't contain his excitement; he started to cry. De Lorimier hugged Garrett while Maria tried to hug them both. The horse just stood there, sensing this was an unusual moment.

Everyone went back out the little door. Allie and Maria explained everything to Garrett, excitedly taking turns giving him the details. When Garrett mounted his horse he looked so proud. He rode the horse to the north edge of the clearing and back. He could see that the horse handled well. Maria explained that his name used to be Buddy but Garrett could change it if he wanted to; Jacob had said so. Garrett said he thought Buddy was a wonderful name. Buddy it would stay.

With the heat of the day, de Lorimier noted that the horses needed to be watered. Thomas suggested they go back to Hess Creek. Garrett knew the way as the two of them had walked to it last summer and again this spring. Garrett confirmed that he remembered the way: straight north through the pine forest for a mile until you come to a cedar swamp, then northwest following the western edge of the swamp for another mile until you hit the creek. On horseback it should take no more than 20 minutes, Thomas reckoned.

It was a pleasant ride back through the pine forest. The old trees were so large and thick that there was almost no underbrush. The track was mostly a bed of pine needles. The air was pungent with the smell of pine gum. When they came out into the sun of the meadow at the edge of the cedar swamp, Garrett pulled up his horse for de Lorimier to ride up beside him. At this point the trail went down into a gully that was perhaps 100 yards wide, before rising to a rocky outcropping. Since June, when he had walked this trail with Thomas, the gully had become flooded. The beavers had been at work. There was only a foot of stagnant water in most places but the muddy base created treacherous footing for the horses. It was not possible to proceed. The bush was too thick with brambles and tangled hawthorns to go around the flooded area. Anyway, they did not have to go all the way to Hess Creek now. They dismounted and walked the horses to where the water seemed to be the clearest and gave the horses a drink. Before heading back, the three riders tied the horses and sat in the warm sunshine on a log surveying the several acres of flooded beaver pond below. The location of the beaver lodge was not evident but the loud slap of a beaver tail suggested it was to their left. At the back of the pond, a Great Blue Heron was carefully picking his way through the swampy water. To their right, where the pond seemed to be the deepest, a pair of mallards were swimming, happily enjoying the afternoon sun.

Surrounded by the silence of the forest and not wanting to disturb the wildlife, de Lorimier, Garrett, and Maria spoke in hushed tones:

"It sure is quiet and peaceful back here," de Lorimier commented as he closed his eyes and felt the sun on his face.

"Yes," said Maria, "this is the first time that I've been back this far. The trail through the pine forest was beautiful."

"You two are sure lucky to have your own horses," said de Lorimier. "Good of Jacob to deliver Buddy to you today, Garrett, and yours was a gift from Jacob, is that right, Maria?"

"Yes. He's very kind to me." Pausing for a moment, Maria continued, "Can I ask you something, Gui?"

"Sure," de Lorimier replied, turning to look at Maria, "ask me anything."

"It's about Jacob. I call him Jacob because I have known him since I was a little girl. Now that he has married my mother, do you think I should call him something else?"

"Oh, I'm sure he'll love you just the same no matter what you call him."

"I know that," Maria replied, "but I was thinking maybe it's different now. I've never had a father. He's my father now. What would you do?"

"Have you talked to your mother about this, Maria?"

"No, but I've been thinking about it. I wanted to know what you thought."

"I think you should talk to your mother. She's the best person to ask. I'm sure Jacob would be very touched if you called him 'Father,' if that is what you're thinking."

Garrett had been sitting on the log saying nothing. De Lorimier wasn't even sure that Garrett was listening to the conversation, as he seemed to be concentrating on watching two rabbits that were at the edge of the clearing to the right. Without turning his head to look at Maria, Garrett, still watching the rabbits, said quietly but firmly: "You should call him Poppy. That's what I called my Poppy before he died. He liked that name. He said it was his favourite name. Jacob would like you to call him Poppy."

"Thanks, Garrett," Maria said as she reached out and touched Garrett's hand, "that's a good suggestion. That's a very good suggestion, don't you think, Gui?"

"Yes," replied de Lorimier, "I am sure Jacob would be very pleased. How old were you when your father died, Garrett?"

"I don't remember. It was just after Maria was born. Maybe twelve? What did you call your father, Gui?" asked Garrett.

"He was always Papa to me," De Lormier replied. "By the way, did you know that I am going to be a papa very soon? My wife is due to have our first baby."

"Congratulations. What are you going to call your baby?" Maria asked.

"If it is a girl, we will call her Marie, which is the French for Maria," he said, with a wink at the girl. "If it is a boy, we will call him Guillaume-Henri. I hope the Yankees go home for the winter so that I can be home for when our baby is born. It will be in just two months."

"Do you think they are going to invade us this fall, Gui?" Maria whispered as she saw the rabbits coming even closer, apparently unaware of the human presence.

"I don't think so but we can't be sure," de Lorimier replied. "But I do think it's time for us to head back. What do you think, Garrett; are you ready to ride back?"

"Yes," replied Garrett, "but first, look at Buddy. What's he worried about? Look what he's doing."

Buddy was putting his nose in the air, nostrils flaring, and one front foot pawing at the ground. He shook his head and then stood perfectly still, listening intently. Then de Lorimier's horse started to act agitated. Maria's horse too was startled by something. He reared back and took several steps towards the pine forest.

"I think they smell or sense something. You're right, Garrett. I have never seen my horse act like this. Maybe we should be going back," de Lorimier half-whispered to Maria and Garrett as he got off the log and took the reins of his horse. At that moment, the three were startled by a loud crash to their right as a large white-tailed deer burst into the clearing. Seeing or smelling the humans, the doe bolted to its left and leapt onto the trail leading back into the pine forest, the white flag of its tail flashing, and it was gone in an instant.

"The horses must have sensed that the deer was close by. That must be why they were so unsettled," Maria suggested to de Lorimier. "What do you think, Gui?"

"I don't know. Something must have been chasing the doe for her to be running so fast. And look, the horses still are not settled. They have had a drink. We should be going back anyway," he replied as he mounted his horse.

Only moments after the riders left the clearing and were riding along the trail in the pine forest, into the clearing sauntered a huge panther, its grey-brown fur glistening in the afternoon sun. He smelled where the horses and humans had been. He took a drink and then lay down on his side and stretched out—all eight feet of him—to enjoy the afternoon sun. There was a black tip at the end of his long tail, which he flicked contentedly. Dinner could wait until dark.

When de Lorimier, Maria, and Garrett entered the clearing at the north end of Thomas's lot, they couldn't see Thomas or Allie. As they rode up closer to the cabin, Maria yelled, "Hello."

Thomas came out the door straightening his hair. His sweater was on backwards. As Maria asked where Allie was, she too came out the door, tucking in her blouse. Her face seemed a little flushed.

De Lorimier suggested that he, Garrett, and Maria would go back to the front now. Thomas and Allie replied that they would follow soon.

"No need to rush," de Lorimier said to Thomas. "There are still a couple of hours until supper. It's a beautiful day."

"Oh, we don't need that long," replied Thomas with a smile, as he put his left arm around Allie's waist and gave de Lorimier a little salute with his right hand. "Thank you, Lieutenant," he said, "and you're right, my friend. It is a beautiful day. A wonderful day. We'll be back by supper."

And they were back before supper. Catherine in particular noticed how happy they seemed to be as they came walking into the back yard holding hands. Allie was happy to see her children and quickly joined in to help Oma and Catherine with final preparations for supper. Thomas went straight to the barn, where Jacob, Garrett, Peter, and de Lorimier were finishing the chores. While Garrett and de Lorimier shovelled out the manure, Jacob fed and watered the cows. Peter and Thomas climbed up the ladder to fork down the hay from the mow. When they were done, Peter leaned on his fork handle and spoke to his brother:

"I have a little story for you, Thomas. When I was walking back from Barclay's today I thought I would stop in and say hello to Lewis and Lena. All they could talk about was how Herse had come by their farm this morning. He was, he said, just dropping by for a visit. He gave Lena a silk scarf, which, he said, came all the way from Paris. He told several interesting stories about his recent trip home. Apparently, Elizabeth was particularly impressed by his story about sailing from Quebec City to Montreal on a real steamship. It is called the *Swiftsure*. It provides regular service now between Quebec City and Montreal. No need for sails, can you imagine? Do you still call it sailing? Elizabeth, apparently, was enthralled by Herse's many stories of what city life in Montreal is like. After having dinner with the family, Herse kindly offered to save Elizabeth the long walk tomorrow to Thomas and Allie's by giving her a ride back on his horse. That was over four hours ago. Where are they? I thought they would be here when I got here. I didn't say anything to anyone. I didn't want anyone to worry about where they were or what they were doing."

Thomas smiled: "I don't know where they are but I have a good idea what they are doing. I wouldn't be too worried."

"You're not concerned about Elizabeth?" questioned Peter.

"From what I've seen of Elizabeth, I'd be more worried about Herse. I hope he knows what he's getting himself into. And, if you ask me, I wouldn't tell anyone what you know. It's embarrassing getting caught out in such circumstances. I've had a similar experience myself quite recently," Thomas said, still smiling.

Thomas and Peter climbed down the ladder from the mow to be met by an excited Maria, who had just come into the barn with news that Captain Herse was back. "And guess what?" she said. "Guess who he brought with him on his horse?"

"Let me guess," said Thomas. "Could it be . . . Elizabeth?"

"Yes," said Maria, "isn't it wonderful? It's been such an exciting day!"

"Yes," said Thomas, "it has been a great day."

Chapter 6
Wednesday, October 20, 1813
Williamsburg Township

"So now we check to see if the honey has gone all through the linen filter. There, you see, the heat of the sun on this glorious afternoon has freed the honey from the wax. Beautiful, eh? Next, we pour the honey into these jars. Your mother is going to be so happy we finally did this. I admit that we've put this off so long we almost ran out of the warm sunny days to get it done. After we finish this, what do you say we fix the problem with the front door? Won't your mother be pleased with us? And then we'll start supper so when your mother comes home with the baby she can just relax and, well, be happy with her boys. What you think, partner? Yes, and I can see that you agree too, Gunner. Now we'll set the wax over here until we heat it up so that we can strain it and get all the little bee parts out of the wax. There's a whole bee. Poor little fella, worked himself to death. You can tell a bee from other insects—they have six legs and four wings. We need nice clean wax for Oma to make her candles for us all . . . your coughing has stopped. I think maybe you're finally asleep. Are you asleep, partner? Your father loves you very much. I hope you always know that. So, let me see, are you asleep?"

Thomas leaned over and looked into the wood box.

"There you are, my son, my handsome little boy. Almost as good-lookin' as your old father. Sound asleep at last and warm as toast in the wood box."

"Almost as good-lookin' as his father? Aren't we full of ourselves today? JT's in the wood box?"

Thomas turned to see his mother, who had just come around the corner of the cabin. She was standing with her hands on her hips; then she came forward to peer into the wood box.

"What, pray tell, is he doing down there in the bottom of a dirty old wood box?"

"I had some work to get done out here, Mother. He was having trouble getting to sleep with all his coughing. I made a deal with him that he could come out here if he lay down on a blanket I put in the box. I talked him to sleep."

"He's got a cough again?"

"Yes, Mother, he has a cough again. We are as worried as you are."

"Where's his mother?"

"Allie and Elizabeth are pickling at the Whittekers'. They took Aleda with them. She'll be home soon."

"She should be here with JT if he's sick again. Does he have a fever?"

"A mild one, I think."

"Did you give him some of my willow tea?"

"No, Mother. Allie will do that when she gets home. She'll be home soon."

"I don't care what you say. She should be here. That little boy has been sick since August. He's so thin. That cough just doesn't go away. I'll take him back to my house. Get some of my tea into him."

"No, no, you won't, Mother. He's finally asleep. Sleep will do him good. He was up most of last night coughing. Allie wanted to stay but I insisted she go. This pickling has been planned for a couple of weeks. She enjoys spending time with Anna. I can look after my son until she gets home. It won't be long now."

"Fine. Suit yourself. Don't listen to me. I came over to tell you that Garrett and Peter are working at Cooks' today but they'll be back in time to do the chores. And I'm making a harvest soup with the last of my sweet apples and the leeks Garrett found. I made extra, so I'll bring some over for your supper. Unless you think that I'd be interfering too much."

"Mother, some of your soup will be good. And don't worry about JT. He's asleep now and should be feeling better tomorrow. I know you're concerned and so are we. I know that . . ."

Before Thomas could finish, he heard a knocking at the front door.

"We're around at the back," he yelled. Then remembering that JT was asleep, annoyed at himself, he looked into the wood box. Relieved that JT wasn't awakened, Thomas went to walk past his mother to go around to the front, when John Cook came around the corner.

Motioning with his finger to his lips to be quiet, in a softer voice Thomas greeted John:

"JT's asleep. I shouldn't have yelled," he said. "Oma and I were just having a pleasant visit, weren't we, Mother?"

Ignoring her son, Oma nodded to her oldest grandson. "Afternoon, John. How's your Kate? Have you talked to your sisters? I never hear from them."

"All well, so far as I know. Everyone is enjoying this splendid weather," he replied. "George is at Casselmans' again."

"And your mother? Have you seen her lately?"

"Yes. She came by with Maria yesterday in the horse and carriage."

"She didn't come by here," Oma said curtly.

"No. She didn't have time to come this far. She just dropped by on her way from seeing Althena Beckstead, back on the fourth concession. She was delivering a message from her sister Margaret. You remember her. She was at Dr. Smith's at Sorel at the same time as Mother. They have stayed in touch over the years through letters. She wrote Mother to tell her that they were forced off their farm in the Thames Valley the day before the battle at Moraviantown. They lost everything but she and her family are alive. She asked Mother to tell her sister."

"I remember Margaret," Oma said matter-of-factly. "Lazy as a coon, as I recall. Never had it so good as when she lived in Dr. Smith's big house with all the food she wanted. I was surprised she had the brains to learn the abc's. Catherine did all the work and taught her more than Mrs. Smith did. They shared a bedroom for four years so Catherine read to her every night. I remember her. She got fat as a sow at Dr. Smith's while we never had enough to eat. Catherine got Sundays off and brought us food every week. How Lena and Christina would look forward to those treats every Sunday!"

"Well, anyway," said John, "she's alive. Her husband and father were in the battle. I guess it was a terrible rout. A lot of men killed."

"Her father, now there was a good man. You must remember him," Oma said, turning to Thomas. "He was a friend of Johannes. Had a farm back on the second concession, Matilda, for a while. Used to come by for a visit now and then. Bought a boar off of us one time, I recall. Big, tall handsome man he was. You must remember him, Thomas?"

"Yes, I remember him," Thomas replied.

"Well, I'll leave you boys. I've got work to do," said Oma as she took one last look at JT, shook her head at her son, and left to walk back across the field to her house.

"Can't offer you my mead yet," Thomas said, motioning to John to follow him into the cabin. "It's not ready yet. Got a jug of rum hid in the barn I could go get. Or, I could make you a cup of tea."

"No, nothing for me thanks, or maybe just a glass of water. Can't stay. Came by to tell you and your brothers that there's another drill planned for Sunday. And I thought you might be interested to have me read parts of this letter sent to Mother. I have it here. The Yankees control all of Upper Canada west of Burlington Heights now. Proctor's a coward. Fled Moraviantown even before the battle started. With British leadership like that, how are we ever going to stop the Yankees if they come this way?"

"It's getting pretty late in the season to come down the river. The Yankees would never get past Kingston and Prescott."

"I'm not so sure," replied John. "Let me read you this letter."

"I got a feeling I'm going to hear this letter whether I want to or not. Go ahead, Professor. Have a seat at the table and let me check on JT. I'll be right back. I'll be all ears."

"It's dated October 10, Burlington Heights," John began.

Sunday, October 10, 1813
Burlington Heights
Upper Canada

My dearest Catherine:

I fear that you will have heard about the awful defeat Tuesday at Moraviantown and are anxious to know if we are all still alive. Many have died but we have been spared, though we have lost everything. We only have the clothes on our back.

Henry is trying to keep a brave face but I know he is not himself. He and my father were with the militia at the battle and saw some terrible, terrible things. Henry's best friend Silas was killed leaving poor Euphemia with three young ones and another on the way. She is in the tent beside us. I don't think that she has stopped crying since she got here. I've been trying to help so I have her little Hattie here with us. Catherine is good with girls that age.

Henry is with my father this evening trying to settle him. Father is drinking heavily. The savagery of the battle and losing everything has just been too much for him to take. I swear that in all my 39 years

I never saw him cry, not even when Mother died. But he's been crying for four days now. Only the drink seems to let him sleep. Having to leave all his animals behind, losing everything at his age—seeing so many men killed—it's all been more than he can bear. He's a broken man. My heart aches seeing him like that but what's a soul to do? Henry has been trying to console him but poor Henry is not well either. What he saw at the battle and worry about Catherine and me is weighing on him bad. Sometimes he just stares off into space.

Anna MacDonald is here in the camp too. You remember her from Sorel. She was a couple years older than us. She worked for Dr. Smith too. She used to do cleaning in the office and surgery. She always had bad nerves, you will remember, so this has put her over the edge. Henry says she tried to do herself in two nights ago. Poor soul. At least that's the gossip.

Henry's just back so I'll finish this letter to you later tonight.

Henry and Catherine are asleep now. She's a great comfort to her father. She's always been older than her age and as smart as her godmother. It relaxes me to write to you so I'll tell you what Henry has told me about what happened that day.

On Tuesday we were following the trail up the river trying to stay ahead of Harrison's army chasing us. We had to abandon everything the day before. They say he had 4000 men, many of them Kentuckians. Leaving our little farm along the river was such a sad thing. 15 years of work and all gone. The summer here was hot and dry so there was not enough water in the Thames to use boats of any size so we had to walk. We pulled a wagon for a while until the wheel broke.

Across the river from Moraviantown is Fairfield, a mission to the Delaware Indians. General Proctor made the decision to face the Yankees near there because they were gaining ground on us. The women and children were sent ahead. The militia and the 41st had a cannon loaded with canisters on the road. Our Indians under Tecumseh were in a swamp on the right on the north side of the river. The Yankees attacked on horses so fast and there were so many that Henry says he doesn't think our cannon got off more than two volleys. Maybe not even that—he only remembers hearing one.

The battle didn't last ten minutes. Henry said that Kentuckians who had daubed themselves all over with red paint like Indians followed the Yankee cavalry. These wretched animals used their scalloping knives on our soldiers. When Henry saw such villainies, he ran into the swamp. That night he came upon a small group of the 41st and thank goodness, got here Wednesday night. He looked like he had seen ghosts. We don't know what happened to Father. I was worried sick. I thought he'd been killed or was wounded somewhere or taken prisoner. Good thing Henry hadn't told me about the Kentuckians. Then on Friday morning a corporal from the 41st brought him to me here. As you probably heard, Tecumseh was killed and after the Kentuckians scalloped him, they say that they cut his skin into strips to be fashioned into razor strops as souvenirs to take back south to Kentucky.

Tecumseh's older sister is here in the camp with us. She lost both her famous brother and her husband but she seems to be bearing up well. She is a very strong woman and beautiful. She wears her thick black hair in a braid that goes right down to her waist. Her name is Tecumapease, which means "Flying over the water" in Shawnee. She raised her brother. She is very kind. In spite of all that she has been through she has been trying to help with all the sick soldiers we have here.

It's now Monday evening, my dear Catherine. I had to stop writing last night because they came to get me. Father was so drunk he fell, but nothing's broken. He's in an awful state. I don't know what's to become of him.

Henry says that at the meeting this morning an officer said that our army was completely "annihilated." That's the word he used but I don't know if that's how you spell it. We lost 28 officers and over 600 men were killed or taken prisoner. In a battle that only lasted 10 minutes!

Henry says that if Harrison keeps coming we will have to walk back to York or maybe to Kingston. That will mean that all of Upper Canada west of Kingston will be lost to the Yankees. I shudder to think of it. For one thing, my old legs could never do it. Too much weight to carry around, I fear. Maybe we'll be in Dundas County yet this autumn. What's to become of us?

Henry says that even the British officers are blaming the defeat on General Proctor, who was the first to run off. Henry says that Tecumseh was twice the leader Proctor was. The talk today is that Harrison isn't coming here because he ran out of supplies. I fear that the Yankees will be back. They won't give up until all of Upper Canada is part of America.

Flour is in short supply. The summer has been so hot and dry that the local gristmills couldn't operate. There's also been a lack of wind so even the windmills are still. I don't know what we are going to do about food or having a roof over our heads this winter.

Catherine is a good reader. I am so proud of her. A nice British soldier was surprised to see her reading yesterday so he loaned her a book about Ireland. I suppose this was also his way to make friends with her. She is pretty and a big girl for 13 and I fear she is going to have her mother's body. I told him that I was writing a letter and he offered to help put it in a message bag for Prescott. I'm to give it to him after dinner. I'll bet your little Maria is a beauty and that you've taught her to read and write by now. We were so lucky to have Mrs. Smith teach us. At least something good came of those terrible five years in Lower Canada.

It's my turn today to work in the tent hospital that has been set up. I hope this letter finds you and your family well. I hope some day after the war we can see each other again and I can meet your handsome new husband.

Please get a message to Athena that we're all alive. Don't say anything about Father.

Love, Margaret

John took a drink from his glass of water. He folded Margaret's letter and put it back into his pocket.

"I better check on JT again," Thomas said, as he got up from the table and went outside. John followed him out.

"Well," said John, "I guess I better get on going home. Pass on the message to Peter and Garrett about the drill. It's at Bouck's again, around noon . . . Margaret's letter brings it home, doesn't it? We've been so lucky here in the east. I can't understand why they're not attacking Montreal. Or Prescott even, to cut off the supply lines. What do you think, Thomas?"

"I don't know what to think. I do know that I remember Margaret's father. I remember him well. I can't imagine him being—what did she call him?—a 'broken man.' I wonder what broke him most: losing everything, or what he saw at the battle? I can't picture him in my mind crying. This is insanity. How did it get so wrong? What are we going to do?"

"That's an easy one. The Yankees attacked Upper Canada. They invaded us to take our homes and make us Americans. That's what is so wrong. What do we do? We fight back to defend our homes. We kill as many Americans as we can until they go home."

"That simple, eh?" replied Thomas, his voice getting quieter. "It's not like they're some other people or something. They're the same as us. Hell, we could be killing our cousins. Allie's older brothers are still down there. Doesn't your Kate still have lots of family in the States?"

"What, you think we should just surrender, give up and join them? Submit to their mob rule and the new American empire?"

"I didn't say that. Tell you the truth, I don't know what to say. I wish I had your certainty. I do know that I hope the Yankees stay at home and I wish my wife and baby were home here by now."

"Yes, well, I have to go too," John said as he started to walk away. "See you Sunday, eh?"

"Sure," said Thomas, "wouldn't miss it for the world. I'll walk out to the road with you to see if I can see her coming."

As John walked west on the King's Highway to his home, Thomas stood on the road looking east. There was no sign of Allie. The sun was lower on the horizon now. With the loss of the direct heat of the sun, the temperature was dropping quickly. Thomas felt a slight shudder down his spine. Why wasn't Allie home by now? It would be dark in less than an hour. A cool breeze came in off the river. Then he remembered that JT was still outside so he rushed back to his cabin.

Thomas reached down into the wood box and brought his son to his breast, wrapping the blanket around him. JT opened his eyes when he saw his father; he smiled, then closed his eyes again. The fever was worse. Alarmed, Thomas brought JT into the cabin and placed him on his bed. The cabin was getting cold. Thomas was annoyed at himself for not starting a fire sooner.

"Stay right there, JT," he said, "I'll put on a fire to make it nice and cosy in here. Don't move off the bed. Your mother will be home soon."

As Thomas hurried outside to get some kindling, he noticed that dark clouds were gathering in the east as a cool damp breeze blew off the cold black river. When Thomas came back into the cabin JT was coughing and calling "Da, Da." Thomas went to the bed and picked up his son.

"You're burning up, my little boy. What am I to do?"

"Drink, Da Da," JT pleaded.

"Oh yes. Of course. What was I thinking of? Let's go in the kitchen. Here. Here . . . have some water. That's good. Drink it. You're such a good boy. Not even crying. Let me put you back in your bed. There now. What's that noise? It must be your mother. Your mother's finally home!"

But it wasn't Allie at the door. It was Peter. Oma had sent him over with some hot soup. When Peter asked where Allie and the baby were, Thomas replied calmly that she would be home soon. He wasn't worried. What could go wrong from Whittekers' to here? She would be home very soon. Peter offered to wait with Thomas until Allie got home but Thomas assured Peter that everything was all right—JT was in bed and doing fine.

When Peter left, the cabin was silent except for the sound of the growing wind outside. Thomas put a bigger log on the fire, lit a lantern, and checked on JT, who was sleeping soundly, but his forehead was still hot. Thomas put Oma's soup on the stove. He heard Gunner scratch at the back door. When he opened the door to let Gunner in, he could feel the cold dampness from the growing east wind.

It was dark now. Where could Allie be? Standing alone in the kitchen, staring at the door, Thomas felt a deep sense of foreboding. He tried to tell himself that he was over-reacting, that there was a perfectly simple explanation for why Allie wasn't home and why she hadn't sent a message. But it wasn't working.

"I'll be right back," he said to Gunner as he rushed out the back door to the outhouse.

When he came back in, he checked JT again and his forehead seemed a little cooler—but maybe that was just wishful thinking, he thought to himself. He dipped a cloth in the water pail and wiped JT's neck and forehead. Again, JT opened his eyes for a moment, smiled a little smile at his father, and went back to sleep. His listlessness worried Thomas. He wiped JT's forehead with the cool cloth again. Thomas decided that if Allie wasn't home in a half-hour, he would have to swallow his pride and ask Oma for help with JT and ask Garrett to ride Buddy to Whittekers' to find out what had gone wrong.

Thomas sat down at the table. Gunner, sensing something was wrong, curled up under Thomas's chair. Thomas tried to will his mind away from worrying about Allie and JT. But thinking about Margaret's father and the prospect of the Yankees attacking Dundas County was not that helpful. He reached down and rubbed Gunner's head. Gunner made a strange little moan—more a note of concern than contentment. Thomas thought again of Margaret and her husband and her father. Even if Allie and the baby were fine, even if JT was better tomorrow, if the Americans invaded the St. Lawrence Valley, they too could lose everything.

Gunner suddenly raised his head and then stood up. He took two paces towards the door and stopped. He uttered a deep growl. The growl stopped, his tail started wagging, and he walked to the door as a rush of wind came and the door swung open. It was George Cook letting himself in.

"*Tabernac*, it's getting cold out there," he exclaimed as he closed the door and rubbed his hands. "There wasn't much of a light here so I thought you were at Oma's. I tied my horse there and came over here after they said you were here."

"Yes, yes, George. You have news of Allie?"

"Allie is fine. The baby is fine. It's my fault that you didn't get a message earlier."

"Where's Allie? Why isn't she home?"

"She's staying the night at Crysler's."

"She's at Crysler's farm?"

"Yes, let me explain. Allie was at Whittekers when Nancy Crysler sent for Anna to come because Nancy's cousin who was visiting went into early labour. Anna took Allie and Elizabeth with her. It was a long and difficult delivery. Nancy said that Anna took a spell before the birth so Allie took over. I guess everyone was impressed with how good Allie was. Nancy says that Allie is a natural at being a midwife. Baby and mother are both going to be fine."

"Why isn't Allie coming home?"

"Well, it was almost dark before the baby decided to come. I was visiting Sally this afternoon. Her father had me helping out in the barn. You know what Ceph is like. Anyway, when I finally got out of there, as I'm going by the Crysler place, Nancy sees me and asks me to take a message to you that Allie and Elizabeth were exhausted and that Nancy insisted they stay over until the morning. I left to come to tell you, when I remembered that I forgot the jams that Sally's mother gave me to give Kate, so I had to go back. Anyway, I'm sorry if I had you worrying."

"Oh, I wasn't worried," said Thomas. "I knew there had to be some good reason."

"I was supposed to tell you that Allie was sorry she wasn't coming home but John Crysler will bring them back in the morning in his carriage."

"Allie will be glad to stay in the big Crysler house. She'll be living like a queen there compared to here."

"I have to get going. I'm already late," said George. "I'm sorry again that I was so late."

"That's all right. I wasn't worried," repeated Thomas as he closed the door behind George.

Thomas checked JT, who was sleeping soundly. He poured himself some soup from the pot on the stove and sat down at the table. Gunner got up from his mat beside the back door and lay down under Thomas's chair, his chin resting on Thomas's foot. It was quiet in the cabin but Thomas could hear that the wind had come up outside even more. Something was banging in the back. He must have failed to properly latch the outhouse door.

"What do you think, Gunner?" he said as he rubbed his dog's head. "Kind of lonely in here without Allie and the baby. They're safe but I still don't feel right. What's wrong with me? You don't know? What good are you? What good is an old dog if he doesn't give advice? What do you think, old fella? I complain about her but when she's not here, when she's not here . . ." He was looking for the words when there was a knock at the door, and Peter let himself in and slammed the door behind him.

"Getting colder out there. That door is sticking," Peter said.

"Yes," replied Thomas, "I know. I know. I was supposed to fix it today. Allie's been complaining about it for a week. What's that you have for me?"

"Oma sent this piece of cake for her favourite son and this little sack of her dried willow tea. She insists you make some for JT. And George tells us you're on your own tonight with JT. How is he doing?"

"He seems to be sleeping well. Hasn't coughed much since this afternoon. I've got the water on. Want a cup of tea?"

The two brothers sat at the table having their tea.

"Good cake," Thomas said. "You and Garrett were working at Cooks' today?"

"Yah. Cut and stacked wood. Made some cash. Weather's been so good we forget winter's not far off. That wind tonight is going to blow off a lot of leaves. Starting to feel more like fall out there tonight. Got your wood ready?"

"No. I'm behind on a lot of things. Separated three tubs of honey today though. I promised Allie I'd do several things today.

Like fix that door. But John Cook came by and interrupted me. He wants us to know that there's another drill Sunday at Bouck's. To shame me for not showing up to these militia things, he read me a letter Catherine got from her old friend Margaret about the battle at Moraviantown. It was a slaughter. Terrible slaughter. Her husband and father were there. Remember her father?"

"I remember him. In fact, I remember the last time we saw him. He came by that fall before he left to go west to the Thames country to be closer to his daughter. He came by the same week that Luke went back to the States."

"That's right. I remember now. You were so disappointed. And I was sorry to see his sister leave."

"The two of you were pathetic, as I recall."

"Oh yes. First love."

"I'm not sure it was 'love' so much."

"Whatever. You have to admit, she was pretty and she had a great body."

"I don't want to hear about it."

"You brought her up. Now I'm getting all excited just thinking about her."

"You don't need much," Peter said, shaking his head. "You never did. Can we get back to the letter. Margaret's family are all safe?"

"Yes, but they've lost everything. Her father has taken it real bad. She says he's a 'broken man.' The Kentuckians scalped our men. John thinks that the Yankees still might invade us before winter. He was really pushing us to go to this next militia drill."

"Garrett and I haven't missed one. We have to be as ready as we can be."

"So, let me get this straight. You've decided now. If your little friend Luke invades Dundas County next month, you'll be ready to shoot him or run him through with your bayonet or stab him with that bone-handled knife he gave you?"

"I guess we have to do what we have to do. We've already had this conversation," Peter said, getting up from the table. "But now that you're in one of your moods I think it's time for me to leave. Anyway, it's time for bed. See you in the morning."

After Peter left, Thomas checked on JT. He seemed to be sleeping soundly. Peter's visit had served to distract Thomas from his unease but it returned as soon as he left. Why was he feeling such a sense of dread? Was it the continuing poor health of JT? Allie and the baby not home? Hearing that Margaret's father was a broken man? The growing storm outside, signalling the coming winter? That the American invasion could still come to the St. Lawrence Valley, that everything they had could be destroyed, "annihilated"? Why couldn't he shake this fear that went straight to his bowels?

"I've got to go again, Gunner. I'll be right back. You look after JT. This time I'll latch that stupid outhouse door," Thomas said as he went out the back door of his cabin.

When he came back, he put another small log on the fire and took the lantern into the bedroom, setting it on the bedside table. He lay down on his back looking at the ceiling. He heard Gunner come into the bedroom and curl up at the side of the bed. He was worried too. The wind outside was growing stronger. Thomas tried to think of pleasant things but at times like this his mind seemed to have a mind of its own. It kept going back to a swirl of worries. He turned out the lantern and turned on his side, curling himself around JT, putting his face next to his son's, listening to his breathing. "Please get better. I love you, son," he whispered. "Everything is going to be all right."

CHAPTER 7
SUNDAY OCTOBER 24, 1813
Williamsburg Township

He awoke at dawn, aroused by a dream of lovemaking. She was right beside him in their little bed. He could see her in the dim light that came in the small back window. Her thick brown hair covered most of her face. It was Sunday morning and they were alone; Elizabeth had gone home to be with her family for the weekend. The children were still asleep.

He rolled over on his left side to face her and carefully used his right hand to move a lock of her hair to reveal her face. She was beautiful. He tenderly touched her cheek and gently brushed her chin as he moved his hand down under the covers to her warm, soft breast. He was going to say that he loved her, but he didn't say that.

"You're beautiful," he whispered in her ear. He moved his body closer to hers as his hand moved farther down, resting his open palm on her firm flat belly.

"No," she said sternly, eyes still closed. "I'm not in the mood."

He wasn't either any more.

He rolled over onto his back and stared at the ceiling. The room was a little brighter now. A rooster crowed. He struggled with the rush of thoughts going through his mind, trying to decide what to say. With his left hand he reached for her hand and squeezed it gently and affectionately. She accepted his hand as a gesture of reconciliation. Finally, he said:

"We have to talk. Allie. We can't go on like this."

She removed her hand from his and said nothing. A rooster

crowed again. The baby in the crib beside the bed stirred and made little cooing sounds.

Thomas rehearsed in his mind what to say next. He sifted and sorted his options. Should he escalate the discussion or leave it all to another time? He didn't have to decide: the baby started to cry. Allie got up, took the baby out of the crib, and brought her back to the warmth of the bed. She rolled over on her side away from Thomas and brought the baby to her breast. "I love you," she said.

Thomas left the cabin without saying goodbye. He did the morning chores and decided to walk to his lot to do more clearing. The Dundas militia had been called out for more drills and for a meeting that afternoon with Captain Crysler, but Thomas couldn't bring himself to go. He had not been to one all summer and autumn and he wasn't in the mood for military drills today.

~ ~ ~

The militia drills this warm fall Sunday afternoon were in a cleared pasture just west of Bouck's farm on the north side of the King's Highway. As they were just two farms east of Crysler's farm, Captain Crysler himself came to the drill but the ranking officer was Captain Merkley. Both men were veterans of the first war, having fought with the King's Royal Regiment of New York—Sir John Johnson's famous Royal Yorkers. Captain Merkley still wore his old green Yorker uniform. The two militia officers were up on their horses surrounded by about a hundred Dundas militiamen, who awkwardly stumbled into line when they were finally called to order.

Captain Merkley spoke first. He was a man of few words with no pretence to eloquence. In his thick German accent, he explained that some recent intelligence had been received that the Yankees might yet decide to launch an invasion to take Montreal that fall. If this happened, the Dundas militia must be ready to act as light troops to assist Colonel Pearson's redcoats at Prescott. The Dundas militia, he explained, would not be used to fight in the line but would be used as skirmishers and scouts. He also explained that in a battle near Niagara earlier this summer it became clear that light flank companies needed to have the skill to prime and load while in the prone position. This, he explained, would be the main new drill for today. Learning this skill might very well save lives. He introduced a young Voltigeur who would demonstrate the manoeuvre.

The Dundas men hated the drill. It involved lying on your stomach and required considerable dexterity. It also meant getting very dirty. The men were near unanimous that the drill was stupid and the likelihood of ever actually using the method very remote. The universal grumblings continued throughout the hour-long drill.

It was a dirty and unhappy group of men who were then brought to order again. This time, Captain Crysler addressed the men. He had been a drummer boy with the Royal Yorkers and he was now only 43, but he looked much older. In a remarkably short time he had made a lot of money in the timber trade, through his ownership of several sawmills along the river. He had been elected in 1804 to represent Dundas County in the Upper Canada Parliament. Crysler's farm was the largest in the area, with several fine barns behind his stately yellow two-storey house.

Just as the Captain was about to speak, several large flocks of Canada geese flew low overhead, their honking loud enough to drown out a man's voice. Everyone looked up to see the large Vs heading south, moved by the sight of these beautiful creatures in their annual migrations, which marked the beginning and end of winter.

As Captain Crysler was also on the staff of Colonel Morrison as an aide, he was resplendent in the red uniform of the 89th with a large sword hanging by his side. When the geese had finally passed, the Captain reminded the men that he, too, had spent his whole adult life in this beautiful county along the great river. They had transformed this special part of the valley in a single generation thanks to their hard work and the generosity of the Crown. He told the men that the war against Napoleon was going well and that he had been assured that major new reinforcements would be freed up and posted to Canada in the spring. "We just need to hang on until then," he said. Just as he was coming to the climactic conclusion of his speech about the need for the men to do their duty, et cetera, the Captain was forced to stop again. Another large flock of Canada geese were flying by, honking quite vigorously. The Captain looked up, turned to the men with a look of exasperation and resignation, and then began to laugh as he had not laughed for a long time. All the men joined in. In the years ahead, Garrett would always enjoy telling the story about the time the geese made everyone laugh.

When the drills were finally completed and the men dismissed, Jacob asked his stepson John Cook if he wanted a ride home, as Jacob had come with his horse and carriage. John was grateful for the ride. As they approached the Marselis farm, Jacob explained to John that he had been instructed by Captain Merkley to stop in to see Thomas Marselis to inquire why he had missed the drill practice again and to tell him that Captain Merkley expected Thomas to be part of the group of militia that had been assigned to do artificer work at the fort. As John was also part of that group and a friend and relative of Thomas's, Jacob asked if John would agree to come with him to speak to Thomas. John agreed.

When they turned into the Marselis lane, Oma met them. She explained that Thomas had worked all day on his lot and that he had come home only to find that Allie and the children had gone to spend a few days with her parents. Oma had tried to talk to Thomas about several things but he was upset and, after doing the chores, he had gone into his cabin. Oma feared that he had been drinking since then. She had never seen him so agitated. She had been waiting at the road for Peter and Garrett to return from the militia drill, hoping that they could console him.

"I'm glad you're here," she said to Jacob and John; "maybe you can talk some sense into him." Jacob tied up his horse to the post outside Thomas's cabin and he and John rapped on the door that was partly open. Thinking it was Peter or Garrett back from the militia drill, Thomas responded:

"Please, just leave me alone. I'm going to finish this drink and go to bed early. I'll be all right in the morning. It's not your fault. I have nobody to blame but myself. We can talk in the morning."

"It's me, John, and Jacob. Can we come in for a minute?" responded John.

"The door is open," said Thomas.

John and Jacob came into the main room of the little cabin. It was quite dark inside. The only light came from the small window. Thomas was sitting at the table, patting Gunner who was sitting beside him. Even Gunner seemed worried about Thomas. Jacob and John sat down at the table across from Thomas, who looked up at them only momentarily and said nothing.

"Are you all right, Thomas? What's wrong?" asked John quietly.

"I'm fine. Little too much to drink but I'll be good in the morning. You came by to ask me about my health?"

"We also came by to see why you missed the drill again today," Jacob explained. "We asked Peter and Garrett where you were but they told us nothing."

"I had other things I had to do that were more important than playing soldier for the afternoon," Thomas replied without looking up.

"We're not playing soldiers. We are doing our duty. We all have other work we should be doing but a full call-up alert has been ordered. Captain Crysler was there today. He rode down from Kingston to tell us that Colonel Morrison is counting on the militia to play an important role if the Americans attack this fall. Most other men are making the effort," said Jacob, perhaps a little too righteously.

"Oh, I know. I've been very bad," Thomas said in a mocking tone. "Are you going to whip me?"

"No. We just need you to say you will come to drills and take your turn at the fort."

"All right. Whatever you say. Are you all done with your big speeches?"

"Don't mock me, Thomas. This is serious," Jacob said sternly.

"What is serious?"

"It's our duty. We have to do what we can to help defend our new country."

"Some country. Some country." Thomas slurred his words. "Who's here in Upper Canada? We Loyalists, who are here because we're losers. The Indians, what's left of them, they're all complete losers, even if they don't know it yet. And a motley bunch of losers from Europe. With the conquered Canadiens, what we have here is a country founded entirely by losers. Great future, don't you think?"

"What? You want to lose everything again? Where do we go this time? What do you suggest we do? Should we just surrender to the Yankees?" Jacob's voice was tinged with anger now.

"What do I know? I'm just a stupid, illiterate Dutch farmer, remember? Would the Yankees be worse masters than the Brits?"

"Don't say that, Thomas. You don't mean that. This is just the rum talking. Get hold of yourself."

"So, you're in favour of war now. What about Luther's warning: 'Nothing good ever comes from violence'; remember Lewis's father preaching this, years ago?"

"You're just baiting me, Thomas. The Reverend Martin Luther was always clear: wars of national defence are just. He wrote a prayer for victory over invading Turks—war was justified to defend against Mohammedanism. We have every right to defend our home from a take-over by America. You know this."

Thomas took another drink, draining his glass. He looked at John, who continued to say nothing. He got up from the table to get the jug of rum and poured himself another drink.

"You have had enough, Thomas," said Jacob. "Give me that jug. What would your father say if he saw you now and heard you talking like this?" This was a low blow that had its effect. Thomas slammed his fist on the table.

"Kiss my arse. Don't bring my father into this. And don't talk down to me. I'm not a boy. I'm certainly not your boy. You're not half the man my father was . . . you're not half the man John's father was either. Everyone knows, Catherine just married you for your money."

"That's enough." Jacob was angry now. "You can get vulgar and insult me but don't insult your sister. Let's go, John. There's no talking sense to him when he's like this."

"No. Go ahead," said John. "I'll walk the rest of the way home."

Jacob walked over to the door and then turned around, more sad than angry now.

"This is just the rum talking. I know this is not you. I came here to tell you that Captain Merkley told Pearson that some of our Dundas men would be at the fort by this Saturday. You have never taken a turn. We all have to do our duty. This is our country and we have a duty to do what we can to defend it. Be there by Saturday, please."

Jacob left the cabin. John poured himself a drink and sat down on the chair across the table from Thomas. John said nothing. The anger slowly drained out of Thomas. He slumped in his chair. He put his hands over his face. John still said nothing. The little cabin was dead quiet until Thomas put his hands down, sat up straight, and took a full breath in, letting it out slowly. He shook his head and allowed a small smile:

"What do you think, Professor?"

"About what?"

"About everything. You're the smart one. You're the one that can read and write."

"Don't start picking on me."

"I'm not. I'm serious. What should we do? What am I going to do about Allie?"

"I don't know about that, but I do believe that we have to do what we can to fight the Yankees. We don't have much of a government yet but if we can get this war behind us, we can have one. Our own. We can build roads. We can build schools. Don't you want JT and Aleda to go to a school? Our parents were the founders of this country. At the very least we have a duty to them. Maybe we are a nation founded by losers. Maybe that will help us to stay humble and, I don't know, try to get along with people. But if we have to fight Yankee soldiers to defend what we have, then I think we have to fight." He hesitated for a moment and continued. "Even if both our wives were born in the States."

"So I guess you think we have to take up our hammers and nails and saws and go to war on Saturday."

"Better a hammer and nails than a musket and bayonet."

"All right. All right. You're right. It's time to go to bed. I'm exhausted. Do you want to stay here?"

"No thanks. My little Yankee wife Kate will be worried and waiting up for me. I'll walk on home."

"I doubt if my little Yankee wife is too worried about me."

"I'll come by Saturday morning. Go to bed and sleep it off. I have to go. It's getting dark."

"John, just a moment before you go . . . you'll see Jacob tomorrow, I suppose."

"Yes. I am helping him cut his corn so long as it doesn't rain. Why?"

"Maybe . . . maybe you could tell him that I'm sorry for mouthing off tonight. I'm sorry. I'm a better man than that. I didn't mean a lot of what I said, but . . . he shouldn't have brought my father into it."

"I'll tell him. Now get some sleep. See you Saturday morning."

"Thanks, John. You're a good man."

"Now don't get all sappy on me. See you on Saturday morning."

Chapter 8
Thursday November 4, 1813
Prescott, Upper Canada

Thomas Marselis, U.E., private, Second Flank Company, 1st Dundas Regiment, Militia of Upper Canada, stood at the top of a hill, facing south, looking across the great river. The air was clear and cool but the sun was pleasantly warm upon his face. He had closed his eyes and thought of his family and his home just down the river. He had only been posted at Prescott for five days but already he missed his family. This was the first time that he had been away for more than a night since he was married.

He placed his father's musket against a big flat-topped rock and climbed up on top of the rock. It felt warm in the afternoon sun. The weather had been rainy and windy for a couple of weeks so it felt good to soak up the warmth of the sun still held in the rock. He took off his boots and spread them out on the rock to dry.

Half-way down the hill to the river was an old oak tree. Thomas liked to think that no one had cut it down by this time because it was so majestic, but it was probably still standing because it was just too large to cut down. Up close, a tree's branches seemed to follow no pattern, no plan, there was only incoherence; from this distance, he noticed, the tree had a perfect symmetry. There weren't many big oaks left this close to the river. He still had some lovely old oaks at the back of his property but none as old as this one. Some hardy dry brown leaves hung on to the branches. Some squirrels scampered at its base collecting acorns, getting ready for the hard winter that they knew was coming soon.

Some hammering down in the fort to the east startled him. The other men from the Dundas militia were still working on the west wall and he could still hear shouting of orders and drumbeats indicating that some of the regulars were still practising their drills in the yard.

He looked back at the river and across the mere 1800 yards to the American side. He thought he saw a canoe coming down the river close to the shore but there was no sign of any Americans. He didn't expect to see any. When he left the rest of the regiment camped at Iroquois Point just a few miles down the river, all the men were convinced that Colonel Pearson had over-reacted by ordering all the militia regiments to assemble. Even Captain Munro said that probably everybody would be released to go home in a week or two. All the men had a lot of work to do on their farms to get ready for winter. There weren't going to be many more nice days like this.

Anyway, there was absolutely no chance that the Americans would attack the fort on this clear bright afternoon. Last night at supper, Peter Loucks had said that he had heard from Sergeant Dillin of the 49th Regiment of Foot that Captain Jackson of the Royal Artillery had said that the Yankees would never try to take Montreal this late in the season and that their movement to French Creek was simply a feint before they moved to attack Kingston.

Thomas checked to see how his boots were drying and then he lay back onto the rock and closed his eyes. This was the time of year that he and his brothers and neighbours got ready to do their best deer hunting. Now that the leaves were off the trees you could see better and within days the first snow would come to make tracking easier. He knew that back home old Gunner would be wondering where all the men were and why they weren't getting ready for the hunt.

Thomas thought of his father and how much he used to look forward to the hunt. Right up until his death, Johannes Marselis always insisted on being the dogger with his favourite dog, Gunner's mother Beauty, and before that her mother, Queenie, whom he had brought up from the Schoharie when he went back for his family in '81.

Just as they had learned to do in the dense forests of the Mohawk or Schoharie Valley, the Dundas County Loyalists would organize runs at selected areas. They would line up on watches about 200 yards apart in a big semi-circle. After they had been given enough time to get into place, Johannes and his dogs would walk through the bush barking and yelling to scare the deer out of their hiding places. Gunner came from a line of small walker hounds with truly remarkable noses. Thomas smiled to himself as he remembered that his father's bark was indistinguishable from his dog's. As the men heard the dog and the dogger coming towards them, they would cock their muskets because they knew they would only get a few seconds' warning, usually from hearing the frightened deer crashing through the bush trying to get away from the dogs, but it was hard to know where they would first appear. And muskets weren't exactly precision instruments.

There was nothing more exciting than hearing the tone of the bark change. As soon as the hound got a good scent and started to get close to the deer, the high-pitched yip-yipping geared down to a deep "Aroo," "Aroo," "Aroo." The trapped deer would soon emerge from the dense bush somewhere along the net and one of the men on a watch would get a shot.

Bang! Bang! The shot startled Thomas and he jumped up, forgot where he was, and awkwardly fell off the rock. Private Lewis Schwerdfager, Thomas's brother-in-law, clapped his hands and bent over in laughter seeing how his joke had frightened Thomas.

Thomas got up on his elbows, looked at Lewis with his big twinkling blue eyes, smiled, and quietly uttered, "I'll get back at you for this, Lewis. You know I won't forget."

"I know," said Lewis, "but it was still worth it. I can hardly wait to tell Allie and everyone that I caught you sleeping on your watch. What if I had been Hawkeye Pearson? You would be in the brig tonight. I can hear him now: 'You worthless, lazy Canadians can't even stay awake on a watch in the afternoon. You are a useless excuse for a soldier, Marselis. This is what happens when your so-called officers don't impose any discipline.'"

"I wasn't asleep, and if it had been Pearson, I would have told him that he could . . ."

But before Thomas could finish his sentence, he was startled again to hear someone behind him yell out, "Hey, great white fisherman."

It was John (Shawindas) Sunday and Big Jacob who had just come into the clearing up the hill from the big oak. The two old Indians gave Thomas and Lewis full hugs when they got to the top of the hill and the four exchanged warm greetings.

"It's really good to see you, you old hound dog," said Thomas with a smile. Then Thomas said something to Big Jacob in Mohawk. Big Jacob laughed.

"How did you know I was up here?" asked Thomas.

John replied, "We ran into young Cook down by the river and he told us you were a soldier today. He said only lucky Thomas Marselis would get watch duty on a clear day like this."

"I can't offer you tea yet. Lewis here still hasn't made a fire. But I do have some tobacco." And with that, Thomas made a little ceremony of handing a small pouch of tobacco to John and Big Jacob.

Big Jacob made a little bow and said, "*Nia:wen*, Thomas."

Thomas replied in Mohawk to the effect of "As soon as we know that those Yankees are not coming, we can get back to something useful like deer hunting."

John replied in English: "Hunting will have to wait, Thomas. I have some bad news for you. The Yankees are coming tonight or tomorrow night."

Thomas looked at John seriously and then grinned: "I don't believe it, John. They wouldn't want to ruin our hunting season."

"I am not joking, Thomas," said John. He shook his head and then continued. "I'm serious. We'll have to fight tomorrow."

"I'm a lover, not a fighter," said Thomas, with feigned indignation.

John continued: "Jacob and I were going up river to join some others to net pickerel on French Creek when we met Old Peter and Captain Jim just above the fort this morning. They were told the Yankees had arrived at the mouth of French Creek yesterday and that there were thousands of them coming down the river tonight or tomorrow night."

Old Peter and Captain Jim had explained to John that they had been rushing up to Tyendinaga to warn Lieutenant Anderson and the group of Mohawk warriors he had assembled to defend Fort Henry. John and Big Jacob decided to turn around and go back to warn everyone at home. Big Jacob said something in Mohawk that ended with the English number 81 and John translated to Lewis, "Big Jacob says that Captain Jim said it was the largest army he had seen since the first war along the Mohawk. Much bigger even than Sullivan's army in '81."

Thomas replied, "Are you sure the Yankees are coming on down the river? We heard they were just getting ready to swing around and attack Kingston. It's too late in the season to fight their way past here, to go down all the rapids and attack Montreal. We'll have winter in a couple of weeks and those poor crazy southern boys will freeze."

John Sunday looked straight at Thomas. "Listen to me, Thomas, they are coming down the river. They unloaded all their boats at French Creek and they are carrying their supplies by land along the old trail on the south side of the river. They have hundreds of horses. They're going to meet the boats at Morristown."

"That's just across the river from here," Lewis said, shaking his head. "I guess we better report this to the Colonel right away."

John Sunday then explained that he and Big Jacob were returning home to Akwesasne immediately to warn everybody to disperse and to hide their supplies. John urged Thomas to warn the redcoats at the fort and then hurry back home to warn his own family and all the other Loyalists to get away from the front until the huge American army passed through. Thomas responded that he wasn't sure if Colonel Pearson would even listen to what John was reporting. Thomas wondered what anyone could do anyway if what Old Peter said was true.

"Do you really think that they're going to attack Montreal?" pressed Thomas. He didn't want to be disrespectful to the old Indian who had been such a great warrior in the first war, but it didn't seem possible that the Americans had finally decided to attack.

John shrugged and then slowly moved his hands out in front of his body and turned his palms up. His eyes narrowed.

"Thomas," he said slowly, emphasizing each word, "your father and I went through a lot. We both lost friends and family the last time. We lost everything to the rebels. Whether the Colonel believes us or not, we have to alert everyone on our side that thousands of Yankees are going to try to take our homes again. You know that your mother never stopped hating them for what they did. Even your father warned everyone that they probably wouldn't stay south of the St. Lawrence forever."

The old Indian shook his head and slowly repeated, "Never again. Never again . . . We're going home, Thomas, to warn and protect our families and you should do the same thing. My son and nephew are both at Tyendinaga and will be fighting with the redcoats when they come east to help defend Montreal. As you know, I lost my brother fighting the Long Knives last time. If we lose again, this time there's nowhere left to go."

"No, wait, John," Thomas pleaded. "Come, come with me and we'll go to see Captain Jackson together. He's a good man. If we talk to him, he will talk to the Colonel."

"No, Thomas. I remember Pearson. I remember how he treated us when he was at Cornwall. You do what you have to do. Do what you need to do. Old Jacob and I don't want to lose any more time. This good weather won't hold for long. We'll warn the rest of your men at Point Iroquois. We're leaving now. You tell the Colonel that we hope the message will get to Fort Henry by tomorrow. Tell him that the American invasion has finally started and their objective is Montreal . . . Listen to me, Thomas. For the British army, all they can do is lose a battle. We will lose everything. This is our only home now. Think about it. Where do we run to next? If they take Montreal or even hold it to siege this winter, we will all be part of the United States in the spring. Your father and mother didn't come up here to lose everything to the Yankees again."

John looked at Thomas and then took both his hands in his. His old face turned solemn, serious, determined. He shook his head.

"You can't talk to people who want to defeat you, people who will take your land again. If your father was here, even he would tell you that you will have to fight these Yankees until you die or they do." He paused again. "Ask your mother, Thomas, ask her if you can just wish the Yankees away. That is all I have to say." Then he looked at Old Jacob. "Let's go."

With that, John Sunday and Old Jacob shook hands with Thomas and Lewis and went down the hill to the river. As they left, Lewis turned to Thomas. "You go down and report this to your friend Captain Jackson. I'll cover your watch, Thomas. Maybe this war has finally come to us after all."

Thomas walked down the hill towards the fort. Colonel Pearson had arranged for ten men from the Dundas militia to be sent from their camp at Point Iroquois to work as artificers on a rotating basis. Thomas had managed to avoid artificer duty all summer. He had just spent four days using his axe and carpentry skills to complete another section of the south wall of the fort and had been lucky enough to be assigned picket watch duty on the one nice day of the week. He had to do artificer duty two more days and then he could walk home Saturday morning.

"I'll be home for supper Saturday," he thought to himself. If he still had a home by then.

Thomas walked through the back gate of the fort, giving a half-hearted "I'm just a dumb farmer" salute to the private on guard duty. The young redcoat ignored him. As he approached the stockade door, Captain Jackson happened to step out.

"Mr. Marselis. How are you, sir?"

"Well, thank you, Captain. It's been good to have some sun. May I speak with you a moment? I'm afraid I've heard some alarming news."

"Let's step out into the sun, Thomas," Captain Jackson said as he took Thomas's arm. "What's troubling you?"

"The Yankees are coming. My father's old friend John Sunday just this past hour ran into Old Peter and Captain Jim who were returning to Tyendinaga and they told John that there are thousands of Yankees at the mouth of French Creek and that they have hundreds of boats. John says that Old Peter was told that the Yankees would be leaving tonight or tomorrow to come down the river to pass by the fort after dark. I am quite sure that John has reliable information. Old Peter was at the Indian fishing camp on the other side near French Creek when the Yankees started arriving. They traded some fish. They saw everything with their own eyes."

Captain Jackson shook his head and responded, "Nobody, not even Wilkinson dead drunk, would try to run down those waters on the American side fully loaded in the dark. There must be a mistake, Thomas. Not even Jonathan is that stupid."

"No, that's the thing. Apparently they have hundreds of horses. They are off-loading all the boats at French Creek and running them down empty. They are taking all supplies overland along the old Indian trail and meeting up with boats at Morristown in the morning."

Captain Jackson thought for a few moments, took a big breath, and then asked Thomas to come with him to see the Colonel.

"No. No thanks," said Thomas. "You know what I think of him. You saw how he treated us yesterday. He yelled at old Mr.

Baker like he was his servant or his dog. Mr. Baker is twice the man that Pearson will ever be on his best day."

"Don't be too hard on the Colonel, Thomas. He is in terrible pain all the time."

"We all have our pains. Pains don't justify pompous arrogance and the way he treats all of us. He thinks that we're just a bunch of stupid farmers. All the men have been talking about how he treated our Colonel Cartwright in public in front of everyone. No real gentleman would do that."

"All right. All right. I'll tell the Colonel what you've said." Then, with a twinkle in his eye and a little smile, Jackson leaned forward and asked, "So, Mr. Marselis, may I take the liberty to inquire whether your family is well?"

Thomas smiled back. "Elizabeth is fine, Captain. I'm sure she would want me to extend her very best wishes to you and to de Lorimier and especially to that handsome young man, Captain Herse."

Thomas gave a little salute, and turned and left the fort to go back up the hill to join Lewis.

Captain Jackson marched across the parade ground and knocked on the Colonel's door.

"Come. What is it?" an irritated voice shouted from inside. Jackson went in to find Pearson at his desk. The Colonel was rubbing his thigh. He had already led an extraordinary life. While he was only 33, Pearson looked much older, with his deep dark eyes. He had spent his whole life in the army, having joined as a second lieutenant at age 16 in 1796. He had an outstanding military record. He had fought in Holland, Spain, and Egypt, where he was severely wounded in the thigh at the Battle of Aboukir. By age 27 he was a major in the 23rd Foot. He suffered a second serious wound in Martinique and then was sent to New Brunswick. There he married Anne Coffin, the daughter of a prominent New Brunswick Loyalist. He was then sent back to the Napoleonic wars where he fought in the bloody battle of Albuera, which cost the

23rd Foot half the men the unit brought into action that day. Pearson was awarded a gold medal and promoted to Lieutenant Colonel. He was injured again and invalided into a staff job in Lower Canada, and then appointed to command the little fort at Prescott with its two hundred men.

"Excuse me, sir." Captain Jackson saluted. "I have just received a report, Colonel, that Wilkinson has assembled several thousand men and hundreds of boats at French Creek and that he is intending to come down the river along the United States shore tonight or tomorrow night under cover of darkness. Their objective is to take Montreal before winter sets in."

"And who gave you this—what did you call it—report?"

"Thomas Marselis, a private in the Dundas militia. I know him personally, sir. He is very reliable. He received the information from some Mohawks who just came from the Indian settlement near French Creek. They say they have many horses and that the Yankees are taking the supplies along the old trail on the south side."

"I don't believe it, Captain. Morrison received orders to stay put because General Prevost has concluded that it is too late in the season for Jonathan to try to run all the rapids and get to Montreal before winter. Kingston is the more likely objective. And do you think that I should rely on what a Red Indian has said to some illiterate Dutch farmer? I've kept our men in their uniforms all day and night for months, ready to march west to help defend Kingston. I got a message on Sunday that the Americans were approaching French Creek. I still have very good contacts on the American side. They will send me a message if the Americans approach Ogdensburg. As you know, I just sent Morton, one of our best young officers, back up the river to see what he could find out. And I specifically instructed Lieutenant Clark of the Incorporated Militia, who knows the terrain, to go as far as Elliott's Point and to stay there and to watch for enemy movement. From there he should be able to see if they are going to cross over to the north shore to attack Fort Henry from the east or come down the river to try to take us. I instructed Clark that as soon as he saw them turn down river he was to instantly take horse and repair to this place, with all possible diligence, alarming the country along the way. I haven't heard from Clark and until I do we're going to stay here, on the ready, in case of attack, and we'll show these Yankee rebels what the British Army can do. If and when they come, Captain, I know that you and the Royal Artillery and your three 6-pounders will make them wish they had never come up here. We just have to hold out until the spring. By then, I have been assured, we'll have finished off Napoleon and we'll get all the men we need to crush the Yankees and make sure they never attack the Canadas again." He stopped for a moment. He rubbed his thigh. "The British Empire will prevail. We have nothing to fear from a raggedy bunch of colonials. Am I clear, Captain? . . . That is all."

This was not the time to ask how two hundred men were going to defend a half completed fort from an invasion by an army of several thousand soldiers. Jackson saluted, wheeled about, and closed the door behind him.

Late that afternoon, after an early supper, several of the Dundas militia gathered together to leave the fort and climb the hill to join Thomas and Lewis, who had started a small fire. As the sun went down so did the temperature, but there was still no wind. It was pleasant around the fire. Several of the local militiamen lit their pipes, pulled their collars up, and put on their toques. Bottles of rum were passed around. Two privates from the 49th Foot who had been sent from Fort Henry to be part of the Prescott garrison asked, in a thick Irish brogue, if they could join the group, and the men shuffled a bit to make room.

A couple of enlisted men from Fraser's Provincial Light Dragoons arrived and stood behind the circle of men seated around the fire. They were arguing about something. Private Antoine Belinge of the Canadian Voltigeurs and his friend Private Joseph Plamondon of the Canadian Fencibles were engaged in an animated conversation in French as they joined the merry group on the top of the hill overlooking Prescott on this clear November evening.

Thomas Marselis got up from his seat near the fire and walked a short distance towards the river. The air was cool. The light of the full moon reflected on the river. It was clear that there were no Yankees coming down the river tonight. Maybe the war would pass them by after all. Maybe the Grand Invasion had been put off again.

Standing there by himself, away from the fire, looking over the river, Thomas reflected on the growing group of men behind him. He could hear Gaelic, French, German, and many variations of English. Then above the voices he heard the scratchy start of their one common language, the fiddle. Clapping started. All the men seemed to know the tune. The clapping, talking, and singing got louder. What a diverse group they were, Thomas was thinking. Men from many countries and two continents, with completely different backgrounds and languages, keeping time to a fiddle on a hill overlooking the St. Lawrence River just east of Prescott, Upper Canada. More soldiers arrived. Some men from the 89th brought with them some logs that could serve as makeshift seats before they would be used to feed the fire. Seated on one of these logs was Private Smith. He stared intently at the fire; his tic was hardly noticeable. The fingers of his left hand resting on his knee kept time with the beat of the music. He did not sing but it was clear that the music had a calming effect on him.

Lewis, who had left the group to go down the hill to get more wood for the fire, shouted up to Thomas as he returned. "Private Marselis, look who I have here," he said as he pointed to Captain Jackson walking at his side.

As Captain Jackson came into the light of the fire, some of the regulars stood up; the fiddle and the talking stopped. A hush fell over the group and even the fire seemed to become quieter, with just the occasional crackle.

"At ease, men. I've just got some news from Colonel Pearson that I thought you would find interesting, especially those of you who are Canadians. Obviously the report that we received that the Yankees would try to pass by here tonight has not proven to be accurate."

He didn't look at Thomas when he said that, but moved in closer to the fire with a paper in his hand. He continued, "This evening Lieutenant Morton brought this pamphlet back from Gananoque. Several such pamphlets were distributed all along the Canadian side and to residents on Grindstone Island and Wells Island. We understand that they are being passed along all the way to Elizabethtown."

Thomas moved in closer to hear Captain Jackson begin to read from the pamphlet.

"It is addressed to all Canadian civilians. It says, '*The army of the United States, which I have the honour to command, invades the Province to conquer, not to destroy; to subdue the forces of his Britannic Majesty, not to war against unoffending subjects. Those therefore amongst you who remain quiet at home, should victory incline to the American standard, shall be protected in their persons and property; but those who are found in arms must necessarily be treated as avowed enemies. To menace is unmanly—to seduce dishonourable. Yet it is just and humane to place these alternatives before you.*'"

Lewis turned to Thomas and shrugged. "So, what do you think? Isn't that a relief? The invasion of the army of the United States is not here to destroy us, only to conquer and liberate us—doesn't that make you feel a lot better?"

Thomas shook his head. "When did we ask the Yankees to liberate us? Liberate us from what?"

CHAPTER 9
FRIDAY, NOVEMBER 5, 1813
Prescott, Upper Canada

Friday was clear and bright. Inside the fort everyone was busy and nervous with anticipation. At one end of the parade ground, Sergeant Joseph Laporte was drilling a company of the Canadian Regiment of Fencible Infantry. Sometimes in French, sometimes in English, the fluently bilingual Laporte would bark out the commands as the 48 men in the company wheeled as one through a variety of manoeuvres. Coming from a long line of *coureurs de bois*, Laporte was a solid muscular man who commanded great respect among his men in spite of his height, which could not have been much over five feet. He was proud of the fact that this group of men from Lower Canada was as good as any company of redcoats anywhere in the British Army.

Standing erect at the side, watching his men go through their manoeuvres with impeccable timing, was the handsome Lieutenant Guillaume Francois de Lorimier. In spite of his youth and shy demeanour, his men loved him. They knew de Lorimier would be right in front of them if and when they saw action in the next few days.

De Lorimier himself appeared to be giving his company his complete attention but his mind was actually elsewhere. He couldn't stop thinking about his young bride and how their first child was due very soon. Last year at this time he was looking forward to getting some real action and experience in battle. Now he just wanted the Yankees to go home for the winter so that he could get back to Caughnawaga to be with his new family. The excitement and glory of military action didn't seem so important any more.

At the other end of the parade ground, Sergeant Louis Langevin was drilling one of the three companies of the Canadian Voltigeurs that were stationed that autumn at the Prescott fort. Watching the company from the sideline were Lieutenants Daniel de Hertel and James M. Pendergast, who were engaged in an animated conversation with their Captain, William Johnson.

The illegitimate son of Sir John Johnson, William Johnson, 44, was a tall, handsome, distinguished-looking officer in his Voltigeur uniform. Raised by his mother, Clara Putman, a Dutch farmer's daughter, William and his sister went to a small rural school until the first war ended, when they moved to Schenectady where William's mother used her mantle-maker's trade to make a modest living. There was no future for the son of Sir John Johnson in the new United States of America, so the father finally took some responsibility for his son and got him a position in the Indian Department at Niagara, Upper Canada, in 1786. While most of the officers in the Voltigeurs were bilingual Canadiens, Captain Johnson spoke Dutch and Mohawk as well. Rather than being embittered by the way he had been abandoned by his father, he exuded an easy-going calmness that endeared him to his men. Colonel Pearson thought Johnson was too familiar with his men because Pearson had little understanding that men could follow a leader out of admiration, affection, and respect, rather than fear.

"Well, Daniel," Johnson said to Lieutenant de Hertel, "the men look good. If the Yankees come, are we ready?"

"Ready for what, sir?" he replied. "If there are ten thousand Yankees what are we to do? We have less than two hundred men here. If they attack us, do we fight or retreat? Do we march west to Fort Henry or do we go east to help defend Montreal?"

Captain Johnson then told his two lieutenants that he had just been advised that Colonel Pearson had called an officers' meeting in the large room in the Stockade House at 1700 hours. Dinner would be served. Johnson surmised that Colonel Pearson would provide a full briefing and that clear orders would be given at that time. He knew that this news would please his officers. Last month Colonel Pearson had ordered the large room to be cleared of supplies and converted to an officers' dining room. The Stockade House was one of only about ten buildings in Prescott and it was the only two-storey stone building. With the fireplace roaring and the lanterns lit, the room would be warm and cosy. With good food and lots to drink, the officers' dinner in October had been the most pleasant evening since the summer, and so tonight promised to be a welcome repetition of that interesting evening. At the October dinner, even Colonel Pearson seemed to let himself go and the officers saw a brief glimpse of a different side of the usually gruff and imperious Colonel.

Lieutenant Pendergast couldn't resist wondering out loud whether the Colonel wasn't preparing a last supper for them all before they went off to the slaughter. Captain Johnson gently reprimanded Pendergast, with the assurance that no one yet knew if the Yankees were even going to go ahead with the invasion, but wherever the Voltigeurs might see action, be assured, said Johnson, that Colonel Pearson would be right there to lead them. Pearson had fought Napoleon and, as he often said, was "always ready for the Yankee colonials," whatever that meant.

The younger officers started to arrive at the Stockade House right at 1700 h. Enlisted men served drinks as they arrived. Lieutenant Daniel de Hertel and Lieutenant John Hebden were engaged in a spirited discussion in French with the other two Captains of the Canadian Voltigeurs, Captain Jacques Adhémar and Captain Jacques-Clement Herse, until Captain Richard Fraser of the Provincial Light Dragoons joined them and, out of courtesy, they quickly switched to English. The discussion continued to centre on the various theories about what Colonel Pearson would be saying when he arrived.

As the sun set outside, the large room took on an amber glow from the fireplace and lanterns. Bottles of rum and wine and pitchers of beer were placed on a side table for the officers to help themselves. The talk got louder.

When the outside door opened, followed by a whoosh of cold air, everybody turned to see if it was Colonel Pearson, but it was just Captain Jackson of the Royal Artillery, who announced to all that Colonel Pearson would arrive soon and that it was "getting bloody cold out there."

But it was getting hotter in the large room in the Stockade House. With the big fireplace, the lanterns, and the body heat from the dozen officers in their wool uniforms, faces became flushed, the windows steamed up, and the talking got even louder. Then someone yelled, "Jackson, Jackson." Everyone joined the chant until Captain Jackson, Royal Artillery, stepped away from the group beside the door. The talking stopped and Jackson cleared his throat and in his thick upper-class English accent, began to sing one of the great British military songs of the Napoleonic era:

Great guns have shot and shell, boys,
Dragoons have sabres bright.
The artillery fire's like hell, boys,
And the horse like devils fight.
But neither light nor heavy horse
Nor thundering cannoneers,
Can stem the tide of the foeman's pride,
Like the British bayoneteers!
The English arm is strong, boys,
The Irish arm is tough.
The Scotsman's blow the French well know,
Is struck by sterling stuff.
And when before the enemy
Their shining steel appears,
Goodbye! goodbye! how they run, how they run!
From the British bayoneteers!

When Jackson finished, to great cheers of "Huzzah" and "More" and "Bravo" and "Encore," he nodded. The room grew silent again. Jackson cleared his throat.

"Here's a new song that I just learned. They were singing it all this summer at Fort Henry:

Come all ye bold Canadians,
I'd have you lend an ear
Unto a short ditty
Which will your spirits cheer,
Concerning an engagement
We had at Detroit town,
The pride of those Yankee boys
So bravely we took down.
The Yankees did invade us,
To kill and to destroy,
And to distress our country,
Our peace for to annoy,
Our countrymen were filled
With sorrow, grief and woe,
To think that they should fall
By such an unnatural foe.
Come all ye bold Canadians,
Enlisted in the cause,
To defend your country,
And to maintain your laws;
Being all united,
This is the song we'll sing:
Success unto Great Britain
And God save the King."

As Jackson finished, everyone shouted, "God Save the King." Not to be outdone, two of the Voltigeur captains stepped forward and began a duet, with all men clapping to the favourite song of the Lower Canada militia during the war.

Le matin, des le point du jour,
On entend ce maudit tambour,
Maudit tambour et maudit exercice,
Toi, pauvr' soldat, tu en as d'la fatigue.
Ils nous font mettre dans les rangs,
Les officiers et les sergents,
L'un dit: recule et l'autre dit: avance!
Toi, pauvr' soldat, t'en faut de la patience.
Nos sergents et nos officiers
Sont bien traites dan leurs quartiers,
Nos capitain' boiv' le vin et la biere
Toi, pauvr' soldat, va boire a la riviere.
Qu'en a compose la chanson
C'est un tambour du bataillon
C'est un tambour en battant sa retraite
Toujours regrettant sa joli' maitresse.

Just then, with an unfortunate lack of timing, the door was flung open and, with the rush of cold fresh air, in came Colonel Pearson. The room went silent. The Colonel shook off the cold, undid his greatcoat, looked up at the men, rubbed his thigh, gave a half-salute, and told the men to be at ease. A private from the 49th arrived with a glass of sherry and took the Colonel's coat.

Captain Herse of the Canadian Fencibles stepped forward to welcome the Colonel and raised his large pewter mug of beer in a form of toast. Colonel Pearson, almost shyly, and certainly awkwardly, gave a hesitant response. In all his years in the British army he had been able to use rank and position to avoid the manly camaraderie that always made him uncomfortable. Most of the officers in the room were Canadians and he still could not, would not, get used to their informality and casual attitude to rank and position. In spite of the fact that he had served for a while as the inspecting field officer of militia in Lower Canada and was married to a Canadian, he had no patience for colonial informality and he still resented the fact that he had been invalided to serve in Canada rather than fighting the real fight against Napoleon. The French-speaking Voltigeur officers bothered him particularly because he had spent most of his adult life fighting the "Froggies" in Europe. But he was a seasoned officer and he knew this was not the time or place for a lecture on "proper British discipline and understanding the importance of rank."

The men continued talking and refilling their glasses until Colonel Pearson moved to the head of the long table and Captain Jackson requested everyone to take their seats. The officers moved to their chairs but, seeing the Colonel standing behind his, they did the same. With everyone in place, Colonel Pearson raised his glass of sherry to propose a toast.

"Gentlemen," he said, "the coming days may prove to be very difficult. I know I can count on all of you to do your duty. Whether we are attacked directly or whether we have to rush to Kingston to help out there, we will face an enemy many times our size. I have received credible information to confirm that close to ten thousand Yankees are camped at French Creek and that they are preparing to either attack us and cut off Fort Henry from Montreal and then use this fort for a base to launch an invasion of Montreal or Fort Henry, or they will proceed directly to attack Fort Henry. In either event, I expect that we shall see some very difficult action over the next couple of days." He stopped for a moment, cleared his throat, rubbed his thigh, and then continued:

"I am waiting for orders from General Prevost. If the Yankees attack us with their full army, are we to stand and fight to the finish, or shall we withdraw from the front and save our men to fight another day? We shall know very soon. Gentlemen, may God be with us all. God save the King."

The officers repeated "God save the King" and followed the Colonel in taking their seats. A cold solemnity overtook the group as the grim reality sank in. For some, or many of them, this might really be their last supper.

The food was then placed on the long table. Platters of sliced roast venison, steaming pots of potatoes, cabbage, carrots, turnips, and plates of freshly baked loaves of bread were served. After the officers completed the first course, the privates removed their plates and returned with johnnycake covered with maple syrup. With dessert finished, large chunks of local cheddar cheese and more fresh bread were placed on the table beside bowls of local apples.

At eight o'clock in the evening just as the officers had completed their meal, a private from the Canadian Regiment of Fencible Infantry rapped on the door, entered, and went over and whispered something to Lieutenant de Lorimier, who then said something to Captain Jackson who was sitting beside him. Captain Jackson rose and proceeded to approach the Colonel and leaned over to give him a message. On Pearson's instructions, Captain Jackson proceeded to the door, opened it, and in lunged Lieutenant Clark hardly able to catch his breath.

"Well, what is it, Clark?" barked the Colonel. "Speak up, man. What is happening?"

The young Lieutenant finally stood at attention and in an excited voice shouted, "Sir, the Yankees are coming. The Yankees are coming."

"For the love of God, Lieutenant, tell us what you mean. When are the Yankees coming?"

Lieutenant Clark then explained to the assembled officers that he had just seen with his own eyes "some three hundred of every description of craft, including several gunboats, coming down the river." He explained that they should be at the fort probably mid-day Saturday, depending on how fast such a huge armada could travel. There was no doubt—they were not attacking Fort Henry. They were coming down the river to attack Prescott. While he didn't have a horse to return to the fort to warn the Colonel as quickly as possible, he explained that he had borrowed a plough horse from a local farmer and rode here as quickly as the old farm horse could take him. He had yelled a warning at the local farmers along the way as he rode to the fort. He then started to cough and seemed spent with exhaustion.

Frustrated and impatient, the Colonel yelled at the young lieutenant, "Go on. For God's sakes, go on. Did you see them yourself? What else did you see? Speak up, man."

The Colonel then caught himself. He stopped talking. He rubbed his thigh and then became more erect, more composed.

Then Clark slowly repeated in a quieter, monotone voice, "The Yankees are coming, sir. It's a huge flotilla, sir. The first of their boats will be here tomorrow."

By now, all of the officers were standing, and turned as one to the Colonel for orders.

Without hesitation, Colonel Pearson calmly instructed the officers to call the alarm and to assemble all the men in the parade ground immediately. Captain Jackson was instructed to take the three 6-pounders around to the hill on the west side of the fort. Colonel Pearson advised that he would address all of the men in the parade ground at 2200 h.

As the officers left the stockade house, Captain Johnson held back so that only the Colonel and he remained. The Colonel looked at the Captain. He was about to say something and then stopped himself. He walked back to the table and picked up his glass, and downed the remaining sherry. Finally, the Colonel looked at Johnson and quietly began, "I know what you are thinking, Johnson. You think it would be foolish to try to defend this godforsaken little so-called fort in the middle of nowhere. You think we should move out in the morning so that we can—how do they put it?—'live to fight another day.' Abandon our post and let the Yankees chase us down the river. I've spent my whole life in the army and I'm not going to start running now."

"Sir," said Johnson, "wouldn't General Prevost want us to return to Montreal? Three companies of Voltigeurs, the Fencibles, and our three guns might make a real difference in the defence of Montreal in, say, a week's time. If we are going to spill blood, shouldn't we do it for something other than a lost cause?"

"I knew that was what you wanted to say, Johnson. No, I didn't get sent out to the colonies to run from Yankees. We didn't surrender at Aboukir. I didn't make major at twenty-seven by running just because the enemy had more men. We lost half our men, good men, at Albuera that day and we didn't surrender. No, Captain. If the Americans want to take our little fort, they are going to have to pay the price. Now let us go. We have work to do."

As the two soldiers stepped outside they were caught breathless for a moment by the cold air and the spectacular beauty of the clear night sky. The moon reflected off the great river and, as their eyes adjusted, they could see clearly all the way to the American side as they walked back to the fort, without speaking.

At precisely 2200 hours, Colonel Pearson marched out to the parade ground in the middle of the fort to speak to the 240 men assembled and waiting. It was an eerie sight here, under the moonlight and in this little strip of land between the St. Lawrence River and the dense primeval forested wilderness of Upper Canada.

Except for the Colonel and Captain Jackson and some men from two of the flank companies of the 49th Foot, most of the assembled men were Canadians. This was their land, their country. Most had only been soldiers for a few years at most. Some of the Canadian Fencibles and Canadian Voltigeurs had seen action; many had not. A couple of the older militiamen had fought with Sir John against the rebels over 30 years ago but they had been farmers ever since.

Colonel Pearson stepped up onto a small stoop and a voice barked out, "Attention."

"Men," began the Colonel, "we have been waiting for this all summer, and now it has come. We expect to be attacked by a large enemy force sometime tomorrow. The army of the United States is coming to take this fort because we are all that stands between them and Montreal. If we can hold out for a couple of days then Morrison can bring reinforcements from Fort Henry. We have to delay the Americans as long as possible and inflict as much damage as we can. I know that I speak for General Prevost when I say that I know that you will do your duty tomorrow. Try to get some rest tonight because tomorrow will be a long and difficult day."

Chapter 10
Saturday, November 6, 1813
Prescott, Upper Canada, on the St. Lawrence River

Saturday was another gorgeous Indian summer day. It was such a contrast to the mood of the men assembled inside the little fort. They tried to keep busy but there was little they could do but wait.

Up the river, on the American side, General Wilkinson had 8,000 men: a company of riflemen, 14 regiments of infantry, 2 regiments of dragoons, and 3 regiments of artillery. There were 300 bateaux for transportation and 12 gunboats for protection. The clear sunny day on Friday had finally allowed them to make progress down the river but the waters were treacherous and the current quickened as the river began to narrow. Here the river was dotted with thousands of small picturesque islands, as this was where the river crossed the ageless granite rock of the Canadian Shield.

The men back at the fort could only wait and watch, looking west up the river for any sign of the advancing armada. The men from the Dundas militia finished the north wall with a new sense of urgency. The Voltigeurs and Fencibles cleaned their firelocks, drilled some more, and waited.

By supper time a rumour spread among the men that one of the dragoons had reported to the Colonel that the Americans had turned back. By darkness even the Colonel began to wonder what had gone wrong. Duncan Clark had said that he had seen the boats coming down the river but there was a general consensus that not even the Americans would try to attack the fort at night, even if there was a full moon. Where were they?

The artillery commander Captain Henry Jackson reported to Colonel Pearson that he was ready for the attack. The guns were loaded and aimed at the level plain just west of the fort where the United States army was expected to land.

Lieutenant de Lorimier was assigned to command the picket duty up on the high point of land. He took with him a couple of the Canadian Fencible privates. When Thomas Marselis heard that de Lorimier was in charge of the lookout, after he finished his supper he and his brother-in-law Lewis Schwerdfager rounded up some firewood and went up the hill.

"Can we make you a fire, Lieutenant?" offered Thomas. "It's getting cooler. Around here a wind from the east usually means a change in the weather is coming. A fire will take the edge off the dampness."

De Lorimier was grateful for the offer and with a little help from one of the privates, behind the protection of the big rock, a compact fire was started and the men moved in a little closer. The conversation soon turned to a discussion of why the Americans hadn't come as had been predicted. The unspoken hope was that the Americans had changed their minds, that it was just too late in the season to launch an invasion of Montreal. In spite of their different backgrounds and ranks, the five Canadian men around the fire enjoyed a warm collegiality, a shared sense of place. Thomas and Lewis talked of their families and their plans to return to their homes tomorrow if there was no invasion. De Lorimier shared with them his hope that if the attack were called off he might be granted leave to return to Montreal to be with his wife, who was having their baby any day now.

"Having children is the most important thing I've done with my life," Thomas told de Lorimier. Lewis agreed.

"You are a lucky man, Thomas, to have such a beautiful family," replied de Lorimier.

"Yes I am," said Thomas. "I am a man that is truly blessed."

"If my baby is a girl I hope she is as beautiful as your little Aleda, Thomas," de Lorimier said to Thomas, and then turned to the two Fencible privates and with a big smile continued, "and you should see Lewis's not so little girl. Some people say she's the most beautiful girl in the St. Lawrence Valley from Montreal to York. She is *formidable*. Herse certainly thinks so. She is all he ever talks about. If the invasion is off, I think you'll see him hanging around Dundas County this winter. What do you think, Thomas? Shouldn't Lewis keep her locked away?"

"Herse is a good man but Elizabeth is too young for him," Lewis replied. Thomas could see that Lewis was uncomfortable with the discussion.

"Shouldn't somebody check to see if the Yankees are coming," said Thomas, changing the subject.

One of the privates got up and moved away from the fire and within moments yelled back, "*Colis*. What da Christ is dat?"

The others jumped up and moved away from the fire to get a better look. There did appear to be several lights up the river on the American side that hadn't been there earlier. As the men were straining to tell if they were lights on the shore or on boats, a gentle breeze came up, bringing with it a thickening mist. The lights were no longer visible as the river became completely shrouded in a thick fog.

For more than an hour the five men stood staring up the river, cursing the fog. Then, for a few moments, a hole opened in the fog and flashes of light were seen on the opposite shore, just 1,800 yards away. The men realized immediately that the flashes were caused by moonlight on bayonets held by men marching on the opposite side of the river. As the fog cleared a little more, several boats could be seen slowly moving down river, hugging the American shore.

"*Vite. Vite. Dites au Colonel. Dites à Jackson. Merde, merde. Les Yankees sont ici.* Mother of God," shouted de Lorimier.

Within minutes the whole fort was alarmed. Jackson and his artillerymen moved the guns and directed them to the other shore. Before they were set up, on the opposite side in the little village of Ogdensburg, someone seemed to be flashing signals.

More boats came into view as more of the fog receded. Finally Jackson was ready and the 6-pounders roared out as they sent their iron hurling across the river, but to little effect.

Colonel Pearson arrived on the scene and started yelling at Jackson to adjust the range. The roar of the cannons was unremitting. One of the cannon balls actually overshot the boats and hit a house in Ogdensburg, starting a small fire visible from the Canadian side. As the fog completely lifted, by the moonlight it became clear by midnight that almost all of the bateaux had now passed down the river, far enough to be completely out of the range of the cannons.

Pearson became frantic, yelling at Jackson and his sweating gunners, but it was clear to everyone after two hours and over 50 cannon balls that the distance and darkness were making the effort futile.

Colonel Pearson regained his composure and confronted Captain Jackson. "Did we get any? Can I report that we at least sank several bateaux? We have to send a message tonight to Montreal. What am I supposed to report to General Prevost?"

Jackson replied, "It is difficult to say, sir. From this distance the bateaux are very small targets. I'm sorry, sir."

"Yes, I'm sure you are, Captain. The damn Red Indians were right, they just had the wrong night. I'm going to report to General Prevost that we must have inflicted some real harm on the enemy and sunk some of their boats. We must have hit some of their boats."

In fact, of the 350 bateaux that quietly rowed past Prescott the night of November 6, 1813, only one boat was slightly damaged, with only one American killed and only two or three wounded. There was now nothing between the large American army of invasion and Montreal except for some Stormont and Glengarry militia at Cornwall and the Dundas militia—a few hundred soldier-farmers without uniforms, armed only with their old muskets.

Chapter 11
Sunday November 7, 1813
King's Highway, Upper Canada

Sunday morning dawned clear and bright. Thomas Marselis and the other men of the Dundas militia were finally going home, but not in the way they had hoped. Before sunrise, the furious Colonel Pearson had awakened Captain Jackson with instructions to go down the river with two 6-pounders and harass the American armada as much as he could all the way to the Gallop Rapids. Along with his four gunners he could take a couple of men from the Provincial Dragoons, de Lorimier and a couple of Fencibles, and the 12 men from the Dundas militia, as they were anxious to re-join their units and there was no longer any urgency to complete work on the fort. The little band of 22 men had rounded up the horses to pull the two 6-pounders and were already on the King's Highway heading east as the sun rose. Within an hour they could see some straggling bateaux. Strangely, they could also see some American infantry walking back up the river along the American shore, but they were out of range.

By the time Jackson reached Johnstown he thought that perhaps a couple of bateaux might be in range. He ordered the men to wheel the guns around in the road and fire one round each. The first was clearly short, but the second appeared to have hit one of the boats; however, from this distance it was hard to tell. It also became clear that the current was moving the bateaux more rapidly down the river and that Jackson's men were losing ground—they would need to quicken their pace. Just as the men urged on the horses to a full gallop, a wheel on one of the carriages broke, throwing one of the 6-pounders to the side of the muddy road. One of the Dragoons and Lewis Schwerdfager rushed over to begin repairing the wheel. Jackson approached de Lorimier: "Lieutenant, while we get this damned wheel fixed, you go ahead. The children we met on the road back there say that Captain Munro and the Dundas militia are on the other side of the Gallop Rapids. Take your two men and a couple of the local men and see if you meet up with Captain Munro to alert them to what is coming. We can't stop the invasion, but maybe we can slow it down."

Just as Lieutenant de Lorimier gave a salute and turned to leave, two large cannon shots were heard up the river.

"Jesus, what was that?" Jackson jerked around and looked up the river. "I hope that was on our side. Why would Colonel Pearson be firing the other cannon?"

What Jackson didn't know was that the American Infantry that he had seen going back up the river were actually going back to get some horses and cannons that they had left behind in Ogdensburg and, when Colonel Pearson saw this, he started to bombard the American village. Within a minute, more cannon shots were heard and this continued for some time. Meanwhile, de Lorimier and his two privates, Thomas Marselis and John Cook, were rushing down the highway as fast as they could manage. To their right they could begin to see the bulk of the American armada. Some of the bateaux seemed to be moored on the American shore and some seemed to be rowing towards the Canadian side.

De Lorimier and the others reached the head of the Gallop Rapids in less than an hour, having passed by more than two dozen farms along the front. Without losing their stride, Thomas and John would reassure the women and their families that the Americans would not likely stop on the Canadian side until after Iroquois Point, or perhaps at the head of the Rapids du Plat. The families told Thomas and John that all the rest of the men of Dundas County were with Captain Munro at a camp just below Iroquois Point.

By noon they reached the home of the widow Shaver. She was an old friend of Thomas's mother. She, too, had come as a refugee from the United States and lost her husband, who had never really recovered from his long imprisonment by the Yankees during the first war. When she saw the first group of Yankees float by the previous day, she proudly reported that she shot her musket at them several times, although she knew they were out of range. She told them that she had wanted to shoot Yankee soldiers for decades; she decided that this was going to be as close as she was ever going to get. Somehow, even if she hit no one, she felt a little better, she said.. She gave the men some apples, bread, and honey and insisted that they all have a tankard of her malt beer, made the old German way.

The men pressed on down the King's Highway until they came to Jacob Brouse's farm just above Iroquois Point, when, to their surprise, Brouse and a dozen men from the Dundas militia emerged from behind Jacob's barn and rushed over to shake hands with Thomas and John, who introduced them to Lieutenant de Lorimier and the two Canadian Fencibles.

Brouse explained that Captain Munro had left some men there to watch for the Americans because a messenger had earlier alerted them to the fact that the huge American armada had sailed past Prescott the previous night without injury and that they were slowly working their way down the American side. Captain Munro and the 200 men of the Dundas militia had camped last night just below the Point, where they had spent the last few days erecting a semi-circular defence of pine logs.

Thomas explained to Lieutenant de Lorimier that at Iroquois Point the river was only a dangerous 500 yards across to Sparrowhawk Point on the American side.

De Lorimier decided that they would wait with Brouse and his men to see what the Americans would do. They were making only slow progress, but a number of bateaux could be seen on the other side just a mile farther up the river.

At about three o'clock in the afternoon, the small group of men waiting on the shore in front of Jacob Brouse's farm saw some American boats turn and begin to head straight for where they were now standing. First, there were just a few bateaux, and then there were four or five large barges coming directly towards them.

De Lorimier took charge.

"All right, men. Form a line. Wait for my order. Wait." A couple of the farmer-soldiers were a little excited and slow to get into line. "Wait, men. Wait. Make ready, present arms. Fire! Repeat. Prime and load. Hurry men, make ready. Present arms. Wait, wait. Fire! Prime and load."

The men were excited as they paused to see if their two volleys had any effect on the advancing Americans. The American soldiers were still mostly out of range but the Canadians had hoped perhaps to scare them away with their warm little welcome.

Thomas Marselis was shaking. This was the first time in his life he had ever fired his musket at another man. Except for a couple of old veterans of the first war, and those who had fought at Ogdensburg, this was the first time for many of the Dundas militia to see action. The war had finally come to them, to their homes. Young Nicolas Ault, who was barely sixteen, stepped out of the line, turned away, and began to vomit. Finished, he wiped his mouth with the sleeve of his old greatcoat, got back into line, and bravely stood at attention again. It didn't look as if the Americans were turning back. Suddenly, young Ault shouted out at the top of his lungs, "Come on, you Yankee bastards. We're ready. Huzzah!"

The rest of the men were startled at first by the young private's outburst but soon they, too, started hollering obscenities at the approaching Yankees. For a few moments they felt a little less frightened, a little less overwhelmed by their extraordinarily hopeless situation.

Hearing the hollering, Brouse's wife and young son came out of their farmhouse and joined in the yelling. Brouse was startled to hear that his young son even knew such words.

Then de Lorimier shouted, "Make ready."

The men fell utterly silent. Their bravado vanished in an instant.

"Present arms. Fire! Prime and load. Make ready. Present arms. Fire! Prime and load."

The firing had no effect. The Americans seemed to be coming at them with even greater speed and determination. The men looked to de Lorimier. By now he could see that their situation was impossible. There appeared to be several hundred men in more than a dozen boats approaching the Canadian shore. There was no brave hollering now. Their choice was clear. Stay and be killed or captured, or disappear into the thick woods behind them.

De Lorimier shouted out: "We'll just get rid of our loads, men. We'll give them one more welcome to Canada and then we have to get out of here. Mrs. Brouse, you'd better get away from here. Get your things. Gentlemen," he shouted, "make ready. Present arms. Fire! Shoulder your firelocks. About turn . . . Men of the Dundas militia, you can return now to your flank company, which, I am told, is not that far away. You can follow Brouse. We are going back to rejoin Captain Jackson who can't be that far back up the highway by now. Hurry. Hurry, men."

With that, everyone was startled by the sound of a rifle shot. Then another. Then another which hit the side of Brouse's house, and another whistled by de Lorimier's head as de Lorimier yelled, "Let's get the hell out of here. *Vite, vite*."

In the confusion that followed, de Lorimier and his two Canadian Fencible privates scrambled back up onto the highway and ran west as fast as they could to rejoin Jackson and the others. This was not an orderly retreat. The men from Dundas militia climbed up to the highway and began to run the other way, east, towards the rest of their militia.

Jacob Brouse picked up his son and took his wife's hand. "Come on, Mother," he said. "We'll go back into the bush and wait to see what the Yankees do. They're heading for Montreal and won't be here long. We could try to hide in the barn but I'm afraid they are likely to be hungry and might find us there."

Meanwhile, Captain Munro and his 200 men from the two companies of the Dundas militia had heard the firing and came out from the brush to the Point, only to see another group of bateaux advancing to the Canadian side. Captain Munro instructed Sergeant Ruler to take his men a mile up river to watch for a possible landing at Grassy Bay. He, Munro, would take Lieutenant Doran and his men out on the rocks of the Point to get closer to the advancing Americans to maximize the effect of their volleys.

Captain Munro quickly assembled his men as they arrived at the bank into a ragged line. The Point was mostly rock, very uneven and quite slippery. This was not a place for precise military movements—not that the band of soldier-farmers were capable of such manoeuvres anyway.

When he could see that about half the men were ready, Captain Munro yelled to the men to "Make ready." The river was fast and noisy here and many men were falling and stumbling as they were trying to get into some kind of order.

In a flourish of military gallantry, Captain Munro pulled out his sword and raised it high above his head. He was pleasantly surprised to see young Loucks suddenly appear at his side with his drum. He began to beat a short rhythm and then stopped. The men looked at the Captain. He shouted, "Make ready. Wait. Present arms. Wait. Fire! Prime and load."

To Munro's surprise, the volley was quite effective. When the smoke cleared he yelled again, "Make ready . . . Present . . . Fire! Prime and load."

Again the volley had been effective, and it was clear that it had made quite an impression on the Americans. Some boats immediately wheeled and turned back towards the American side. A couple of the boats that were caught in the strong current of the narrows simply turned downstream and quickly passed the Point.

For a moment the Americans seemed to be in disarray or even in retreat. When a few of the other bateaux that were closest to the American side turned back and pulled into the shelter of the bay just above the narrows on the American side, several of the Dundas men hollered out, "Huzzah! Huzzah! They've turned back."

Capital Munro signalled to his drummer to beat the drum again. Again he raised his sword and shouted out the command, "Make Ready. Wait. Present arms. Wait. Fire! Prime and load."

The Dundas militia fired several more volleys with almost military precision. They were surprised at how well they seemed to be doing, when a soldier ran up to Captain Munro. "Sir, sir," he said, trying to catch his breath, "Private Haines advises that as many as fifty boats with hundreds of infantry, artillery, and even cavalry are coming ashore in Grassy Bay. There are too many for Ruler's men to stop from landing. Sir, we can't stay out here on this Point or we'll be trapped. We'll be cut off. There's too many Yankees. We can't stay here."

Captain Munro could also see by now that farther up there were even more boats coming down the river and some appeared to be heading directly for the Canadian shore. If he had any doubt about what course of action to follow, it was immediately dispelled when a large blast came from a gunboat in the river. He heard it hiss over his head and crash into the trees just 50 yards from where he was standing. Another blast roared out, hitting the water only 20 yards from shore.

Captain Munro ordered the drummer to beat a retreat as the men began to pull back off the rocky point. The terrain was too rough to even assemble the men as a group until they got back from the river to a small clearing beside the King's Highway. He climbed a small elevation and then stood up on a large pine stump. The men gathered around waiting for instructions. While he was still out of breath, Captain Munro made an effort to seem composed as he shouted out, "Men. We gave the Yankees a good welcome but there are just too many of them. All we can do is harass them as much as possible now and then disperse. The current is just too strong for them to land on the Point so the larger barges will probably land up at Grassy Bay and the smaller craft continue down the river to disembark at the head of the Plat Rapids. Lieutenant Doran will take his men up the river to join Ruler to make their landing as difficult as possible. It is prudent to retreat from the front and wait in the bush until Colonel Pearson arrives. I will take the balance of the men down the highway to alert our families that the Yankees are coming. We will harass them as much as possible if we can and then we, too, will back off to let them pass until the Prescott soldiers get down here. Everybody understand? May God be with you."

Jacob Doran gathered his men and started marching at a quick pace west along the highway to join Ruler and his men at Grassy Bay. As they came around the bend in the road they could see several more men standing along the shore shooting randomly at three American boats which seemed to be hovering just out of range. Then Ruler's men heard some shouting up the road and realized it was the Dundas militiamen who had been at Prescott. There were twelve of them running down the road towards them.

"Thomas, Lewis, John. We're here. We're here." The voice was unmistakable. Garrett came running towards them.

"Here we are, Thomas. Peter and I are here. We are so happy to see you, aren't we Peter?"

"Yes, Garrett. We are all together again just like you wanted." Garrett tried to shake Thomas's hand, and then Lewis and then young John.

"Is everybody all right?" asked Thomas, "Luke, Fred, Peter? No one is wounded?"

"We are all alive and well," replied Garrett. "What do we do now? There are too many of them."

While everyone was pleased to be reunited, the grim reality and urgency of the situation overwhelmed them. There were thousands of American soldiers coming down the St. Lawrence to either pass by or pass through their homes. The extent of immediate danger to their families was not yet clear but there was really nothing they could do anyway. An army of such size was unstoppable. Not even Montreal could withstand such a massive invasion.

Another wave of a dozen or more bateaux sailed safety through the Gallop Rapids just as Captain Jackson and his men came down the highway. Jackson yelled at the closest militiamen to help his gunners set up the two 6-pounder guns, and in a matter of minutes they were positioned on the road to fire at the passing armada.

"There," yelled Captain Jackson. "There. That schooner. That must have some of their officers. Aim at that schooner, men." The horses were freed from the gun and led to the side of the road by Garrett and John Cook, who tied them to a tree. John told Garrett to stay with the horses while he went back to help with the guns. Both guns fired but missed the schooner which shifted direction, and moved more to the American side to be out of range.

After two more rounds from the 6-pounders, one of the American gunboats came through the rapids and immediately swung left to approach the Canadian shore. Within minutes the American gunboat was able to return Jackson's fire.

The situation became chaotic. Canadians were standing on the shore shooting randomly at the passing bateaux, barges, and schooner. An American gunboat steadily approached the Canadian shore, its cannon fire becoming increasingly dangerous. Jackson and his two guns were firing as rapidly as possible.

Thomas and Peter Marselis and Lewis Schwerdfager had never seen anything like this. Because of the noise of the cannons, no one could hear anyone else, so there was really no one in charge. Thomas yelled to Peter and Lewis to try to find Ruler and to get him to make some decisions. Thomas yelled that he would speak to Captain Jackson.

It was becoming increasingly clear that while Jackson's guns had forced some of the American bateaux and barges to move closer to the American shore, the gunboat and six other bateaux filled with soldiers were not intimidated by the firing from the shore and were continuing to move to the Canadian shore.

Peter and Lewis found Ruler, but he seemed utterly bewildered and confused by the situation. Nothing in his life experience had prepared him for leadership in such circumstances.

Lewis grabbed Ruler. "John. Get hold of yourself. What are we going to do? That looks like Forsyth's men in the bateaux that are getting close to the shore up there. John! Somebody has to make some decisions."

"Where's Sergeant Loucks? Where is Doran? Yes, get Doran. He will know what to do," Ruler muttered.

Lewis and Peter found Sergeant William Loucks with a small group of men who were standing on the shore firing at some of the bateaux that seemed to be getting closer.

"William. Ruler is dazed. You have to take command. We need to get organized. If Forsyth's men get on the land we could all be killed. That bastard will take no prisoners."

"Where do you see the Forsyth Rifles?" Loucks yelled back. Jackson's guns roared again.

"Those bateaux coming in over there to the right. I'm sure that's Forsyth's men."

"All right," said Loucks, "get as many men as you can round up. We'll go a little way up river and try to organize some concerted firepower. Let's go."

About forty of the soldier-farmers of the two flank companies of the Dundas militia got word of Loucks's decision to move up river as a group to concentrate some fire on the six bateaux that had come within a hundred yards of the shore. There was a clear level field of winter wheat between the highway and the shore just above the little beach where the bateaux seemed to be heading.

By now, Jacob Doran and his men had arrived. Jacob was not fit enough for so much running. He was coughing and gasping for breath. He waved his men to go on ahead; he would catch up with them later.

Down on the narrow plain, Loucks shouted orders to move into echelon as they had practised a couple of times in September. No one seemed to remember just how that worked, but they could see the riflemen taking aim at them. They could hear bullets whistling through the air. Loucks shouted for the men to "make ready" and there followed a couple of ragged volleys that didn't seem to inflict much damage. Loucks marched the men closer to the edge of the field, where there was a stone fence just before the beach began.

Within fifty feet of Loucks's group, a huge shell from one of the gunboats exploded, sending dirt and stones flying, but no one seemed to be hurt. Loucks shouted for the men to run up to the stone fence for cover and to fire at will. Now the men were more comfortable. They were not used to fighting in the open in ranks like the redcoats. Getting shelter behind a rock fence and shooting their muskets when ready—this they could do. It was not that different from deer hunting. While this procedure didn't have the same shock effect as a concerted volley, it proved to be quite successful, as the balls from the militia muskets struck some soldiers in the bateaux. The lead bateau turned back. Then a second bateau turned back.

Thomas Marselis aimed his musket just above the head of a tall American he could see in the lead boat. He pulled the trigger and saw the soldier lunge back and fall into the river. Thomas's heart was pounding in his ears. He could feel his bowels turning to water. He got back down behind the stone fence to reload, when Jacob Doran ran up beside him.

"I think I got one," said Jacob, panting.

"Me too," said Thomas.

Thomas stood up to reload, when a musket ball whizzed by his head. He jumped down. Jacob rolled over and reloaded on his back, staying out of danger.

"Where did you learn that?" Thomas yelled.

"Don't ask," shouted Jacob, as he rolled back onto his elbows and took another shot.

But by now, many of the Dundas militia were running very low in ammunition. Their muskets were too hot to touch. While the approaching bateaux with soldiers either turned back or slowed their advance, the larger gunboat, also filled with soldiers, kept advancing.

It was then that Thomas heard Garrett yell his name and he looked back across the field to see Garrett leading the four horses pulling one of the 6-pounder guns. Thomas and Jacob crouched down as they ran back to the road where they could see Captain Jackson coming with the other horses and gun.

"We have to get out of here before our retreat is cut off," Jackson yelled to Thomas. "We can't stay any longer. Macomb's whole elite brigade has disembarked just above Iroquois Point. We have to get back to Prescott to join the Colonel before Forsyth's riflemen cut off our retreat. You can tell Loucks and the rest of your men to stay behind that fence and to keep up the fire as best they can to buy us some time to get out of reach before nightfall."

"Many of us are running low on powder and balls, Captain, and that gunboat is getting very close," explained Thomas.

"Just do the best you can. Stay as long as you can and then come back to the fort. Good luck, Thomas." Jackson gave a little salute.

Thomas took Garrett by both arms and looked straight into his eyes. "Garrett, you stay with Captain Jackson and help him with his horses. He needs your help, Garrett. We'll all be together again tonight at the fort. We'll have a big fire and lots of food. Go now and be careful."

"But what about Mother and . . . and everyone? We can't leave them alone. The Yankees will kill them." Garrett's face was filled with pain and a fear that went right to Thomas's insides. He had been so preoccupied with the fighting, he hadn't thought about his family all afternoon. He couldn't show his fear to Garrett.

"No, Garrett," he said. "They will be all right. The Yankees are going on to Montreal. They won't stay long in Dundas County."

"They are trying to kill us. Why wouldn't they hurt our family? You're lying to me so I won't worry."

"No. I'm not. Individually they aren't bad people. They are just doing what their officers are ordering them to do. They don't hate us, Garrett."

"Mother hates Yankees," interrupted Garrett.

"Yes, well, that's different. Listen to me, Garrett. Go with Captain Jackson. We'll all be together tonight. I have to go back to help Lewis." And with that Thomas ran across the field towards the stone fence to join the others firing at the approaching Americans. Just before he reached the fence Thomas fell to the ground, his musket flying from his hands.

Loucks saw Thomas fall and saw the terror in his face.

"My God, man, are you hit?" he yelled to Thomas.

Thomas grabbed his musket and ran to the fence. "No," he said, "I just tripped."

The stone fence proved to be the perfect defence. Forsyth's men were forced to abandon their plan to land on the beach which was so well fortified and they moved about a mile farther down the river to the next possible landing ground. This allowed Sergeant Loucks to begin to send men a few at a time back up to the highway to retreat to Prescott. As the sun began to set, the last of the Dundas militia stole away from the fence, moved unmolested across the field, up to the highway past the Gallop Rapids, and started walking back to the fort. The skirmish at Iroquois Point, November 7, 1813, was over.

The Dundas men were walking in various groups. Curiously, some of the men seemed to trudge along mostly in silence, perhaps still trying to come to grips with what they had been through during this Sunday that none of them would ever forget. Other groups were animated in excited conversation, still filled with the adrenaline of the afternoon.

Towards the end of the line of militiamen, walking slowly, were the two Marselis brothers. Neither had said much. Peter assured Thomas that everybody back home was well and had missed him.

"I was looking forward to getting home tonight," Thomas said. "I never thought I would be walking back to this damned fort. Are you sure everyone is well?"

"Everyone is fine," said Peter, "everyone is fine. But I wish I could be as sure as you that they'll be just as well tomorrow. Do we really know that several thousand Yankee soldiers won't cause harm to our farms or to our families as they pass on down through?"

"I'm not sure," Thomas replied, "but I know that I'm feeling very uncomfortable, maybe even guilty that I'm walking up the river while thousands of Yankee soldiers are marching the other way towards everything in this world that I love. How did it come to this?" He paused, then continued: "I'm scared and angry. The whole lot of them doesn't have to be evil. All it would take would be a couple of drunken soldiers thousands of miles from home to do something cruel or stupid. I'm sure some of them are angry too, freezing their asses off up here. We are at war, for God's sakes. We just spent the afternoon trying to kill them. Damn, I may even have killed one myself. Poor bastard!"

Peter had never seen Thomas so distraught. Seeing him this way gave Peter a sick feeling in the pit of his stomach. Thomas was always the brave one—the optimistic one. How often had he heard his brother say, "Don't worry, it will all work out; this too will pass"?

Thomas uttered a long audible sigh and then wiped his eyes with his coat sleeve. He took another big breath and looked at Peter. He could see the fright in Peter's eyes. He thought of his father. He wanted to say something to reassure his younger brother, but no words came. He felt drained. The adrenaline was wearing off. His stomach felt queasy. "We could all be brave if it weren't for our stomachs," he remembered his father saying, talking about the time he was hit at the Battle of Klock's Field. Thinking of his father again seemed to make him feel a little better. He looked at Peter again. He reached out and put his arm around him.

"Don't worry, Peter," he said, "we'll get the bastards tomorrow. Everything is going to be all right. Everything is going to be all right."

While Thomas was trying to reassure Peter as they walked back west towards the fort at Prescott, the United States army of invasion was preparing to march east along the Canadian shore. The forward advance group, particularly Forsyth's men, thoroughly looted Peter Shaver's store which had just received a boatload of goods from Montreal, including rum, brandy, sugar, gloves, cravats, and buttons. The following army later that day purloined his potatoes and apples. By the afternoon of the 7th, Forsyth's men and some others from the Twentieth U.S. Infantry Regiment reached Jacob Doran's farm on the border of Matilda and Williamsburg. Doran, like Shaver, was with the Dundas militia up river or at the fort. His wife Catherine and stepdaughter Maria were alone when they arrived. The U.S. Infantry officer was courteous and explained that the men had been warned not to loot the farms along the river as these sturdy German and Dutch farmers from the Mohawk Valley, all born in America, would soon be good Americans again. The United States would pay good Spanish silver for any supplies that were needed, he assured them. Catherine, who spoke fluent English, feigned ignorance of the language. Some of the Yankees spent the night in the Dorans' new barn. In the morning, the soldiers were gone and so were the little pigs and four chickens. Catherine and Maria and the Bouck boy from next door spent the morning leading all the rest of the animals back into the cedar bush at the second concession and hid them there for the next two days as the rest of the army marched past.

By the early evening of the 7th, Forsyth's riflemen had gorged themselves on Bouck's honey, had been shot at by old man Garlough before he fled into the bush with his cow and two goats, and had seized Haines's Tavern and its rum and brandy and settled in for the night. Over 6,000 regular troops would follow them through Williamsburg over the next three days: four brigades of infantry (over 5,000 men), the Elite Brigade commanded by Brigadier General Alexander Macomb (over 1,000 men), 460 cavalry from the First and Second U.S. Light Dragoons, and 348 in two regiments of artillery under Brigadier General Moses Porter. This U.S. army of invasion was the most serious attempt ever by the United States of America to conquer the Canadas.

Thomas had been right. The Yankees had not yet molested the Marselis family but the forward advance—the hated First U.S. Rifle Regiment commanded by Lieutenant Colonel Benjamin Forsyth—spent the night only ten farms up river from the Marselis farm.

Chapter 12
Monday November 8, 1813
Prescott, Upper Canada

The skirmishes at Iroquois Point the previous day had made an impact on the American commander General Wilkinson. Jackson's guns, the Dundas militia, and what Wilkinson referred to as the "active, universal hostility of the male inhabitants" of Upper Canada had not been expected, and so he decided that the Canadian side had to be cleared of any resistance from Iroquois Point to the Long Sault Rapids, a distance of some 20 miles. Macomb had secured the Canadian shore just down from Iroquois Point so Wilkinson decided to undertake the major operation of moving the bulk of his army to the Canadian side at the narrow point in the river just above Ogden Island. Particularly daunting was the task of ferrying across the St. Lawrence River 250 artillery team horses and the 400 horses of his two cavalry regiments.

Wilkinson's advance scouts, some of Macomb's Elite, and a few of Forsyth's riflemen reported that all of the Dundas County men had either fled away from the river to the bush or were with the militia either above them at Prescott or farther down the river closer to Cornwall, so the way should be clear except for women and children. But Wilkinson also had intelligence that the British commander at Kingston, Lieutenant Colonel Joseph Morrison of the 89th Foot, was moving east towards Prescott to follow him.

While Wilkinson realized that he was in danger of being attacked from the west by Morrison's men, who could join with the soldiers at Prescott commanded by Pearson, he was confident that his position was strong as he estimated his own strength to be over 7,000 men (even though many were sick) and Morrison's combined forces he estimated to be less than 1,000. At the same time, he also knew his supplies were low, estimating that there were only ten days' worth of rations of bread and twenty of meat remaining.

On the afternoon of November 8, Wilkinson called a full council of war with all of his senior officers and the decision was made to prepare to attack Montreal with all dispatch. The enemy force was trailing from the west and the solution to the shortage of food and the coming winter was to attack and secure Montreal, where the American army of invasion would have all the comfort and supplies they needed.

The weather had turned bad late Sunday night. Monday morning was stormy and cold. The men of the Dundas militia spent a miserable night. They hadn't been prepared for the change in the weather and they certainly hadn't planned on spending the night at Prescott. Some of them had found room inside a storage building in the fort, others had slept on the barracks floor, but most had spent the night outside in tents in the fort's parade ground.

The morning was an anxious time for everyone at the fort. Colonel Pearson had been advised that Morrison had left Fort Henry with his men on the 7th to come to Prescott. Pearson's orders were to wait for Morrison's arrival, probably on the morning of the 9th, and together the two groups would catch up with Wilkinson to harass his rear. It was clear now to Pearson that their orders would be to engage the enemy, in spite of the overwhelming odds against them.

For the men of the Dundas militia, the wait was agonizing. As they sat around waiting in the security of the fort, their families, their homes, their barns, and all of their worldly possessions were vulnerable to the 7,000-strong American army marching through their beloved Dundas County on the way to Cornwall and Montreal.

The cold rain had stopped by early afternoon, but there was still a bitter wind coming in off the river. Inland from the fort, in a sheltered gully, several men from the Dundas militia had made large bonfires for warmth and to try to dry their clothes. Around one of these fires stood the three Marselis brothers, John and George Cook, Jacob Doran and his two sons, and Lewis Schwerdfager. The nine men were related by birth or marriage; their conversation was dominated by their unrelenting worry for the safety of their families and farms and their agonizing frustration that they were helpless to do anything. The men who had farms away from the front didn't have the same sense of fear as these men, all of whose farms were right on the river, on the very King's Highway down which the American army was marching. Their wives and sisters and daughters and mothers were completely unprotected.

It was Peter who raised first what others had been thinking: "What will Oma do when the Yankees get to our farm?"

"I don't think that she will be serving them tea," Lewis answered, trying to break some of the nervous tension. It didn't work.

Peter continued: "Lena and Allie will have the good sense to stay out of their way and keep quiet, but I shudder to think what Oma might do or say."

"She hates Yankees, all right," replied Thomas, "but I don't think she would do or say anything that would put the children at risk. Lena may be there, too. Oma might listen to her. Or, on second thought, maybe she won't. I've got Father's musket; there are no firelocks there so she won't be able to shoot anyone."

"I don't know," said Lewis, "I wouldn't want to be the man to face Oma with her butcher knife."

"Why would a Yankee soldier want to attack Oma?" asked David Doran.

"They wouldn't have to try to attack her. Oma would happily kill a Yankee soldier for dirtying her precious kitchen floor," Lewis replied, with nodding heads all around. "The bigger fear is that she would attack one of them just for coming onto her land."

The men continued to fret about the safety of their families and their frustration that they were doing nothing, when a private with the 49th approached Jacob. Because Jacob was wearing his old green Yorker uniform and was obviously one of the older militiamen, the private asked if he was one of the militia officers, as he had a note to deliver. Jacob replied that he was a lieutenant and, pointing to John, advised that John Cook was the man to deal with notes. The private handed John the note and returned to the fort completely unaware that he had just handed the paper to probably the only militiaman there who had the ability to read it.

The note was from Captain William Johnson requesting that all the Dundas militia officers meet with him at the south end of the parade ground as soon as they could be assembled.

It didn't take long for John and Jacob to round up the other officers and to present themselves to Captain Johnson. With Johnson was Captain Richard Fraser of the Provincial Light Dragoons and Lieutenant Charles Anderson of the Indian Department. Johnson thanked the men for coming and got immediately to the point:

"I have orders for you from Colonel Pearson. Colonel Morrison will be arriving here within a matter of hours with the 89th. During the night we will all leave together on the gunboats and the sixty bateaux that have been assembled. In the meantime, Colonel Pearson has ordered Captain Fraser here and his dragoons to lead what remains of the Dundas militia and Lieutenant Anderson's Indians to Iroquois Point this afternoon. We don't have room for the horses on the bateaux and Colonel Pearson knows how anxious you are to get back to your homes. Colonel Pearson doesn't believe that it would be appropriate to have the Indians on the bateaux with the regular men. Your orders are to get to the enemy as quickly as you can and to get as close as you can. Your mission is to learn as much as possible about their numbers, position, and condition. This is an important task, as we will be relying on your intelligence and advice when we come to join up with you early tomorrow morning. Any questions, gentlemen?"

When there were no questions, and before dismissing the men, Captain Johnson spoke to Jacob:

"It's Mr. Doran, isn't it?"

"It is, sir."

"I see you're wearing your old Yorkers' uniform. You fought with my father in the old regiment?"

"I did, sir. I had the honour to serve with Sir John throughout the first war, sir. He was a great man."

"Thank you for that, Mr. Doran. May I ask what is your rank with the militia?"

"I am a lieutenant, sir."

"Well, then, Lieutenant, let me take this opportunity to say how proud I am to serve with men from the old corps. My father will be so pleased when I tell him that you and I had this conversation."

"Please extend my best wishes to Sir John, sir, and assure him that the Yorkers and their sons and daughters hold him in the greatest esteem."

"That is very kind of you, Lieutenant. Let me now ask Captain Fraser to provide details. Captain Fraser."

Captain Fraser stepped forward. He was a tall handsome Scot with a large handlebar moustache.

"Gentlemen," he began, "we have an important duty. The militia will have to march back the twelve miles to Iroquois Point. I know that you men just came from there yesterday but now you will be attacking, not retreating. I will have a couple of my men ride ahead to make sure that the way is clear. Lieutenant Anderson's Mohawks, whose behaviour cannot always be predicted, will join you, but they are excellent warriors. The Yankees are frightened to death of them. A few of them speak English but most of them do not. I understand that one of your men, a Private Marselis, is a fluent Mohawk speaker and is familiar with their ways. Lieutenant Anderson has asked that he be assigned to assist him over the next few days, as we need a local man who knows the county. I trust this is satisfactory. That is all. Please have your men make ready and assemble outside the fort doors at fourteen hundred hours."

Jacob was pleasantly surprised at how smartly the men assembled and responded to commands. They were in relatively straight lines and most men were properly standing at attention when Captain Fraser rode up at precisely 1400 hours. He dismounted from his large black stallion. He ordered his twelve dragoons to dismount. Not all of their horses were quite so impressive. In fact, two of them looked more like old heavy workhorses and the rest appeared to be Canadians of varying sizes and colours. Captain Fraser stood erect, resplendent in his red uniform with blue facings. There was a twinkle in his eyes, as he had a couple of surprises in store. In a few moments, from the other side of the fort, Lieutenant Anderson appeared, leading his 30 warriors in single Indian file. They were truly impressive in full battle attire, fully painted, waving muskets and tomahawks, and uttering the occasional blood-curdling whoop for full effect. They halted beside the militiamen, many of whom had never seen such a display.

And then the double doors of the fort were flung open and a small colour party with two drummers drumming and a piper piping marched out of the fort to the front of the militia. Colonel Pearson then appeared at the fort doors and marched smartly to Captain Fraser. The drumming stopped. He took the salute. Captain Fraser ordered his men to mount. From the far end of the fort, Captain Jackson of the Royal Artillery released a thundering shot from one of his 6-pounder cannon.

To the sound of the drumming and the piper playing a cheery tune, the little band of Canadian militia, dragoons, and Indians marched down the hill to the King's Highway and wheeled left on to the road, heading east along the Canadian shore of the St. Lawrence River.

The pretence of military order dissipated soon after the advance group was down the hill and onto the King's Highway out of sight of the fort. Fraser's twelve dragoons rode on ahead. The Dundas militia broke up into various groups in no particular arrangement, military or otherwise. Anderson and his 30 Mohawks lagged even farther behind.

This ragged group, all Canadians, made the trip back to the field just east of Iroquois Point where many of them had camped the night before. John Loucks, an 18-year-old Dundas County boy, and one of Fraser's dragoons, had ridden ahead. He returned with news that the rear of the American army was only a mile ahead, just approaching Peter Shaver's farm. Fraser made the decision to camp for the night and to wait there for the arrival of Morrison and Pearson.

The area where they made camp already had a number of lean-to's and other forms of temporary shelter. From the nearby Brouse farm, some basic supplies were obtained, including some straw for bedding. The Mohawks camped down closer to the river.

After a hearty early supper of army beef, potatoes, carrots, and turnip, the men gathered around a large bonfire just at sunset. Most of the men were nervous about what was coming. Jacob Doran and his sons knew that the last of the United States Army would pass by their farms by noon of the next day so they would be home soon, the danger to their families having passed. For those men with farms farther east in central or eastern Dundas County, they could only hope that the last of the American army would pass by their farms and be gone by Tuesday night or Wednesday.

The Marselis brothers were talking with Jacob Doran and his sons around the campfire when Lieutenant Anderson approached them. Charles Anderson was a small, wiry man in his early thirties. He was the son of a Scot surveyor and a Mohawk mother. He had his mother's deep brown eyes and high cheekbones and his father's curly red hair. He had been raised by his mother along the Grand River in Six Nations country until she died when he was 15. His father retrieved him then and he was brought to Glengarry County to live with his father's wife and family but, never really fitting in, he joined the Indian Department when he was 18, serving in a number of positions until the start of the war.

Anderson explained that he had been given orders to take his warriors that evening back into the bush, perhaps to the second or third concession, to move east circling past the United States Army but beyond their sight, so that by daybreak they might be able to determine how far east the main part of the army had progressed. They were to travel as far east as possible, but it was recognized that if the weather didn't clear, even with the local knowledge of Private Marselis, it might not be possible to travel at night because in this part of Dundas County much of the second concession had not been cleared as a road and in most places was still no more than a trail. Anderson, Thomas Marselis, and the warriors were to stay hidden in the bush until they were provided with additional orders.

Anderson's scouting party made good progress along the second concession trail. There were a few isolated cabins and clearings along the way and the occasional new farm. Darkness came early that cold, cloudy evening. There was no moon and travel became difficult. When they arrived at the farmhouse of the widow Reddick at about 8:00 in the evening, Thomas advised Lieutenant Anderson that he knew Mrs. Reddick's late husband who had been a friend of his father's and who had also fought with the Royal Yorkers. Perhaps they could use her barn and two sheds as shelters for the night. Anderson agreed and he and Thomas, keeping the Mohawks back and out of sight, rapped on the door of the small farmhouse. Mrs. Reddick met Thomas warmly at the door and he and Anderson were invited in. She explained that she had been warned of the invasion on Sunday and fearing that the U.S. army might come back to the second concession to pillage crops and animals, she had sent her oldest daughter and son to lead their two cows back to the fourth concession where her brother had a cabin and barn. She was only too glad to give permission to Anderson and his men to use the barn as shelter for the night.

The Mohawk warriors were pleased to settle into the cosy barn for the night, as it had been a long day. Most of the men climbed the ladder and made their beds in the hay and straw in the upper mow. Too exhausted to eat, most of the warriors were quick to fall asleep. Too excited to sleep, Thomas and Lieutenant Anderson sat outside the barn on a bench in a little alcove talking.

"We've had quite a day," said Anderson.

"Yes, quite a day," replied Thomas, "and tomorrow's not going to be easy either. I still don't understand why we would take on an army ten times our size."

"Colonel Morrison knows what he is doing. He probably knows a good deal more than we do. Maybe our job will be to just try to slow them down to give the Lower Canada forces more time to get organized. I don't know." Anderson looked at the sky. "It looks like it may be clearing in the east. If we get some moonlight, should we wake the men and carry on? What do you think?"

"The track east of here gets very wet. There is a large boggy area that we will have to go around and that would be difficult even with good moonlight . . . anyway, your men are very tired. They should get some rest for tomorrow, don't you think?"

"Agreed. By the way, where is your farm from here?"

"Not that far. Another four miles and you come to an old Indian trail. Take it south to the river and there is my family's farm. To get to my own property that I am just now clearing you would have to go back one more concession. It's good land."

"You married?"

"Yes, two children. Boy and a girl. You?"

"No, still looking for the right girl."

"Where did you learn Mohawk?"

"From my mother at Six Nations. You?"

"You're from Six Nations?"

"Yes."

"I lived there from the summer of 1808 to spring of 1810. I lived with the Monture family."

"I had left by then. Do you mean Chief Joe Monture?"

"Yes. He took me in. I was in bad shape for a while. I'd been out west. Coming back with a full load of furs we got into some bad weather on Lake Erie. Some of the men drowned. I broke my leg when I got to shore. We were near the mouth of the Grand. I couldn't go on so the Mohawk Chief took me in for the winter. Ended up staying for two years."

"I knew the Monture family well. My mother was Christian. A good Catholic like my father. The Montures are real Haudenosaunee. What kept you there so long? Wait, let me guess. A girl? Am I right?"

"Right you are," said Thomas. "I fell in love with the Chief's niece."

"The Six Nations have some beautiful women. Why did you leave?"

"I got a message that my brother Peter was ill in the summer of 1809 so I went home. He recovered well and I went back to Six Nations in the fall. Then I got a message just before Christmas that while I had been home, I got a girl in a family way. So, I had to do the right thing and go back in the spring and marry her. My son had already been born. That's my story."

"Any children at Six Nations?"

"No. But I enjoyed my time there. Great people. Very smart. Very generous. Good hunters. Any of these men from Six Nations?"

"No. These are mostly Tyendinaga men. Christians. Catholics mostly. Strong supporters of the Crown. Got a couple of good men whose families were originally from Akwesasne."

"What are their names?"

"Captain Jim and Kenewe. Why? You know some of the praying Mohawks from Akwesasne?"

"My father was quite close to a number of them. They fought

together in the first war with Sir John." Thomas then stopped talking, hesitated, and finally asked:

"Ever hear of a Mohawk at Tyendinaga called Jeremiah Sunday?"

"Hear of him? He's here. You saw him today. Big guy. Fearless warrior. He calls himself Kenewe now. Only uses his Indian name. Very smart guy. Speaks good English. Renounced Catholicism. Haudenosaunee true believer now. Wolf clan. You know him?"

"Yes," said Thomas, his heart racing. "Haven't seen him for many years."

"I'll introduce you tomorrow."

"Yes," said Thomas. "Tomorrow. It really is going to be quite a memorable day."

"We better get some sleep. We should be on the trail at daybreak. I left my kit and musket in an empty horse stable in the barn. There's room for another man there."

Thomas was physically exhausted but he didn't sleep well that night. He couldn't get his mind to slow down. He thought of his wife and family. He thought of Jeremiah Sunday. When he finally got to sleep, he had a nightmare about Nancy's death that woke him in a cold sweat.

Meanwhile, in Williamsburg Township that cold late afternoon, the American forward advance, particularly Forsyth's riflemen and some cavalrymen from the Second Regiment of the U.S. Light Dragoons, did come to pass through the Marselis farm at Lot 21, Concession 1. An older woman stood at the open door of the main house with her hands on her hips. She was yelling something in Dutch or German as the men passed by. No soldier approached her or the house. Some of the Forsyth riflemen took potatoes from the shed beside the barn. The doors were locked on the nearby log cabin and a baby was heard crying inside so no soldier tried to force entry. One of the U.S. cavalrymen, who had lost his horse by drowning several days before when one of the bateaux had overturned, was tired of walking. He noticed a lovely little black horse in the barn. Beside the horse was a new saddle neatly hanging from a hook. The U.S. cavalryman saddled up the little black horse and quietly led it out the back door of the barn.

Chapter 13
Tuesday, November 9, 1813
Dundas County

The weather did improve overnight. With a fresh breeze from the east, dawn broke clear and cool. Thomas and Anderson were already up. The young Canadian dragoon John Loucks had awakened them in the early morning just before daybreak. He brought a message from Captain Johnson ordering Anderson's scouting party not to proceed farther but to stay at the Reddick farm until further orders were provided. Loucks explained that Morrison had arrived at Prescott earlier than expected, having made the 70-mile trip from Fort Henry in just 21 hours. Morrison didn't want to wait, so he ran the Gallop Rapids in the dark and was already approaching Iroquois Point, where he would rendezvous with the militia and assess the situation after determining how far back he was from the rear of the U.S. army. Loucks explained that Johnson would send word whether Anderson was to return to the militia camp at Iroquois Point or go directly south to the river.

Anderson did not receive any objections when he sent word to the Mohawks in the mow that they did not have to rise early. He also sent a message asking Jeremiah to come down as Anderson had something to show him. Meanwhile, Thomas and Anderson were sitting on their bench in front of the barn enjoying the warmth of the early morning sun rising in the east.

"With this clearer weather, the Yankees should be making better time," Anderson commented to Thomas. "Perhaps Morrison has changed his plans and given up trying to catch them. But he sure made a fast trip from Fort Henry."

"This weather isn't going to last," replied Thomas. "Whenever we get a wind from the east like this we are usually in for a bout of bad weather. My guess is that we will have a cold rain or snow flurries by tomorrow. My mother always says that she can feel the dampness of these easterlies in her bones. If my mother were here she would give us a full weather prediction. She's never wrong about the weather, or anything else, come to think of it."

"Your mother is still alive?"

"Oh, she is very much alive," replied Thomas. "At least I hope she is. I reckon that the advance group of the U.S. army would have gone through our farm yesterday. She doesn't like Yankees. She was badly treated by them in the last war. Civil wars are hard and bitter. Her own father disowned her for being married to a Loyalist. She and my father lost everything to the rebels. They had to start over here in Canada. She is very angry that the Yankees are again threatening everything she has worked to create over the last thirty years. She is very—how shall I put it?—strong-willed. I just hope that she left the Yankees alone."

"After my mother died at Six Nations, my father brought me to Glengarry to live with his family. He came from Scotland after the war but most of our neighbours were Loyalists who had fought with the 84th—the Royal Highland Emigrants—or with Sir John's Royal Yorkers. I understand well the bitterness you talk about. That generation will never forget and never forgive. You're right—civil wars are the worst. And the refugee experience scars people for life."

"My father tried to put it behind him, but watching his younger brother die in his arms haunted him all his life." Thomas paused, then continued. "Heavens, how did we get onto such a morbid discussion this early in the morning?"

At that moment a tall Indian emerged from the barn door. Anderson beckoned to him.

"Let me introduce you to Thomas Marselis. He says he knows your family."

The tall muscular Indian wore a beaded deerskin vest over a white shirt. He had tight deerskin leggings. His moccasins were trimmed with fur. His head was shaven. He had deep blue eyes. There was a large scar on his left cheek. He walked with a limp.

He came closer to Thomas, looking at his face intently. He put out his hand to Thomas. The two men shook hands but they both seemed more focused on looking at the other's eyes. Neither man spoke. Words did not come easily to Thomas. Finally, the big Indian smiled and in a slow deep voice said:

"Good morning, little brother." He spoke in the Mohawk language.

Anderson assumed that this was a gesture of affection. He did not understand the greeting to be literally accurate. Thomas finally replied awkwardly:

"Good morning, Jeremiah. It's been a long time. Maybe ten years. Do you remember?"

"I remember," he said slowly, still speaking in Mohawk, still carefully watching Thomas's eyes.

"So, how do you men know each other?" Anderson asked, also speaking in Mohawk, sensing a certain unease which he did not understand.

"Our families were close during the war," Thomas replied, "and Jeremiah's uncle was one of my father's best friends. They fought together in the war. They both lost brothers on the same day at the Battle of Klock's Field."

Again, Jeremiah didn't say anything. He seemed to be studying Thomas's face. Finally he put his big hand on Thomas's shoulder and in a low quiet voice he said, "Come, little brother. Let's go for a walk."

Anderson did not understand the mixture of awkwardness and affection that seemed to define the relationship between the two men but he could see that they wanted to be alone. He watched them walk across a clearing towards a stand of ancient pines.

The sun was rising now. It was a clear cool day.

At about nine that morning a young dragoon, Private Edward Shaver, rode into the Reddick farmyard. He brought orders for Anderson to take his scouting party straight south to the river. They were to carefully determine whether the American army had advanced east past there and then to send a runner back with the intelligence. Morrison and Pearson's men were ready to move east. Anderson ordered Thomas and Jeremiah, who had just returned to the yard, to round up the Mohawks and prepare to move south.

The leader of the Mohawks seemed to be Captain Jim. His Mohawk name was Shagaunnahquodwaby. He wore a British army red coat that was too small to cover his barrel chest and long arms. Around his neck he wore a large silver gorget. He was heavily tattooed. He carried an intricately beaded bag from which there protruded a large war club. Around his waist he wore a belt and hanging from the belt was a large Indian tomahawk with red feathers hanging from its handle. His head was shaved, except for a long braid of hair that began at the back of his head. His weathered dark face was given a particularly fearsome look by tattooed horizontal lines on both of his cheeks and under his eyes. He wore deerskin pants and beaded moccasins.

Anderson, Thomas, Jeremiah, and Captain Jim were the first to arrive at the edge of the clearing. They crouched behind some smaller cedar trees. Thomas recognized the farm as Big Red Casselman's. (Big Red was with the militia at Point Iroquois.) They could see the back of the barn and part of a small one-storey farmhouse on the other side of the barn and to its right. No one seemed to be there. Apparently the U.S. army had gone past the farm by now as no soldiers were in sight. There was a large maple tree at the edge of the clearing, which Captain Jim offered to climb to see if the Yankees could be spotted down the road to the east. He scampered up the tree like a man half his age. From the higher vantage point, Captain Jim could see a mile on both sides of Casselman's farm. Captain Jim climbed down from the tree and reported that there were no Yankees to the west and just a few stragglers to the east, about three farms away. It would seem that the American army had passed through. Anderson decided to send Thomas to the farmhouse to ensure the way was clear, with instructions to then proceed back west to meet up with Morrison and tell him where the rear of the U.S. army was and advise him that Anderson would wait there for Morrison with his warriors.

As Thomas walked out into the clearing towards the back of the barn, all he could think about was that he was getting close to home. Soon this ordeal would be over. He reckoned that the Yankees would be past Dundas County by end of day. Would Morrison catch up with them? What would he do if he did? What would be gained by engaging them? The U.S. army was too large. A lot of men would die for nothing. Was his family safe? Thomas's mind was elsewhere when a loud shot rang out. He dove to the ground. He wasn't hit. Who was shooting at him? He thought he could hear a woman's voice behind the barn. He raised himself up onto his elbows to get a better view of the barn. He was shaking with fear and was completely confused by what was happening. He turned and saw Anderson, Jeremiah, and Captain Jim running in a crouched position towards him. They dove to the ground beside him.

"Shit. We thought someone had shot you. Are you all right?" Jeremiah was beside Thomas trying to catch his breath. He spoke in Mohawk. "Where did the shot come from?"

"Behind the barn, I think. Did you hear a woman's voice?" Thomas replied, his voice still dry and shaky. They could hear a dog barking. Anderson turned to Jeremiah:

"What do you think? Should we try to run up behind the barn and see what's on the other side?"

Captain Jim wasn't waiting for a decision. The big warrior was already up and running towards the barn. The other three quickly followed. Anderson and Thomas went to the right side of the barn and Jeremiah followed Captain Jim to the left.

Thomas crouched down and carefully looked around the corner of the barn. Standing just in front of the back door of the farmhouse was Mrs. Casselman. She was pointing a musket towards the front of the barn but Thomas couldn't see what was there. He thought he heard a child scream. Then he saw a child in the doorway just behind Mrs. Casselman. There was a small dog by her side, barking and growling.

"Leave my horse and you can go," she yelled.

"You stupid, stupid woman," came a man's voice from inside the barn, "throw down that musket and go back into your house."

"You're not taking my horse," she yelled back. The child came out the door screaming, trying to pull her mother back in the door. The dog kept barking frantically.

"Throw down that musket and get into your house. I don't want to hurt you. I can shoot you dead right now, you stupid woman," he yelled back. "Don't make me shoot you."

"You can't steal my horse. No damn Yankee is stealing my horse."

"I'm not leaving here now without the goddamn horse. Please put the musket down," and with that he fired a warning shot that struck the house above the door. The child screamed and pulled at her mother, who stumbled. Her musket went off, the ball hitting the ground in front of her.

A man came out of the barn and ran towards the woman, yelling something that Thomas couldn't make out, but seeing the soldier in a Forsyth Rifle uniform running towards Mrs. Casselman, Thomas sprang from the side of the barn, running to catch the soldier from behind. The dog leapt at the soldier who hit the dog with the butt of his rifle, sending it yelping to the ground. Just then, Thomas reached the soldier and leaped on his back, also crashing into the woman and the child.

Another shot rang out. There was a second soldier? Thomas looked back and saw Anderson lying on the ground behind him. Distracted by the shot and the sight of Anderson on the ground, Thomas released his hold on the soldier for a moment. The soldier wheeled and struck Thomas on the side of his head with the butt of his rifle, sending Thomas sprawling to the ground on his back. The soldier pulled out his knife, coming at Thomas. Thomas looked up and saw the face of the soldier as he raised his long knife above his head. Thomas could see that the soldier was just a boy, a frightened boy soldier with a pimply face who was about to kill him. There was no hate in his face, no anger. His eyes seemed to say "I'm sorry, but . . ." Thomas raised his feet to try to push the soldier away. Lying on his back he kicked at the soldier, but missed him. The knife was coming towards Thomas. The soldier's body suddenly lurched back. His eyes opened wide. His mouth opened and uttered a desperate cry of agony. His limp body fell to the ground, face down. Just below his neck, squarely between his shoulder blades, was a large Indian tomahawk with red feathers hanging from the handle.

What happened next was always a blur to Thomas. He remembered Anderson jumping up from the ground yelling to him to get into the house. He remembered seeing Anderson leaping over the soldier's body and pushing Mrs. Casselman and her child through the door and back into the house. He remembered leaping to the door, another shot, and then darkness.

Outside, Jeremiah and Captain Jim were pinned down at the side of the barn. They couldn't risk coming around to the front and getting into the sights of the second rifleman holed up in the barn. And maybe there was more than one shooter. They saw Anderson pull Thomas the rest of the way inside the door.

They couldn't see the rifle barrel barely protruding from the little open window at the front of the barn or the Casselman dog scratching at the closed barn door beside it, but they could hear the dog barking furiously. And then they heard behind them the blood-curdling screams and whooping of the Mohawk warriors running across the back pasture towards the barn.

The American soldiers to the east had also heard the shots in the barnyard. Several of them were now galloping west along the King's Highway towards the Casselman farm with some infantrymen running behind. A couple of rifle shots rang out. When the warriors saw the approaching American soldiers they ran past the barn out to the stone fence beside the road to take cover. Captain Jim and Jeremiah joined them.

There was considerable exchange of gunfire to little effect on either side, as both the Indians and the American soldiers took cover at a distance of over 300 yards, well outside the effective range of their muskets and rifles. Neither side attacked, as they had no idea of the other's strength. After only a few minutes of sporadic shooting, the Americans withdrew and the Indians pulled back to the barnyard.

When Thomas came to, Mrs. Casselman was wiping his forehead with a wet cloth. She explained to Thomas that he had hit his head on the side of the door when he had leaped to try to get into the house. Outside in the barnyard, Anderson was tying the rifleman to a hitching post. He had thrown his rifle out the window and quickly surrendered to Anderson when he heard the warriors running by the barn to the road. The Skirmish at Casselman's Farm on the morning of November 9, 1813, was over.

~ ~ ~

"I told you that I would never make a good solider." Thomas was talking to his two brothers Peter and Garrett and to his two nephews John and George Cook in Big Red Casselman's woodworking shop. "I'm not making this up. Just as the action really heated up, I ran into the edge of a doorway and knocked myself out. When I finally woke up, it was all over. Garrett, your big brother was not a great hero today. If we had just a few more soldiers like me, the Yankees couldn't lose."

When word got back to the Dundas County militia camped just below Iroquois Point that the way was clear east to Big Red Casselman's farm, the local militiamen were quick to head down the King's Highway to their farms and families. Contrary to their orders, many of the soldiers with farms west of Casselman's just dispersed and went home. They would spend this cold Tuesday night in their own warm beds. Jacob Doran and his sons finally got home but promised to rejoin the others in the morning. Any of the militiamen with farms still farther east from Casselman's had to be billeted for the night in the homes and barns of families along the river. The Marselis brothers and John and George Cook kept walking, looking for Thomas, until they finally came to the Casselman farm, where they found him making a fire in the little stove in the woodworking shop. Besides being a farmer, Big Red made extra money as a carpenter. His sturdy chairs were popular all along the river all the way to Glengarry. Thomas had been invited to spend the night in the Casselman house but he didn't want to intrude. It was a small house. Mrs. Casselman and her daughter had been through a traumatic event that day and this was Big Red's first night home in nearly two weeks. Thomas accepted the offer to spend the night in the woodworking shop with Anderson, but Anderson had changed his mind and decided to go with his warriors who had been given the Bakers' barn next door. His presence wasn't a condition of the offer but Anderson sensed that the Bakers would prefer him to be with his warriors. The prisoner was securely tied in a small storage shed. Anderson made it clear that if he tried to escape the Indians would scalp him. Peter was told to check on him periodically.

It didn't take long for the wood stove to heat the shed. The closing darkness and cold easterlies outside made the woodworking shop especially cosy. They ate the supper that Mrs. Casselman had brought them. Thomas lit the lantern and briefly related the events of the day. Peter and George soon fell asleep in a corner. It was left to John and Garrett to pry the details of the day out of Thomas. Garrett was the most curious and confused.

"How old was the man that tried to kill you?" asked Garrett.

"He was just a boy really. He was pale and thin and covered in pimples," replied Thomas.

"Why was he stealing the horse?"

"I guess he was just tired of walking."

"The family loved their horse. Maybe he would give it back later."

"No, Garrett, I don't think he was planning to give it back later. But I don't think he wanted to hurt anyone. I guess he just created a situation that he couldn't get out of. A lot of bad things happen that way. If he had his time back, I'm sure he and his friend would have left the old horse in the barn."

"Where is his body?" asked Garrett.

"Jeremiah, one of the Indians, and I buried him in the back pasture under a grand old maple tree. When Peter wakes up, remind me to tell the two of you about Jeremiah. Jeremiah was grateful to get the Yankee's rifle, his cartridge box, greatcoat, and boots. Jeremiah insisted that I take this wool vest that the soldier wore under his Forsyth uniform. It looks like a good warm one. Do you want to try it on?"

"No," said Garrett firmly.

"All right then. It's too small for John and George. I'm sure somebody will be glad to use it. Look what I found in the vest pocket. It's a little miniature pewter horse. I guess he liked horses, like you. Do you want it?"

Garrett took the little pewter horse. He studied it but said nothing. John Cook continued the discussion:

"Why didn't you use your bayonet?"

"It all happened so fast. I didn't think of it," Thomas explained. "Most of it is a blur to me. I was walking across the pasture not paying attention and then I heard a rifle shot. I fell to the ground. Next thing I know I'm looking around the corner of a barn, another shot, and Mrs. Casselman's musket goes off, and I see this soldier running to grab her. Another shot. I thought Anderson was hit when he fell to the ground and then the boy was over me with a knife. Then he's dead with the tomahawk in his back. I dive to the door, trip, and hit the side of the doorway knocking myself out. Seriously, I did everything wrong. I think I better stick with farming and beekeeping and mead-making. I told you I'd never make much of a soldier."

"Mrs. Casselman says you saved her life."

"I did not. Anderson got Mrs. Casselman and her daughter into the house. Captain Jim saved my life when he killed the soldier. Poor bastard never knew what hit him."

"You feel sorry for the horse thief that tried to kill you?"

"He was just a boy that got into a mess. He didn't hate me. I didn't hate him. He looked a lot like George's friend Adam, only with more pimples. Poor bastard never knew what hit him."

The shed door opened with a rush of cold air and in burst Herse and de Lorimier.

"Mercy, it's getting cold out there," exclaimed Herse. "Now, where's the famous Marselis everybody is talking about? You and Anderson and some Indians pushed back a whole company of Yankee cavalry, killed one soldier, and captured another. Where's our hero?"

Herse came over to shake Thomas's hand.

"It wasn't like that at all. I never even saw the cavalry. I was out cold at the time. And it wasn't a company of cavalry—Anderson said that it couldn't have been more than a dozen cavalrymen and some infantry. Our Mohawks outnumbered them," Thomas explained.

"That's not the way we heard it, is it, Gui?" said Herse to de Lorimier.

Guillaume de Lorimier smiled and embraced Thomas.

"We're just happy that you are all right, *mon ami*." He rubbed his hands together. "This is a cosy cabin you have here. Very nice. Good to see you safe. We rode ahead to scout things out. Morrison and our army will be here in the morning. They're camping at Point Iroquois tonight. Do you think we could join you here tonight?"

"Of course, please settle in," said Thomas. "Be my guest."

"Where's your prisoner?" asked Herse.

"He's tied in the little storage shed next door. I just checked on him."

"I'll have Private Therien stay with him. It will be better for him in there than in a tent. It's getting full in here," said de Lorimier as he stepped outside to give instructions to the private.

The arrival of de Lorimier and Herse woke up Peter and George. Herse threw Peter his pack saying that he had brought a gift to celebrate the victory at the Battle of Casselman Farm. The men all laughed heartily when Peter took out two jars of brandy from Herse's pack. The excitement of the day, the warm dry heat of the wood stove, the brandy, and the easy familiarity of friends all contributed to a pleasant evening of conversation and camaraderie. George fell back to sleep. De Lorimier and Garrett talked about horses. Herse talked with Peter about Elizabeth. Thomas and John talked about mead-making, grafting apple trees, and the weather. Seven men doing what men do in such circumstances—talking about everything except what was on their minds.

After Thomas put one final log in the stove and turned out the lantern, it was only minutes before the sound of the outside wind was drowned out by the deep breathing and heavy snoring of most of the men. Sleep would not come to Garrett. He was exhausted but not sleepy. There were too many things to worry about. He knew that everyone was avoiding any talk of what was coming in the next couple of days. He had heard Peter complaining that Colonel Morrison was foolish to even think about taking on an enemy that outnumbered them by almost ten to one. He couldn't stop thinking about the story of Thomas nearly being stabbed by a Yankee. He couldn't get the image of a tomahawk in a boy's back out of his mind. He tried to think of pleasant thoughts to block out the bad ones. He thought of his horse. Peter said that he would be seeing Buddy in just one more day. He pictured in his mind the day they went swimming bare balls at Jacob's farm. He remembered the warm September day that he had gone riding with Gui and Maria, the day they saw the deer. He remembered the day the geese made all the men laugh. But he could not fall asleep.

Garrett heard someone bump into something and then the door opened and someone went outside. The rush of cold air came in again a couple of minutes later when the man returned.

"Is that you, Gui?" Garrett whispered.

"Yes," said Gui. "I'm sorry I woke you, Garrett. I had to have a pee. I couldn't wait until morning."

"You didn't wake me. I can't get to sleep."

"There's nothing to worry about, Garrett. Everything is going to be all right."

"That's what Thomas says but he just says that so I won't worry. But I can tell that even Thomas is worried about tomorrow and I know Peter is afraid. If everything is going to be all right, why is Peter so afraid?"

"It's normal to be a little afraid. I'm nervous about tomorrow too. I try not to worry about things I can't do anything about. Worrying can't help."

"I can't make my mind think like that."

"I know it's not easy. By the way, did you get a new bit for your horse?"

"Yes. Oma bought it from a man from Montreal."

"He's going to need some good brushing when you get home tomorrow. How's Maria doing with her new horse?"

"Good. She loves her. She's a good little horse."

"After the Yankees leave, we'll have to go for another ride back to Thomas's property before we get snow."

"Yes, that would be fun."

"Has Sally had her puppies yet?"

"Yes," replied Garrett slowly.

"Are they weaned yet?" de Lorimier enquired in a quiet voice.

"Not yet," Garrett sighed.

De Lorimier said nothing for a few minutes and then continued: "I was thinking of asking Thomas if he could save one of his puppies for me and I could take it back to Louisa May as a present. What do you think?"

There was no answer. Garrett was finally asleep. Apart from the snoring inside and the winds outside, there was no sound in the little shed.

"Thanks, Gui. You're a good man," whispered Thomas.

"*De rien*, Thomas," he whispered back. "Your brother is a beautiful person. He loves so much, so deeply; he can't stop worrying about people." He switched to Mohawk. "By the way, Maria tells me you're a Mohawk speaker. You never mentioned that."

"Yes," Thomas replied in Mohawk, "learned the basics from my father who was fluent. Then I lived at Six Nations for a couple of years. Where did you pick it up?"

"I'm half-blood. My mother was Mohawk. I grew up at Caughnawaga. My father is the Indian agent there. He is Captain of the Caughnawagas now."

"Do you know John Sunday?" Thomas asked.

"John, from Akwesasne?"

"Yes," said Thomas. "He was a close friend of my father's from the first war. My father was a Yorker."

"My father was a translator with the Indian Department in the first war. Probably knew your father. And yes, I know John. Good man."

"Small world," said Thomas.

Another man stumbled from the back of the shed, groping in the dark and stepping over bodies to get to the door. It was John Cook, who grumbled, "I might as well get up and have a piss. I'm not sure what is worse—all the whispering of you two in Indian or Herse here competing with Peter over who can snore the loudest. Now I can't get back to sleep either."

"Oh, so you are awake?" said Thomas. "Somebody in here has been doing a lot of farting. Are you sure you are just going out for a piss?"

Thomas started to laugh. De Lorimier struggled unsuccessfully to muffle his laughter. John feigned insult and indignation with an "it wasn't me," but then he punctuated the utterance with a real ripper to trumpet his point, as he stepped out into the cold night air.

CHAPTER 14
WEDNESDAY NOVEMBER 10,1813
Williamsburg Township

"Good morning, Private," de Lorimier greeted the young American soldier.

"Good morning, sir," he replied as he stood and saluted de Lorimier, who awkwardly saluted back.

"Private Therien here has been good to you?"

"Oh yes, very good sir. We talked all night. He is the first Canadian I ever met and I am the first Yankee he ever laid eyes on. He was kind enough to untie my wrists this morning. We made out pretty good considering he's a Frenchie. We were both hired hands before the war and we both like hunting and fishing. And know what else? We both have the same name, almost. He's Francois and I am Francis."

"Yes, well, that is very good," replied de Lorimier. "It is my job this morning to ask you some questions. Do you understand?"

"Ask away. Ask me anything."

"Well, to begin, what is the rest of your name?"

"I am, sir, Francis Miller from Warren County, Kentucky. Next to Bowlin' Green. Private, Forsyth Rifles. Joined up last spring 'cause the recruiter offered to give my poor sick aunt five dollars. They promised me two meals a day and six dollars a month. Have to say I never heard of Canada but I'm glad the war is over for me. No hard feelings, you understand."

"Well, yes, thank you for that. Now, Private Miller, what can you tell me about the strength of your army?"

"I can't be sure, you understand. I heard that we had over eight thousand men come down the river but a lot of men got sick since then. I know that the First, Second, Third and Fourth Brigade have over a thousand men each. General Macomb's Elite Brigade has over a thousand men. That's my brigade. I was with the First U.S. Rifle Regiment under Colonel Forsyth. Hand-picked because of my skill with a rifle. Tim and I got separated from our regiment on Monday."

"Tim is the soldier that was killed yesterday?"

"Yes sir. The war is over for Tim. God rest his soul."

"Tell me about your cavalry and artillery."

"Both Colonel Luckett's First Regiment of U.S. Light Dragoons and Major Woodford's Second Regiment have over two hundred cavalry each. Bringing all those horses by Prescott in the dark on Saturday night was not easy. The poor animals hated the bateaux."

"What about artillery?"

"General Porter has three companies of over four hundred men, according to what a sergeant told me. And you never seen so much firepower. I helped load twelve 24-pounder guns and even more 6-pounders. We have some big Howitzers too—a 5.5 inch and an 8 inch. And some big mortars. My friend James operates a ten-inch mortar. It's a big army. They say it's the largest U.S. army ever. The bigwigs are planning to take Montreal next week."

"Where is the main part of the army now?"

"I don't know nothing about any of that, sir. Like I told you, Tim and I got separated Monday. All I know is everybody is talking about these awful rapids we still have to get by. Have to say this is the biggest river I ever saw. Bigger than the Mississippi. Imagine that. Colonel Forsyth and the rest of our company were supposed to take the lead and clear the shore of all the Canadian farmers but there is a lot of confusion. A pile of men are sick. They say that even General Wilkinson out in his boat is deathly ill. Others say he's just drunk. Do you think you could untie my ankles, sir?"

"I think we'll keep you tied for now, Private. You understand. How did you get so separated from your company?"

"It's complicated, sir. Tim has a lot of problems with his nerves. Night before last he wanted to do himself in. He cries a lot. He can't help it. He hates it up here. We found a large store of honey a couple days ago and we ate too much. Tim loved the honey but we both got the shits so bad we couldn't walk. Tim got bad, bad cramps. Real bad cramps. He got to thinking that maybe we could go off into the bush, build a cabin, and wait it out until spring. There's lots of deer around here. No locked doors. Then Tim got to thinking if he got a horse he could get home somehow. I know what you're thinking. It was a stupid idea. But when you're cold and scared and sick, you don't think straight. It's just too damnable cold up here, beggin' your pardon sir. No offence, but you can have this country. I don't understand why President Madison wants it so bad. There's a lot of land to the west to settle where it's not so cold. All they gotta do is chase the Indians out."

"Just so you know, Private, we like it here. My father's family has been here for a hundred and seventy-five years, my mother's much longer. We don't know why you are up here either." Turning to Thomas, de Lorimier continued: "Do you think, Thomas, that you could watch the prisoner for an hour so that Therien could get a break? I have to report this information."

"Yes sir," said Thomas, "and with Garrett and John, I think we should be able to handle him. Three Canadian farmers should be able to watch one Yankee big-mouth."

When de Lorimier and Therien opened the door to leave, they hesitated, as it was raining even harder.

"You were right about the weather, Thomas. It's a hard cold rain. Not fit for man or beast outside today." De Lorimier pulled the door shut tightly behind him.

Inside the shed it was warm and dry. The prisoner, though, was nervous. He doubted that these men not in uniforms would be as gentlemanly as the Lieutenant, especially the one from yesterday. He was right. The first to speak was Thomas.

"You tried to kill Anderson yesterday, you Yankee bastard."

"He'd be dead today if I'd wanted to kill him," the prisoner sneered. "You think I can't hit a man at twenty yards with my rifle? I just shot to wing him. If I wanted him dead, he'd be cold dead right now."

This was a different man talking. There was a hard belligerent edge to his voice now. He glared straight at Thomas's eyes. He braced himself for what was to come. And it came. Thomas lunged forward and took a swing at the prisoner but it was just a glancing blow, as the Yankee soldier leapt to one side and then raised his fists to defend himself. John pulled Thomas back. Thomas pushed John away. John shrugged his shoulders and sat down on a box in the corner.

Thomas pointed his shaking finger at the prisoner: "If you weren't tied, I'd beat the shit out of you, you little bastard. You'd wish you never saw this country. I don't want to hear any more of your sob story." Thomas stomped to the door. "You look after him, John." Thomas slammed the door behind him.

The prisoner was relieved to see Thomas go. He didn't know what to make of the two remaining. They both just stared at him but didn't speak. John sat on his box and Garrett paced nervously. The silence unnerved the prisoner and he misread the situation:

"I've never done anything to that fella. The Frenchie soldier was a good man. He understands that this is a war and I was just following orders. Who is that other hothead farmer?"

"He's my brother," said Garrett. "He doesn't like you because you are not a good person. You tried to take someone else's horse and you weren't going to give it back . . . why do you want to take our land?"

"I don't want your goddamn land. You can keep your frozen farms. But I have to tell ya, I don't get it. We're giving you a chance to be part of the United States of America. Why wouldn't you want that? You're just like us. Why wouldn't you want to be an American? Don't you see? It's just a matter of time before this whole continent is ours. We'll be the richest and most powerful country in the world."

John stood up and walked over to the prisoner. In a quiet voice, he spoke slowly to him:

"You have no idea who we are or where we came from. You know nothing of our history. It is this ignorance combined with your blind Yankee arrogance that brought your army here. We came here as refugees from America twenty-nine years ago. We can be neighbours but we have our own country now. So, sit down and shut up."

"I don't take orders from some farmer," the prisoner sneered, "even if he thinks he's some big talker. Enjoy your precious country because you're not going to have it much longer. By the end of the week when Montreal falls, you'll be Americans whether you like it or not."

"It's not over yet," John snapped back. "The Canadiens will fight to the finish and we have more British soldiers coming."

"You think so? If the British gave a good goddamn about Canada they'd have thousands more soldiers here. It's all over for you but you're just too stubborn or stupid to see it." The prisoner waved his hand dismissively at John, turned around, and sat down in the corner on the straw.

John was left standing there trying to think of a reply. No words came. Everything the prisoner said angered him all the more because, John knew, much of what he said was true.

Unbeknownst to the little group at the Casselman farm, Morrison and his army had made it down the river the evening of the 9th all the way to Haines's Tavern just a little more than a mile to the west. Camping there for the night and then awakening to the cold rain, the troops prepared to continue their march down the river. The first of the army to arrive at the Casselman farm was Captain William Johnson with his company of Canadian Voltigeurs, together with Herse's company.

As the rain had intensified, Captain Herse had sent messages to Captain Johnson to meet him in Casselman's woodworking shop at 9 a.m. to receive de Lorimier's intelligence from the prisoner and to make plans for the further advance of the rest of the army. While John Cook and Garrett stayed with the prisoner in the nearby storage shed, Thomas was sent to get Lieutenant Anderson to come to the meeting.

Waiting in the woodworking shop for the others to come, Peter, George, de Lorimier, and Herse helped themselves to the soup that Mrs. Casselman had left on the wood stove. Captain Gore arrived first with his Sergeant, Marmaduke Kearns. They, too, were grateful for the hot soup. Waiting for Johnson and Anderson, Herse and Gore reviewed the situation. Both officers were still unclear whether it was Morrison's intention to engage the much larger American force. Peter remembered Sergeant Kearns from the time that he carried out the training at Jacob's farm in July; they both agreed that it seemed like more than just four months ago. De Lorimier and Duke Kearns had become quite good friends from their months together at Prescott and they waited anxiously for orders for the coming days.

Anderson and Thomas arrived next. They quickly removed their outer coats and hung them up near the wood stove. The little woodworking shop that usually smelled of pine was now redolent with the smell of wet wool. Anderson and Thomas filled their cups with Mrs. Casselman's soup and pulled up chairs to warm themselves in front of the wood stove.

Captain Johnson arrived finally with apologies for his lateness. He explained that he had received information that Colonel Morrison had left early this morning with Mulcaster in one of his gunboats with fifty men to go to Hamilton, New York, just across the river, to recover seven small boats and their considerable cargo which had been stolen by the Americans in the last week of October. Hamilton was now defenceless and Morrison had concluded that these supplies could prove to be critical in the days ahead. In the meantime, Johnson was ordered to bring the rest of the army to Casselman's. The main troops of the line (the eight companies of the 49th Regiment of Foot and the five companies of the 89th) were to camp there to wait for further orders. The Light Company and the Grenadiers of the 49th Foot, the three companies of the Canadian Voltigeurs, the two companies of the Canadian Regiment of Fencible Infantry, Jackson's Artillery, and the Mohawk warriors were to proceed east along the King's Highway until they came in sight of the rear of the U.S. army, where they were to stand down and wait for further orders. Colonel Pearson was to command this advance force and he would be arriving shortly.

De Lorimier debriefed the officers on his interrogation of the American prisoner. If the prisoner was telling the truth, his information confirmed everyone's worst fears about the size of the American army. Thomas wanted to speak up to say that he didn't think anyone should believe a single word spoken by the Yankee horse thief, but he knew it wasn't his place as a mere militia private to say anything, and besides it might appear that he was contradicting de Lorimier.

~ ~ ~

Early that morning just after daybreak, while de Lorimier was interrogating the Yankee prisoner, the American General Wilkinson sent General Brown with his Second Brigade, Macomb's Brigade, two 6-pounder guns, and Luckett's First Dragoons east down the shore of the river to scour the Canadian bank to the bottom of the Long Sault Rapids. The rest of the army under General Boyd was to wait until mid-morning to provide some distance to prevent the British and Canadians from attacking as Brown's army traversed the long and dangerous Long Sault. At about 10 a.m. Boyd started to follow down the King's Highway, with his army of over 3,000 men, on shore and in the flotilla that went alongside. Just as Boyd's U.S. forces were under way, Colonel Pearson arrived at the Casselman farm.

The officers of the light companies that made up the Advance Group were still holed up in Casselman's woodworking shop getting shelter from the unrelenting rain when Lieutenant Christopher Hagerman, Kingston law clerk and aide to Colonel Pearson, entered the crowded, steamy shed to announce that Colonel Pearson had arrived and ordered all officers and men to assemble promptly on the King's Highway in front of the Casselman farmhouse. Hagerman explained that in Colonel Morrison's absence, Colonel Pearson was in command and that he had decided to advance until they reached the rear guard of the enemy.

Apparently oblivious to the driving cold rain, Pearson rode tall in the saddle, leading his Advance Group in the march east along the King's Highway. He led a diverse group of officers and men. The three companies of the Voltigeurs were, by now, experienced light company fighters. Like the officers from the two companies of the Canadian Regiment of Fencible Infantry, most of the officers were from well-off French Canadian families and nearly all were bilingual. The men were mostly habitant farmers. Jackson's Royal Artillery, the Light Company and Grenadiers of the 49th, were now seasoned veterans, having served for more than a decade in North America. Some of the officers were Canadian. Most of the men were English or Irish. Added to the Dundas militia, all of whom were farmers, many of whom spoke Dutch or German, and combined with Mohawks, the group was a remarkably polyglot and multicultural mix. However, the officers and men of the Advance Group on this cold and rainy morning shared one firm belief. They were, to a man, convinced that Pearson was a crazy and dangerous fool who seemed determined, just for his own warped sense of glory, to lead them all to their annihilation. Soaked to the bone, trudging through the mud, the men knew that they were closing in on a hostile army of several thousand men.

After less than an hour of marching east, Pearson came upon John Parlow, an old farmer who was standing on the side of the highway in front of his house. Beside Parlow was his young grandson, holding his hand. Pearson brought his horse up directly in front of Parlow and yelled down to him:

"Tell me, how long has it been since the American army passed by here?"

Parlow looked up at Pearson, shook his head, and replied:

"You needn't follow them, for they are ten to your one."

"Never mind that, my man," Pearson replied. "We are not asking your opinion."

Equally indignant, Parlow replied, "You may not be asking my opinion, sir, but I'm giving it to you just the same. Up on your fancy horse in your fancy uniform you may think you know what you are doing, but you don't. There must have been five thousand Yankees pass by here in the last two days. They have gunboats, large artillery, and hundreds of cavalry. The last of them went by here less than a half-hour ago. You get much closer to their ass and they are going to turn around and wipe you out. Nobody can say I didn't warn you."

"You, my man, are speaking to a British officer. I suggest you keep a civil tongue," Pearson replied sharply.

"Yes, well, bigwig officer or not, I suggest to you, sir, that you are a damned fool if you keep going."

Pearson had had enough. He pulled his horse to the right and, saying nothing more, he proceeded to lead his men farther down the road, the men marching four abreast.

Only a few minutes after his exchange with the farmer Parlow, four men on horses were seen in the distance galloping towards Pearson. The Colonel called a halt to the march until the men came into closer view.

It was young Hagerman who spoke first:

"They're Yankee cavalrymen, Colonel; what should we do?"

Pearson did not reply but he took out his spyglass for a better look, using both his hands to steady the glass. Finally, he responded, almost casually:

"There appear to be four of them riding this way. They are Yankee cavalry all right."

Then, looking more intently into the glass, Pearson said quietly and slowly, "I think there is also a column of infantry behind them marching this way. Here, Hagerman, take a look and tell me what you see."

Hagerman took the glass and peered down the road, then exclaimed to Pearson, "Sir, there's a large group of Yankees coming this way. They seem, sir, to display a certain disposition to attack us."

Pearson calmly ordered Hagerman to have all of the officers come forward to receive orders. The officers quickly responded. The rain seemed to let up slightly as Pearson instructed the officers to prepare for attack and to bring the two 6-pounders forward immediately.

Jackson had the two 6-pounders in place within minutes. Pearson himself gave the order to fire. Hagerman, who still had the spyglass, could not contain his fear:

"Sir, they're still coming. There's a whole dragoon company and what must be several hundred infantry backing them up. We must turn back now, Colonel, or we will all soon be dead or prisoners."

"Nonsense, Hagerman. We are not going to retreat just because some Yankees are coming our way," replied the Colonel. "Jackson, extend our compliments to Jonathan again."

Jackson fired another round, this time using shrapnel shells for the two 6-pounders.

"Sir," yelled Jackson, "they're still coming. If we don't move back now they'll soon have these two guns. I implore you, sir, we must pull back. It's raining too hard to use our muskets."

At that moment, Hagerman, still looking through the glass, shouted frantically to Colonel Pearson:

"Sir, their cavalry has just charged over the line of fences. They can't be much over two hundred yards away. We must pull back."

Pearson ordered Jackson to fire the 6-pounders again. This time one of the Yankee cavalrymen was thrown from his horse, hit by flying shrapnel. This had the effect of causing the cavalrymen to hesitate and hold back momentarily and, finally, to cease their forward attack. Pearson then ordered Johnson's and Herse's Voltigeurs to form into file and fire a volley. That done, the men struggled to reload in the pelting rain. To cover for them, Pearson ordered Anderson to move his Mohawk warriors forward and to advance across the muddy field towards the cedar swamp to Pearson's left. At that moment, musket balls whizzed just over the heads of Pearson and Hagerman. Johnson yelled to Pearson that the rain was too heavy for successful reloading. The American infantry continued their advance.

Seeing that the situation was hopeless, Pearson finally ordered his little band to turn around and retreat quickly. Anderson and his Mohawk warriors did not see the retreat or hear the command, and so they kept advancing across the field towards the swamp, yelling blood-curdling whoops.

Whether it was due to the Indian war cries or Pearson's withdrawal—the reason wasn't clear—the Yankees stopped their forward advance. When Pearson saw this, he ordered the withdrawal to stop. He then ordered the two Fencible companies and the Grenadiers of the 49th Foot to assemble into rank and file formation in the field at the side of the road and to march forward, bayonets fixed. Seeing the redcoats advancing, the American commander ordered a full brigade of infantry to resume their attack. Pearson ordered Jackson to fire another round of shrapnel and while it could be seen that this had the desired effect of wounding a couple of U.S. infantry men and throwing an officer from his horse, it did not stop the U.S. army from resuming its attack.

Pearson could see that this was not the time nor the place to try to stop the American advance. Again he shouted to his officers to order the retreat of the men. As the soldiers were pulling back, Anderson's warriors fired an intermittent volley and then turned to join in the retreat.

Just then, about noon that day, Colonel Morrison arrived at the scene and resumed command. He ordered a complete withdrawal of the Advance Group to await the arrival of his main army.

He saw immediately that this was not the right place to engage the enemy. The narrow road was boxed in on the south by the river and by a muddy ploughed field on the north. The back and forth skirmishing was over for now, as the U.S. army stopped its forward advance when it saw the British and Canadians withdrawing. Morrison ordered his men to stand down, reload if they could, and wait for further orders.

For the Marselis brothers and the other remaining men of the Dundas County militia, the two hours from the time they left the Casselman farm until Colonel Morrison arrived were utterly confusing and, apparently, a complete waste of time. Being at the rear of the Advance Group, they could hear the occasional roar of Jackson's guns but they had no understanding of the back and forth confusion of the two hours of skirmishing. To these men, standing in the pouring rain, wet to the bone and so close to their homes, the confusion confirmed their conviction that Colonel Pearson was completely unhinged. Why would any military leader taunt the rear of a far larger enemy? What would be achieved? Why put the whole Advance Group at risk for no benefit?

When Colonel Morrison arrived at noon and told all the men to stand down but gave no further orders, the Dundas militiamen began to wonder whether their new commander was any saner. As they sat at the side of the King's Highway, which was now nothing more than a muddy trail, the grumbling of the men of the Dundas militia intensified.

"*Tabernac*," exclaimed Peter, "does anybody know what they're doing? I'm so wet I got water running down the crack of my ass. Do the officers not realize that there isn't a dry musket in the whole gang? They say there's a big Yankee army right up ahead of us. Why are we staying here sitting in the mud? Would anybody notice if we snuck back to Stata's farm? At least we could get some food there."

Jacob Doran responded by insisting that everyone should just sit and wait for further orders. He explained that the officers were now conferring with Colonel Morrison and decisions would soon be forthcoming.

But they were not. The rain kept coming. Garrett was sitting beside Thomas sharing a pine stump on the side of the road, his knees pulled up to his chest.

"I'm really cold, Thomas," Garrett said.

"Me too," Thomas replied. "Be patient. We should be moving soon. We're only a couple of miles from home. With any luck, we'll be sleeping in our own beds tonight. Oma will be so happy to see us, especially you Garrett, especially you."

"Why don't we go home now?" Garrett asked.

"Don't be silly," Thomas replied. "You know we can't go home yet. We have to wait till the last of the Yankees have passed. If Morrison and Pearson would leave them alone, they'd be moving down to the rapids right now. I don't understand why we are taunting them."

Garrett didn't say anything more. He pulled his legs closer to his chest. Then he muttered something to himself and rested his forehead on his knees.

Huddled in his greatcoat beside Garrett, Thomas tried to remain still. The coat was like a large sponge for the rain but his body warmed the coat from the inside and so long as you didn't move, the coat provided some insulation. His feet, on the other hand, were numb by now, his leather boots and wool socks well past providing any protection from the cold. His thoughts turned again to Allie and the children. As difficult and spoiled as Allie was, Thomas knew that he had no one to blame but himself for the many problems in their relationship. His thoughts went to that warm afternoon in the summer of 1810 when he had come home for a brief visit. Oma said that Allie had deliberately set out to seduce him but he remembered being a very willing participant. Very willing. He returned to Six Nations the next day. It shamed him to think that he had hardly thought of her after that. He didn't love her that afternoon. He hardly knew her. No man could have resisted the way she looked that day, the way she acted. It was John Cook who had sent him a message to Six Nations. Thomas knew that he came back only out of a sense of duty, not love. He came back when the ice went out. He married her on May 8, 1810, her 18th birthday, the week before JT was born. He also admitted to himself that he had not done enough to disguise his feelings in the early days. After JT was born, he tried to be more affectionate but by then Allie seemed to direct all her attention and affection to the baby. Most of the time she didn't seem to care if there was little love—little intimacy—in their relationship. When Allie became pregnant again, she shunned Thomas even more. For months they shared the same bed in purely literal terms. This, in turn, caused Thomas to be even more distant. He knew now he should have been more accepting, more understanding. Her parents had spoilt Allie and she suddenly found herself living in a musty two-room cabin with two difficult infants and one resentful husband. And she was just a hundred yards away from a hurtful and meddling mother-in-law who never missed an opportunity to be sure that Allie knew that she was not good enough for her son. Thomas knew that he should have tried harder to get their own place sooner. He shouldn't have been so proud—if he had accepted the offer of money from Allie's father that first summer, they would be living in their own house by now.

The more he thought about it, the more Thomas had to admit to himself that Allie had tried to adjust to her difficult situation. Certainly no one could say that she wasn't a good mother. And there were times that she surprised Thomas, times when she showed signs that maybe she did love him. There were even a few times when she showed real affection, even passion. His mind drifted to that Saturday afternoon in late September when she had been just like a little girl playing the trick on Garrett with de Lorimier and Maria. She had been so happy that day. He remembered how when they were alone in their cabin without a roof she had taken the initiative. She came to him with a fervent urgency.

Memories of her enthusiasm that afternoon, her unquenchable desire, aroused him every time the thoughts came to him. Even now, sitting on the side of the road in the cold and rain and mud, the memory of that day stirred him. He closed his eyes and pictured her in his mind's eye. God, she was beautiful.

A massive explosion in the distance startled Thomas out of his daydream. Both he and Garrett jumped to their feet and looked to the river. The huddled group of Dundas militiamen at the rear of Morrison's Advance Group turned in unison to see a puff of smoke rise from a gunboat downstream in the middle of the St. Lawrence. Their first instinct was to take cover from the next cannon ball that was sure to come. It was Lieutenant Hagerman, who still had Colonel Pearson's spyglass, who shouted out to the officers at the front that the gunboat seemed to be one of theirs and it seemed to be firing at something farther downstream. Another explosion; another little puff of white smoke.

Only a few minutes later while all the men were standing on the road wondering what was happening, Captain Johnson rode back to the rear of the Advance Group to explain to the Dundas militiamen that Colonel Morrison had received a message that Captain Mulcaster, R.N., had got his gunboats through the Rapids du Plat and they were now bombarding Wilkinson's fleet of six boats moored next to Crysler's farm. Mulcaster's gunboats were heavily armed, with 6- and 18-pounder guns, and his lead gunboat, the *Nelson*, had a long 24-pounder gun and a 32-pounder carronade. It was this large gun that Morrison's men could now hear cannonading. This threat forced Wilkinson to unload onto the shore his two 18-pounder guns which had been stored in artillery scows ready to go down the Long Sault Rapids. Presently, they began to respond by firing back at Mulcaster's gunboats. This long-range artillery bombardment continued but there was little harm done to either side.

Mid-afternoon saw the arrival of the rest of Morrison's army, what he now called his "Corps of Observation." Having spent the morning and half the afternoon skirmishing back and forth, advancing and then retreating, Morrison's army of rank and file now sat or stood in the unrelenting rain on or beside the King's Highway in Dundas County, Upper Canada, waiting for orders that didn't come. The misery and frustration of the men was palpable.

By late afternoon, just as darkness began to fall, the whole of Boyd's army rose up and marched two more miles east past Crysler's yellow house, well out of range of Mulcaster's guns and closer to the head of the rapids, where they set up camp for the night in the fields surrounding Cook's Tavern. To the considerable consternation of Michael and Abigail Cook, their tavern was now the headquarters of the U.S. Army.

Seeing the movement of the Americans, Morrison ordered his men to advance. With pomp and some ceremony, with drums drumming and pipers piping, Morrison's army finally began to march east. Marching at the head of the parade, high on his horse, sword drawn, was Colonel Morrison, followed by the staff officers, including Captains Crysler and Sherwood of the Militia of Upper Canada. Following them, also on horseback, was the commanding officer of the 49th Regiment of Foot, Lieutenant Colonel Charles Plenderleath, leading his eight companies of infantry, numbering just over 300. They marched four abreast as the muddy road did not allow a larger phalanx.

After the 49th came Major Miller Crawford leading his five companies of the 89th Regiment of Foot. The four Advance Companies were led by Colonel Pearson, including the Grenadier and Light Company of the 49th and two companies of Fencibles. Three companies of the 89th commanded by Captain Barnes and the Royal Artillery commanded by Captain Jackson followed them. There followed then the Light Troops led by Major Heriot, comprising the three companies of Voltigeurs and the Provincial Light Dragoons.

At the end of the parade were the Dundas County Militia under the command of Captain Merkley, and Lieutenant

Anderson with his 30 Mohawk warriors. All told, Morrison's Corps of Observation had about 1,200 men in arms.

As they marched east from Casselman's, the first two farms appeared to be abandoned—presumably the women and children had fled from the front two days earlier when the American army had first begun to traverse the front of Dundas County. However, when the front of Morrison's army came to the Garlough farm, the Dundas militiamen and Mohawk warriors at the end of the parade heard a chorus of loud huzzahs at the front. In a minute the reason became clear. Standing at the side of the road at the gate, wearing a wool toque and an old greatcoat, dog on a leash in one hand, loyalist flag waving from the other, old Mrs. Garlough was cheering the arrival of the British and Canadian army. As the Dundas militia marched past her, she started waving and yelling excitedly to the many men whom she recognized, although it was difficult to make out what she was saying because of her strong accent and the constant barking of her dog. Some of the men saluted her. Others yelled greetings. The drummers and pipers switched their tune to the classic "The Girl I Left Behind Me." Mrs. Garlough threw her toque in the air. Her dog barked excitedly.

To his complete surprise, marching along the muddy road, Thomas started to weep. He quickly tried to wipe his tears so that no one could see this uncharacteristic display of emotion. "Don't be silly," he said to himself, "get hold of yourself, man."

He couldn't remember the last time he had cried. Probably seven years ago when Nancy died. Was it the music (drums and parades can have that effect)? Was it because he was physically exhausted? (He had not had a decent night's sleep since he left home 11 days ago.) Was it the sight of Mrs. Garlough's happy toothless smile? (Her wrinkled old face was truly radiant.) Or was it because he missed his family so much and now he was only minutes from home? He pictured in his mind's eye Allie and the children anxiously waiting for him at their gate.

There was now just a single drumbeat. Left. Right. I had a good job but I left. Left. He was thinking of Allie again, about the harsh things they'd said to each other when they were last together. He so wished he could take those words back. Left. Left. He heard another roar of huzzahs from the redcoats at the front. Was this for Allie? They were almost there. The Marselis farm was coming up. They were marching four abreast and Thomas was on the river side so he could not see clearly.

Thomas couldn't wait any longer. He shouted to Garrett who was on the other side, two rows up:

"Is it Allie? Is it Allie at the gate?"

"Yes. We're home!" said Garrett as he broke from the ranks and ran ahead.

John and George Cook, Thomas, and Peter also dropped out of the ranks as Jacob yelled back to them that he would return after the army made camp up ahead and after he had instructions.

There was a woman at the gate, all right. But it wasn't Allie. It was Oma, by herself. She was wearing Johannes's old green Yorker coat and his faded three-sided soldier's hat. She was neither smiling nor waving. She stood at attention, shoulders thrust back, chin up. She wore a look that was both proud and defiant. There was a quiet dignity to her. She could have been a general reviewing her troops in a march past.

When Garrett reached Oma, her demeanour completely changed. She returned to being a mother. She grasped Garrett and pulled him to her ample breasts. She said something to Garrett as he joyously hugged her back. Oma reached out and touched John and George and Peter and Thomas as they arrived at the gate to greet her.

"Come," she said as the last of the parade went by. "Enough of all this hugging. I've been waiting for you boys. I've got a big pot of soup on the stove. Shouldn't Jacob and his sons and Lewis join us? I have lots of soup."

As the others went to Oma's house, Thomas went to his cabin. It was dark inside. Dark and lonely. He lit the lantern. He changed into dry clothes. He washed his face and hands and combed back his hair. With his beard and worried eyes, he hardly recognized himself in the little mirror over the sink.

Thomas joined the others who were already changed into dry clothes and seated around Oma's big kitchen table gobbling Oma's soup and bread fresh out of the oven. She told the men how on the first day, Monday afternoon, the advance of the Yankee army arrived. These men in blue uniforms were bad. Many of them were on horses. They stole anything they could get their hands on. Yesterday a much larger army came through, both cavalry and infantry. One of their officers was a real gentleman. He knocked on Oma's door and offered to buy food and blankets. Oma told him that she didn't have anything to sell to a Yankee. He accepted this. When some of his men stripped the squash and pumpkins from the front garden, the officer came back and left a Spanish dollar on the front step. Oma pointed to the dollar in the middle of the kitchen table.

Oma explained to the men that on Monday evening after the first group had gone through, afraid for the safety of themselves and the children, Allie and Elizabeth took the children back to the third concession to Elizabeth's home. One of the Schwerdfager boys had come to get Oma as well. It was safer to leave, he insisted. Oma sent the boy home with a message to Lena that no Yankee was going to evict her from her own home again. She would die first. Then, Oma explained, John Loucks rode in that evening to tell her to get away from the front because he had just seen the large American army coming down the river on the Canadian side. John was telling all the neighbours to get out of the way. He had to set fire to the bridge at Nash's Creek and that should slow them down but they would be arriving soon. Oma told John she was staying but that evening she was sure she saw the white moose at the edge of the bush at the back. This was a bad omen, which she could not ignore. She was very relieved to see that her three sons were still alive. She insisted that the men have more soup, then repeated that the white moose was a bad sign, a very bad sign.

The five men took turns telling Oma about their many adventures over the last several days. As the adrenaline faded and the men began to feel the effects of their exhaustion, Oma got out blankets and a pillow so George could use the daybed in the kitchen. John would spend the night at Thomas's cabin with him.

As Thomas and John were putting on their boots to go outside, Garrett too got his coat and was putting on his boots. He explained that he was going out to see Buddy before he went to bed. Oma couldn't put it off any longer:

"I've something I have to tell you, Garrett," she said as she held Garrett's two hands in hers.

Garrett could tell from his mother's tone of voice and her face that it was not good news.

"I'm sorry, Garrett," she said, "that first afternoon, Monday, one of the Yankee soldiers in the blue uniforms took Buddy. I didn't know it until morning. I'm really sorry, Garrett; we'll get you another horse when this is all over."

Garrett was about to say something and then stopped. He looked at his mother and then at the others. No one spoke. Garrett slowly took his boots off and hung up his coat on the peg beside the door. His head down, not looking at anyone now, Garrett walked over to the bottom of the stairs. "I'm going to bed now," he said, as he went upstairs.

"Fucking Yankee bastards!" said Peter.

When Thomas and Peter got back to Thomas's cabin and sat down at the little kitchen table to light their pipes, Thomas slapped the table and stood up.

"I've got an idea. It's too early to go to bed. Getting my second wind. I just made a new batch of mead—apple mead—it's called cyser. You remember? I was making it when you came by with the letter about Moraviantown. It should sit for a few months but I'm sure it's drinkable. What do you think, John?"

"You talked me into it," said John, "and anyway, we should wait up till Jacob comes back. I understood that he was still planning to come back here tonight to tell us what has been decided for tomorrow."

John and Thomas sat at the table smoking their pipes and sipping the mead. They had been friends all their lives. John had always looked up to the older Thomas, admiring his quiet strength. To John, Thomas was more like an older brother than an uncle. John admired Thomas's broad knowledge of so many things and his exceptional skills in canoeing, fishing, hunting, beekeeping, and languages. He admired Thomas's physical strength and endurance. And, of course, John wished that he had travelled west like Thomas, had seen the many wonders beyond Dundas County. At the same time, Thomas had always admired John's obvious intelligence and character and was deeply envious that John had learned how to read and write. Having learned the basics from his mother as a young boy, John had devoured every book he could get his hands on. The Reverend Schwerdfager had once called John the "cleverest" boy he had ever met.. Everyone knew that John had great faith in the future of Upper Canada and that some day he would be a leader in the new colony.

Thomas poured John another drink of mead.

"One last one before we hit the sack," he said to John. "Am I looking forward to sleeping in my own bed! If there's a battle tomorrow, someone's going to have to wake me up 'cause I think I could sleep for a couple of days."

"If Jacob doesn't come soon, I think that probably means that Morrison has decided that there's just too many of them. Anyway, this miserable weather setting in must have the Yankees re-thinking their plan to attack Montreal before winter. Even if they get to Montreal in two days, how would they lay siege to the city from a winter camp? The poor bastards would freeze to death. It doesn't make sense for us to provoke a battle now."

"I don't know," replied Thomas, "but I can see Morrison continuing to harass their rear just to slow them down getting around the Sault. Maybe we'll just have another day of back and forth like today. At least nobody gets killed. I just wish we had enough men to really put it to the bastards, but we don't."

"You've changed your tune in the last day, Thomas. It was only yesterday that you felt sorry for the poor soldier that tried to kill you and yet this morning at Casselman's I thought you were going to kill his partner with your bare hands."

"Yeah. I hated his arrogance. This war is getting a little personal now. I could castrate the bastard that stole Garrett's horse."

A rap came at the door. It was Jacob. Thomas invited him in and took his still-wet coat.

"You look like you could use a drink, Jacob. Sit down here," said Thomas, "and tell us that there'll be no battle tomorrow."

Jacob took the drink, swallowed it in several gulps, and placed his glass on the table, inviting another. He sat down and took off his wet boots and socks.

"The rain and sleet has returned," Jacob began. "It's miserable out there. Got bad news. Morrison called a full War Council in Crysler's house this evening. Morrison has made the house his headquarters. I was there with Captain Merkley. There was a full discussion of the options for tomorrow. It seems that two thousand of the Yankees are now down river below the Sault. So that means they've still got around six thousand men—five times our number. Nevertheless, Morrison thinks that he has ideal ground for a fight. With the large clear field behind and east of Crysler's farm all the way to Bush Creek, Morrison thinks he can employ European field tactics. If they don't attack us, we are going to attack them. The Dundas militia will be part of the light troops led by Pearson. We will have responsibility for the right side, along the river, and we will have one of the 6-pounders. The Yankees have made Cook's Tavern their headquarters."

"I hope Morrison knows what he's doing," John responded solemnly. Thomas said nothing.

"It could be an awful rout but we are taking a stand tomorrow.

It's a little crowded in here. I'll go tell Garrett and Peter and find room in the house to bed down for the night. We are to report at Crysler's farm first thing in the morning," continued Jacob as he pushed on the door to leave. A rush of cold air came into the little cabin. Jacob stepped back in and turned to Thomas and John: "We can't be late, boys. First thing in the morning we have to be on the road. Oh, I almost forgot, Thomas. Apparently Anderson thinks you could help him with his Indians so you will be fighting with them. See you in the morning, boys."

Jacob left the cabin, slamming the door behind him. John and Thomas looked at each other. It was John, shaking his head, who spoke first.

"Damn it. I hadn't planned on dying just yet. We could die tomorrow. Think I'll write my wife a little letter. Do you have a pen and some paper?"

"Yes," said Thomas, "on the shelf over there. When you're done, maybe you can do a letter to Allie for me. I have some things I need to say."

Their letters done and placed on the table, the two men went to bed, John taking Elizabeth's bed in the main room.

But sleep did not come easy to Thomas. He thought of Allie and his children. He could not resist the waves of fear and anger that came over him when he thought of how this invasion was putting at risk all that his family had worked for, all that he loved. His thoughts turned to the unfairness of it all: that a decision made by a handful of politicians in faraway Washington to send thousands of young American boys to invade another country would have such consequences both for Canadians and the young American boys, some of whom would also die tomorrow, thousands of miles from their homes, cannon fodder for old men's arrogant imperialist ambitions.

Thomas then heard John's heavy rhythmic breathing. John was asleep. Thomas tried to will himself to sleep as well but at these times his mind had a mind of its own. His mind wanted to think of his mother and brothers and sisters and the fear and anger this invasion created for them. He thought of what must be going through Garrett's mind tonight. Thomas had no doubt that at this same moment Garrett was lying awake in his bed worrying about the coming day. And then, as always at times like this, the picture of Nancy lying in her bed came into his mind. He had been haunted by this memory for years and he knew it was hopeless to resist what was coming:

It is just before dawn on that hot summer night in July. Thomas and Garrett have insisted that Oma get some sleep and that they will sit up with Nancy. Nancy cannot sleep. The pain that has been racking her body for months comes in unrelenting waves. Thomas is sitting on the chair beside Nancy's bed. Garrett is curled up on the bed beside Nancy, his cheek next to hers. He is gently stroking her wet hair with his fingers as this helps to calm her some nights, but it does not seem to help tonight. Even in the low light from the lantern on the bed stand, Thomas can see the tears.

Lying in his bed now, over seven years later, Thomas could feel his heart throbbing as it did that night, threatening to burst his chest open. He struggled to put the scene out of his mind but it continued:

Nancy is hardly recognizable. She is half her normal weight, her face so thin she looks twice her age. The pain that has been so unrelenting for so many months has caused a steady facial wince that persists even when she falls into sleep. She no longer has the strength to move her arms but she moves her long thin fingers as though beckoning to Thomas. Thomas reaches down and gently takes her hand and gives three small squeezes, a long-standing secret Marselis family message for I-love-you. Their father has been doing this since before anybody can remember. Nancy weakly gives three back. Then she opens her eyes and stares directly at Thomas. She closes her eyes and whispers something Thomas cannot make out. Garrett raises his head to look at Nancy. To hear her, Thomas gets off the chair and kneels beside her bed, putting his ear close to her mouth. He can smell Nancy's putrid breath and feel Garrett's on his cheek. Nancy whispers to her two brothers: "Please do it now. I cannot take this any longer. If you love me, you will do this for me. The pillow. Please, Thomas, please." Nancy opens her eyes, filled now with a determination that has been gone for weeks. The look is now more accusatory than begging. Garrett too notices the change. He looks at Thomas, his nod almost imperceptible, its meaning unmistakable. Garrett is quietly sobbing now. He rises from the bed and then leans over to kiss Nancy on the forehead: "I will always love you, Nancy," he says. Garrett gets up and stands beside the bed. He reaches down and gives Nancy's hand three slow squeezes. He looks at Nancy a final time. He leaves the room. Nancy and Thomas are alone now. Thomas is still holding her hand. She signals her love to her brother and then releases his hand. She gives Thomas one more look, relaxes, sighs, and then closes her eyes, confident now that the awful pain will finally be gone.

Chapter 15
November 11, 1813
Early Morning on the St. Lawrence River, Dundas County

It was still dark when the three Marselis brothers, their brother-in-law Jacob Doran, and their nephew John Cook were out on the King's Highway walking towards John Crysler's farm. The rain had stopped but there was still a bitter east wind in their faces as they quietly trudged down the road the mile and a half to Morrison's headquarters at Crysler's farm.

Oma had got up in the middle of the night and started a fire. She boiled eggs and fried bacon for the men. She made Garrett's favourite toast and blueberry jam with honey. There was little conversation at the table. After eating the morning meal, each man was given two boiled eggs in the shell and a small apple to carry in his pocket for eating later.

Jacob got up first from the table to put on his coat; it was important to arrive at the camp by daybreak, he stressed. The others quietly and quickly followed, putting on their boots and hats and warmest coats.

"Well, here we go," said Thomas. "Lambs to the slaughter."

No one laughed. Oma glared at Thomas as she shook her head. She was about to scold him when she stopped herself. She closed her eyes and, unexpectedly, especially for her, tears began to stream down her cheeks. Oma opened her eyes and briskly wiped away her tears, regained her composure, and gave the men an order:

"You boys be careful. You hear me? Don't take any chances. And don't be late for supper. I'm making a fish stew with new potatoes."

Oma stood at the door touching each man as he stepped out into the cold. Garrett was the last to get to the door. Oma pulled his fur hat down tighter on his head and then held his face in her big hands, looking at him straight in the eye. She brought her face so close to Garrett's that their noses touched.

"Be careful, son," she whispered to him, her voice now trembling and the tears now back. "I know you can't stay here. You have to go with the men. This is what your father would want. He'd be proud of you today. Be careful, son. Stay close to Thomas. I'll be waiting for you to come home soon. Fish stew for supper."

"Everything is going to be all right," he whispered back to his mother as he went out the door.

The men said little as they walked along the road. They walked slowly and occasionally stumbled, as it was still so dark it was hard to make out the edge of the road. They could hear and smell the big river to their right but they could not see it. But it was there, as it always had been, as it always would be. The men knew, though, that very little else would remain the same after this day.

It was Thomas who finally spoke.

"Just think if the Yankees could see us coming. Wouldn't they be frightened? Five farmers with old muskets from the first war. No uniforms. All of us scared shitless. I sure hope Morrison knows what he's doing."

"He seemed quite confident last night," replied Jacob. "He's convinced that the open fields behind Crysler's and the Jones's will allow him to use field tactics. He reckons that this will give him a real advantage, even against a much stronger force. And we'll have our gunboats in the river."

"Well, I guess we'll soon find out," replied Thomas. "I hope you're right, but then again, what are we afraid of? What did Wilkinson say? He's just here to liberate us. That can't hurt so much."

As they got to the Baker place, one of the original old log cabins right at the edge of the road on the river side, they saw a lantern as the door opened and the form of a man could be seen. He shook hands with another man and then the door closed.

Jacob called out: "Is that you, Mr. Baker?"

"No," came the irritated reply. "It's not Baker. He's too feeble to go to war again, but I'm not. It's me, Levi. Wait for me and I'll walk with you if you don't mind not walking too fast. Who's there?"

The men identified themselves as Levi joined them. They started walking east again but slower, to accommodate Levi.

"I know what you're thinking," he said. "You're thinking that an old drunk with a wooden leg is just going to get in the way. I don't blame you boys for thinking that way. I admit that old Conrad and me, well, we took on quite a snootfull yesterday after the Yankees went through. There's a lot of them. Yes, there's a lot of them. But Conrad and me, we got to talking at supper last night and when the Loucks boy rode by to tell us that we were making our headquarters at Crysler's place, well I knew right off that there was something I could do. Something maybe all those officers might not have thought about enough. If there's a real battle today, there's gonna be a lot of boys hurt, hurt real bad. After I lost my leg in the first war I served as a surgeon's mate. I know something about all that. I know how to put on bandages and tie men down. I reckon I can help." He paused a moment and then continued.

"So last night Conrad and me, well, we decided I'd go to Crysler's. Do what I can for hurt boys. I cagg'd myself. I won't take another drink until we've beat the fuckin' Yankees. This is our only home now and we're not giving it up without a fuckin' good fight."

It wasn't long before the men could see large bonfires in the distance. They soon learned that these were in the fields behind Crysler's barn. The soldiers had burned cedar fences all night to ward off the cold and dampness.

The six Dundas County farmers arrived just as dawn was breaking and just as the drums were beating reveille for the soldiers to begin their morning meal and to get ready to assemble. The camp was all military bustle, but it was obvious that the soldiers had spent a miserable night. It was also clear that there was quite a difference between the 49th and the 89th. The men of the 49th were seasoned veterans, having spent over ten years in Upper Canada. They knew Canadian winters. They all wore their grey greatcoats. Not a redcoat could be seen among them. But the newly arrived 89th were completely ill prepared for the beginning of a Canadian winter. They were wrapped in ragged blankets pulled over their wholly inadequate brick red coats.

Near one of the first bonfires that the men came upon was Sergeant Duke Kearns of the 89th. He rose immediately to greet the Dundas County men. He explained that they had arrived just in time, as Captain Crysler had just ridden by to tell some other farmers who had already arrived that the militia were to assemble in the paddock behind the horse barn. Captain Merkley was waiting for them there now. They thanked Duke for the directions and proceeded through the camp which was becoming now a real hive of activity: bugles and drums sounding, men hustling about.

There were already a couple of dozen Dundas County farmers standing around and leaning against their muskets or standing beside the cedar snake fence that surrounded the paddock. They were all bundled in their winter clothing. Most had spent the night in their own beds or billeted in nearby farmhouses. They were noticeably drier than the regular troops, but they still looked more like a frightened group of confused farmers than soldiers ready for battle.

Lieutenant Christopher Hagerman, Militia of Upper Canada, came by on his horse. The Kingston law clerk who was serving as an aide to Colonel Morrison got the attention of the Dundas County men and advised them that Captains Merkley and Crysler were with Colonel Morrison at that very moment and that they would be returning shortly with orders. On behalf of the Colonel he thanked all the men for coming. He rode off.

More militia arrived from the west over the hour that followed. There were about 80 Dundas County men in the paddock when Captain Crysler and Lieutenant Hagerman returned on horseback. Captain Crysler thanked the men for coming. He explained that a decision had been made the night before that the United States was going to be provoked into a battle today. They would have to turn and fight, as they could not take a chance on an attack while they were disembarked to get past the Long Sault Rapids. To threaten their rear, the Voltigeurs and Mohawk warriors were going to be sent soon to attack the north end of the American camp in the field behind Cook's Tavern. Even earlier, Mulcaster's cannons would begin to shell the southern part of the camp. This combined assault should force the Yankees to mount a rear-guard action to drive back the British and Canadians.

Captain Crysler explained that an Advance Group under Colonel Pearson had already been sent that morning down the King's Highway to Davis Point. The American pickets would have seen Pearson's men by now and should report to their commanders that an attack along the river road might also be imminent. This was just a bluff. What Colonel Morrison wanted was for the Yankees to send their army west, back through the maple bush, so that the battle would take place in the open fields just west of the bush. That would also mean that they would have to cross Bush Creek and its ravine.

Captain Crysler explained that there were many important roles for the Dundas militia. They were to be divided into three groups. Some of the younger men who were good shooters would be assigned to back up and fill out the ranks of the Voltigeurs, who would be operating out of the cedar swamp at the north end. These men had been selected by Lieutenant Rose and would go with him. The ten chosen men would be issued new muskets and cartridge boxes and more powder and balls if these were needed. Others would be given various tasks to support the main army of the centre—for example, some would help with the artillery horses and with ammunition supply, while others would be used as stretcher-bearers. These men would go with Captain Merkley who would be arriving soon. The third group of men would leave immediately to provide support for Colonel Pearson's Advance Group, who were already at Davis Point.

Captain Crysler explained that the 30 Mohawks under Lieutenant Anderson would also be part of the light company group under Major Heriot, as would be the dozen Mohawk warriors from Akwesasne who had arrived the previous night.

Captain Crysler then asked Lieutenant Rose to come forward to read out the names of the men who had been chosen to supplement Heriot's skirmishers.

Wearing an elaborately embroidered buckskin coat that went down to his knees, moccasins, and a raccoon fur hat, the heavily bearded 44-year-old Lieutenant Rose came forward. All the men in the Dundas militia knew of his background in the first war and the strong role he played in organizing the Dundas County militia during the past year. He was renowned as a trapper and hunter. Having been captured and raised by Indians as a boy, he had acquired many of their ways and their language. He made no speech; he just listed the following names from memory:

"John's boy, William Serviss from Matilda; John and George Shaver; Johann Strader's boys, Jacob and John from Matilda; also from Matilda, John Van Camp's sons, John and Peter; and from Williamsburg, Stephen Garlough, George Cook, and Adam Nudle. Follow me now."

The chosen young men scurried out of the paddock to follow Lieutenant Rose.

Captain Crysler invited Lieutenant Doran to come forward and then he asked Lieutenant Hagerman to read out the list of men who would go immediately with Lieutenant Doran to join Colonel Pearson's Advance Group. These men were directed to line up in front of Lieutenant Doran just east of the paddock.

Private Jacob Merkley Jr.
Private Nicholas Ault

Private Alexander Beckstead
Privates Joseph and Martin Barkley
Private John Cook
Private Nicholas Dillabough
Private Peter Fetterly
Privates Garrett, Peter, and Thomas Marselis
Private Joseph Helmer
Private Peter Holmes
Privates John and Henry Van Allen
Privates William and John Stewart
Privates Frederick and Nicholas Baker
Private Daniel Shell

These selected Dundas County men shuffled out of the paddock and awkwardly stood around waiting for instructions from Jacob. He asked them to line up in pairs and, with some confusion, this was finally completed.

"Good. Listen up, men," Jacob began. "I know we don't have uniforms but that doesn't mean that we can't look sharp. We've practised marching a few times so this is what I want us to do. You will shoulder your muskets on my command and then we will march through the rest of the camp down to the King's Highway. We will make a smart left wheel onto the highway and march past Crysler's house, then down the road to Davis Point. Please try to stay in step. Ready? Shoulder your firelocks. March!"

For Jacob's sake, the men tried to get into step. There was much shuffling until finally they got into the rhythm. Jacob led them down the road, helping out with a "left, left, left-right-left." After the ragged left wheel unto the King's Highway, the men shuffled into step again. The highway ran directly in front of Crysler's house. As the Dundas men approached it, coming out the front door onto the veranda with Hagerman was an officer with a large cocked hat with a red and white tassel on top. He had gold braid hanging from his right shoulder and a long sword hanging on his left side. Hagerman whispered something to this senior officer. The officer stood erect and, looking straight out at Jacob, gave a crisp salute. Jacob smartly returned the salute. As excited as he was, Jacob waited several minutes, well past Crysler's house, to eagerly report to the Dundas men that Colonel Morrison himself had just recognized them.

They marched past the Nine Mile Road and then past Jones's farm. In just another 300 yards they marched past Adam Bouck's farm, over the repaired bridge crossing Bouck's Creek, and then up a slight incline to Davis Point and John Haines's farm, where the 200 men of Pearson's Advance Group were camped on both sides of the highway.

Jacob and his Dundas County men were met by the 19-year-old Prince Edward Islander Lieutenant Samuel Holland, acting commanding officer of the Grenadier Company of the 49th Foot. Jacob knew that Lieutenant Holland was more experienced than he looked—he knew he was a veteran of the bloody battle of Queenston Heights the previous year—but most of the rest of the Dundas men were unimpressed by this small boyish-looking soldier in the oversized grey greatcoat with a sword hanging on his hip that nearly touched the ground.

Holland stood at attention and saluted Jacob, who had not expected this formality, but Jacob quickly saluted back and in an official-sounding voice announced:

"Lieutenant Doran, sir, Dundas County militia, reporting for duty, sir."

"Thank you, Lieutenant," Holland replied. "Have your men stand at ease . . . now, let me begin by saying that if the Yankees are enticed to attack us in these fields, this Advance Group under Colonel Pearson may be sent out into the battle. We'll have to see, but our primary responsibility is to assist and protect our six-pounder. We have an ideal overview of the whole planned field of battle and our gun can play an important role. I leave you now with Lieutenant Doran."

The young officer then saluted Jacob and wheeled to march away, when he stopped and turned to the men:

"I almost forgot. Lieutenant de Lorimier of the Canadian Fencibles has asked that a Thomas Marselis report to him promptly. He is with his men over there across the road next to the river." Lieutenant Holland then turned and marched off towards the rest of the 49th who were camped beside Haines's barn.

Thomas promptly found de Lorimier, who explained that he had been ordered to relieve the two Fencible privates who had been assigned forward picket duty the previous evening. They would have had an uncomfortable night and be anxious to be relieved. De Lorimier's orders were to replace the pickets and then to see if he could get close enough to see the American camp and determine if there was any sign of them embarking yet on a rear-guard action. He was to report back to Colonel Pearson no later than noon.

De Lorimier explained that he wanted to take Thomas because Thomas knew the area and because Peter Fetterly had asked if it was possible for someone to look in on his mother and sisters. They would be right on the route that the Americans would be taking if they mounted an attack along the King's Highway. Peter had not been able to persuade his mother last night to leave her home. It was Peter's hope that maybe someone else could encourage her to get out of harm's way. De Lorimier knew that Thomas knew Mrs. Fetterly—she was an old friend of Thomas's mother—and thought perhaps he could persuade her to leave her home, at least for the rest of the day.

De Lorimier and Thomas walked quickly down the hill from Davis Point along the King's Highway until they reached the edge of the ravine that surrounded Bush Creek. They walked along the west side of the creek until they reached a temporary bridge across it and then entered the maple bush along a trail that cut through it about 200 yards north of the highway. The pickets were supposed to be hiding on either side of this trail near the east side of the bush where they could have a partial view of the American camp just a short distance farther to the east.

The two pickets quickly stepped out of their hiding places when they saw de Lorimier and Thomas. Wet and cold, they lost no time in heading back to Davis Point, excited that they had finally been relieved.

Just as the pickets were trotting off to the west, a small exchange of musket fire could be heard to the north. De Lorimier motioned to Thomas to crouch down and follow him as he ran to the eastern edge of the maple bush to try to see what was happening. Hiding behind a clump of cedar trees at the edge of the maple bush, from their somewhat elevated position de Lorimier and Thomas had a good view of the huge American camp just a half-mile away. De Lorimier was surprised that the Americans didn't have their own pickets at the edge of the maple bush, but then a further exchange of musket fire suggested that there were American pickets out of sight to the north and maybe they were coming into contact with Heriot's advance scouts.

"That's a big army," said Thomas, looking at the size of the camp. "There are still a lot of men that haven't gone by the Sault Rapids. Maybe they think they have enough soldiers to protect themselves and they won't turn back to attack us. What do you think, Gui?"

"I don't know," replied de Lorimier. "The plan is to have Heriot's skirmishers attack from the north and for Mulcaster's gunboats to begin firing at their camp. This should be soon. Let's wait here for a while and see what happens. Then we can swing down and talk to Mrs. Fetterly."

"Do you really think we could stand up to that many men?" Thomas continued, pointing at the large camp to the east.

"I don't know," replied de Lorimier. "We'll just have to do our best."

"Captain Crysler said this morning that about a dozen Mohawks from Akwesasne came into the camp last night. Did you see them?"

"Yes, just for a minute. Just saw them come through. They didn't stay in the camp long. They had some supper and got a supply of powder and balls. Then they left to camp at the edge of the swamp with Anderson's warriors. Why?"

"I was just wondering who they were. A couple of them may be old family friends. I think I have mentioned John Sunday to you before."

"Yes. Good man. He was one of them. Your Alex Rose was talking to him. I'm told Rose is to take some of your men to join Heriot's men as well. Rose speaks some Mohawk, I'm told. How did he learn Mohawk?"

"Actually, it's Seneca that he speaks. Rose is well known in these parts. He was born in the Schoharie Valley where my family came from. Before the first war, '71 or '72 thereabouts, a raiding party of Indians from the south attacked the valley. His parents were killed and he was taken away. He was two or three years old. The Chief adopted him. Some years later when he was about eight he ended up with a chief of the Seneca tribe. When the Chief died, the story goes, he was sold to a blacksmith near Niagara for a bottle of rum. He soon escaped from his new master and spent the last couple of years of the war as a drummer with the Yorkers, my father's regiment. When most of the Yorkers settled in Dundas County he came here with them. He's a tough fellow. Hard as nails."

The conversation was interrupted by cannon fire. One of the shots sounded very much like the 24-pounder on Mulcaster's *Nelson*, the others most likely from the smaller British gunboats. Soon after, shots could be heard from the east, presumably from the American gunboats down the river in the lee of Cook's Point.

The sporadic exchange of fire by the gunboats did not have any noticeable effect on the American camp from what Thomas and de Lorimier could tell, but they could not see that part of the camp closest to the river, where the British shells were most likely falling.

"It must have been good to see Allie last night. I miss my Louisa May so much," resumed de Lorimier.

"No, I didn't see her last night. I got home but Allie wasn't there. She and Elizabeth had moved back from the front with JT and Aleda to avoid the invasion. They stayed with Lewis and Lena. We only saw Oma. She refused to move."

"Any problems with Oma?"

"No. The Yankees left her alone. No raping, but lots of pillaging. They took any food they could find. Oma had hid a lot but they stole cabbages and several baskets of potatoes. And, the bastards, they stole Garrett's horse."

"That's too bad. Poor Garrett. How's he holding up otherwise?"

"As good as any of us, I guess. He understands that people are going to die today."

Neither man spoke for a minute. When de Lorimier spoke he didn't look at Thomas. He was looking away, his voice very soft.

"I have . . ." He hesitated. "I have a bad feeling about today. This is how I felt watching my mother die. My life is so good now. I have a beautiful wife. We're having our first baby soon. Maybe my life is too good. I have this, this dread in me."

"We're all scared, Gui," Thomas replied. "Nobody wants to die."

"If I have to die, I want to go fast. I watched my mother die for months. Did your father die fast?"

"Yes," Thomas replied slowly. "I think he knew he was sick for a while but one morning he just didn't wake up. My sister . . . my sister, I watched my sister die for many months. I still can't get it out of my mind."

At that moment, both men heard the crack of a broken branch. Thomas stepped behind a maple tree. De Lorimier crouched down behind a cedar and cocked his musket, waiting. Another sound. More than one man was walking towards them from the north: there was a rustling of feet on dry leaves, then no noise, silence. Thomas waited but couldn't resist peeking around the tree into the clearing to the north. Nothing. This reminded him of deer hunting when the deer went perfectly still because it had detected the smell of man. But the rustling was more than a deer. Who were they and where were they now? Thomas looked over at de Lorimier. Thomas could see from the expression on de Lorimier's face that he was equally perplexed. Still no sound. All that Thomas could hear was the sound of his own breathing. He could feel his heart racing. He could see nothing moving in or near the clearing. Who were they? Where were they now? Thomas turned and placed his back up against the tree, trying to think what to do. His eyes focused. He blinked. Like a ghost, there, not 20 paces away, was an Indian warrior standing motionless with a wide smile on his wildly painted face.

"*She:kon*, Thomas," he said quietly. It was Jeremiah. Then, louder, he yelled out, in Mohawk: "It's friends. It's Thomas."

"Shit. You scared me," said Thomas. "How did you get behind us?"

As he said that, Thomas and de Lorimier turned to see John Sunday and three other Mohawk warriors, covered in war paint, carrying tomahawks and muskets, step out into the clearing.

"*She:kon*, Thomas," John Sunday said, smiling and raising a hand of greeting to Thomas and de Lorimier.

After some good-natured ribbing and greetings all around, John explained that the Mohawks had been sent ahead by Lieutenant Anderson to scout through the cedar swamp and then down through the maple bush to see if there were any American pickets this far forward. The five Mohawk scouts had had a brief exchange of fire with advance pickets to the north, but the Americans had pulled back as soon as they saw the Indian warriors.

It started to rain again just as another exchange of gunboat fire erupted to the south. With the assurance that the maple bush seemed to be clear of pickets and that no American attack seemed imminent, John and Jeremiah decided to return north to rejoin the rest of Heriot's men and the other Mohawks. Thomas and de Lorimier explained that they would now return and report to Pearson's Advance Group after going down towards the river to the Fetterly farm to pick up the King's Highway and to see if they could get a better view of the American camp from there.

The men shook hands as they prepared to go their separate ways. Jeremiah held on to Thomas's hand and put his other hand on Thomas's shoulder.

"Take care of yourself, little brother, and always watch out for what's behind you," Jeremiah said with a half smile. He spoke in Mohawk.

"Thanks for the advice, big brother," Thomas replied with a playful push to Jeremiah's shoulder, and feigning an upper-cut punch to his stomach. He too spoke in Mohawk.

Carefully working their way towards the river, far enough inside the maple bush to stay out of sight of the Americans, de Lorimier and Thomas reached the southern end of the bush where they could see the Fetterly barn and house just a small field away.

"Let's wait here for a few minutes," said de Lorimier. "Let's see if there is any sign of Yankees here . . . How do you know that big guy back there?"

"Jeremiah? It's a long story. Big family secret. He's John's nephew and he's my half-brother. Not something Oma talks about a lot."

"Family secret, eh? I guess we all have those. He's not a fellow I'd want to mess with. You have to watch those wild and crazy half-breeds!" de Lorimier said, relishing his little joke. "It looks pretty clear. Let's go visit Mrs. Fetterly."

The two men crossed the field behind the Fetterly barn and went around to the small clapboard house that faced the King's Highway. Thomas knocked on the front door.

"Mrs. Fetterly," he shouted at the door.

"Who's there?" came a voice from inside.

"It's me, Thomas Marselis. We need to talk with you."

The door opened a crack and then slowly opened wider. Fifty-three-year-old Anna Fetterly stuck her head out. "Come in out of the rain," she said. "You'll catch your death of cold out there and your mother will blame me!"

Thomas and de Lorimier stepped through the door into the front room of the little house. When their eyes adjusted to the dim light (curtains were pulled over the two front windows), sitting at the table they saw 11-year-old Catherine. "Would you like some tea?" she asked.

Thomas introduced de Lorimier and then quickly explained that they weren't dropping by for tea and that there was about to be a battle all around this house and they had to leave immediately, at least for the day. Ignoring Thomas's pleas, in a raised voice, Mrs. Fetterly called out:

"Come in here, Beth. Rosie will be all right. It's Thomas Marselis and a handsome soldier."

Pretty 14-year-old Elizabeth Fetterly came through the curtain that separated the front room from a room at the back.

Thomas greeted Elizabeth and then turned to her mother, his voice more insistent this time.

"Mrs. Fetterly, you can't stay here with your two daughters. Your Peter and George are really worried about you. You must come with us now. You can probably come back tonight."

"Thank you for your concern, Thomas, but we're not going anywhere. Those Yankee boys have taken everything from the barn—my ducks, my geese, my pigs, my sheep, my four beehives, all of my potatoes, cabbages, and oats. They even took Peter's pantaloons from the workshop. My poor dear Peter would roll over in his grave if he knew some rebel was wearing his wool pantaloons. Oh yes, and they took my dried apples. What are we going to eat this winter?"

"You know that everyone in the county will help you out, you know that," interrupted Thomas.

"Maybe so," she continued, "but I'm protecting what I've got left. I have all my preserves in here and two things that can't be replaced and can't be moved. Ask your mother, Thomas, what I have sacrificed to bring my dear granny's silverware and china to Canada in the last war. The Yankees didn't get them then and they're not stealing them now. They'll break in here as soon as I leave, sure as shootin'. No, I'm not leaving. They're cold and hungry and they'll steal whatever they can carry. I couldn't stop them yesterday from taking my animals and emptying the barn but when one of them tried to open my door last night I told him that the first man, well, I would shoot him with my husband's musket, which was cocked and aimed at the door. He went away. They won't break the door down so long as I'm in here. The girls can go down to the cellar."

"We don't have time to argue any more," replied Thomas. "They could be coming now."

That was when a loud mooing sound came from the back room.

"That's our little Rosie," explained Mrs. Fetterly. "We lost my Peter in February and my beautiful Hannah this spring. It's been a hard year. Beth and Catherine agree: we're not letting the Yankees take our Rosie—she's been with us too long—best little milker in the county, one of the family really. You tell Peter and George that we're safe. We'll see them tonight or tomorrow."

It was clear that there was no changing her mind. Thomas and de Lorimier stepped back out into the light rain and onto the King's Highway.

When de Lorimier looked east down the road he was shocked to see four American cavalrymen riding down the road towards them. Realizing immediately that they would soon be overtaken, de Lorimier signalled to Thomas to follow him. They ran to the Fetterlys' outdoor bake oven at the side of the road. Staying out of sight of the cavalrymen, de Lorimier took aim and fired. Thomas did the same. Neither discharge hit a horse or rider, but they pulled up quickly. Not knowing that they only faced two lone Canadians, the Americans turned their horses around and road back to their camp at Cook's Tavern to report that an attack was imminent.

With the same sense of alarm and disregard for any appearance of dignity, Thomas and de Lorimier ran as fast as they could in the opposite direction, back towards their camp.

Chapter 16
Noon, November 11, 1813
John Haines's Farm, On the St. Lawrence River, Upper Canada

"Where are my brothers?" Thomas shouted ahead to John Cook as he stepped up onto the level land of Davis Point. Thomas was alarmed by the look on John's face. He knew something was very wrong. He knew that the Advance Group, now camped on Davis Point, had been watching him running back to the camp with de Lorimier since they had broke out into the field west of the maple bush.

He could not understand why Peter and Garrett were not with the other Dundas militiamen to greet them as they scampered up the last ridge.

"Where are my brothers?" he repeated, quite breathless from running up the hill and even more alarmed that John did not answer immediately.

"Get your breath, Thomas," John finally replied. "Sit down here. This is going to sound strange. Peter was arrested. He was taken away for striking an officer . . . striking an officer in the face of the enemy. It's a serious charge. Garrett and Martin have gone to try to find him. There is nothing you can do right now. Here, sit down on this ammo box. Let me explain what happened."

De Lorimier, too, was alarmed and impatient to hear the story, but there was a private waiting anxiously to escort him immediately to report to Colonel Pearson. He hurried off past several tents that had been erected to give the men shelter as the light drizzle had continued since mid-morning.

Thomas sat down on the ammo box beside the 6-pounder that had been positioned at the edge of the ridge. John leaned against the gun carriage as he explained to Thomas what had happened.

After Thomas and de Lorimier had left, John explained, Pearson's Advance Group was ordered to get ready for a possible attack. Under instructions from Corporal Moore, the Dundas County men manoeuvred the horses so that the 6-pounder was placed at the eastern edge of the embankment at the highest point. From there, they had a good overview of the whole cleared area that Morrison had chosen for the field of battle and to protect the Advance Group if the Americans attacked on the highway. According to Moore, with a range of over 500 yards their gun could reach nearly all parts of the field. Peter and Garrett were part of the group that was using the horses to position the gun and ammunition cart when artillery officer Lieutenant Henry Kersteman arrived. Nobody was sure what Garrett did wrong, if anything. Kersteman started to yell at him. Garrett was confused and did not reply. This made Kersteman even angrier. As he stepped forward as though to strike Garrett, Kersteman slipped in the mud and fell face down on all fours, his hat falling into a puddle. As he got up, humiliated, his anger turned to rage. John could not make out all of what Kersteman was yelling but he did hear:

"I'm going into battle and what do they give me for gunners? Stupid Dutch farmers and imbeciles."

Pointing at Garrett he continued, "In England, morons like you would be put away, not operating my artillery."

Garrett did not know what the word meant but Peter did. Peter ran over to stand beside his brother. When Kersteman advanced towards them, Peter stepped forward, pointed his finger at Kersteman and quietly said something to him that John could not make out. Kersteman stepped back angrily and then turned to the Corporal beside him, ordering him to arrest Peter. Peter said something else to Kersteman which John couldn't make out, but the remark so angered Kersteman that he drew his sword. Raising it as though to strike Peter, Kersteman took a step forward and with full force brought his sword down towards Peter's head. Peter moved quickly to one side and raised his musket with two hands so that the sword merely hit the musket barrel. As it did, Peter swung the butt of his musket, catching Kersteman on the side of his head, knocking him to the muddy ground. Somewhat dazed and still on one knee, Kersteman yelled at the Corporal to arrest Peter immediately. Just then, hearing the commotion, Colonel Pearson rode up on his horse and, without dismounting, demanded that Kersteman explain what was happening. Kersteman, covered in mud, pulled himself erect, saluted the Colonel, and insisted that "the stupid farmer hit me. He must be arrested and summarily executed for assault and threatening an officer in the face of the enemy."

Peter was arrested and he offered no resistance as he was taken away.

Colonel Pearson told Kersteman to follow him to Morrison's headquarters as the officers had been summoned for a meeting there. After they left, Martin Barkley and Garrett spoke to Corporal Moore and received permission to see if they could determine where they had taken Peter. Corporal Moore also suggested that they seek out Captain Wrightwick, who had intervened when Kersteman had lost his temper and struck a private in the 49th last week.

"Don't think you're special," said the Corporal. "Kersteman is a bad-tempered arse hole to everybody. He even beat his pretty new wife so badly that she left him two weeks ago and returned to Kingston. Rumour has it that she's now shagging a lieutenant in the Quartermaster's Department at Fort Henry. But he's good with the gun. They say he studied under Colonel Henry Shrapnel himself. If he weren't so good, especially with the shrapnel, the bigwigs would have sacked him weeks ago."

Finally, John told Thomas that all the men, both Canadian and British, who witnessed Peter's encounter with Kersteman would confirm that Peter only struck Kersteman in self-defence.

When Thomas could not find young Barkley and Garrett in the Advance camp, he started walking back west along the highway towards Loucks's farm. To his right he could see the men of the 49th and the 89th beginning to line up along the fence line running back from Loucks's farm. Bugles were sounding; officers on horseback were yelling commands; ensigns were positioning regimental colours. It seemed to Thomas that Morrison was going to a lot of trouble to organize for a battle that might not come. Maybe the Yankees would keep moving down the river and not turn back and attack.

What Thomas didn't know was that at that moment, in a meeting with his senior officers, Morrison confirmed a strategy that had been agreed to the night before in the Council held in John Crysler's farmhouse. Impatient because the Yankees had not attacked yet, in spite of Morrison's massing of his troops to threaten their rear, Morrison ordered Heriot to push even closer to the American camp with his three companies of Voltigeurs, with Anderson's Mohawks scouting ahead. They were ordered to harass the American camp in such a way that Wilkinson would have to conclude that he was going to be attacked by Morrison's full army. The Yankees could not ignore a direct attack on the northern edge of their camp by 200 light troops and over 40 Mohawks whose blood-curdling whoops would give the impression of an even larger force.

Thomas was walking down the highway just a few hundred yards east of Loucks's farm, when a violent thunderstorm struck. He took shelter under one of the few large white pines still left along the side of the road. Two soldiers who had been marching east along the road also ran under the tree. They were two privates from the 49th, the very two, it turned out, who had escorted Peter to the headquarters at Crysler's farm. They explained that they were returning to the Advance camp. They told Thomas that Peter had been put into the custody of Captain Crysler, who had then made the decision to release Peter to be a stretcher-bearer for the

89th on Peter's promise that he would present himself to Captain Crysler after the day's "activities" were over.

Thomas was grateful to hear that Peter was no longer in custody and he decided to return to the Advance camp on Davis Point with the two soldiers when the thunderstorm had subsided somewhat. While he was still cold and wet and anxious about what the day would bring, he was relieved that no action was going to be taken against Peter, at least not that day.

While many of Pearson's regulars were seeking protection from the rain in their tents, waiting for orders to move, the Dundas militiamen had no tents. Thomas found most of them taking shelter under a crude lean-to that they had constructed from some boards they had found in John Haines's barn. They were a sorry lot huddled together, wet to the bone, their silence and their eyes revealing both the misery of the morning and the dread they felt for what the afternoon was to bring.

While the Dundas men waited under their lean-to for orders, Heriot's men broke out of the bush and came into full view of the American camp. They were too far away for their musket balls to do any damage but the ranking American officer, John Parker Boyd, realized he had no alternative but to marshal his troops to drive back the Canadians. While many of Wilkinson's men had already gone down the river, Boyd was confident of easy victory as he still had quite a formidable army. With between 2,200 and 2,400 infantry under his command and 200 mounted cavalry, he had six 6-pounder guns. He knew that he vastly outnumbered the British and Canadians.

Boyd had been given clear orders by Wilkinson. If the enemy got too close, he was to "turn and beat them back." He sent Swartout's Fourth brigade of 900 men to march to the north end of the bush where Heriot's skirmishers were pressing most heavily on the American pickets. Behind Swartout came two more units of the brigade, the Fourteenth and Eleventh Infantry.

Heriot's Voltigeurs and Anderson's Mohawks fired several times, but they were so badly outnumbered they were forced to pull back under the cover of the woods. The Americans sent more men west to chase the Canadians back, including Brigadier General Covington and his Third Brigade numbering between 900 and 1,000 men. They followed a trail through the centre of the bush, closer to the river, not far north of the King's Highway—the trail, in fact, that Thomas and de Lorimier had been on less than an hour earlier.

As the three American brigades moved cautiously through the woods, the Canadians and Mohawks managed a few last hurried shots and then they were forced to completely retreat all the way to the western edge of the maple bush and to keep under cover in the cedar swamp to the north.

Thomas and the other Dundas men heard these last shots and ran out from under their lean-to to the edge of Davis Point. It was just before two o'clock. It had finally stopped raining. They could see the six militiamen assigned to Frasier's Provincial Light Dragoons now hurriedly galloping their horses back towards the British lines. They could see that young John Loucks, who had been the closest to the river, was riding as fast as his old horse could take him towards the Advance camp.

It soon became clear why the dragoons were returning so quickly. While the men had heard the firing in the woods, they knew now without any doubt what many had suspected and what Morrison had hoped for. Emerging from the western edge of the woods and coming out into the open fields all the way along the tree line was the first of the American army of over 3,000 men in arms who presented themselves and readied for battle. The men could clearly see Boyd's three brigades organizing themselves around their regimental colours and preparing for attack.

From their perch on top of Davis Point, Thomas and the other men of Pearson's Advance Group had a clear view of Morrison moving his men of the 89th and 49th into position. He marched them forward from the Nine Mile Road to a lane that ran directly back from Charles Jones's barn. The British were now lined up facing their enemy. There was less than a mile of open field separating the two armies. Suddenly, with a great flurry, Colonel Pearson and Lieutenant Kersteman rode into the Advance camp. Kersteman dismounted and yelled commands to his artillerymen and the militiamen assigned to support them. His orders were unnecessary. They were already formed up and prepared to operate their 6-pounder. Corporal Moore didn't need Kersteman to tell him that the battle was about to begin and that they should lose no time in taking advantage of the ideal position of their gun. Still mounted on his horse, Pearson gave the command to Kersteman to fire. The first volley landed right in front of the line of blue coats now advancing out of the woods and into the open area. Kersteman ordered Corporal Moore to adjust the aim and release a second volley. From this distance he was still using round shot.

Thomas and John had been assigned the responsibility of bringing forward reserve ammunition, so they stood beside the wagon some 25 yards back from the 6-pounder, the wagon positioned there so as to be well removed in case of a hit from enemy artillery. There was nothing that Thomas could do yet but watch events unfold.

He saw Barnes move his three companies to the edge of Casselman Creek, almost parallel to the 49th. He saw Kersteman's next round shot land immediately in front of the lead Americans, but it did not do much damage as it landed with a thud in the deep mud. Then he heard a loud explosion and saw the bodies of many Yankees fly into the air: it was the 24-pounder from the *Nelson* now shelling the American brigade closest to the river.

Then Thomas saw a frightening spectacle which alarmed everyone around him. The Sixteenth Infantry was advancing at a rapid rate across the field and appeared to be swinging somewhat to their left towards the Advance Group. Pearson saw this and yelled to Kersteman to redirect the 6-pounder and change to shrapnel. Corporal Moore ordered his Royal Artillery men to rotate the gun slightly and ordered shrapnel to be brought forward from the wagon. So preoccupied were they by the scene around them, neither John nor Thomas understood that last order was for them. Then Thomas heard Kersteman yell: "Where's the shrapnel? Where's my shrapnel? Tell those stupid bastard farmers to bring me my shrapnel shells now!" Thomas understood that order, and he and John hurriedly carried forward the box of shrapnel shells.

Corporal Moore carefully took out from his bag a 6-inch-long tapered hollow beechwood tube which was already filled with a powder mixture.The tube was marked with ribs, each rib equal to a half–second of burning time.

"Cut it at six seconds," Kersteman yelled. "Move it, move it now!"

Corporal Moore cut it and tapped it into a small hole on the top of the ball. At the same time Gunner Thomas Gosling used a rammer to drive a cloth bag of black powder to the bottom of the gun's barrel. Moore then pushed the fuzed 6-pound ball into the muzzle of the gun and rammed it down until it was against the bag of gunpowder. Immediately, another gunner standing at the back of the gun pushed a small wire into the tiny aperture at the top of the barrel to pierce the bag of black powder. Then he carefully put a short length of goose quill (which had already been packed with powder) into the hole, ready to be ignited.

Kersteman was now ready to lay his gun. He had the wind against him. He saw the dark blue flag of the Sixteenth Infantry. With his right hand on the screw beneath the breech, he raised the barrel a couple of inches. He took another look down the length of the barrel. Considering the moisture still in the air so soon after the rain, he made a further adjustment, raising the barrel another inch.

Satisfied, Kersteman stepped back and yelled, "Fire." At this, the gunner at the rear of the piece carefully ignited the quill tube. Within a moment, the cannon discharged with a loud thunderous roar, sending sparks flying from the end of its barrel. Both Thomas and John jumped away as the gun recoiled back towards them. A mass of thick, choking smoke hung over the big gun and its gunners.

Thomas then looked over at the fields and saw, about ten feet or so above the first column of U.S. infantry, the shrapnel shell explode, driving the 27 musket balls inside the shell directly at the enemy. The devastation was immediate and deadly. It was a perfect shot, right on target. Thomas could see immediately the awful effect rendered on at least a dozen of the Yankee soldiers, who now lay in pieces on the muddy ground.

Kersteman, too, saw with pride that his aim had been right on. He looked at Pearson, who nodded approvingly.

"Again," he yelled, "again. Let's give those Yankee bastards another one."

Thomas helped one of the gunners push the 6-pounder back into place and stepped aside to get out of the way, to allow the Royal Artillery men in their blue uniforms to perform the ritual again, with cool precision. About one minute later, Corporal Moore stepped back and nodded to his Lieutenant. Kersteman stepped forward, made a small adjustment with the screw, then stepped back and yelled again, "Fire." Through the dense smoke Thomas and the other men saw that Kersteman's aim was right on again. Mud and body parts flew into the air and, it seemed, the advance of the Sixteenth Infantry was stalled.

Moments later Thomas heard the two other cannons fire and again he heard the loud thunder of the 24-pounder mounted on the *Nelson* in the middle of the river. Beyond the range of enemy artillery that had yet to appear, Morrison's three pieces pounded the Yankees without fear of retaliation. Without the protection of artillery and too far from the enemy to use their muskets, the Sixteenth withdrew to the shelter of the woods to re-group. For Thomas and the other men in the Advance Group on the top of Davis Point, the sense of relief was palpable. Kersteman ordered his artillerymen to hold fire. Some redcoats yelled, "Huzzah!"

Their exhilaration was short-lived. From their elevated perch, the men of Pearson's Advance Group could see clearly that while the Sixteenth may have been temporarily repulsed, two regiments of American soldiers (the Fourteenth and Eleventh Infantry) emerged from the woods at the north end. They saw them form into companies one behind the other. Beside them, also emerging from the woods to the north, came two more full regiments (the Twelfth and Thirteenth Infantry). The four regiments of American infantry were moving quickly *en masse*. It was clear that they posed a serious threat to Morrison's left, where the 89th were assembled facing east to prepare for the attack coming across the open field directly towards them. Another full regiment (Ripley's Twenty-First Infantry) were marching in parallel to the four regiments attacking from the northern edge of the woods.

The men of Pearson's Advance Group from the hill at Davis Point could hear Heriot's Voltigeurs and Anderson's Mohawks taking aimed shots at the blue-uniformed columns advancing towards Morrison's 89th. The skirmishers could slow the advance somewhat, but they could not stop the hugely superior force of American infantry who were advancing so quickly that it appeared to the men at Davis Point that Heriot's men might be overtaken. Suddenly, they saw Heriot, who was mounted, exit the woods, yelling to his men to run to the cover of the 89th. They could see the Voltigeurs emerge from the woods, running for their lives because the American Infantry was right behind them, probably now no more than 100 yards from the British left flank.

The only way that Morrison could repulse the serious threat to his left flank was to execute a parade-ground manoeuvre, wheeling the 89th from its position in line facing east to face northeast to meet Ripley's men head-on. This they did with perfect precision. The men on Davis Point could see the American infantry continue to advance directly toward the 89th, but the 89th stood silent and stock still, firing not a shot.

"Why are they waiting so long?" John said.

"I'm sure they know what they're doing," Thomas replied. He was far less sure than he was pretending. Thomas had never seen a European-style battle with opposing armies carrying out frontal attacks like this. In truth, he too could not understand why Morrison and the officers with the 89th were waiting so long to open fire. The Americans had certainly started to fire—their sporadic shots evidenced by little puffs of white smoke at various places along the American lines.

"Mother of mercy, what are they waiting for?" John repeated, not really expecting an answer from Thomas.

But the answer came with one loud explosion, easily heard by the whole of the Advance Group. In spite of the large cloud of white smoke hanging over and surrounding the right three companies of the 89th and drifting the mere 100 yards to the American lines, it was clear that the front ranks of the right three companies of the 89th discharged their weapons in perfect unison. The effect of 150 musket balls on the American lines was immediate and obvious. Many American soldiers could be seen falling to the muddy ground. Two seconds later another concentrated volley came from the two companies on the left wing, hurling another hundred musket balls at the American infantry. Within seconds the right three companies repeated their disciplined firing, followed soon again by the two companies on the left. This steady concentration of musket fire "by wings" devastated the American ranks. Meanwhile, Jackson kept up a regular bombardment with his two 6-pounders.

The American Eleventh and Fourteenth Infantry could not stand up to this devastating series of volleys by the five companies of the 89th Regiment of Foot. The Yankees began to turn and run.

Back somewhat and to the right of the 89th, waiting patiently in reserve, were the eight companies of the 49th Regiment of Foot commanded by Lieutenant Colonel Charles Plenderleath. Seeing the American infantry turning back in confusion, Morrison decided to bring Plenderleath's men into the action. He ordered them up beside the 89th, and the two battalions, to the sound of the bugle, their standards flapping in the breeze, proceeded to march in echelon, bayonets fixed, towards the fleeing enemy, pausing occasionally to fire by platoons.

The retreat of the Americans back towards the woods provided enough distance from the British lines that Pearson could now safely order Kersteman to "fire at will." Again, the men of the Royal Artillery from their elevated position on Davis Point turned their 6-pounder towards the fleeing Americans and began to bombard them, this time with round shot.

"Bring me more round shot, Thomas," Corporal Moore yelled to Thomas. Thomas was startled to hear his name. He had been watching the action on the field so intently that he had almost lost track of where he was. He and John took a box of round shot from the wagon and carried it forward to the artillerymen who were methodically loading their field piece. Kersteman got off only two more volleys before it was obvious that the American First and Fourth Brigades could not stand the withering fire from the advancing red and grey line and the continuing damage caused by the three field pieces. They were forced to withdraw to the cover of the wood, their retreat soon afterwards followed by the complete withdrawal of the Eleventh, Twelfth, Thirteenth, and Fourteenth Infantry.

The 89th and 49th slowed their pace and finally halted as the Americans fled beyond the range of musket fire. But Heriot's Voltigeurs and Anderson's Mohawks continued into the woods, chasing the retreating Americans. Even from their distance from the woods, Thomas and the others could hear the ululating howls of the pursuing warriors anxious for the spoils of victory. Morrison's army of the centre and left, through their disciplined firepower and professional manoeuvring, had completely repulsed an army twice its size.

Loud huzzahs could be heard among the ranks of the 89th and 49th. Most of them were alive. They had beat back a much larger force. Their exultation was short-lived. Almost at the very moment that the last American soldier had left the field for the cover of the woods, a serious threat emerged on Morrison's right flank, along the King's Highway, right in front of Pearson's Advance Group.

Hundreds of American soldiers were rushing west along the King's Highway past the Fetterly farm. Pearson, still mounted, had the best view. He could see the first of these reinforcements arriving at the east side of Bush Creek. The bridge across Bush Creek was destroyed. To get around the water at the lower end of Bush Creek, the American infantry were forced to go to their right off the road. The banks along the ravine were muddy and slippery, but this did not stop them. They crossed the creek at the narrow point where some logs had been laid out and began to scramble up the 20-foot-high west side of the ravine, many of them slipping and sliding in the mud. As they got to level ground, they returned to the highway and began to form into ranks only 200 yards east of Davis Point. It was clear that they were preparing to attack the Advance Group. Pearson had not expected this major threat, but he immediately ordered the two companies of the 49th and the two companies of Canadian Fencibles to form into a line along the easterly edge of Davis Point. The Americans were still too far away for an effective volley by the musket men but they were in perfect range for Kersteman's gun.

Even before receiving the order from Pearson, Corporal Moore had his men swing the 6-pounder to the right and prepare to fire on the soldiers assembling on the highway.

More American men came streaming up onto the dry level ground on the west side of Bush Creek. The line of reinforcements went all the way back to the Fetterly farm. There seemed to be no end of them.

Pearson rode up beside Kersteman. Only several feet away from Pearson, John and Thomas could see the alarm in his eyes and could hear the fear in his voice as he shouted to Kersteman,

"Hurry man, hurry!"

The gun roared. The cannon ball missed its mark, going over the heads and to the right of the American soldiers. Thomas could see that Pearson was not pleased.

"Adjust the bloody gun, you fool," he yelled to Kersteman.

Thomas could see the desperation in Kersteman's eyes. The Lieutenant had not adjusted enough for his elevated position and had overestimated the distance between him and the Americans. As Kersteman lowered the barrel with the small screw, Thomas heard someone yell, "They're still coming! There are too many!"

In fact, there were over a thousand American soldiers assembling to attack Pearson's small Advance Group of 200. It was the whole of the Third Brigade. At the head of the three Regiments of the Third Brigade on foot, sword raised and waving his men forward, was Brigadier General Leonard Covington. Beside him was an ensign with their colours flapping in the strong east wind. Beside the ensign was the bugler, his notes clearly audible to Thomas and the others on Davis Point, now less than 200 yards away.

Kersteman's gun roared again. This time the cannon ball landed short, stopping in a useless thud in the deep mud in front of the American army. Kersteman had over-compensated. The Americans began to advance.

Pearson could not wait. He rode over to Captain Harry Ormond of the 49th who was also mounted. The order was given to commence firing. Standing beside Captain Ormond was Sergeant John Cronsby, who stepped forward and shouted the order:

"Make ready!" his voice boomed. "Fire!"

In almost complete unison, the two hundred muskets of the four companies in the Advance Group let loose a powerful volley. Some met their mark but most fell short, as the Americans were still a little out of effective range.

Covington ordered his men to halt. They reciprocated with

a ragged volley of their own. To Thomas's horror, he saw two men from the Canadian Fencibles fall to the ground in agony. Thomas recognized one of them as the Plamondon boy. The battle was very personal now.

Another roar from the 6-pounder. This time it was somewhat more effective. A few American infantrymen could be seen falling, to be quickly replaced by their back-up.

Sergeant Cronsby was ready with another volley. "Fire!"

Another roar from the 6-pounder. Another volley from Sergeant Cronsby. This time, the brave American general at the head of his men, Covington, sword in hand, fell to the ground. Kersteman's gun was deadly at this range. Stretcher-bearers appeared immediately to remove Covington to the rear, to the shelter of the bush.

Recognizing his vulnerability to the 6-pounder operating from the protection of the elevated position on Davis Point, Covington's replacement, the Pennsylvanian Colonel Cromwell Pearce of the Sixteenth U.S. Infantry Regiment, decided that Kersteman's gun had to be taken. He immediately sent his light company of riflemen to run forward along the road to the edge of Davis Creek. Within 100 yards of Pearson's Advance Guard, and somewhat sheltered by the little bridge, the creek bank, and a few trees, Pearce's skirmishers—about 50 had come forward—could now take direct aim at Pearson's men. The American riflemen, no longer under any threat from Kersteman's gun, as it was now too high, started picking off men in the line, to devastating effect.

Pearson knew what had to be done and acted quickly. He rode over to the Canadian Fencible company closest to the river. He spoke to their commanding officer, Lieutenant Guillaume de Lorimier. Pearson knew de Lorimier from his time at Prescott. While he was only a colonial and not a "real" British soldier, Pearson knew that de Lorimier was a solid officer who enjoyed the strong support and confidence of his men. Pearson ordered de Lorimier to prepare his men so they would be ready to go down the hill towards the river and then come directly up onto the highway to make a full charge and drive back the American riflemen. Before giving the order, Pearson rode back to Captain Ormond of the 49th, ordering him to be ready to send his Light Company forward down the hill to the left of the road, in order to provide support to de Lorimier.

Pearson then rode over to Kersteman and ordered him to direct his gun to the right to discourage as much as possible more skirmishers being sent forward along the highway to support their riflemen.

When Pearson was talking to Kersteman he was only a few feet away from Thomas and John, who were standing beside the ammunition wagon waiting to be ordered to bring forward more canisters. Thomas could see now that Pearson wasn't alarmed or fearful. He seemed perfectly calm. He had a plan. He had faced overwhelming odds before. He spoke slowly to Kersteman, who was noticeably more agitated and fearful, but Pearson's voice seemed to have a calming effect.

Kersteman said "Yes, sir," and wheeled to advance closer to the gun. Pearson sat up straighter in his saddle to get as good a view as he could of the situation. Thomas looked up at him. He saw him shift in the saddle and remembered that he had been told that Pearson suffered constantly from acute pain in his thigh from earlier wounds in the Napoleonic wars. Until that moment, since the first time he had seen him the previous summer, Thomas had had nothing but contempt for the overbearing arrogant British officer. Thomas saw him differently now.

Just as Thomas turned away from watching Pearson, he heard a strange sound. A thump and then a piercing cry. He looked back to see Pearson's horse rear up and then crash to the ground, his front left leg flailing in the air, his head frantically thrashing back and forth. He saw the panic in the horse's eyes and then he saw Pearson's arm. Pearson was pinned under his horse.

Thomas and John rushed around to the back of the horse to

avoid the hooves of its thrashing front leg. Grabbing a shoulder and an arm, they pulled the colonel free of his horse. Pearson lay on his back on the muddy ground, gasping for air.

Several other men quickly surrounded the fallen officer. Captain Ormond rode up, dismounted, broke through the surrounding men, and bent down on both knees beside Pearson.

"Colonel, can you hear me?"

"Of course I can hear you, you fool. There's nothing wrong with my ears. They just got my horse. Poor fellow. He landed on my bad leg. The pain is terrible, terrible, but I'll live."

Pearson closed his eyes. When he started to speak again, his voice caught. Eyes still closed, breathing heavily, he rubbed his left thigh and weakly waved to Ormond with his right hand, beckoning him to lower himself closer to Pearson's face.

"Harry," he said in a half-whisper, "we've got to stop Jonathan's skirmishers on the road. The Yankee riflemen are too good. They'll just keep picking us off. Keep Holland's Grenadiers here to protect the gun, but you're going to have to take your Light Company and some of de Lorimier's Canadians and drive them back. Go now." He opened his eyes. "Stick it to 'em, Harry," he said. "The Yanks will run when they see your blades."

Ormond rushed back to the line. He ordered de Lorimier to send one of his companies (about 50 men) down the bank to approach from the right the American skirmishers, whose firing was now so damaging to the men in the Advance Group. Sergeant Joseph Laporte would take half the men, Sergeant Daniel McLeod the other half. De Lorimier chose to lead the men himself, knowing full well the danger this entailed.

At the bottom of the hill, right at the mouth of Davis Creek, there was a small level landing. De Lorimier decided to take his men there to assemble for their final charge against the American snipers across the creek. Some of his men would have to wade across the creek, which was two to three feet deep there, and some would try to storm the bridge to get to the other side.

On de Lorimier's order, the Canadians began to scramble down the muddy embankment. In doing this, they were completely exposed to the American rifle fire.

The first to be hit was Private Bujold. There was no scream. Most of his neck was torn away as he was thrown to the muddy ground, writhing in agony, holding his neck with two hands. The men could see that the pain wouldn't last long. Then, to the horror of the men in his platoon, Sergeant McLeod was struck in the leg. He fell to the ground, tripping another soldier, who then landed on top of him. Sergeant Moses Brown, drawn sword in hand, leapt over the edge and ran as fast as he could down the bank to take McLeod's place at the head of his platoon. As the men reached the bottom of the bank they ran to the small landing where, by now, de Lorimier was waiting. Somewhat protected by a small hill, de Lorimier quickly assembled the men and then, on his order, Sergeant Laporte bellowed out in his loudest voice the order that chills the spine of even the most experienced infantrymen.

"Fix your bay-o-nets!"

Out of their scabbards and clicked into place at the end of the barrel in two seconds, the bayonets were held chest-high pointing at the enemy. The two sergeants looked at de Lorimier. With his pistol in his left hand, de Lorimier held his sword high in his right. As he brought his sword down, his right arm fully extended, sword now directed at the Yankees, the two sergeants yelled, "Charge!"

De Lorimier ran towards the road followed by Sergeant Moses Brown with his platoon. Laporte led his men to the right to wade across the creek, which at this point was two feet deep. De Lorimier and Brown reached the road where the footing was better, but they were now fully exposed to the Yankee sharpshooters.

Brown's men spread out taking turns running forward, then crouching, others seeking shelter in the ditch between dashes towards the bridge. The American riflemen had not expected this direct assault. They realized they only had time for perhaps one final shot before they were in direct hand-to-hand combat.

Thomas and many of the others left on Davis Point had moved even closer to the edge of the bank to get a better view of de Lorimier's attack. Thomas lay on his stomach to avoid being hit by a marksman. He watched de Lorimier lead half of his men in a frantic dash to the bridge. He could see Laporte leading the other half, wading across the creek. He saw Laporte assemble his men along the bank on the east side. They began to edge forward, staying low out of the sight of the American riflemen. But de Lorimier and his men were fully exposed. Thomas saw one man running beside de Lorimier take a direct hit. As he fell to the ground, two other men leaped over him, still running towards the enemy. Brown, Chretien, and de Lorimier were the first to reach the little wooden bridge over Davis Creek. It was no more than 10 feet across and perhaps 20 feet long. A Yankee soldier stood up to get one more shot. When he saw the three Canadians crossing the bridge he turned and fired at them. The force of the direct hit seemed to lift Chretien's whole body, throwing it over the side of the bridge into the creek below. Brown charged the now defenceless American soldier. Thomas could see Brown thrust his bayonet into the stomach of the soldier. It seemed to stick in the soldier's body, so that he had to put his foot on the man's chest to get it out. Seeing this, one nearby American rifleman threw down his weapon and began to run. Another, though, with sword drawn, lurched at Brown and struck his arm. Brown's musket fell to the ground as he grabbed his dangling arm. The American swordsman now lunged at de Lorimier. Their swords met. De Lorimier swung his sword, but the American adeptly stepped aside and deflected the blow. De Lorimier swung again, but the movement caused him to lose his footing and he fell to the muddy ground. The Canadian, young John Christy, stood over the American and now, with two hands, drove the bayonet down through the chest of the American.

As de Lorimier got back on his feet, he was joined by about a dozen of his men, who had now crossed the bridge. The

Americans did not retreat. No longer able to use their rifles, but realizing that they still outnumbered the Canadians, they stood and fought. What followed for the next few minutes was a chaotic clash of flesh and steel.

When two American soldiers charged de Lorimier, he was forced to use his pistol to stop one, but the other succeeded in knocking him to the ground, his sword falling to the mud. The bigger American soldier had de Lorimier pinned to the ground, pummelling him with his fists. Another Canadian, Thomas could not tell who it was, saw the American on top of de Lorimier, rushed forward, and thrust his bayonet into the soldier's back. De Lorimier threw the soldier to one side and got up. He saw Laporte and his men coming to the rescue. Now outnumbered, most of the Americans that could still walk or run began a ragged withdrawal.

But a large bearded bear of a man was not retreating. His left arm dangling uselessly at his side, he grabbed the musket lying beside an injured Canadian writhing on the ground. He raised the musket over his head and drove its bayonet down through the neck of the Canadian Fencible. He then turned to see de Lorimier, who had grabbed somebody's musket. De Lorimier was charging him. Remarkably nimble for a man his size, the big American wheeled to meet de Lorimier and knocked the musket out of de Lorimier's hands. He then drove his bayonet completely through de Lorimier's arm. He pulled out the bayonet and smashed the butt of the musket against the side of de Lorimier's head. De Lorimier fell to the ground, limp.

Chapter 17
2:30, November 11, 1813
John Haines's Farm
Dundas County on the St. Lawrence River, Upper Canada

The skirmish at the Davis Creek Bridge lasted no more than ten minutes. With the arrival of Laporte's platoon, the remaining American riflemen withdrew as best they could. While the 49th waited for orders to go down the highway to help rescue de Lorimier's dead and wounded (with Pearson down, there was a temporary vacuum of leadership), the Fencibles did not hesitate. They ran down the road to the bridge as fast as they could. Thomas and John Cook joined them.

Thomas went directly to de Lorimier. Laporte was already there. He was sitting on the ground with de Lorimier's head carefully cradled in his lap. Laporte was sobbing as he gently stroked de Lorimier's hair.

"He's hurt bad. Real bad," Laporte said to Thomas as Thomas bent down to get a closer look. The Sergeant's eyes met Thomas's. The Sergeant slowly shook his head.

"The arm wound doesn't look too bad—the bleeding has mostly stopped—but he got an awful blow to the side of his head. See this. He still has a heartbeat. He doesn't seem . . ."

Before Sergeant Laporte could finish his explanation, de Lorimier's head jerked violently to one side. His eyes opened wide in a wild far-off stare. He cried out, "*Maman, Maman! Je ne peut pas voir. Maman! Ou est-tu? Maman!*"

Almost as suddenly, his cries stopped. He whimpered something now in Mohawk. His head lowered back into Laporte's lap. His mouth stayed open, breathing heavily. He stared at the sky. "Mother, Mother," he whispered in Mohawk, "I am sorry, Mother."

Laporte gently stroked de Lorimier's forehead. Laporte's touch seemed to soothe him. As Laporte looked up to Thomas, he saw John grab Thomas's shoulder.

"Come on," John shouted, "we got to get out of here. The Yankees are coming fast. We've got to get back up to the Point. Ormond is signalling a retreat. Come on. We've got to get the wounded out of here. You and Laporte bring Gui. I've got to get help for this man here."

Thomas tried to lift de Lorimier as Laporte rose to his feet but realized that de Lorimier's left arm was still bleeding profusely, his uniform now soaked with blood. He could not lift him by that arm.

"I'm not leaving him," said Laporte as he reached down and picked up de Lorimier, carrying him like a baby in his arms. "You get Janvin over there. Michel's a good boy."

Thomas saw the soldier that Laporte was referring to. It took only a few steps to reach him. He was lying face down in the mud. Thomas got down on one knee as he turned him over. The boy's bowels and intestines lay steaming on the ground beside his body. Thomas's first reaction was to try to put the intestines back. It was no use. The soldier blinked. To Thomas's horror, the boy reached out and grabbed his arm. "*Aidez-moi*," he whimpered, "*s'il vous plaît. S'il vous plaît.*"

Then Thomas felt the soldier's grip release. Still on one knee, Thomas turned his head to avoid vomiting in the dead boy's face. He threw up again. And again. A pounding in his ears blocked out all other sounds. On all fours now, Thomas heaved again but there was nothing left. Free of the retching, some clarity came back to his mind. The pounding in his ears subsided. He heard clearly now the bugle sounding retreat. He couldn't help this boy. Private Michel Janvin, Canadian Fencible, was dead. Thomas looked around to see if there was someone else he could help. He realized that he was the last remaining man standing on the east side of the creek. He saw Laporte up ahead crossing the bridge carrying de Lorimier. Some other men were helping the wounded climb the ridge up to Davis Point. As he began to climb up onto the road to run towards the little bridge, he heard to his left a man yell out, "Help me!"

Thomas stepped over towards the man, who was lying on his back, his head resting on a stone. Both his hands seemed to be holding his stomach. Thomas leaned over to help him, then saw that he was a Yankee soldier.

"Please," said the soldier quietly. "Help me. I'm hurtin'." Thomas saw the desperation in his eyes. He was young, a boy really.

"I'm sorry," said Thomas. "Just wait. Your men will be here soon."

Thomas started to run west along the road. He crossed the bridge and caught up to Laporte. One of his Grenadiers, a giant of a man, had come down the hill and taken de Lorimier from Laporte.

Thomas was one of the last to get up over the ridge to the level land on Davis Point. What was left of the Fencibles and the two companies of the 49th was now spread out at the top of the ridge. They were waiting for orders. Were they to get in one last volley or retreat right away? Thomas looked back and from this elevated position, he could see hundreds of Americans, bayonets fixed, swarming forward along the road. He could also see for the first time what was causing all the noise just to the north of them. Barnes's 89th were taking heavy fire from a larger force of Americans that was pushing them back as well. He then saw that some Dundas militiamen and the Royal Artillery men were hitching the 6-pounder to the limber and getting the horses to move back, as someone must have decided that there were too many Americans attacking. It was clear that they did not have enough men to successfully defend Davis Point and they could not risk losing the 6-pounder. Now Thomas understood why Kersteman wasn't firing when de Lorimier's men were retreating.

Soon, the American forces were arrayed along the east side of Davis Creek on the very land where only minutes before de Lorimier had been struck down. The body of Michael Janvin, Canadian Fencible, was now surrounded by hundreds of American soldiers. They were now close enough that they began a sporadic volley. They were still a little out of range so it did little damage but it added to the confusion among the ranks of the Fencibles and the 49th. The bugle was no longer calling a retreat, but nobody was giving orders to reply to the American fire either.

While it was only a few minutes of confusion, to most of the men it seemed much longer. During these few minutes, Thomas found Laporte and de Lorimier. De Lorimier was lying on the muddy wet ground beside about a dozen other wounded men. Other soldiers were comforting them but there was no one to provide medical attention. One of the wounded Fencibles was screaming in agony. Thomas could see that John Cook was trying to calm the man, but to no avail. To his right he could hear Kersteman yelling at the men who were trying to manoeuvre the horses to pull the gun back. He could see that there was some problem. This must have been the explanation for the delay in beginning an orderly retreat. No one seemed to be in charge. Captain Ormond was nowhere to be seen. What Thomas didn't know was that after being injured by his falling horse, Colonel Pearson had been taken by stretcher to John Haines's house just a hundred yards away. Captain Ormond was in the house with him. Morrison's whole army had only two doctors. Ormond's aide had taken his horse to fetch one of them. Unaware of the deteriorating situation, unaware that hundreds of Yankee soldiers had now reached Davis Creek and were starting to cross it, Ormond had not provided orders.

Moreover, the junior officers of the 49th (both Light Company and Grenadiers) were not clear whether the bugle signal to retreat was directed only to the Fencibles down at Davis Creek Bridge or intended to apply to the whole Advance Group. It was clear that Kersteman had been ordered to move the 6-pounder back, but others were confused.

"How is Gui?" Thomas asked as he leaned over Laporte's shoulder to see what he was doing to de Lorimier. Laporte was applying a better tourniquet out of a torn shirt.

"Same. No change," replied Laporte. "When he comes to he is confused. Keeps asking for his mother and whispering something in Mohawk. What the hell is going on? We've got to get these wounded men out of here if we're pulling back. Where is Ormond?"

Laporte motioned to Thomas. "Here, push down on this cloth right here. Let me see if I can get somebody to make some decisions."

Leaving Thomas to care for de Lorimier, Laporte jumped up and ran closer to the eastern edge, where he spoke to a Sergeant from the 49th Light Company. Together they ran to young Lieutenant Samuel Holland, acting officer in command of the 49th Grenadiers.

Lieutenant Holland, the 19-year-old son of a Prince Edward Island Loyalist, who had already seen action at Fort George and Stoney Creek, had been waiting for orders from Captain Ormond.

"You've got to take command, Lieutenant," urged Laporte. "We have to get out of here."

"Where's Ormond? Where the Christ is Captain Ormond? Shouldn't we wait for the Captain?" replied Holland.

"There's no time, sir," Laporte pressed. "You have to give the order to retreat."

"All right then, Sergeant, I'll take command. I agree. I say we get out of here. There are too many of them. We don't have our gun. But we need to buy a little time to get the wounded back."

Holland seemed to be gaining confidence as he spoke. He continued:

"Laporte, you take your men and try to move back your wounded as best you can to the other side of Bouck's Creek. Surely Morrison will send men to help hold our line there when he sees how many Yankees are coming down the road. Sergeant, line up your Light Company and fire at will. They're getting close enough now. See if we can slow them down. I'll take my men a little to the right. We can get closer there. We'll try to hold the line for three or four minutes . . . Christ almighty, look at them coming . . . Go, Laporte, get your men out of here."

Laporte yelled to his men to withdraw. Many didn't hear the order because the firing had re-commenced. Laporte reached the wounded men. By now, John Cook was beside Thomas, who was kneeling over de Lorimier.

"The boy is dead," explained John.

"How many wounded men are there?" asked Laporte. "Are there others?"

"These men here. Maybe ten still alive. I don't know how many can stand being moved," replied John. "I'm not sure but I think there are some others in Haines's house with the Colonel."

"The Colonel is in the house?" both Laporte and Thomas repeated in unison.

"Yes, I think Ormond is in there with him. I know that one of the gunners was taken in there too when he was picked off by a Yankee sniper earlier."

"All right, John, Thomas and I will help organize the rest of our men to move the wounded back. For those that can't walk, we can put together makeshift stretchers by taking the coats off the dead and putting our muskets through the sleeves. I'll show you how to do it. You go to Haines's house, John, and tell them that we're moving back to the other side of Bouck's Creek. Kersteman should have the gun back there by now."

As John arrived at the front door he met Captain Ormond coming out. Ormond had been in the house with the injured Colonel Pearson, but hearing the commencement of the firing he had just come out to see what was going on.

Captain Harry Smith Ormond, a 29-year-old son of a New Brunswick Loyalist, had been with the 49th for 14 years. Prominent in the Battle of Queenston Heights the previous year, he had seen a good deal of action in the war already. But he had made a mistake. He had not anticipated such a quick turn of events.

"What's going on? I leave the field for five minutes. Men are retreating. Others are firing at will. What the hell is going on? Shit, Jenkins has my horse. What the hell is happening?" Ormond, bewildered, was shouting at John.

"We're pulling back behind Bouck's Creek. The Yankees have crossed Davis Creek. Hundreds of them are coming at us. We've got to get out of here," John replied, breathless from running to the house. "The 49th are trying to hold them back to give us time to move our wounded. We don't have long."

"Shit! Shit!" Ormond punched and kicked the air and then could be seen to will himself to be calm. "You," Ormond said, pointing to John, "you, you go back and tell whoever is in charge to hold on as long as they can. I'll have to get Colonel Pearson out of here. We can't have him taken prisoner. Who is in charge, by the way?"

"I don't know," John replied, shaking his head.

"Shit. Shit. Shit." Ormond was punching the air as he turned to go back into the Haines's house.

As John returned he could see that the situation had grown more serious and more confusing. Some men were too wounded to be moved. They would soon be prisoners of the Americans. There were ammunition supply problems for some of the Canadian Fencibles and for the 49th which had stayed at the edge of Davis Point, firing at will. Out of ammunition, or experiencing musket problems, or unwilling to hold the line any longer as the waves of American soldiers got closer, many were now helping the wounded move back or retreating outright on their own. While unplanned infantry retreats are never very orderly, this one was becoming particularly ragged.

In the few hectic minutes that followed, Holland continued to stand his ground, but it became increasingly clear that his position was becoming untenable. He was relieved to see Captain Crysler ride up with orders from Colonel Morrison to retreat at once. Barnes's 89th had taken heavy losses and had been ordered to withdraw as well. Davis Point could not be held. Kersteman's gun was safely pulled back. All the men of Pearson's Advance Group withdrew immediately to the western side of Bouck's Creek and formed up there in the meadow in front of Adam Bouck's farmhouse. Colonel Crysler advised that Colonel Morrison would try to send reinforcements; the bridge at Bouck's Creek must be held or all could be lost. Orders were to take as many of the wounded back as possible but not let the removal of wounded delay a speedy retreat; those who could not be removed quickly were to be left on the field.

Orders given, Captain Crysler rode off. Lieutenant Holland shouted orders to all who remained that they were to retreat immediately to the meadow in front of Bouck's farmhouse. It was only 300 yards away but it meant giving away the high ground of Davis Point to the enemy. Just as the last man of Pearson's Advance Group crossed the bridge over Bouck's Creek, the first of the American Sixteenth Infantry appeared over the ridge and clambered up onto Davis Point. As more arrived, they formed into ranks to prepare their bayonet charge. The Yankees knew that they had the British and Canadians on the run.

~ ~ ~

To the surprise of most of the men of the Advance Group, as they began to form up in Bouck's meadow, Colonel Pearson reappeared and resumed command. With the pain in his leg and thigh relieved somewhat by several ounces of diluted opium, Pearson was back up on a borrowed horse and issuing orders. The Light Company and Grenadiers of the 49th and what remained of the Canadian Fencibles were formed into a single line ready to fire when the Americans came into range. Kersteman and the Royal Artillery men were hurriedly setting up their gun to resume firing. Some men of the Dundas militia who still had operating muskets were ordered to fill in some of the gaps on the line. Others were helping with the horses to re-position the 6-pounder and the ammunition cart. The remainder were ordered to carry the wounded the further 300 yards to Crysler's house and the two outbuildings.

Thomas Marselis and John Cook gently rolled de Lorimier back onto their makeshift stretcher and proceeded to carry him to Crysler's farm. He was unconscious now but still breathing.

When they arrived at Crysler's, a corporal from the 49th, his head bandaged and his arm in a sling, took one look at de Lorimier and ordered Thomas and John to take him to the shed beside the main house.

One of the double doors at the front of the shed was open when they arrived. As they manoeuvred their way through the door with de Lorimier, the first thing that met John and Thomas was the overwhelming smell of guts and blood and vomit. Then they heard the screaming and moaning of the wounded as they lay on the dirt floor lined up in a row. There were perhaps a dozen men. Many seemed more dead than alive, covered in blood and mud. At the far end of the shed a young soldier was screaming in pain. Kneeling over him was a tall soldier who appeared to be trying to calm him down. He was wiping his face with a dirty rag. The screaming stopped. Thomas assumed that this soldier was in charge so he called out to him and asked where to put the new patient. Hearing Thomas, the tall soldier turned, and John and Thomas recognized him immediately as Duke Kierens of the 89th. Duke's right hand was bandaged, his swarthy face drawn, his dark eyes showing the strain of the horrid situation.

"Welcome to my hospital," Duke said in a tired voice, "which is becoming a morgue as you can see. Got another one for me, do you?"

"We do, Duke," Thomas replied. "It's de Lorimier."

Duke stood up. "Put him there," he said, pointing to a corner to his right.

John and Thomas lowered the stretcher and gently laid it on the ground. Duke stepped over and kneeled down beside de Lorimier. With remarkable gentleness he wiped de Lorimier's face with his rag. He put the rag on the ground and then cupped de Lorimier's face with his two hands. Without looking up and still holding de Lorimier's face in his big hands, he asked: "Passed out from lack of blood?"

"Maybe that too," said Thomas, "but he got a bad blow to the head. Been unconscious now for maybe twenty minutes or half an hour. What do you think? Will he make it?"

"There's nothing the surgeons can do for him. That's why they sent you here. They're doing the surgery in Crysler's house. They patched me up there and sent me out here to look after these poor bastards." Standing up now and turning and pointing to the soldier he had just been attending, Duke shook his head slightly and said:

"This boy finally died. Thank the Lord. I almost strangled him with my own hands a few minutes ago. He kept begging me to. He was in awful pain. Poor little bastard."

Thomas's heart seemed to stop when he heard this. Nancy's face appeared in his mind's eye. He could feel his bowels turning to mush. There was a ringing in his ears that drowned out all other sounds. He couldn't breathe as a giant cold grip of panic pressed on his chest. He reached out and put his hand on the wall to steady himself.

"You all right?" he could hear John say to him, a voice in the distance.

"Yes, yes, I'm good now. Just felt a little faint there for a moment," Thomas replied. "I'll just step outside for some fresh air."

With Thomas outside, Duke explained to John that he had taken a glancing musket ball to the back of his hand even before Barnes's men had been forced to retreat. It probably broke some bones. He couldn't pull a trigger any more so he was sent back to help out with the injured. He explained that he had just seen Garrett, who was doing stretcher duty for Barnes's 89th. Pointing to another soldier who was lying on the ground with a blanket over him, Duke said that another Dundas County man and Garrett had just brought him in. Looked like he might be going to make it. They probably saved his life, he said. They had made several trips over the last hour. They had just left to see if there were any more dead or wounded that needed to be removed from the field. Duke had told them not to go back as the retreat now under way was making it even more dangerous out there, but the two were fearless and insisted on returning to the front.

Just then the artillery could be heard again: a loud roar, and then another.

"I hope that's our gun," said Duke. "I hope that means we've now taken up new positions and are using our guns to stop the Yankee advance. If the Yankees have finally brought their artillery to the action, we'll not even be able to hold here. There are just too many of them. If they had artillery and a better ammunition supply system, they'd be kicking our asses this afternoon."

"I'd better go see how Thomas is doing," replied John, "We're supposed to get right back to Bouck's farm to help with ammunition supply. The Yanks are still pressing. I know you'll do what you can for de Lorimier, Duke."

John leaned over for a final look at de Lorimier. He touched his cheek. Just then, two more men arrived with another stretcher and a wounded man. One of the stretcher-bearers was Peter Marselis.

"Peter, is that you?" John exclaimed.

Peter looked up and saw John. He lowered the stretcher and slowly raised his hand in greeting to John. As glad as he may have been to see John, he did not smile. The strain on his young face was palpable. He turned to Duke.

"This one died on the table, Duke, just as Surgeon Korb was sawing off his arm. Can we just leave him here?"

"At least you're not in jail, Peter," John said, trying to distract everyone from the horror of the disfigured body on the stretcher between them.

"I wish I was," Peter said. "Henry and I have seen some awful things this afternoon, John. I'm not cut out for this."

"Nobody is," said John, "nobody sane anyway. Heard anything about George or Luke? Do you know if they're safe?"

"No, nothing. Still with the Voltigeurs. What are you doing here?"

"Thomas and I brought de Lorimier here. He's hurt real bad. That's him over there. Thomas is outside somewhere. I take it you didn't see him when you came in. We have to get back to Bouck's where Pearson is taking a new stand. The Yankees drove us off Davis Point. I've got to go. Take care of yourself, Peter."

"Have you been to Crysler's house where they're doing the surgeries?"

"No," replied John, "we were directed here. Why?"

"Just tell Thomas that I told him to go by the house just for a moment before he goes back to the front. I guess I'll see you one way or the other tonight. Make sure Thomas goes by the house."

John left the shed. He found Thomas at the back. He was talking to young Ceph Garlough, who had just come from Bouck's farm.

"John," Thomas said, "Ceph says that the fight has started again. Kersteman's gun is doing real damage and Jackson now has his 6-pounder going again too. We have to get back right away, as there will be more wounded."

"All right," replied John, "but you won't guess who I just talked to. Peter. He has been through a lot but he's good. Nothing physical. He insisted that you go by Crysler's house for a moment just before we go back. He wants you to see something."

"See something. Why? Why would I go there? I've seen enough horror already. Hell, enough for a lifetime. I'm not going there. Any change in de Lorimier's condition?"

"No. Duke will be there if he comes to. I'm serious, though. Peter made me more or less promise to have you look into the house. I don't know why either, but Peter was not in a joking mood."

"Fine. Let's go. We have no time to waste. Are you sure Peter is all right?"

"He's good. It's been a tough day for all of us. And it's not over yet."

They crossed the yard past Nancy Crysler's garden and walked up the steps to the veranda. While John waited outside, Thomas walked through the open door to witness a scene of indescribable horror. He stopped, his breath taken away by the smell.

The dining room table had been moved in front of the large window in the front parlour to the left. This table was the operating platform. At that moment an older man, Surgeon William Woodforde, was sawing off the leg of a soldier above the knee. The soldier was being held down by a rope around his waist and by two soldiers. Other patients were on various other makeshift tables. Some were screaming in agony. To the right and at the base of the stairs was another operating platform, made by a door set on two wooden chairs. At that table, facing Thomas, was a young surgeon who appeared to be using a pair of forceps to extract something from the back of a naked soldier who was lying motionless face down on the makeshift operating table. Assisting the surgeon, her back to the door, was a woman. Her hair was tucked up in a scarf. She wore an apron over her dress. Another woman—it was Nancy Crysler—came through the door from the kitchen carrying a pan of steaming hot water. She set it on the floor beside the operating table. When the other woman turned to dip a cloth into the water, Thomas could see that it was Allie. Allie, whom he hadn't seen in days, was washing the injured soldier's back. She did not see Thomas.

Thomas took a couple of hesitant steps so as not to slip on the floor covered in blood and then said her name. When she turned he could see that her face and apron were splattered in blood but she was still the most beautiful thing he had ever seen.

"Thomas," she said haltingly, "you're alive."

"I'm alive. I didn't expect to see you here."

"How are you holding up?"

"Not bad. You?"

"I'm trying to do what I can. They just keep bringing them in. It's horrible."

"Yes," he said, "it's horrible. I've missed you."

"Yes, me too," she said.

Then the surgeon said something to Allie.

"I can't talk now," she said. "I'll see you tonight. Before you go, look in the back room." She pointed to the door at the right.

"I have to go too," he said.

"Be careful," she said. "I love you. Tonight."

She turned away to wipe the soldier's back. Thomas was too overwhelmed to think clearly. He followed her instructions and walked over and into the back room. Lit only by a single window the room was almost dark, but he could see that it was filled with injured men, screaming and moaning, some lying on blankets on the floor, others on a few crude benches. Lying on one of these benches was a soldier with a bandaged stump where his right arm used to be. Holding up his head was Levi. Holding a cup, helping the soldier to drink, was Oma. She, too, was covered in blood. Down on her knees, wiping the face of a soldier lying on the floor, was Elizabeth.

Elizabeth saw Thomas first and called out his name. Oma and Levi turned to see him. He held up his hand in a half-motion of greeting. He looked straight into his mother's eyes.

"I have to go," he said. "I'm already late. John is waiting for me. Peter and Garrett are alive. I'll come back tonight."

He didn't give Oma any time to say anything.

Thomas went out the side door and yelled to John who was still waiting on the front veranda.

"Come on," he said to John, "we have to get back. I'll tell you who was in there on the way. You won't believe it."

Within just a few minutes, Thomas and John got back to Bouck's farm. By now the renewed battle was well under way. Firing was constant, the effect brutal. On and on it went. Ready . . . Present . . . Fire! The opposing lines, just 150 yards apart, blazed away at each other. There were two or three times the number of American soldiers but they still had no artillery. Kersteman's 6-pounder was making the difference. From this close range, every discharge of his gun had a devastating effect on the American line.

Sitting erect on his horse, Pearson was shouting commands. When he saw Thomas and John arrive he yelled to them:

"Leave the wounded where they are for now. One of you give this private a hand taking ammunition to the men on the line. And you," he said, pointing to John, "help Kersteman. One of his gunners has been hit."

Thomas grabbed several 10-round packages of cartridges from the half-barrel on the ammunition wagon and ran, head down, towards the back of the line. He had to step around some wounded soldiers that had been dragged back from the line and just left on the field. He could see that the Fencibles were only in single lines.

As a Canadian Fencible turned to Thomas to receive a package of cartridges to put into his haversack, he was hit in the shoulder. He was knocked backwards and fell over. The soldier screamed in agony. Sergeant Laporte saw this and yelled to Thomas to take the soldier's haversack and musket and fill his place in the line. His heart racing, Thomas stepped up and loaded as fast as he could. His hands were shaking so badly he could hardly manage to bite off the end and to get the powder into the pan. He heard the order to "fire" and the discharge, so he knew he had to hurry: it would be only 30 seconds before the next volley.

He rammed home the cartridge. Still trembling, he waited, heard the order, "Ready," then "Present," and "Fire." He felt the recoil in his right shoulder and knew he had to hurry if he was going to be ready for the next volley. Before he could do that he heard Laporte yell the order:

"Fencibles. Fix your bay-o-nets!"

When this was done, he watched the men on either side of him to know what to do next. Then he heard Laporte again.

"The Yankees are withdrawing. Follow me. We're crossing the bridge and forming up on the other side. Ready. Let's roll!"

Thomas followed the man to his left as they trotted in line, crossed the bridge, and were immediately ordered to form up. Thomas was not familiar with these manoeuvres so he just tried to watch what the others were doing.

The U.S. Sixteenth Infantry had fought hard and well to capture Davis Point. But their officers had made no plans for ammunition re-supply. That, and the damage from Kersteman's 6-pounder, meant that the American commander, Cromwell Pearce, had no choice but to withdraw from the Point to the protection of the trees.

Similarly, Barnes's 89th, to the left of Pearson's Advance Group, were able to push back the American Twenty-fifth Infantry as they, too, ran out of cartridges. Jackson's guns had been very effective. Morrison's right flank was now restored. With no artillery support and the failure to organize ammunition supply, again the Americans had to withdraw. Pearson's Advance Group recovered the high ground of Davis Point. It was about 3:30 p.m. Morrison's men were back to where they had been an hour earlier. But there was no time for rejoicing because, finally, the American artillery had arrived.

Chapter 18
Late Afternoon
November 11, 1813
Dundas County

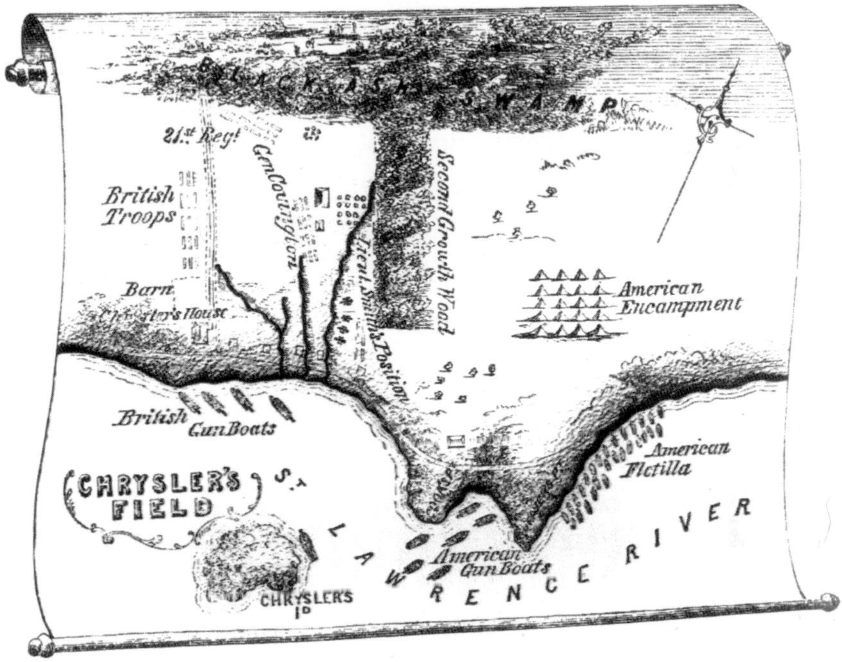

The first of the American guns to appear, coming out of the woods on the east side of Bush Creek, about 800 yards distant from the front line of the 49th and 89th, were the two black 6-pounders commanded by Lieutenant Armstrong Irvine of the United States Second Artillery Regiment. He quickly wheeled them into position. His first shots fell short of their target. He reloaded and continued to hammer away at the British lines. Jackson responded with his three bronze 6-pounders, but both sides were barely within effective range. Then, just minutes later, four more 6-pounders emerged on the King's Highway passing the Fetterly farm. Lieutenant Henry Craig commanded these guns. Craig recognized that to be effective he had to get on the other side of the creek. He led his four gun detachments north along the east side of the ravine surrounding the creek about 400 yards from the highway where the creek was much shallower. Using shoulder harnesses to steer the guns, Craig's men guided his four 6-pounders down into the ravine and across Bush Creek, and struggled up on the far side. The horses were difficult to manage as they slipped in the mud and were surrounded by the noise of musket fire and the shelling from Jackson's guns. But Craig finally got his four artillery pieces in place, immediately in front of the 49th and only 400 yards away. He opened fire on the 49th Foot. One of the first to fall was young Ensign Sylvester Richmond, carrying the regimental colours of the 49th. Several other soldiers were hit. It was soon clear to Morrison that the 49th's position was untenable. They were within cannon range but too far away for an effective musket response. They must either withdraw or charge.

Morrison ordered their commander, Lieutenant Colonel Charles Plenderleath, to attack Craig's guns. At the time this order was given, the 49th were a mere 120 yards from the two American infantry regiments that poured on a hail of musket fire. The 49th plodded relentlessly forward through ploughed wet and heavy ground intersected by two snake fences which they had to pull down. The combination of Craig's guns and the infantry fire had a devastating effect on Plenderleath's men. The charge of the 49th Foot was repulsed. Within ten minutes, 11 officers out of 18 were killed or wounded, as were over half of the men in the line. Plenderleath, with a canister bullet in his thigh, had to decide whether to retreat immediately or try to hold out. He decided to pull his men back a safe distance and then he ordered his men to fire by platoons.

Barnes, of the 89th, seeing Plenderleath's desperate vulnerability, moved his three companies forward on the right of the 49th and began firing at the American lines, but with negligible effect as they were still a little beyond range. The infantry lines continued to blaze away. For Barnes there was no going back. He continued to order his men forward in spite of their mounting losses.

But Craig had not expected Barnes's tenacity. With the supporting American infantry still on the east side of the creek, Craig realized that his four guns were in danger as Barnes relentlessly pushed even closer. Craig decided to leave Lieutenant William Smith with his one gun to provide some cover and he ordered the withdrawal of the other three. Craig's men were forced to retrace their steps and pull their guns back down the bank of the ravine, and to ford again the muddy creek they had just crossed not 20 minutes before.

Barnes continued to advance against Smith's gun, the only one still on the west side of the creek.

To try to save Craig's retreating guns from being taken by the advancing redcoats, German-born and French-trained United States Colonel Jean-Baptiste de Barth Walbach, U.S. Army Adjutant General, saw the necessity to send in the Second Regiment of the United States Light Dragoons, who were now assembled on the King's Highway in front of the Fetterly farm, waiting to be deployed. Numbering over 150 sabres, the Second Dragoons prepared to mount what would become the only cavalry charge by a regular cavalry regiment in the whole of the war.

Because Barnes's men were still on the other side of the creek, the objective of the cavalry charge was to turn the right flank of Plenderleath's 49th Foot before they could overtake Craig's retreating artillery. The attack had to be fast and aggressive, as the Second Dragoons would be exposed on their left to the gauntlet of Pearson's Advance Group and Barnes's three companies of the 89th Foot.

The cavalry squadron was quickly assembled along the King's Highway in columns of four. Following their leader, the Virginian Major John T. Woodford, the Second Dragoons carefully rode their horses off the highway to their right to where the creek was only a couple of feet deep. They assembled quickly on the other side because, by this time, Jackson had begun to direct his artillery towards the advancing cavalry.

To no small anxiety, the men of Pearson's Advance Group saw the squadron of cavalry gallop up to the level ground of the King's Highway. They saw the leader ride to the front and draw his sword. The other dragoons followed his example and then the whole squadron began to gallop somewhat faster. Thomas heard the bugler sound the call and saw the horses accelerate. The danger was clear: if the horsemen could get around the flank, they could wheel about and charge the British line from the rear.

Now at full speed, their horses lunging forward, the riders "gave point" with their sabres fully extended just above the right side of their their horses's heads. The squadron of mounted horsemen charged towards the right flank of the 49th Foot.

Thomas Marselis and the other men of Pearson's Advance Group had a good vantage point on Davis Point to watch in horror the battle unfold and see the progress of the powerful cavalry charge.

As soon as the U.S. horsemen left the King's Highway to cross Bush Creek, Pearson had ordered his men to align themselves along the edge of the Point with muskets ready.

Filling in as a musketman in the ranks of the 49th Light Company, Thomas tried to hold his musket still. He hoped that the soldiers on either side of him couldn't see it shaking, but the old soldier on his left could see or sense Thomas's fear.

"Steady, lad, steady," he said in his thick brogue. "Steady boy. My guess is we'll only get one volley. Make'r count. Aim a little high with this fair freeze. Steady. Wait."

The old soldier's words did have a soothing effect on Thomas. He took a deep breath, but he jumped when he heard the roar of Kersteman's gun just to his right. He steadied himself again. The cavalry were coming fast. Then he heard the command: "Make ready." He pulled back the hammer. "Fire!"

Some horses and riders tumbled to the ground; it wasn't clear whether this was from Kersteman's gun or the musket fire. The old

Irish soldier was right: before Pearson's four companies could get off a second volley, the cavalry charge had roared past them, but the sabres were now coming alongside Barnes's 89th, whose first volley was almost right into the faces of the horsemen. The effect was devastating. More horses and riders tumbled to the ground and some could be seen turning back. As the remainder rode by, Barnes's men, with cool discipline, reloaded and got off a second volley into the rear of the cavalry rushing past.

At the same time, the right flank company of the 49th were ordered to carry out another drill book manoeuvre to meet the threat. They wheeled four paces back to the right, again with perfect precision. They waited a moment and then fired in unison. The 49th volley slammed directly into the faces of the men and horses of Woodford's squadron of cavalry.

Thomas and the other men on Davis Point were thrilled to see dozens of horses and their riders fall to the ground. Some of the dragoons stopped their horses to fire their pistols before rushing off to their right to the protection of the bush. Thomas and the other men in Pearson's Advance Group then saw the squadron's leader, Woodford, gallantly rush forward, leap a fence, and ride directly into the lines of the 49th, who rushed out to attack him with their bayonets fixed. Seeing the bayonets and realizing that he was alone, just before contacting the 49th he wheeled his horse about, took the fence again in good hunting style, and rode quickly off to the right to join the others in the protection of the maple bush.

Watching the American cavalry retreat in disorder, Thomas and the others yelled a jubilant "Huzzah!" On the field where they had launched their attack lay over 30 dead or wounded American dragoons and their horses. Even from the distance of Davis Point, the horrible wailing of injured horses could be clearly heard.

Barnes's men now pressed forward to capture the one remaining American gun west of the creek, Smith's 6-pounder. They stopped momentarily to fire another volley and then, with bayonets fixed, they charged Smith and his gun. Within moments, they overran the gun and the wounded Smith and his men were taken prisoner. Barnes's 89th gave out a spirited cheer.

For a moment there was a pause in the fighting but it didn't last long, as Jackson and Kersteman adjusted their guns and began an artillery barrage against the rear of the retreating American army. Irving replied with his two guns, but to little effect.

Morrison decided to press his advantage and ordered his whole army forward to the west side of the ravine surrounding Bush Creek. From there he was within musket range of the American infantry, now re-armed and lined up along the western edge of the bush.

Morrison waited for the Americans to renew the combat. It didn't happen. Instead, many of the American infantrymen seemed to be retreating into the trees. Could it be that they were now in full retreat? Could the battle be over?

Just then a new supply of American soldiers arrived and emerged from the tree line into the open. It was Mordecai Myers' company of the Thirteenth Infantry of about 600 fresh men. While many of the Americans were retreating, Myers brought his men forward. He was immediately met with musket fire from the 89th and 49th and with a heavy bombardment from the Royal Artillery. Myers' Light Company was forced to kneel behind a two-foot-high stone fence. This protected them somewhat from musket fire but did nothing to lessen the impact from Jackson's three guns and Kersteman's 6-pounder, still up on Davis Point and in a good position to send continuous volleys of shrapnel. Myers realized that he too might have to retreat.

Meanwhile, more of the American troops were breaking and running to the protection of the trees. Morrison now realized that Myers' men had been brought forward simply in an attempt to check Morrison's further advance. He knew now that no new attack from the Americans was forthcoming. He could risk ordering Pearson's Light Companies from the right and Heriot and the

Mohawk warriors from the left to advance into the bush to keep up the pressure on the retreating Americans, who were running helter-skelter back into the trees.

When Thomas heard Pearson yell out an order behind him he turned, as he did not understand what was said. The old Irish soldier beside him grabbed his arm.

"Come on, lad. Just follow me. We're goin' Yankee hunting."

Thomas could see sergeants lining men up but he still wasn't clear on what was happening. He followed the old soldier to the road where he now could see that Pearson was forming up the whole of the Advance, or at least those left who were still able-bodied enough to fight, to go down the hill from Davis Point, cross the creek, and attack any American soldiers that hadn't retreated. While they were being roughly assembled on the road, Thomas looked back to see what the other Dundas militiamen were doing. He saw Jacob Doran collecting several of them just off the road in Haines's front yard. He thought of asking whether he should go back and join the group with Jacob when he realized that this would look as if he was afraid to go into action. Anyway, who would he speak to?

The old Irish soldier saw Thomas looking back at the other men of the Dundas militia.

"Listen to me, lad," he said, "you're better off coming with us. We may get shot at, but we got them on the run. It's still better than what your friends are getting ordered to do. Believe me, you're better off coming with us."

"What do you mean?" Thomas asked.

"While we're chasing the Yankees and taking their wounded prisoners, those men, poor buggers, are being sent out into the field to bring back our dead and wounded. I've done that. Yes sir, I've done that. I'd sooner take me chances as a soldier. Once you do what they're goin' to be doin' now, well, you never forget the horror of it all. Never. Believe me, lad, believe me, you're better off coming with us."

Thomas didn't have a chance to decide. At that moment, Colonel Pearson rode up beside them and shouted out the order to move forward at double time. The 49th Light Company, Thomas among them, was heading over the crest of Davis Point down the King's Highway, leading the others in pursuit of the fleeing Americans.

As Pearson's skirmishers moved forward, the Royal Artillery were ordered to cease firing for fear they would hit their own advancing men. This allowed Myers' Thirteenth Infantry to emerge from behind the stone fence and to accelerate their fire. Several soldiers in the 49th who were leading the charge took direct hits from the American sharpshooters. Pearson had underestimated how many Americans were still in the action. While other Americans might be retreating Myers's soldiers were not giving up the fight. They knew they still outnumbered Pearson's men.

Thomas heard a scream to his left. He turned to see a Canadian Fencible fall hard to the ground, his musket bouncing ahead of him so close to Thomas that he had to jump quickly over it. In doing so, he slipped and landed face down in the mud, his own musket flying to the ground.

Thomas was ashamed at what immediately came into his mind: *If I just stay lying here, I won't die today. It's getting dark, the battle will be over soon. I can't do anything anyway; my musket is too wet to fire. I don't want to die, especially as the battle is almost over. I'll just lie here until the danger passes. I'm exhausted. I'm too young to die. I've done my share. Pearson should never have sent us forward; most of the Yankees were already retreating.*

Thomas put his head down. He felt the cold mud on his cheek. He felt his heart racing. He heard the sporadic firing of the American sharpshooters. He heard the horrible shrieking of the wounded horses off in the distance to his left. He heard men running by him to his right. He heard another shot.

Keep your head down, Thomas. No need for heroes this after-

noon. We've nearly won, the battle almost over. Stay down. There's nothing you can do anyway. Your family needs you more.

Thomas heard a voice he recognized. He lifted himself up onto his elbows. He saw Sergeant Laporte. His left arm seemed to be dangling at his side but his right arm was held high, sword in hand, waving the men forward. He was at the edge of the creek.

"Keep coming, my boys. Run!" he yelled at the top of his voice. "*Allons-y! Vite, vite!*"

Thomas saw the young Canadian soldier beside him. He was wounded in the leg. He couldn't get up. His dark eyes burned into Thomas. Thomas jumped up, grabbed his musket, and started to charge towards the creek.

Run, you little bastard. Run so fast the Yankee sharpshooters can't hit you. Get across that goddamn little creek. Run. Run for your life.

Chapter 19
Late Afternoon
November 11, 1813
Dundas County

By the time Thomas and the others got over the creek and up to the top of the ravine, they noticed that the shooting by the Americans seemed to have stopped. By the time they charged forward to the stone fence, the Yankee sharpshooters had gone—gone with all of the rest of the defeated American army, back to their base camp at Cook's Tavern. The battle at Crysler's farm, November 11, 1813, was over.

It was 4:30. The cold rain had begun again. Most of the men were sent back to join the rest of the army, but Corporal Green ordered Thomas and a half-dozen other soldiers to join him in seeing if there were any wounded American soldiers left behind. Green's party went first to the King's Highway and walked the few hundred yards to the gate of the Fetterly farm, where they found the bodies of five American soldiers lined up in a row. Having had to retreat so quickly, the American soldiers had been unable to bury their dead or arrange to take them with them. Thomas went through the gate and walked up the short lane to the Fetterly farmhouse. He rapped on the door just as he had earlier that morning, and Mrs. Fetterly cautiously opened it just as she had before. Thomas explained to her that the battle was over and the Yankees were defeated. He urged her to keep her daughters away from the front gate as there were bodies there and they probably wouldn't be buried until tomorrow. Mrs. Fetterly's response was terse: "Let the bastards rot." She asked whether Thomas knew anything about her sons or whether any of her neighbours or Dundas militia were wounded or killed. Thomas replied that he didn't know but he tried to reassure her by saying that her sons would probably be home soon. After checking for wounded in the maple bush behind the farm, Thomas said, he was going home—home before dark, he hoped.

Green's men crossed the field behind the Fetterly farm and then spread out several yards apart to comb the bush for American soldiers. They crossed the trail that Thomas and de Lorimier had taken earlier that morning. To Thomas, it seemed such a long time ago, almost like another day. So much had happened. He thought of de Lorimier. He wondered who else was injured. He thought of what Peter and Garrett and Oma and Elizabeth had been through. The scenes kept rolling before his mind's eye: de Lorimier limp in Laporte's lap; Laporte crying; the blank look of trauma in Peter's eyes; the horror of the surgeries in Crysler's house; the blood on Allie's face; the bodies of the American soldiers lined up at the Fetterly gate.

As they approached the north end of the bush, Thomas heard one of the soldiers to his left yell for the others to join him. The other men arrived to find one of the privates standing over a Yankee soldier who was lying on his back, his face covered in blood, the top of his head missing.

"Looks like the Mohawk warriors have been here already," Corporal Green remarked, "and look, there's another one over there."

The men turned to where Corporal Green was pointing to see that there were actually two more American soldiers who were also dead and scalped. One of the other privates went to his hands and knees vomiting.

Before the men had time to do anything with the bodies they heard a noise at the edge of the clearing. It sounded like a sheep baaing. They looked in the direction of the noise and then saw a large man with a full beard, his face covered in blood, his eyes blinking fiercely, emerge from behind a large maple tree to the men's right. He was using the tree to hold himself partly erect though his legs were buckling beneath him. His mouth was moving as though he was trying to say something but no words emerged, just a "baa." His legs wobbling, his bulging dead eyes staring blankly ahead, he kept uttering "baa." He fell to his knees. Matter oozed down onto what was left of his forehead and into his eyes. The top of his skull has been sliced off.

"Oh my God. Oh my God. Mother of mercy. Do something, Corporal," a private pleaded. "Stop him from making that noise. Put him out of his misery. I can't take this any longer, Corporal; please put him down!"

The private put his hands over his ears and turned away, uttering his own mournful cry of agony.

Thomas, too, had had enough. He turned to Corporal Green: "I'm sorry, Corporal," he said, "I'm going home."

Thomas walked away from the others without waiting for any reply or permission. He walked west through the bush until he stepped out into the clearing. The battlefield was before him. He knew that it would still be filled with death and destruction so, looking away from the field to his right, Thomas followed the edge of the maple bush until he saw where the logs lay over Bush Creek. He crossed and walked up the side of the ravine and kept to his left until he got to the King's Highway. As he got to the little bridge that crossed Davis Creek he could see that at least here the dead and wounded had been removed. He saw the spot where de Lorimier had been struck down. He climbed back up the hill to Davis Point.

Barely conscious of the soldiers coming and going, camped still on both sides of the highway in front of Haines's house, Thomas continued to walk as in a trance down the middle of the road, determined to stop for nothing until he got to his home.

Then he heard someone call his name. He looked up to see Jacob Doran coming down the steps from Haines's front veranda and walking towards him.

"Thomas," Jacob called out, "you're safe and sound?"

"I'm safe," replied Thomas, "but I wouldn't say I'm sound. What are you doing here?"

"We just finished bringing in the last of our wounded. The house and the two barns are full. Now I have to report to Captain Merkley that there are no more of our wounded on the field. I reckon they'll now try to bring in some of the Yankee wounded before it gets too dark."

"How's everyone else? Peter, Garrett?"

"They're both uninjured though I understand that Peter had a close call. An Indian saved his life. The last I saw Garrett he was with de Lorimier. He's taking it pretty bad."

"De Lorimier didn't make it?"

"No. He's still alive, but barely."

"What about your boys and Luke?"

"My boys are good. Overwhelmed by all this, but I guess that's true of us all."

"What about Luke?"

"Luke is safe. He's gone looking for George. We're all worried; George and a couple of other young men are missing. They should have returned by now."

"Where's his brother?"

"John is with Captain Merkley. He's part of some officers' meeting at Jones's. They're making plans for tomorrow. I think they're organizing a mass burial for the morning. With so many wounded in Crysler's house, Morrison has moved his headquarters to Jones's. I have my horse tied out back. After I report to Captain Merkley, I'll tell Oma and everyone that you're safe. Catherine brought the horse and carriage to take Oma and Elizabeth home, but no one would leave until they heard that you were safe, and when Catherine learned that young George was missing, well, she is beside herself with worry. Captain Johnson has gone with Luke to look for them."

"Have you seen Allie?"

"She's waiting at Crysler's for you. She's exhausted but she's refused to go home until you return. I've got to get going. I'll tell everyone that you're safe."

As Jacob left, Thomas started walking back up the road to Crysler's with even greater determination. The light rain continued. He was soaked to the bone but he was hardly aware of how cold he was as his mind was preoccupied, overwhelmed by the events of the day. George's death, he knew, would devastate the family.

As he rounded the corner at Bouck's, Thomas saw Peter walking towards him. Peter hugged his brother when they came together, then the two continued walking up the road.

"Jacob told us you were coming. Thought you could use some company," Peter said.

"Thanks," replied Thomas. "It's good to see you. Thank God this day is almost over. George is still missing?"

"Yes. It doesn't look good. Oma, Catherine, Garrett, and Elizabeth are all waiting for Luke to return. They're in the small barn behind Crysler's. Staying out of the rain. The barn where de Lorimier is. Where I saw you earlier this afternoon. De Lorimier is hanging on but Duke isn't very hopeful. He says there's nothing we can do for him but wait."

"Jacob says you nearly got killed?"

"It was a close call. Early in the battle, Heriot's Voltigeurs were driven back by a large American force. At the north end, in the cedar bush at the edge of the swamp, you know where I mean. We used to hunt there. Several of the Voltigeurs were killed or wounded while retreating. But we recovered and the Yankees were driven back. I was sent with some others to fetch the wounded. We found some back there. We put the wounded on stretchers. I went by myself a little farther back into the swamp to see if there were any others. That's when I saw some blood on some leaves. I followed the trail of blood. It's not easy tracking back there, as you know. It gets really tangled. I found the body. It was a young

Mohawk warrior. A boy really. He had dragged himself into the swamp to hide. I found him lying behind an old hemlock stump. He was light enough that I could pick him up and put him over my shoulder and carry him for a while. When I laid him down for a moment for a rest, I heard someone crashing through the brush. I assumed it was one of our men so I yelled out asking for help to carry the Indian boy.

"To my horror, into the clearing came a Yankee soldier. He pointed his musket at me and told me to shut up, to not say a word. From the looks of him, he was being chased and didn't want to shoot me and give away where he was. As he came closer I could see the desperation in his eyes. When our Voltigeurs pressed back he must have run into the swamp to get away. He must have got turned around and was now trying to find his way back to the U.S. camp. He could see that I wasn't armed but he still told me to lie down on my stomach. I started to get down but that was when I got to thinking that maybe his musket wasn't loaded, that this was just a bluff, and that when I was down he would run me through with his bayonet or knife or something. I was trying to decide what to do—I was so scared—when we both heard a noise in the brush. He stepped forward quickly and pointed his musket at me, its bayonet pushing against my stomach. His eyes told me that if I made any noise he would run me through. At that moment a ball entered his head just above his right ear and passed through to the other side. He fell lifeless in the same instant.

"Two Mohawk warriors came into the clearing. They had been looking for the boy and had come across the trail made by the Yankee soldier. Fortunately for me, they arrived just in time and one of them was a crack shot. The shooter was a tall muscular fellow who spoke good English. They were both very saddened to see that the boy was dead. The older man was particularly upset. He got down on his knees and held the boy in his arms, rocking back and forth, uttering this awful cry of despair. The shooter told me that this young man was the older man's son; the son's name was Atonsa. I expressed my sorrow for their loss and thanked them for their help before I left. I never got the father's name but the shooter, the big guy, told me his name was Jeremiah."

"Where are the Mohawks now?" Thomas asked.

"I don't know," replied Peter, "but I heard someone say that with the battle over he thought they had lost no time taking their dead and wounded across the river and back to Akwesasne before dark. Somebody else said they lost at least four men, one scalped by the Yankees. He said that the Mohawks fought with great courage. They were fighting to defend their homes too, I guess. I owe my life to that Jeremiah."

Explaining to Peter his relationship to Jeremiah would have to wait as, at that moment, the Crysler farm came into view and they saw Garrett running towards them. While Garrett hugged his brothers tightly, the usual exuberant joy was missing from his eyes. They told a story of pain and continuing anxiety.

Garrett got between his brothers. He held their arms as though leading them to safety. Neither brother resisted this show of affection. The three men increased their pace as they got closer to the barn.

Standing outside under the overhang of the roof, Elizabeth was the first to see the three brothers walking up the road, arm in arm, towards them. The brothers saw Elizabeth go into the little barn and then re-emerge with Oma, Catherine, and Allie. Catherine stood with her arms around Oma and Allie waiting, but Allie broke free and ran towards the men.

She hugged them and slapped them on their shoulders and hugged and slapped them again, a mother dog lovingly chastising her pups for running away. Then she put her arms around her husband and buried her face in his chest and then raised her head to look directly into his eyes.

"I'm home," he said to her.

"Yes, and it's about time," she replied, "you had me worried sick." Then she hugged him again, holding him tight, then stepped back.

"You're wet," she said, "very wet. I've got to get you out of those clothes."

"Sounds good to me," he said, with a sly twinkle in his eye.

She returned the smile and took his hand, giving him three squeezes. He squeezed back, three times. Then her face turned sombre.

"George is missing," she said.

"Yes, I heard."

"Luke has gone on horseback with Captain Johnson to try to find him."

"Yes, I heard," he said as he kept her hand in his and walked to the barn door to greet his mother, sister, and niece.

They all stepped into the barn to get out of the rain. While it was called a barn it was really just a shed, lit only by a lantern which Duke had lit that hung from a rafter. Duke had left to carry away a soldier who had died, leaving the care of the wounded inside to the women. There were only four still alive. One was a Canadian Fencible who was sitting in a corner with a bandaged foot but otherwise looked like he was resting comfortably. Another, a Voltigeur, lay moaning beside him. The other two lay motionless on the floor, sleeping. One of these was de Lorimier.

Looking at de Lorimier, Catherine said that he was a strong young man and that his body was healing. The others didn't seem to share her confidence.

In spite of what she'd been through, Oma didn't seem that exhausted. Relieved to have her four children and granddaughter with her, she seemed more calm than tired as she quietly recounted some stories from her day. She was trying to distract Catherine, who paced back and forth in the little barn. Elizabeth sat back down between the wounded Fencible and the Voltigeur. She put her hand on the knee of the Fencible and gently stroked the matted hair of the wounded Voltigeur, soothing him as best she could. Allie sat on the straw beside de Lorimier, touching him occasionally. The three brothers sat slouched on a bench, spent, waiting for Luke's return, saying very little. After, what they had seen all afternoon, they prepared themselves for the worst.

It was dark now. Peter was the first to fall asleep, his head slipping down to rest on his brother's shoulder. Then Allie gave in to her exhaustion, curled up on the straw beside de Lorimier. Then Elizabeth fell asleep. The rest in the room were all a little surprised by the volume of Elizabeth's heavy snoring.

"Who would think that such a pretty young thing could snore like that—even louder than an old drunk?" Oma said, matter-of-factly, and then she continued: "But, I have to say, she was a real trooper today. She never stopped . . . and Thomas, you should know that Allie was . . . exceptional. She never flinched from the horror of it all. Dr. Korb told me that he couldn't have got through the afternoon without her. A 'natural,' he called her. She did well today. Real well. She's a much stronger woman than I thought. Maybe I'm going to have to . . ."

Before Oma could complete her sentence the door to the barn burst open and in walked Luke and George. George was alive and well.

George didn't hesitate for long to begin telling his story about why he was late. He explained that after the 49th and 89th had successfully stopped the American infantry attack at the north end of the battlefield, Heriot's Voltigeurs (with George among them) and the Mohawks were ordered to chase them back into the bush. Several American wounded soldiers were captured. George and Adam Nudle continued farther into the bush and into the cedar swamp to the north, searching for American wounded or stragglers. When it looked as though there were none left, Adam suggested that the two of them continue on the trail through the swamp because Adam's family farm was only a mile away. Adam wanted to be sure that his mother and sisters were safe.

So, George said, they had followed the trail for just a few minutes when they heard soldiers ahead talking. George and Adam cocked their muskets and carefully snuck up on the soldiers. It was just like deer hunting in that swamp, George commented. As they got closer they could see four soldiers in blue uniforms standing in a clearing, none of them holding a musket, two of them smoking their pipes. Adam and George stepped into the clearing and ordered the Yankee soldiers to sit on the ground. Somewhat to George's surprise, they offered no resistance and complied.

George stopped his story for a moment, smiled, and then said: "It was only then that we thought—shit, what do we do now? Maybe," George said, still smiling, "maybe we should have thought of this before we took them prisoners!"

George went on to explain that they had no rope and, they realized, if the four soldiers were standing again, it might be impossible to keep them from running away or even attacking them. With the return of the rain, it wasn't even clear that either of their muskets would fire.

Then, said George excitedly, something extraordinary happened. A lovely little chestnut mare sauntered into the clearing The large letters "US" were stamped on her saddle. And then a black stallion came into the clearing, following the chestnut mare.

"I reckoned that they must have picked up our scent," George explained, "and that's when Adam got an idea. He told the soldiers to take off their boots and to throw them to one side. He then ordered two of them to sit with their backs to a tree on either side. He took the reins off the black horse, cut them in two and used one half to tie the first pair to the tree, and then he repeated the procedure, tying the other pair to another tree. I know what you're thinking, Thomas; I'm not making this up."

George then explained that Adam told him to guard the prisoners while he took the chestnut mare for help. That was how Adam met up with Luke and Captain Johnson as he came out of the swamp. Captain Johnson rounded up some Voltigeurs and

Adam led them all back to the clearing where Captain Johnson and the Voltigeurs took over from George. Adam decided to walk the rest of the way home and so George and Luke rode back to Crysler's, George riding the chestnut mare and leading the little black stallion behind him.

"So," said George, "here we are safe and sound."

"Now tell them the rest of the story, George," Luke said. "Tell them what happened next."

"Well," George continued, talking more slowly now, "Captain Johnson said that I should keep the chestnut mare—spoils of war, he called it. Captain Johnson said—what was Wilkinson's word?—'liberate,' that's it—he said that I should liberate this pretty little Yankee chestnut mare. And—here's the best part—there was a Canadian liberated today, after all." George turned to Garrett: "And guess what, Garrett, it was a little black Canadian stallion and his name is . . . Buddy! That's right, Garrett, we got Buddy back. We got Buddy back! He's going to be happy to see you. Oh, that horse is going to be happy to see you. So, Oma, if Garrett agrees, you won't have to walk home tonight. I tell ya, I'll never forget this day!"

"November eleven, a day we'll all remember," said Thomas, holding Allie's hand now and walking towards the door. "Come on. The Yankees have left, their tails between their legs. They'll think twice before they come up here again. Let's go home."

Historical Afterword

While George Cook and Adam Nudle were rounding up their American prisoners that evening, Boyd, the American General, decided that it was too dangerous to stay on the Canadian side of the St. Lawrence so, under cover of darkness, the American flotilla proceeded some four miles down the river to take refuge on the American side.

The next morning, November 12, Wilkinson was with his senior officers on Barnhart's Island, three miles above Cornwall, when he received a letter informing him that the other half of the planned invasion to take Montreal under General Hampton, this time from the south, had also been beaten at Chateauguay, Lower Canada, on October 26. Within five days, Hampton had fully retreated across the border to a small village in northern New York State. This news provided a convenient additional excuse for Wilkinson at the meeting on Barnhart's Island to decide to completely abandon the invasion. While he tried to justify his decision to his superiors during his court-martial. some months later, the fact is that a force that he had outnumbered by four to one had soundly trounced his army. Wilkinson had lost at least 280 killed, at least 237 wounded, and over 100 taken prisoner. (Morrison's losses were 22 killed, 148 wounded, and 9 missing.)

Wilkinson also knew that the weather was worsening and that the morale of his men had been completely broken. As one of his officers wrote about the battle in a private letter the next day:

> Our troops retreated with great precipitation to the boats, and crossed the river, leaving the British on the field . . . we lost several boats by fire of the British

> Gunboats. What appears most extraordinary in this affair is that nearly 1,000 of our troops crossed to the American side during the engagement! This misfortune has greatly chagrined the officers, and disheartened our troops. The taking of Montreal is no longer thought to be a work of ease; and many wish themselves honourably out of the expedition. [extract of a letter from Ogdensburg, N.Y., dated November 13, 1813, printed in the *Quebec Mercury*, December 14, 1813, p. 396.]

During the evening of the 11th of November, in addition to Crysler's house, several of the other farmhouses along the river in the vicinity of the battle were used to shelter the wounded and to serve as temporary makeshift hospitals. Dr. William "Tiger" Dunlop, Assistant Surgeon with the 89th, spent the evening of the 11th and the whole of the next day tending to the wounded. In his memoirs, he wrote of the local Loyalists of Dundas County as follows:

> I found their hatred to the Americans was deep-rooted and hearty, and their kindness to us and our wounded, (for I never trusted them near the Americans wounded) in proportion strong and unceasing; my only difficulty with them was to prevent them cramming my patients with all manner of Dutch dainties, for their ideas of practice being Batavian, they affirmed that there was infinitely greater danger from inanition then repletion, and that strength must come from nourishment. "Unless you give de wounded man plenty to eat and drink it is quite certain he can never get through."
>
> —Quoted in *Tiger Dunlop's Upper Canada* (McClelland and Stewart, 1967), p. 16.

With Morrison's victory, the "grand invasion" came to an end. The single biggest American offensive of the war was finished and the all-important supply route along the St. Lawrence was safe. (To avoid this vulnerability in the future, the British government ordered the army to build a canal system from Kingston to the Ottawa River, a canal that would never be used for the purposes it was built for, but is today a major tourist attraction and a World Heritage Site—the Rideau Canal. The little village at the Ottawa River end, Bytown, was subsequently to become the capital of Canada, renamed Ottawa.)

The war carried on in 1814 with several more battles in what is now southwestern Ontario, but the American will to fight wore down and regiments of Wellington's veterans—the conquerors of Napoleon—were soon to arrive in Canada. The war that in later years would come to be known as the War of 1812 was officially concluded on Christmas Eve, 1814, by the Treaty of Ghent with the *status quo ante bellum*. For the United States the St. Lawrence campaign, its best opportunity during the war to conquer the Canadas, was an unmitigated disaster. The United States would never again invade Canada.

What happened to the main characters in this account of the battle at Crysler's Farm?

Lieutenant Colonel Joseph Wanton Morrison received many awards for his brilliant victory at Crysler's Farm. He fought at the Battle of Lundy's Lane on July 25, 1814, where he was badly wounded, too severely wounded to see any more action in the war. He was subsequently assigned to service in India but contracted malaria there and died on the way home to England on February 15, 1826. He was buried at sea.

Captain Henry George Jackson, R.A., received a gold medal for his role at Crysler's Farm. He was a Major of Artillery during the 1837-38 troubles in Upper Canada and was subsequently promoted to Lieutenant Colonel. He died at Warley, England, in 1849. His account of the battle contained in a letter to his cousin Sir George Jackson is still one of the best primary sources available to historians of the battle and was followed faithfully in this story.

Colonel Thomas Pearson led a detachment of light troops in 1814 and fought at the battles of Chippewa and Lundy's Lane, where he was wounded in the arm. In the Siege of Fort Erie he was wounded again, this time to the head. After the war, Pearson returned to command the 43rd Foot and then the 23rd Foot. He was knighted and promoted to Major General in 1833 and to Lieutenant General in 1841. He died in 1847.

Captain William Johnson of the Regiment of Canadian Voltigeurs, illegitimate son of Sir John Johnson, went on half pay after the war and died at Lower Canada in 1836, aged 66.

On November 13, when much of Morrison's army had moved down the river to Cornwall, a private of the 89th Foot "accidentally" fired his loaded musket, while trying to use it to light his pipe, killing **Lieutenant Henry Kersteman**. Kersteman left a grieving young widow in Kingston.

Sergeant Marmaduke Kearns of the 89th Regiment of Foot returned to Ireland. He was awarded the Military General Service Medal with Crysler's Farm Clasp by Queen Victoria.

Captain John Crysler, Dundas Militia, ran into serious financial problems soon after the war. He was forced to sell his large house on the front, lost most of his businesses, and eventually moved to a modest residence in the north of Dundas County, in a small village now called Crysler, Ontario, where he died in 1852, age 84.

Lieutenant Christopher Hagerman, Dundas Militia, served in the Niagara campaign in 1814 and then returned to his law practice in Kingston after the war. He subsequently served as a member of the Legislative Assembly of Upper Canada and was appointed a Judge before he died in Toronto in 1847 at the age of 55.

Guillaume-Francois de Lorimier, Lieutenant, Canadian Regiment of Fencible Infantry, died on November 12, 1813, from his wounds sustained in the battle. His widow, Louise Loudel, gave birth to a son, Guillaume-Henri, the next month at Kanawake.

John (Shawindas) Sunday, Mohawk warrior, returned to Akwesasne. He was awarded the Military General Service Medal with Crysler's Farm Clasp by Queen Victoria. William Sunday—a descendant, we assume—is today a Chief and highly respected elder of the Mohawks at Akwesasne. In 1980, he was charged for actions taken to assert an aboriginal land claim to an island in the St. Lawrence. He was found not guilty in a Cornwall court. He was represented at the criminal court trial by the author, who is honoured to say that Bill is still a dear friend.

Sergeant Joseph Laporte, Canadian Regiment of Fencible Infantry, returned to Lower Canada. He was awarded the Military General Service Medal with Crysler's Farm Clasp by Queen Victoria.

Peter Marselis married Barbara Empey at the age of 29 in 1819 but died just two years later, without issue. His brother **Garrett**, unmarried, died the same year.

Lewis Schwerdfager, the son of the famous Reverend John Samuel Schwerdfager, and his wife **Lena Marselis**, had their eighth child in 1815. Their oldest daughter, **Elizabeth**, married John Haines that same year; they had seven children.

Catherine Elizabeth Marselis (the widow Cook) and her new husband **Jacob Doran** lived at the Doran farm on the river in Dundas County until Jacob died in 1837, aged 84. Catherine, born in the province of New York in 1770, died in 1846. Her oldest son, **John Cook**, and his wife **Catherine (Kate) Hess**, had eight children after the war. John ran for Parliament and served with distinction as the member for Dundas County from 1830 to 1845, always a strong supporter of public education. Catherine's younger son, **George Cook**, married **Sally Casselman**, the daughter of **Cephrenus Casselman**; they had nine children.

Catherine Elizabeth Marselis (née Kling), called **Oma** in this story, lived another 17 years, dying at the age of 80 in 1830. The tombstone of her husband, the Loyalist **Johannes Marselis**, musketman in Sir John Johnson's King's Royal Regiment of New York, one of the founders of Upper Canada, is the oldest tombstone in the memorial cemetery at Upper Canada Village, built to mark the location of the historic Battle of Crysler's Farm, now a major tourist attraction in Dundas County, Ontario. Just a few miles up the river, the little fort at Prescott was named **Fort Wellington** at the end of the war; this is now a National Historic Site and is often used as the location for War of 1812 re-enactments.

Thomas Marselis and his wife **Allie** celebrated their 50th wedding anniversary before Thomas died on July 23, 1861. (Allie lived to be 86, dying on October 13, 1878.) They had ten more children. The year after the war they had a son they named Peter. They had another son in 1818 whom they called Jeremiah. As a young man, Jeremiah moved to the north end of Dundas County to clear a farm near present-day Morewood, Ontario, where he eventually built a fine red brick Georgian home. In that house, in 1925, was born his great-granddaughter, **Annie Kathleen Marselis (Marcellus)**, my mother, to whom this book is dedicated.